Margery Allingham's
Albert Campion returns in

MR CAMPION'S
FAULT

by

Mike Ripley

severn
House

This first world edition published 2016
in Great Britain and the USA by
SEVERN HOUSE PUBLISHERS LTD of
19 Cedar Road, Sutton, Surrey, England, SM2 5DA.
Trade paperback edition first published
in Great Britain and the USA 2016 by
SEVERN HOUSE PUBLISHERS LTD

British Library Cataloguing in Publication Data
A CIP catalogue record for this title is available from the British Library.

ISBN-13: 978-0-7278-8625-5 (cased)
ISBN-13: 978-1-84751-729-6 (trade paper)
ISBN-13: 978-1-78010-790-5 (e-book)

All Severn House titles are printed on acid-free paper.

Severn House Publishers support the Forest Stewardship Council™ [FSC™],
the leading international forest certification organisation.
All our titles that are printed on FSC certified paper carry the FSC logo.

Typeset by Palimpsest Book Production Ltd.,
Falkirk, Stirlingshire, Scotland.
Printed and bound in Great Britain by
TJ International, Padstow, Cornwall.

To Catherine Aird, a stout supporter of the Brigantes tribe.

Author's Note

Much of this novel is set in the West Riding of Yorkshire where, in 1969, I was a schoolboy.

New Hall Prison has been a women's prison since 1987 but back in 1969 it was a detention centre for young offenders, known locally as New Hall Camp. HMP Wakefield, now a high-security prison, still exists on Love Lane.

My fictional mining village of Denby Ash is loosely based on the village of Flockton, where I was born and raised. There was indeed a Grange Ash colliery and it had a pyramidal muck stack which dominated the landscape, though that – along with the Yorkshire coal-mining industry – is now long gone. Ash Grange School, however, is a figment of my imagination, although Willy Elliff's fish-and-chip shop did exist (perhaps it still does). I was there on 22 November 1963 when someone burst in and announced that President Kennedy had been assassinated. They say you can always remember where you were when Kennedy was shot, and it's true.

I am indebted to my friend Reg Gadney for many things, but in particular the story of his father Bernard Gadney's exploits as England rugby captain in 1936.

Yorkshire was certainly not a natural hunting ground for Margery Allingham and taking the Campions there may be a risk, though I am sure Albert would have risen to the challenge.

Mike Ripley,
Essex.

Contents

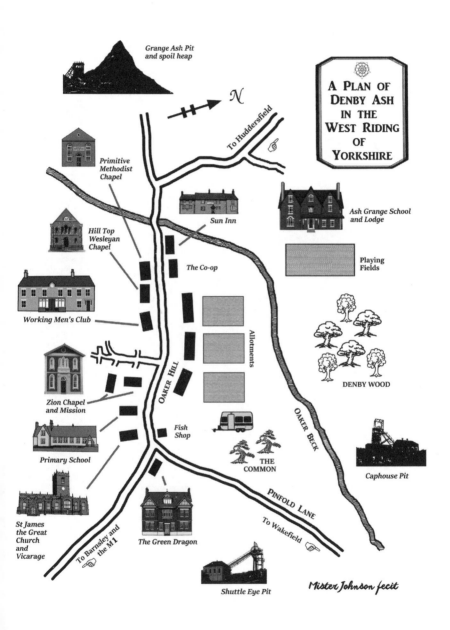

Grange Ash Pit and spoil heap

N

To Huddersfield

A PLAN OF
DENBY ASH
IN THE
WEST RIDING
OF
YORKSHIRE

Primitive Methodist Chapel

Sun Inn

Ash Grange School and Lodge

Hill Top Wesleyan Chapel

The Co-op

Playing Fields

Working Men's Club

Allotments

OAKER HILL

DENBY WOOD

Zion Chapel and Mission

OAKER BECK

Fish Shop

Primary School

THE COMMON

Caphouse Pit

St James the Great Church and Vicarage

The Green Dragon

PINFOLD LANE

To Wakefield

To Barnsley and the M1

Shuttle Eye Pit

Mister Johnson fecit

ONE
Tremors

No one in Denby Ash, neighbours, relatives, the milkman, the rent man, the local priest, the ladies on the brass cleaning rota or fellow members of the Mothers' Union would ever say that Ada Braithwaite was a woman given to hysteria, flights of fancy or deliberate attention-seeking. None of them would dare. She was, by general consent, a woman who did not make a fuss and got on with life; whatever life threw at her.

And life had, in fact, thrown quite a lot Ada's way.

At the age of fourteen she had gone from school into service at Ash Grange when it was known as 'the Big House' and its owners were, in practice if not in title, Lords of the Manor. Ada worked honestly and hard and the lords and ladies of the Big House were grateful, for this was wartime and if good domestic staff were hard to find in 1939, by 1945, under the looming shadow of a bright new socialist age, they were an endangered species. As were – although they did not yet realize it – the owners of Ash Grange themselves, whose fortunes and standing were based not on gifts of the royal prerogative, nor on rewards for victories in battle from a grateful nation, but on the ownership of land which, by geological serendipity, floated on a black sea of coal.

One morning, in her second year as a scullery maid there, the vicar of Denby Ash called at the Grange and informed Ada that her father had been killed on active service at a place called Tobruk, which was in North Africa, and if she was so inclined she could borrow an atlas from the vicarage to find where it was. The beefy, red-faced cook at the Grange, Mrs Stott, to whom Ada saw herself as understudy, put a comforting ham hock of an arm around her and told her she did not have to – a drop of hard work was what she needed to take her mind off things. She received the same advice from Mrs Stott a year later when she was informed, again by the vicar, that her mother had left the village – and Ada, her only child – to follow a Canadian corporal she had 'struck up with' who had been posted to a signals unit in Southampton. Although Ada was just as unaware of the location of Southampton as she was of Tobruk, the vicar made no offer of the loan of an atlas this time and neither did Mrs Stott offer a consoling embrace. The wartime death of a father was one thing, the desertion of a mother quite another and years later, when a letter arrived addressed to her, care of the vicarage and bearing a Canadian stamp, Ada flung it to the back of the fire without opening it.

On VE Day, Ada Lumley, as she was then, plucked up her courage, handed in her notice and left Ash Grange in search of her own brave new world. She found a job in a textile mill in Huddersfield seven miles away, and discovered a world of dance halls, picture houses, trams, charabanc trips to the Dales and even – for the first time – the coast and the delights of Hornsea and Bridlington. She also discovered young men, and eligible young men discovered her. Ada never, in her mind, set a spark but where there was a flicker of a flame, if she did not exactly fan it she certainly encouraged it to come closer, out of the draught. There was a dalliance – she would put it no higher than that – with the rather fusty, bespectacled accountant of the textile mill where she worked, a man of twenty-eight in years but fifty-eight in demeanour and attitude. Then a much more passionate, even exotically fiery, relationship with a Polish Spitfire pilot who had ended the war on the side of the victors but had found his native country still occupied.

But of all the interested young men who tempted her with port-and-lemons or half-pints of Webster's mild served in the dimpled glasses with handles which were reserved exclusively 'for ladies', the one whose cap was pitched successfully at Ada was that of Colin Braithwaite, a miner at Grange Ash, one of the three collieries which encircled the village of Denby Ash like protective, outlying forts.

And so, after five years of freedom, Ada Lumley returned to Denby Ash to become Mrs Colin Braithwaite, solemnizing the event in the village church of St James the Great under the wistful eye of the vicar who had, until that moment, been the bringer only of bad tidings.

The Braithwaites embarked on married life by moving in to Number 11 Oaker Hill, a two-up, two-down terraced council house still known locally as one of the 'pit houses' which had been built in 1906 by the colliery owners who had built Ash Grange for their own accommodation, and had been rented exclusively by miners ever since. Ada kept the house warm and clean, did the washing on Mondays, scoured the back-door steps on Wednesdays, washed the windows on Thursdays, did the baking on Tuesdays and the grocery shopping at the local Co-Op on Fridays. She made sure that Colin's snap tin and flask were full every morning before he bicycled to work at the pit at 6 a.m., and that there was hot water for a bath on his return, followed by a cooked tea on the table by 5 p.m. For his part, Colin went to work with never a day off sick, brought the coal in and laid the fires every morning, and placed his pay packet on the kitchen table every Friday. The couple visited 'the club' once a week, usually on bingo nights when women were welcomed rather than tolerated, but for Saturday night socializing they divided their custom fairly between the two public houses which bookended the village: the Sun Inn at the 'Huddersfield end' and the Green Dragon which marked the 'Barnsley end' of Denby Ash. They paid their dues into the village holiday club which allowed them an annual coach trip and a week's bed-and-breakfast in Scarborough or Bridlington, or, in an adventurous year, Morecambe.

Colin's workmates and Ada's neighbours – especially the neighbours – all expected the couple to plunge into parenthood and no one could explain (though many wondered) why it took Ada a further five years to fall pregnant with Roderick, their first and, as it turned out, only child.

A healthy son was not a blessing Colin Braithwaite was to enjoy for long, for on one fine spring morning in 1960 the vicar of Denby Ash was once more recalled to mournful and tragic duty. Ada was pegging out washing on a line stretched between the back door and the coalhouse ten yards away at the end of a cinder path, to make the most of an unseasonably good drying day, when the vicar's head appeared around a flapping white sheet and suggested that Mrs Braithwaite come inside and sit down.

Perhaps it was because mining communities were used to sudden and shockingly violent occurrences, or perhaps it was the unexpected appearance of the vicar wading through a sea of festooned clothes' lines, but by whatever osmosis, the news which broke over Ada Braithwaite's bowed head spread within seconds to the women of the street. Abandoning their washing, some with wooden pegs gripped between fingers or even teeth, Ada's neighbours drifted instinctively towards the back door of Number Eleven. Idle chatter and cheery gossip stopped as if by edict, the only sounds coming from the flapping of wet sheets and the distant hum of a coal lorry. They stood in a semicircle around the back door, a silent congregation waiting patiently for a sermon.

The vicar of Denby Ash wisely chose the role of newsreader rather than prophet and when he emerged from Ada's kitchen to face a dozen or more blank-faced women, he kept his bulletin to the bare essentials. Colin Braithwaite had, in the middle of that morning's shift, been killed at the coalface when a large stone had dislodged itself from the roof of the shaft he was crawling along and crushed the life out of him.

Obviously, in the circumstances, Ada would need all the support and comfort her neighbours could offer. There was no question it would be forthcoming; there never was in Denby Ash. It was a small community and almost eighty per cent of the population relied economically on its three collieries, as had been the case for more than a century and a half. The hewing of coal deep underground was a dangerous business and widowhood, even at a relatively young age, was accepted as a trial of life without hysteria, bitterness or appeals for compassion to an implacable God. The community of Denby Ash simply got on with it.

The funeral expenses of Colin Braithwaite were covered by an insurance policy underwritten by the National Union of Mineworkers. Ada received modest compensation from the Coal Board and was allowed to remain in her council house as long as the rent could be paid. To that end she went back to work, not to the Huddersfield mills but to the kitchens of Ash Grange she had left as a brash teenager seeking freedom. The Big House was now a boys' school, but boys needed feeding and Ada knew all too well the quirks of the kitchens there.

Ada worked hard to make sure that her fatherless son, Roderick, wanted for nothing. She accepted no charity but baked cakes for several and pulled her weight in the network of good causes marshalled by the church and the Mothers' Union with military efficiency. She was not flighty with the men and did not gossip about the women of Denby Ash. There were few – very few, but there usually is at least one – who had a bad word to say about her. She had not had an easy life, but then who in the village had? Ada was not the first mother to be widowed by the mines and would not be the last, but she had never complained of her lot.

She was certainly the very last person anyone in the village would have expected to be visited by a ghost.

The floor trembled, the walls shook. A china mug leapt from a shelf and smashed in the sink. In a wall cupboard, more crockery rattled and attempted to join it, lemming-like, in a suicidal plunge. Plaster dropped from the ceiling like volcanic ash; the kitchen table moved, crablike across the linoleum floor, spilling a salt pot and a sugar bowl; pipes rattled and hummed; a three-legged wooden footstool lost its battle with gravity and tipped over; an overhead bulb swung wildly from its flex, its glass shade tinkling ominously. The iron doors of the coal-fired cooking range creaked on their hinges and from the front and upstairs rooms came groans, as if the whole house was in pain.

'Eight seconds,' said the man, consulting his wristwatch with some difficulty as the woman was clinging to his arm for dear life. 'Does it usually last that amount of time?'

Ada Braithwaite released her grip and used her free hands to brush away plaster dust from her cardigan.

'Sometimes it goes on for ages,' she said, dry-mouthed. 'Sometimes it comes back two or three times a night.' Then, despairingly, she added: 'There's no rhyme or reason to it.'

Bertram Browne wiped a hand across his balding head to dislodge a lozenge of flaked paint and realized he was sweating profusely.

'Does it affect your neighbours?'

Mrs Braithwaite shook her head. 'Mr and Mrs Lee at Number Ten are both pensioners and go to bed early. They'd sleep through anything. They brag about it and say that not even Doodlebugs during the war could wake 'em, not that any Doodlebugs ever fell closer than Huddersfield, to the best of my knowledge.

On t'other side' – she bent her head towards the wall connecting them to Number Twelve – 'Percy and Phyllis will still be at the club or at the Green Dragon if they're flush, and they'll be there till chuckin' out time or later if they can manage it. *She's* never noticed owt much, though she did once say an empty bottle had fallen off a windowsill and smashed. Put it down to the coal lorries thundering up the road all day. Seemed upset she wouldn't get her fourpence deposit back.'

'So the phenomenon is localized both in place and time, I think you said.'

Mr Browne found that the best way to stop his knees knocking and his heart pounding was to imagine himself back in the classroom. There he was in command.

'If you mean it only 'appens to this house and always on Thursdays, then yes, I did say that,' Ada said carefully, worrying that Mr Browne might have judged the way she had clutched at him as a bit too forward. 'And now you've seen it with your own eyes, so I'm not lying, am I?'

'I never said you were, Mrs Braithwaite,' Browne said formally, as if in court. 'When Roderick told me how upset you were, I believed him immediately.'

'It was good of you to let him stay at the school tonight.'

'Think nothing of it. The boy's at that age when boys don't need extra distractions, especially things like this . . .'

'Like what, Mr Browne? What is it we just saw?'

The woman, white-faced and wide-eyed, was suddenly a distraught stranger to Bertram Browne, a thin substitute for the competent and stoic Ada Braithwaite who had invited him into her home.

'What do you think it was, Ada?' he said more gently, answering one question with another – an almost unforgivable sin in a schoolmaster's lexicon.

'Ah knows what they'd say round here, reet enough,' said Ada, her face set in Yorkshire granite. 'They'd say it was my late husband Colin come back to haunt me.'

Bertram considered draping a comforting arm around Ada's shoulder, but he had lived in the West Riding long enough to know that would be an unacceptable, not to mention potentially dangerous, action. Instead, he smiled his most innocent smile.

'*You* don't believe that, do you, Ada?'

'O'course not, Mr Browne. I may not have your learnin' but I'm not daft.'

Bertram Browne, MA (Cantab) felt that his education was distinctly lacking as he pulled up the collar of his coat and tightened his scarf against the cold night air on his walk back to Ash Grange School.

Towards the end of the war he had, as a young, very green lieutenant of the Royal Engineers, played a small but terrifying part in the crossing of the Rhine, and a few weeks later he had found himself helping the walking dead survivors of Bergen–Belsen concentration camp, which was even more terrifying. With peacetime came Cambridge, where he suffered from an imagined inferiority complex caused by the ribbing from fellow undergraduates of his broad Yorkshire accent and the snobbery of dons who had grumpily put up with the influx of young ex-servicemen under edict from the government only on sufferance (there had, after all, been a war on). Any sniping, real or imagined, aimed at Bertram soon dissipated when it became clear that he was an above-average student and a more-than-adequate scrum half on the rugby field. Even the crustiest of the dons regarded 'young Browne' with new respect when, in his third year, he was seen 'walking out' with a frail Jewish girl, a trainee nurse at Addenbrooke's Hospital, who spoke with a thick Hungarian accent and who bore a tattoo on her left forearm comprising the letter 'A' and a five-figure number.

The couple – her name was Rebekka – seemed very much in love, but on the eve of marital bliss, which is always the time when fate strikes its cruellest blow, Rebekka, who had survived horrors unimaginable, was run over in a gruesomely mundane road accident within sight of the hospital where she worked. A distraught Bertram Browne resigned himself to bachelorhood, entered the teaching profession and returned to his native Yorkshire, one of the spikiest and meanest-spirited of his Cambridge tutors asking cruelly which of those three activities was supposed to be a penance.

Yet nothing in his past life, or his present one as a senior master at Ash Grange, had prepared him for Ada Braithwaite's appeal for help on that dark, wintry night.

He had known Ada since she had come to work at the school. She had, in fact, 'caught his eye', being closer to his age than any other available female he regularly interacted with, and though no classical beauty she was far from unattractive. He also admired her spirit – that of a born survivor in the face of adversity – which perhaps reminded him of Rebekka, and when the widow Braithwaite's fatherless son Roderick gained a place at Ash Grange as a scholarship day boy, he offered if not a protective wing to shelter under, then at least a watchful eye. Young Roderick was

in no need of special treatment or favouritism as he proved a
hard-working and responsive pupil in all his lessons, and not just
those taught by Bertram Browne, in which he positively shined.
Thus it was in Mr Browne that Roderick confided that there was
'trouble at home' with things going, literally, bump in the night
and his mother 'at her wits' end', though of course she would
never admit that.

The story of the haunting of 11, Oaker Hill came to his attention in an essay sheepishly handed in by Roderick as part of his
regular homework. Mr Browne, noting the domestic detail in the
essay, had the sensitivity to take the boy to one side rather than
question him in class, and ask where Roderick's inspiration had
come from. The story, repeated twice for good measure, convinced
Mr Browne that the lad was being brutally honest and sincere in
relating what he had, or thought he had, seen.

During a free period early one afternoon, Bertram had managed
to get Ada alone in the school kitchen, told her what Roderick
had told him and offered to help in any way he could.

The widow Braithwaite had reacted with suspicion at first, then
with an involuntary spark of anger (soon quenched) that her son
should be discussing 'her business' with others. Knowing he would
get such a reaction, for he was a Yorkshireman after all, Bertram
Browne stressed that it was important that the matter be kept very
much to themselves and not provide entertainment for idle
gossip-mongers.

Reassured, Ada had said she would be grateful if Mr Browne
would give his opinion on things, but she had one question: 'What's
a *poltergeist*?'

'It's from the German and means "noisy spirit". Supposedly it's
some sort of psychic manifestation which disrupts things, throws
things about, smashes your best china, that sort of thing.'

The widow Braithwaite had nibbled at her lower lip and nodded
sagely. 'That sounds like what we've got, all right,' she'd said calmly.

And having seen what he had seen that evening, Bertram Browne
had to agree.

But what exactly had he seen, felt and heard?

Not being superstitious in the slightest way and not religious
'so you'd notice', as the residents of Denby Ash would say,
Mr Browne had dismissed any supernatural influence almost

immediately but he could offer Ada no alternative, rational explanation. Instead, he had hinted that he had a colleague at the school whom he thought could help and he would consult him the next day. Until she heard from him, he said, it would be best if they did not discuss the events of that night with anyone.

'You know what they're like round here, Mr Browne,' Ada had said. 'I've no intention of telling them my business. Oh, tongues will wag – they always do – but not with any help from me. And you'd better go now, Mr Browne. It's getting late.'

'At least let me help you clear up some of this mess,' Bertram had offered and had seen Ada's sinews stiffen even before his lips stopped moving.

'When I need a *man's* help to tidy my own house, then I'll put an advert in the *Huddersfield Examiner*, thank you very much.'

At the top of Oaker Hill, his breath steaming and the night carrying the promise of a frost before dawn, Bertram Browne quickened his pace. The sodium street lamps of Denby Ash ended on Oaker Hill by the village's branch of the Co-Operative. From here on, Bertram's walk back to the school would be in darkness, for the only other source of light, the Sun Inn, was already, thanks to a conscientious – some would say pernickerty – landlord, empty of customers, closed for business and thoroughly blacked-out as if expecting an air raid.

Technically, the Sun Inn was the last inhabited dwelling in Denby Ash proper. Beyond it there was the short, narrow bridge over the Oaker Beck (known locally as the 'Okker Dyke') and then the Huddersfield road and, half a mile down it on the right, the playing fields and buildings of Ash Grange School.

Although he could not see it, Bertram knew what lay in the darkness away to his left. Everyone did, for the recently decommissioned Grange Ash colliery, or rather, its enormous spoil heap, dominated the daylight landscape and was almost as well-known a landmark as the towering Emley Moor television transmitter mast had become before its dramatic collapse earlier in the year.

There was little moonlight available through the cloud cover but Bertram had no fear of the dark, nor of wandering off course. As long as his shoes continued to clatter on tarmac, the road would take him to the main gate and driveway of Ash Grange School. It was a walk he could do safely virtually blindfolded. The road ahead was, if not quite Roman, relatively straight, headlights could be seen a good way off and the night was still – an indicator of snow perhaps? – which meant any vehicle would probably be heard before seen.

And yet he was taken completely by surprise when a form travelling at speed loomed out of the darkness.

His initial thought was that he was confronting a large and aggressive rat with red coals for eyes; and a rat which was scuttling directly towards him in menacing silence.

Only when it was far, far too late for him to do anything to avoid the inevitable did Bertram Browne realize that bearing down on him was a very metallic freewheeling vehicle, not a fleshy rodent, and that what he had taken to be burning demonic eyes were in fact the glowing ends of cigarettes being smoked by the driver and a passenger.

Then there was only brief pain and longer, total darkness.

TWO
Situation(s) Suddenly Vacant

Ash Grange School for Boys
Denby Ash,
Nr Wakefield,
West Riding,
Yorkshire.
[*Head:* A.J.B. Armitage, MA(Cantab)]

xiv.xi.MCMLXIX

My Dear Perdita,

I realize that I have been very lax in my duties as god-father; duties which I do not recognize as ending with the marriage of a godchild although I may have inadvertently given that impression by not having been in touch since your wedding to Rupert, who I am sure is proving a fine husband as he comes from a very fine family. Please, once again, accept my apologies for not attending the wedding itself, which unfortunately clashed with an unavoidable meeting of the Headmasters' Conference. I hope my gift arrived in time and that it will be appreciated in the future. (My wife insists that a case of port wine is a most unsuitable wedding present, but I maintain that anyone who has a case of the '63 will have 'a wine for life' as the poet – though I'm not sure which one – would have said.)

Pleasantries aside – and you know we waste as little time as possible on pleasantries here in Yorkshire – there is a reason I am writing to you now; a selfish reason, I admit. I am well aware that convention rules that godparents do what they can to assist the prosperity and health of both the body and soul of the godchild, with nary a thought for the time and cost involved. However, I now find myself in the position of a godparent requiring assistance from their spiritual ward.

I doubt if the press down south has carried reports of the tragedy which has affected us at Ash Grange, but up here it made something of a splash, meriting a paragraph in the *Yorkshire Post*, though hardly the sort of publicity we would seek. I refer to the tragic road accident which resulted in the death of our senior English master Bertram Browne. It has proved a double blow for the school as it has left us short-staffed and Gabbitas and Thring are unable to supply a suitable replacement until next term.

With that we must and can cope, but Bertram's death has left us with a more pressing problem as he was involved in – nay, he was the originator, producer and director of – a musical version of *Doctor Faustus* which is to be the centre-piece of our Speech Day celebration at the end of this term. (And lest you discard this letter at this point, let me assure you that I was never *totally* convinced about Bertram's musical adaption of Marlowe, but he was set on it and we are now committed to it, the programmes having been printed and paid for.)

In short, as we like to be in Yorkshire, where fair words often cost money, Bertram's death has left our nascent musical production without a guiding hand on the tiller, so to speak.

To be blunt, as we also like to be in Yorkshire, I am at a loss when it comes to things thespian, or I was until I remembered my goddaughter. I am also aware that unemployment in the acting profession is rife and therefore it is statistically possible, if not probable, given the rather cruel reviews of the musical show *Lucky Strike* which I read in the *Daily Telegraph* earlier this term, that you may be in need of a theatrical challenge on the getting-back-on-the-bicycle-after-falling-off principle.

And whilst I appreciate that two performances of a syncopated *Doctor Faustus* in the School Hall here at Ash Grange (one for the staff and pupils, one for parents and visitors) hardly reeks of greasepaint and West End crowds, a 'producer/director credit' as I believe it is called, for an original (nay, experimental) dramatic production would surely fit well on to one's curriculum vitae. There would, of course, be a small stipend with the post, which will be called Assistant Drama Teacher and which will run until the Christmas holidays.

Although our pupils are all boys, we have several female members of staff and accommodation and board would be provided in the Headmaster's Lodge as guests of my wife and myself.

I do hope you will feel able to ride to our rescue on the flimsiest of obligations to a most recalcitrant godfather. Please convey to your husband both my best wishes and the enclosed note for his attention.

In order to further save the school unnecessary postage, would you please also deliver the enclosed letter to your mother-in-law, Lady Amanda?

Warmest regards,
Brigham Armitage

Post Scriptum:
I hope it is clear from the desperate tone of this request that the vacant positions in question require filling *immediately*.

'For a man who believes words are not cheap and should not be wasted, he doesn't half go on,' said Rupert Campion across the breakfast table. 'Do you actually know this character?'

'He's my godfather,' said his wife casually.

'But do you actually *know* him? I'm sure I've got several godmothers whom I wouldn't know from Adam and certainly not Eve.'

'Given your family's peculiarities that should be counted as a blessing,' Perdita said without lifting her eyes from the letter she held in one hand as if balancing it against the triangle of toast in the other. 'My parents were less conspicuous consumers of godparents and appointed only one from each sex. My godmother, being an actress, naturally abdicated all responsibility as soon as her agent offered her a spear-carrying role in some overblown medieval epic being filmed in Spain by Italians. She put her dogs – ghastly little chow things – into Battersea, gave her clothes to Oxfam, her furniture to the local church and jumped on the first plane heading for sun, Spain and fame. The last I heard, she'd married a bullfighter, but that was probably wishful thinking on her part.'

Rupert watched his wife's prim baby face as her large, round blue eyes followed the paragraphs of the letter again as she spoke, and not for the first time wondered how such a perfect young mouth could produce, when required, the voice of a middle-aged governess.

'I haven't seen *her* since my christening, if indeed she was there,' continued Perdita, 'but dear old Brigham was always good for a card and a postal order on birthdays and Christmas when I was a kid. He was an old army chum of daddy's and turned up to the funeral in a slightly mothy uniform and brown shoes so highly polished they glowed like amber.'

There was a slight catch in her throat at the memory, which Rupert knew wasn't acting.

'I haven't seen him since and only invited him to the wedding to make up the paltry numbers on my side of things, but as he says, he couldn't make it.'

'He seems to have followed your career with interest, though.'

'Humpf!' Perdita made a most un-governess-like noise as she bit into thickly marmaladed toast. 'Not much of a career to follow so far! And trust him to see the really bad reviews.'

'It wasn't your fault that *Lucky Strike* was a pig-in-a-poke, darling.'

'Pig-in-a-poke? It was an absolute stinker! Book and lyrics by an unrepentant Marxist, which I could forgive had he not also been an illiterate, unrepentant Marxist with music by a tone-deaf, shovel-fisted pub pianist who would be defenestrated by an angry mob if he tried any of his tunes in an East End gin palace on a Saturday night. As for our so-called director – well, we soon discovered he couldn't direct the crowd singing "Abide With Me" at the FA Cup Final, or not without giving all of them individual nit-picking notes.'

Rupert, who had witnessed this sore inflamed on several occasions, wisely changed the subject. 'Your godfather sounds a bit of a rum cove, but headmasters are supposed to be odd, aren't they? "Facts, facts, facts!" and all that sort of thing.'

'That's Charles Dickens in *Hard Times*,' said Perdita primly, 'and I don't think Brigham is a Mr Gradgrind. I remember him as a bit of a softy, but his letter is a bit odd. I mean, this reference to Gabbitas and Thring. Isn't that a joke from those wonderful Molesworth books where two Victorian undertakers go out at night and kidnap unsuspecting young men off the street, dragging them away to force them to become teachers?'

'I bow to you on the Dickens, darling,' said Rupert, pouring milk on to a bowl of very noisy cereal, 'but Gabbitas and Thring are not fictional. At my school they were known as "Rabbitarse and String", which I think was coined by W.H. Auden. They're an employment agency for teachers at all the best schools.'

'You mean at socially divisive schools.'

'Steady on, dear. Bolshevism at the breakfast table does not become you.'

Perdita snorted in half-hearted disgust, which Rupert only found charming.

'Typically, you regard the move to Comprehensive education as Bolshevism.'

'No, I do not; and in any case, I bet Godfather Brigham's establishment is fee-paying and exclusive.'

'Not as exclusive as your old school.'

'As Pop would say, it flipping well *should* be exclusive, the fees they charged.'

Perdita smiled. 'I had forgotten that you were only following the family tradition and your father certainly turned out all right. You'd better read your letter.' She launched a folded sheet of paper in the general direction of her husband, who rescued it before it crash-landed in the butter dish.

'Your godfather certainly believes in saving on postage,' observed Rupert. 'Did you say there was another letter somewhere for Mother?'

Perdita held up the large buff envelope – an envelope more usually associated with official demands from the Revenue – which bore the smudged crest, possibly depicting books quartered with leopards, of Ash Grange School.

'It's in here,' she said. 'Watermarked stationery, sealed and addressed in copperplate to "Lady Amanda". I'm surprised it's not scented. I just get the standard brown job they probably use to send out the detention slips. I'll pop it round at lunchtime. As it happens, she's taking me shopping this afternoon.'

'Carnaby Street or the King's Road?'

'Probably both. Your mother wants to buy me a present; it's possibly a reverse dowry of sorts – due recompense for me taking you off her hands. I've had my eye on a little black number by Kiki Byrne, but if I'm going to the frozen north I might go for one of those black-and-white optical check wool suits from Foale and Tuffin. Are miniskirts allowed in Yorkshire?'

'You're not seriously thinking of taking the job, are you?'

Perdita sighed dramatically. It was, Rupert noted silently, her stock 'Blanche DuBois' sigh.

'What other choice do I have? After the *Lucky Strike* debacle producers are not exactly beating a path to my door and it's too late to get into the back line of the chorus for *Dick Whittington* at the Palladium with Tommy Steele unless there's an epidemic of twisted ankles. There aren't any other jobs going.'

'Oh yes there are,' said Rupert soberly, holding the single sheet of paper before him as if it were a bloody dagger.

'What is it? What does Brigham say?'

'It seems Ash Grange is not only short of a thespian, but also a games master. I've been offered the job.'

'Games master? What are you talking about? Are you sure it doesn't say "groundskeeper"?'

'Why on earth should it say groundskeeper? I'm not a groundskeeper.'

'You're not a games master either,' said Perdita logically.

'I know that – and you know that – but your godfather seems to think that anyone who is an Old Rugbeian is qualified.'

'Old?' Perdita's eyes widened in realization. 'You mean your old school, don't you?'

'Yes, and it seems that Brigham Armitage is an Old Boy too.' Rupert floated the letter back across the table. 'Look, he even signs off *Floreat Rugebia.* That's the school song.'

'So we're both off to the frozen north then.'

'We are?'

'I've got nothing better – not until the Panto season finishes – and you seem to have been lassoed by the old school tie. Anyway, you can't refuse.'

'Why not?'

'Because if I'm going to make a fool of myself with a hair-brained musical based on *Doctor Faustus*, I'd like to know that my darling husband is making an even bigger fool of himself on the rugby field.'

The two women assured the taxi driver they could manage their parcels and bags perfectly well as they were bulky but not heavy, and the cabby's disappointment was short-lived as the older woman tipped him generously anyway.

'I thought The Cavendish would be a good place for tea,' said Amanda, gathering up her shopping trophies. 'Albert will be joining us. He's only just around the corner in Jermyn Street having a haircut and, if I know him, treating himself to some new shirts.'

Perdita, distributing her own shopping bags into a more symmetrical and comfortable pattern, said: 'I do hope he has. I will feel far less guilty that way.'

'No need for guilt, my dear; banish that thought immediately,' instructed her mother-in-law.

'But you've been so ridiculously generous . . .'

'And you would deny me that tiny pleasure? How mean of you! Now, don't be silly. Think of them as early Christmas presents and, anyway, you'll need the warmer things if you're going to the frozen north.'

Perdita knew better than to argue further and followed Amanda into The Cavendish where the two women were greeted by a porter who relieved them of their packages, and by Mr Albert Campion, who beckoned them to a table with a teapot in one hand and a silver jug of milk in the other.

'Perfect timing!' He greeted them both with a kiss. 'A splendid choice of venue, Amanda, the lovely old Cavendish – of course, they've done it up. I've not been here since it reopened a couple of years ago, but I remember it from the war when it was called a "social first-aid centre for servicemen". No wonder the Luftwaffe bombed it. Now, do let me be Mother.'

Once tea had been poured and savouries or fancies selected, Amanda prompted Perdita into repeating the news of her recent offer of employment. Mr Campion listened in polite silence but Amanda noticed the smile behind his spectacles growing in luminescence.

'How splendid!' he exclaimed when Perdita had told her story. 'A chance to enter a world where the youth of this country are instructed in all languages, living and dead, the use of globes, algebra, writing, arithmetic and every branch of classical literature known to man. Terms: twenty guineas per annum.'

'I beg your pardon?' said Perdita between mouthfuls of scone.

'Ignore him,' said Amanda briskly, 'he's just being clever. It's what he does.'

Not for the first time, Perdita wondered if strangers or newcomers to the world of the Campions ever mistook the pair's exchanges for bickering. She had observed her in-laws long enough to have decided that their rapid-fire cross-talk was a well-honed double act and everyone in the performing arts knew that the basis of a truly successful double act was love. They had, after all, been married for almost thirty years now and their act was well rehearsed and always performed with a twinkle in the eye. More telling, Perdita had noticed, were the delicate, minuscule gestures which they exchanged when no one was looking at them; sometimes when even they themselves were not looking at each other. The way their fingertips met as if by accident across a table; the soft, comforting smile when they saw their partner enter a room; the relaxed snugness of their bodies when the two of them sat next to each other; the lithe smoothness as they walked down a street side by side – apart and yet, somehow, together.

'I'm not trying to be clever, darling, merely quoting an appropriate source, should we be in need of inspiration,' said Mr Campion over the rim of a tea cup.

'Source?' queried Perdita.

'Don't let him draw you in, dear,' said Amanda, selecting a daintily trimmed smoke salmon sandwich.

'In to what?'

'His little joke. He was just waiting for you to mention your godfather's school in Yorkshire so he could quote Dickens at you. I think that was the advert Wackford Squeers put in the newspapers for Dotheboys Hall in *Nicholas Nickleby*. Somebody mentions Yorkshire and schools and it's the first thing Albert thinks of. Don't ask me why his mind works that way; it's a mystery.'

'It must run in the family,' said Perdita gently. 'Rupert quoted Dickens too this morning when he heard what was in the letter. He went for *Hard Times*, though.'

'Ah, of course, Mr Gradgrind,' murmured Campion as if to himself. 'Clever boy.'

'Well, I don't think either of you are being quite fair,' said Perdita, feeling she should ride to her godfather's defence. 'I'm sure Yorkshire's not horrid and the schools there have moved on a bit since Dickens' day.'

Mr Campion smiled at his daughter-in-law and it was a beam of genuine affection.

'Yorkshire is not horrid at all, my dear, though a fair bit of wuthering does take place on the higher ground, so I'm told, and I am sure the schools have moved on since Dotheboys Hall closed for business. Although' – he paused mischievously – 'if the schools there are performing a musical version of *Doctor Faustus* then one might think that perhaps they have moved too far.'

Perdita reached for another sandwich. As a 'resting' actress it was a natural reaction to take advantage of free food whenever and wherever it was offered.

'I may have let Rupert believe that it was a piece of experimental musical theatre,' she said coyly, 'which might just have been inspired by that hippy show *Hair* with all its nudity and . . . well, hair . . .'

'Darling, that's delicious!' Amanda laughed. 'Did he fall for it?'

'Pretty much, and to be fair Brigham's letter was a bit vague, so when Rupert was out I telephoned the school and got "the full S.P." Did I say that right? It's something Lugg would say, isn't it?'

Mr Campion nodded his approval. 'Correct on both counts, I'm sorry to say. Pray, continue. What did our esteemed headmaster have to say?'

'It turns out it's not a musical at all – well, not a musical like *My Fair Lady* or *Oliver*. It's actually the play – the real Marlowe deal – done pretty straight as far as I can work out, but with musical accompaniment from the school brass band. That probably makes it sound even more awful than it should.'

'On the contrary,' said Campion, patting Perdita's arm. 'I would take that as a good sign – a sign of quality.'

'You would?'

'But of course. Yorkshire insists on excellence when it comes to brass band music, just as they do with their cricket.'

'Are they any good at rugby?' the girl asked innocently.

Mr Campion allowed his brow to furrow. 'I'm told it's a hot-bed of professional Rugby League rather than Rugby Union which, as I am sure you know, is a game designed for hooligans and berserkers played by gentleman amateurs. Why do you ask?'

'Well . . .' Perdita strung out the moment whilst rearming her plate with more sandwiches. 'It seems that this poor chap Bertram Browne, the one who died in a road accident, was not only the English master and did the drama productions but also coached the boys at rugby. My dear godfather has had the brilliant idea that I can do his dramatic duties whilst Rupert stands in for him on the playing fields, chasing the school teams round the goalposts or whatever it is coaches are supposed to do. It would only be for a couple of weeks until the end of term, and it means we don't have to be apart.'

'And Rupert is happy with the prospect of the sporting life?' said Mr Campion, supressing a smile.

'If it means he can be with his beautiful wife, of course he is,' said Amanda firmly.

'Oh, naturally,' her husband agreed quickly. 'It's just that I don't remember the boy enjoying the game when he was at school. He could play well enough but the game simply didn't interest him. Still, with his thespian training he should be good at the morale-boosting team talk. Once more into the breach and all that. More tea?'

'Godfather Brigham says it will only be for a couple of fixtures,' said Perdita, holding out her cup and saucer, 'because term's nearly over and there's always the chance that games will be called off due to bad weather at this time of year.'

'I told you,' smiled Campion, 'it always wuthers in Yorkshire, especially on the heights. Make sure Rupert packs his thermal long johns and wish him luck. And of course, all the best with your production of *Faustus*, which I'm sure will be splendid, though you may have casting problems.'

'I will?'

'Probably. From memory – admittedly a very unreliable and cobweb-strewn one – somebody has to play Helen of Troy. You know, the beautiful face that launched a thousand ships. Always a difficult casting choice in an all-boys' school.'

'Perdita will manage supremely,' said Amanda, 'and we will be the first to shout "Bravo" and "Encore" when the cast take their many, many curtain calls.'

'We will?'

'We certainly will, for I too have received a job offer from Brigham Armitage.' Amanda snapped open the gold clasp of her Morris Moskowitz black leather handbag and, delving into its capacious interior – Mr Campion referred to it as her 'doctor's bag' – produced the letter Perdita had delivered and handed it across the table. 'Required for one Speech Day: an inspirational speaker with experience of the modern world and the white heat of modern technology. I paraphrase, of course, but it clearly means me, not you, though you are welcome to accompany me.'

Mr Campion scanned the letter out of politeness, folded it and handed it back. 'The headmaster has chosen wisely,' he said, 'and I would be honoured to stand by your side and pass you the Lower Fifth's trophy for raffia work, or the Snodgrass Shield for Greek translation or whatever gongs you'll be handing out, and I promise not to pocket the Footling Cup for smoking behind the Fives' Court. I always felt short-changed that I never got one of those when I was a whining schoolboy with a satchel and a shining face.'

'That's Shakespeare,' said Perdita confidently, 'not Dickens.'

'Almost,' said Amanda. 'He's just showing off again.'

'Seriously, my darlings, I think it's a splendid idea,' said Campion. 'The two of you will perform your respective duties admirably and Rupert – well, it will be an experience for Rupert; probably a good one. When do we go north?'

'Rupert and I are needed immediately, according to godfather Brigham, but Speech Day isn't until the end of term in December. We were thinking of driving up there tomorrow.'

Mr Campion reached fondly for his wife's hand. 'Why don't we make a long weekend of it around Speech Day, darling? We could go tramping on the moors, pop over to Haworth and worship at the Brontë shrine or take a run up to the ruined abbeys at Fountains, Jervaulx and Rievaulx. They're all pretty impressive, even in deep midwinter in darkest Yorkshire.'

'Winter in Yorkshire . . .' Amanda murmured to herself, then turned to Perdita as if she had had a revelation. 'Never mind reminding Rupert to pack his thermal long johns, my dear – let's go and buy you some right now!'

THREE
Great North Road

I f a bright red second-hand five-year-old Austin Mini Cooper had seams, then Perdita's was bulging at them as its stubby snout nosed its way up the A1, its windscreen wipers squeaking in protest at the morning drizzle and the spray of lorries thundering past.

Rupert had been amazed at both the amount of luggage Perdita had insisted on bringing and the fact that it had all fitted into the Mini, but had said nothing. When they had married, Rupert and Perdita had agreed unreligious but eminently sensible additional vows that they would not quarrel or dispute any matters pertaining to money or to driving. And just as Rupert refrained from commenting on the plethora of bags and cases accompanying his wife, so Perdita bit her tongue and said nothing when Rupert chose to follow the A1 north rather than the recently extended M1 motorway.

It was only when they were free of London and almost through Hertfordshire that she questioned her driver's grasp of geography, albeit tangentially.

'There's another sign for Biggleswade,' Perdita said conversationally. 'It must be the fifth one we've passed. Why is Biggleswade so popular? *Where* is Biggleswade, anyway?'

'It's in Bedfordshire, darling, and I think its main claim to fame is that it has more signs than any other place bypassed by the A1. Nobody goes there but everyone knows they've passed a turning to it.'

'One of the joys of travelling the Great North Road,' sighed Perdita, digging into a shopping bag at her feet for the emergency packet of travel sweets she always carried on long journeys. 'How long will it take us, do you think?'

'Another three hours,' said Rupert. 'We can stop for lunch if you want to.'

'I've brought sandwiches and a flask of tea so let's push on. Though I'm happy to do some of the driving if you want a break.'

'If Dick Turpin can make it to York in a day on a horse, then I think I can manage Huddersfield or thereabouts in a car.' Rupert grinned.

'You won't mention Dick Turpin when you're in Yorkshire, will you, darling?' Perdita said, pointedly looking out of her side window.

'Why not?'

'Turpin was an eighteenth-century Essex thug. His famous "ride" from London to York – two hundred miles in a single day – was a story made up later and based on a *seventeenth*-century Yorkshireman called John Nevison who supposedly robbed a man in Gad's Hill in Kent at four a.m. and then rode to York by eight p.m. the same day to establish an alibi.'

'Did the alibi work?'

'Yes, it did. No one believed he could have ridden that far in sixteen hours, but he had witnesses to say he was in York that evening so he couldn't have been in Kent that morning.'

'Clever fellow.'

'Not that clever,' she said, her hands busy rustling something inside the shopping bag now balanced on her knees. 'He was hanged about ten years later, though he went to the scaffold like a true gentleman. Humbug?'

'Yes, please. Where did you learn all that?'

Perdita stretched out an arm and pressed a black-and-white sweet into her husband's mouth.

'From dear old Brigham Armitage, no less, a story he told me when I was little. The curse of the schoolmaster, I suppose. You have to teach an innocent child a fact a day.'

'A bit like the Drink-A-Pinta-Milk-A-Day campaign,' mumbled Rupert as he tackled a hard, minty mouthful. 'When you spoke to him yesterday did he say any more about the teacher you – we – are replacing?'

Perdita unwrapped a sweet for herself and popped it between

her teeth, then daintily kissed the stickiness off her fingers before answering.

'A little. It was strange really, almost as if he was rehearsing a funeral oration. Perhaps he was. Lots of what you might expect: trusted colleague, admired by the boys he taught, driving force behind the school's drama productions and an inspiration on the rugby field . . .'

'Oh dear,' said Rupert, 'I'm going to be a terrible disappointment.'

'The late Mr Browne – that's Browne with an "e", if it matters – used to play for something called the Sappers Rugby Club in his youth apparently, though I've no idea where that is.'

'It's based in Chatham in Kent, I think,' said Rupert, 'at the home of the Royal Engineers. Quite a famous old club, though the Sappers always were a sporty lot. The Royal Engineers played in the first-ever FA Cup Final, you know. That's the other sort of football.'

'The one with the round ball?' Perdita asked impishly and, when Rupert nodded, said smugly, 'See, I do take an interest.'

'So Mr Browne was an ex-military man?' Rupert persevered.

'I got the impression Brigham likes to recruit teachers from the services. Probably thinks it's good for discipline in the classroom.'

'That's another reason I'll be a disappointment – I didn't even get to do National Service.' Rupert frowned but kept his eyes firmly fixed on the road ahead. 'I'm not sure I fancy trying to impose discipline in a classroom.'

'You won't have to, will you? You can shout at them across a muddy field or blow your little whistle or something. It's me who has to drum the Romantic poets into reluctant young brains and then try and get them to remember their Marlowe. *This is hell, nor am I out of it.*'

'*Faustus?*'

'Yes, but I was thinking of Yorkshire.'

'We're not there yet,' grinned Rupert. 'We could turn back and say the car broke down.'

'Oh, we couldn't do that, I've promised,' said Perdita sweetly. 'A goddaughter's word is her bond and all that.'

They pulled into a lay-by near Norman Cross and got out of the tiny car to stretch their legs, eat sandwiches and drink tea from the plastic cups which topped Perdita's flask as northward-bound lorries thundered by them, close enough to make the Mini rock on its chassis.

It was an early luncheon or a very late breakfast, but Perdita was determined to get to Denby Ash before it got dark, and so naturally she insisted on driving the rest of the way. Rupert did not object as he knew her to be an excellent driver, and stoically folded his legs into the well of the passenger seat amongst the bags, books and roadmaps whilst Perdita adjusted the rear-view mirror – automatically checking her hair and make-up as she did so – turned the key in the ignition and set off in a racing start.

Perdita talked constantly as she drove – something Rupert knew she only did when she was worried. Would she be able to control classrooms full of bumptious Yorkshire boys? Would they laugh at her accent? Would she laugh at theirs? Would she even understand them? It was an all-boys' school: had they ever seen a woman before? Of course they had; she was being stupid. They all had mothers, didn't they? And hadn't Brigham Armitage told her that as well as his wife, Celia, who was school secretary and school nurse, it seemed, there was at least one other female on the teaching staff? But they were probably qualified as teachers, whereas Perdita was only qualified to act; surely they would know she wasn't a real teacher?

'Not if you act the role as well as I know you can, my love,' Rupert had soothed, his eyes flicking nervously to the speedometer. 'Think of it as a part in Rep., a part you've been doing for weeks and the critics love you for it.'

'Regional theatre critics are not usually spotty, sniggering, twelve-year-old schoolboys. Well, not all of them.'

'Probably more than you'd think, in my experience,' Rupert agreed with a wry smile. 'But don't worry about it – you'll be fine. The little oiks will all fall in love with you at first sight. It's me they're going to be pelting with mud and scragging in the scrum, not to mention what might happen in the showers.'

'I don't think I want to hear any more on that subject,' said Perdita, tight-lipped. 'It's nothing you need to go to a psychiatrist for, is it?'

'No, no. Nothing like that,' said Rupert hurriedly. 'It's just that a favourite trick when I was a boy . . .'

'When I was a lad,' teased his wife, trying out her stock Yorkshire accent, 'nobbut a whippersnapper.'

'Yes, back then in those innocent days before I was entrapped by gorgeous, sexy actresses. When I was at school . . .'

'Excuse me?'

'What?'

'Use of the plural; you said sexy actress*es*.'

'I may have been chased by several but I only let one catch me.'

'Don't get above yourself, darling – you could always find yourself thrown back into the ocean. Anyway, you were about to confess something unspeakable which happened to you in the showers at school.'

'It wasn't really unspeakable,' said Rupert, looking out of the side window to avert his discomfort. 'Not on the scale of man's inhumanity to man, or even boys' inhumanity to other boys, come to think of it, but it was rather intimidating at the time. If the sports master felt that you hadn't played a game to your full potential, he would throw your towel into the shower with you, or sometimes you would find it waiting for you, on the floor, already wringing wet. It was supposed to be an incentive to improve your performance for the next game.'

'That's bullying, plain and simple,' Perdita said firmly.

'My father called it psychological warfare.'

'You told your parents? Good for you.'

'I mentioned it to Pa,' Rupert said casually. 'In passing, as it were, not complaining, just fishing to see if he'd gone through the same rotten treatment when he was a pupil.'

'And had he?'

'Just the once. He said he ignored it completely and the following week, after the game, he went into the showers *wearing* his towel, came out dripping wet, got dressed without making any attempt to dry himself and went off to Latin Prep as if absolutely nothing untoward had happened.'

'Which showed the bullies they couldn't win. Good for him.'

'That much was true, though he claims he caught double pneumonia as a result of two hours of translating Juvenal whilst wearing damp clothes. I never had the nerve to follow his example; I just smuggled an extra towel into the changing room.'

'Well, that showed initiative,' Perdita said kindly, reaching out her left hand to pat her husband's knee without taking her eyes off the road, 'and it won't be a practice you'll permit at Ash Grange, will it?'

'Absolutely not. My motto shall be *Cave salacones!* – which I think means "Bullies watch out" but I'd better check that with the Latin master. The school does have a Latin master, I presume?'

'Oh, yes. Godfather Brigham insists on Latin being taught, otherwise his brighter boys won't get into Cambridge.'

'But it's not a requirement any longer.'

'I know that; you know that. Brigham is delightfully behind the times,' said Perdita then paused as the thought struck her. 'Of course, he can't be too far behind the times. He has no qualms about employing women as teachers and not just cooks and skivvies, and he's also asked your mother to preside at Speech Day to show how a woman can succeed in a man's world.'

'Plus,' said Rupert, wagging a finger to emphasize his point, 'he's forward-thinking enough to allow a musical version of Marlowe's most famous play and it's not a logical choice for the end of term before Christmas, so that's doubly radical.'

'Mmm,' murmured Perdita thoughtfully, 'my jury's still out on that one. But talking of forward-thinking: what the devil is that *thing*?'

The *thing* which had caught her eye, looming out of the dull morning to the left of the road, was indeed unmissable. It was a structure of sweeping upward curves of concrete which at first glance could have been mistaken for a giant sculpture of some form of alien butterfly landing on planet Earth for the first time. On closer examination, the *thing* was clearly man-made and served as the flamboyant saddle-shaped roof of a rather mundane petrol station, which seemed, to Perdita, to be a rather ostentatious way of keeping the rain out. To Rupert, however, it was a landmark, and he greeted it like a homeward-bound sailor.

'We're at Markham Moor in Nottinghamshire,' he enthused, 'and that famous garage there marks the beginning of the north for most people.'

'It's bizarre,' said Perdita huffily. 'What on earth is it supposed to be?'

'I'm not sure it's supposed to be anything except a modern piece of architectural design. All garages, perhaps even houses, will look like that in twenty years' time.'

'I very much doubt that,' said Perdita. 'It's a ridiculous piece of design; there can't be two of them in the world.'

'Actually,' said Rupert in what he felt was his best school-masterly voice (so convincing, he thought, that he should be wearing a gown), 'the same design – which technically is called a hyperbolic paraboloid – was used for the TWA Flight Centre at Idlewild airport in New York, the one they've renamed after President Kennedy.'

'Your mother told you that, didn't she?' Perdita flashed her husband a sideways glance.

'Yes,' said Rupert, slightly deflated. 'The first time I saw it I thought it was a spaceship landing and folding up its wings, like something out of Dan Dare.'

'Were you in the back seat with a bag of sherbet lemons and a copy of *The Eagle*?' Perdita said with a sly grin.

'If you must know, it was the year before I met you and Mother was giving me a lift to an audition in Sheffield at The Playhouse. I didn't get the part and I can't even remember what I read for it, but I certainly remember that garage. For me, it's always marked the start of the north, although I suppose technically that's probably the Yorkshire border.'

'Oooh!' Perdita's left hand left the steering wheel and shot to her shocked, open mouth. 'I've just had a terrible thought,' she said mischievously.

'What?'

'I think I forgot to pack the passports.'

FOUR

'No extras, no vacations, and diet unparalleled.'

When she first caught sight of Ash Grange, Perdita was reminded of her father-in-law's assertion that a fair amount of 'wuthering' took place in Yorkshire and yet was immediately reassured that the house was clearly sturdy enough to withstand the slings and arrows of the most atrocious

weather. In fact, she was quite prepared to believe the house would
be impermeable to light artillery.

Local antiquarians would cheerfully claim that Ash Grange
could trace its origins back to a fifteenth-century farmhouse which
was expanded and possibly fortified as a sturdy manor house during
the seventeenth century. Mysteriously, no traces of either incarnation had ever been reliably identified and so local pride had to be
content with a mere one hundred years of documented history.
There were many among the mining community of Denby Ash
who took delight in pointing out that the village's brass band pre-
dated the Big House and its rather privileged (if not downright
stuck-up) occupants by a good thirty years.

Such a claim to historical precedence was beyond dispute as
the earliest Minute Books of the Denby Ash Colliers Brass Band
dated from 1838 whereas all architectural guides to the county
placed the construction of Ash Grange as part of the neo-Gothic
revival much favoured by industrially wealthy Victorians in the
1860s, and most dated the house from 1868, its construction coming
immediately after that of the church of St James the Great at the
opposite end of the village which straddled the road from
Huddersfield to Wakefield.

Described, confusingly, as 'part Georgian, part neo-Gothic or
perhaps Jigsaw Gothic' in style, Ash Grange was solidly built of
dark Yorkshire sandstone blocks with grey-black stone roofing
tiles, its powerful vertical lines drawing the eye of the awestruck
beholder up to the pointed arches of its first-floor oriel windows
and then on to the crenellated battlements under the roof and
beyond to the twin towers of clustered chimneys. The only
softening of the Grange's severe, rather militaristic façade was an
ornate ten-segment rose window. This circular aperture, which
would be called a Catherine Window in a Catholic church, was
– or so the architectural journals agreed – an inferior copy of the
White Rose window designed by church architect John
Loughborough Pearson for Christ Church at Appleton-le-Moors
in distant North Yorkshire. The window perched above a stone
porch in which nestled a solid oak door and, between the porch
and window, a coat of arms which now designated the Grange as
a place of learning. In a painted stone relief were four white roses
(were there any other kind in Yorkshire?) at the corners of an open
book whose pages displayed the two words of the motto of Ash

Grange School for Boys: *Turpe Nescire*, which can be translated as 'It is a disgrace to be ignorant' although one retiring science teacher had suggested it be expanded to read 'It is no disgrace to be quiet and ignorant.' His suggestion had met with stern disapproval on school grounds except in the senior staff room where his last few days in post were greeted with constant winks and nods of harmonious agreement.

The actual house – the Big House – formed only a small part – perhaps a sixth – of the area of Ash Grange School. To the rear of the original mansion, where once a kitchen garden and a large brick coalhouse had taken pride of place (the house had been built with the profits from coal so domestic supplies of the noble fuel were suitably protected), there now extended large blocks of concrete and glass rectangular buildings which served as classrooms and offices, their windows giving panoramic views to the east, over the tarmac tennis courts, a cricket pitch, two rugby fields, a pavilion and a brick changing room block before what had once clearly been a manicured parkland gave way to the rising ground and mixed foliage of Denby Wood. It was Denby Wood which had over the years effectively camouflaged from the view of the Grange two of the three sources of the wealth which had built it: the collieries known as Shuttle Eye and Caphouse.

The Victorian builders of the Grange had deliberately sited the house so that the winding towers and slag heaps of the pits which paid their bills were effectively hidden from polite society, or at least the society which congregated around the Grange. The third colliery, Grange Ash, which formed the apex of the industrial 'black triangle' of Denby Ash, was more problematic for the delicate sensibilities of the inhabitants of the new house as it lay to the south of the site chosen, across the Huddersfield road and even in the 1860s its pyramidal spoil heap was rising to heights which would have impressed a pharaoh. To disrupt, if not completely mask, this unsightly sightline, Victorian landscapers planted a phalanx of yew trees to guard the twisted driveway by which the Grange was approached. For almost forty years this man-made extension to Denby Wood protected the owners and staff of Ash Grange from the dirty and noisy reminders that their luxury was provided by the sweat of men, often naked, working in cramped, dark and dangerous conditions underground, and of

women and children pushing and pulling tubs of black gold at
the pit head. Yet with the introduction of motor lorries to transport
that solid harvest around the turn of the century, Grange Ash
colliery and the very coal which was being ripped from it began
to take revenge on the Big House. Not even the thick, disciplined
ranks of yew trees could cushion the incessant rumble of heavily-
laden coal trucks bound for the mills and railway sidings in
Huddersfield or the dusty rattle of their return journey to the pit.
Gradually the yew trees became discoloured from the constant
powdering of coal dust as fine as icing sugar, which reached as
far as the Grange itself, darkening the windows. Moreover, the
procession of trucks on the Huddersfield road produced a seismic
disruption producing potholes and cracks not only in the main
artery through the village but along the length of the mazey
driveway, resulting in many a twisted ankle and broken carriage
wheel, especially in winter. More than one skittish and superstitious scullery maid would maintain that such disturbance in the
very fabric of their surroundings was divine retribution for greedy
pit owners digging too deep.

Now the pit owners were gone; politically thanks to nationaliza-
tion in 1947 and in reality thanks to generous compensation
payments by the government to the owning family, which, in the
words of their accountant, had made them 'terminally well-off'
and prompted a move to the island of Guernsey.

A well-founded fear of punitive death duties and a fifty-two per
cent rate of surtax, and the less accurate predictions of a lifetime
of socialist election victories ensured that the sale of Ash Grange
went through smoothly and the energetic and idealistic Brigham
Armitage, assisted by his wife, Celia, quickly began to convert
the house into a school.

Having left the motorway, the young Campions had approached
Denby Ash from the direction of Barnsley which necessitated
driving the length of the village to reach Ash Grange. Perdita
slowed to within the regulation thirty mph limit in order to
familiarize herself with the local geography, and the first landmark they encountered after passing the official white metal sign
which confirmed they were entering Denby Ash was, to Rupert's
delight, a pub.

A large wooden sign in red lettering across its side wall
announced proudly that it sold Barnsley Bitter; a smaller, traditional

inn sign hanging from a corner iron bracket identified it as the Green Dragon. It was a big, detached brick building strategically placed in the 'v' of a fork where, according to a modest fingerpost sign, the Barnsley road met the Wakefield road. A large white plastic banner hung across the frontage of the pub, proclaiming without modesty in large red print that the establishment was 'Famous For Basket Meals'.

'That looks like the local restaurant,' chirped Rupert, 'though I'm not sure I can remember how I liked my baskets cooked.'

'Don't be a clot,' said Perdita, indicating left and waiting for a coal lorry to thunder by before she turned, 'or a snob, and if we should go there don't you dare ask for soup-in-a-basket. I'm used to your sense of humour but there's no need to impose it on the natives.'

From the fork guarded by the Green Dragon, which sat like a stopper on the bottle that was Denby Ash, the road rose westward into a fading afternoon sun in a long hill running along the side of a valley. As was almost traditional in English villages, the nearest building to the pub was a church, set on a slight rise away from the road, a free-standing wooden signboard displayed the name of the church and details of its services. Rupert decided to show he was paying attention.

'I spy, with my little eye . . . the church of St James the Great, and next to it there's the school!'

'That's the village primary school,' Perdita said patiently. 'Ash Grange is at the other end of the village at the top of this hill. Godfather Brigham said if we kept going we'd come it eventually.'

Rupert leaned forward in the passenger seat, turning his head to give a running commentary on his view through the windscreen and his side window.

'I spy a row of houses, then another and another,' he said. 'In fact, if it wasn't for those little alleyways between them it could be one long continuous sausage of a house.'

'Ginnels,' said Perdita primly.

'I beg your pardon?'

'They call them ginnels up here – those passageways between the rows of houses. It's how people get to their back doors.'

Rupert, suitably impressed at his wife's local knowledge, concentrated on the left side of the road where more modern houses were clustered in small cul-de-sacs where the contours of the hill had allowed. Between them were detached buildings set back from the edge of the road as the church had been, and in Rupert's personal game of 'I Spy', many of them indeed seemed to be churches.

'I spy with my little eye something called the Zion Chapel. Do you think they placed it deliberately near the working men's club on the principle of know-your-enemy? And now my little eye can't quite believe it's now spying a Wesleyan Chapel as well, not to mention' – he paused for dramatic effect – 'a *Primitive* Methodist Chapel, whatever that is. The churches believe in outnumbering the pubs round here, don't they? It's not like Norwich, is it?'

'Norwich?' laughed his wife. 'What on earth are you talking about?'

'Isn't it Norwich which has a church for every Sunday but a pub for every day of the year?' posed Rupert.

'I'll take your word on that,' chuckled Perdita, 'but I wouldn't worry about the bodies and souls of the local inhabitants here. Their needs, both spiritual and temporal, seem to be well catered for and there's another pub to even up the odds.'

'So there is.'

Although clearly older and more picturesque, the Sun Inn made no attempt to compete with the bold claims of its larger competitor, yet it occupied, at the western edge of the village, a similar strategic position guarding the solid stone bridge which carried the road on towards Huddersfield just as the Green Dragon protected the fork in the road at the eastern end. Rupert imagined the two pubs almost as victualing customs posts guarding the entrances to Denby Ash, with the large working men's club he had 'spied' exactly halfway between the two acting as some sort of United Nation's demarcation line. Perhaps there were gregarious customers who could not make the journey from one pub to the other without a refreshment break. Or perhaps the locals were so fiercely loyal to either the Sun or the Green Dragon that the issue divided the village and the idea of visiting both was akin to breaking a local taboo.

Then Rupert's alcoholic reverie was shattered as Perdita accelerated and the Mini Cooper jumped over the hump of the stone bridge with stomach-plunging enthusiasm, as if joyous to be free of the village.

'So that was Denby Ash,' Perdita said cheerfully, thinking she had jolted, quite literally, her husband out of his irritating 'I Spy' mode.

'But what the devil is *that*?' said Rupert, pointing a finger at the windscreen, or rather the black, pyramidal peak which loomed suddenly large to their left.

'That's what they call a muck stack in these parts. Impressive, isn't it?'

'In a dark, satanic sort of way I suppose it is,' admitted Rupert. 'Is it a mountain of coal?'

'I think it's the stuff they pull out of the ground that *isn't* proper coal – stuff nobody wants. Technically it's "spoil" but it can still burn and some of these big muck stacks are permanently smoking, a bit like Vesuvius or Etna.'

'They don't blow up, though, do they?' Rupert asked nervously, recalling a visit to Pompeii as an undergraduate.

'Not usually, though there was that one which slid down the hill and caused the Aberfan disaster in Wales,' Perdita said soberly.

'God, that was awful; those poor children in that school.'

'Don't worry, dear – that couldn't happen here. Ash Grange was the stately home of the mine owners once upon a time and they would have made sure they built it a safe distance away from any dirt or danger.'

Rupert studied his wife carefully, unconsciously imitating the expression his father adopted when he peered over the top of his spectacles at someone.

'That's a bit harsh, isn't it, darling?'

'Perhaps I'm getting more Bolshie the further north we come,' Perdita said vaguely.

'Then it's a good job your godfather's school isn't in Scotland.'

'In fact,' said Perdita as she braked and indicated, 'it's right here.'

'We are a small school,' said Brigham Armitage, gripping the lapels of his Harris Tweed jacket as if they were the straps of a parachute, 'and of course we are very young. Indeed, I suspect that your husband is older than we are.'

Perdita smiled, acknowledging the gallantry of her godfather, who knew perfectly well how old she was and that she too had seniority over his school.

'We have three hundred and thirty boys on the school roll. They range from eleven to fifteen in age and we organize them in eleven forms each of platoon strength or as near as we can get. Ideally, we envisaged a proper House system, though we do not as yet have any distinguished old boys – or benefactors – after which we could name them. Were you in Kilbracken at Rugby, young Campion?'

'Yes, actually I was,' said Rupert smartly, slightly uncomfortable, though not knowing quite why, at being in a headmaster's study.

They had been met at the oaken door by a prim, blue-rinsed woman wearing a cardigan buttoned to the neck as if it was a uniform, who had introduced herself as Mrs Celia Armitage and informed them that 'the headmaster' (not, Rupert noted, 'my husband') was ready and waiting to receive them.

'Thought as much,' said the headmaster, 'always was the best house when it came to school plays and things dramatic. Sadly, we don't have that sort of tradition here at Ash Grange, but then those things take time and growth. Fortunately, the Comprehensive system is helping us enormously.'

'*It is?*' Perdita squeaked in surprise, the blue china cup and saucer she held rattling loudly and the Rich Tea biscuit she had been dunking surreptitiously quivered dangerously.

'Oh, yes, my dear, it most certainly is. If the Labour government pushes ahead with its plans for Comprehensive Schools then more and more parents will opt for private education for their children and I envisage we will be fully fee-paying within the next three years.'

'You're not at the moment?' asked Rupert.

'Only about sixty per cent of our boys are private pupils,' said the headmaster. 'The remainder come via the local education authority after sitting the eleven-plus. Of course, the local authority is strongly Labour and supports the Comprehensive ideal.'

'It does sound an attractive ideal,' Perdita said, turning her face up and smiling sweetly at her godfather.

The hairs on the back of Rupert's neck began to stand to attention. Had he really married a Bolshevik? Fortunately Brigham Armitage, although he had the demeanour and sartorial smartness of an off-duty church warden, did not seem at all worried by radical concepts, especially not when issued from a perfectly pretty mouth.

'Which of course it is,' said Mr Armitage, returning Perdita's smile from underneath a neatly clipped moustache, 'in theory. Equal opportunity in education is a perfectly sound ambition. The problem is, my dear, that in practice it will mean catering to the lowest ability and the brighter children will be held back.'

'The brighter children or just selected children from privileged and richer families?' Perdita asked, noting that her husband was staring fixedly into his teacup and shuffling uncomfortably in his chair.

The headmaster, as headmasters are trained from birth to be, remained unflappable.

'Some of our best pupils are county boys as we call them and not only do they not pay fees but many win scholarships from the various foundations and charities in the mining industry, which even covers the cost of their uniforms and their bus fares. As long as they are pupils at Ash Grange, our aim is to get as many of them as possible into the five per cent of young people who go on to university, whatever their background. If that is condoning privilege and selection, then so be it.'

For the second time since they had entered school premises, a strident electric bell rang out, the sound bringing the same relief to Rupert as it would to an out-matched boxer reeling from a first round battering.

'That's the end of final period,' said the headmaster, 'and we should remove ourselves to the staff room where we can catch your new colleagues or at least some of them before they disappear.'

'Do some of them live off the premises?' Rupert asked, thinking it an innocent enough, non-political issue.

'All of them,' said Mr Armitage. 'My wife and I are here all the time, of course, and the senior staff are on a rota. Two of them are on duty every night to supervise the boarders. We have about thirty boarders, mostly sons of army families, at the moment but Celia hopes we will have many more in the future. She rather likes the idea of being a den-mother. We never managed to have children of our own, you see.'

Brigham Armitage eased himself from the captain's chair and stood to attention behind his desk. He raised his right hand to his face, almost as if he were about to salute, but with finger and thumb stroked the wingtips of his moustache to ensure every individual hair was in its proper place, then he tugged down on the hem of his waistcoat and buttoned his jacket, all with clipped military movements.

'If you would follow me, I'll lead the way to the staff room,' he announced, 'if, that is, we can avoid being trampled by a herd of boys thundering to leave now that school is finished for the day, then I'll give you a brief tour of the premises, just to get your basic bearings.'

He ushered the young Campions towards his study door. 'I am sure you have a preconceived notion of us,' he said genially, 'especially if you've read *Nicholas Nickleby*.'

'You mean Dotheboys Hall?' said Rupert with convincing innocence. 'That thought had not crossed our minds.'

'Oh, I'm sure it did. The comparison is always made by people from down south, but we have broad shoulders here in Yorkshire. We are used to being characterized as a race of skinflints who wear flat caps, like their beer with a big head and only listen to brass band music, and whenever I tell a southerner that I run a school in Yorkshire, they inevitably call me Wackford Squeers.'

'Surely not,' soothed Perdita, slipping an arm around as much of her godfather's shoulders as she could reach. 'He was a perfectly horrid man and you're a perfectly sweet one. Ash Grange isn't anything like Dotheboys Hall, is it?'

Mr Armitage smiled, his heart obviously melting at his Bolshevik goddaughter's flattery.

'Only in one respect, I hope. The advertisement for Dotheboys, according to Dickens, claims that the school offers "No extras, no vacations and diet unparalleled". Well, we do supply extras and we certainly have vacations, but when it comes to offering a diet unparalleled, I have to say we are inordinately proud of our catering and our diet – as you can see' – he patted his well-filled waistcoat – 'is indeed unparalleled. But then, I have to say that as my good lady wife is in charge of catering and that is the one area of the school where the headmaster has absolutely no authority what-soever. Do not, however, repeat what I just said in the staff room. As far as the staff – and the boys come to that – are concerned, the headmaster is all-knowing, all-powerful and absolutely everywhere at once.'

Rupert and Perdita dutifully followed the omniscient and omnipotent Brigham Armitage along a high, windowless corridor which led into the bowels of the school. As was clearly the highway code of traffic within the establishment, they walked on the left and a trickle of schoolboys pulling on coats and scarves, or struggling with heavily laden haversacks or satchels, marched in procession in the opposite direction. To a boy they were quiet and orderly and all greeted the headmaster with a polite 'Good night, sir'. The older ones, or at least those over five feet tall, all gave Perdita a second if not a third glance. Rupert wondered whether he should scowl at them but restrained himself on the grounds that boys were apt to be, when all was said and done, boys.

Along the length of the corridor, well above head height and out of reach of the casual juvenile vandal hung an eclectic series of framed oil paintings without any apparent linking theme. Yet two of them, hanging side by side, struck a chord of recognition in Rupert.

'Excuse me, Headmaster,' he said formally as there were boys in the corridor, 'but those two paintings look rather familiar.'

'Are you an art lover, Mr Campion?' Mr Armitage stopped in his tracks, acknowledged a brace of boys hurrying past with a respectful nod and then concentrated on the paintings Rupert was pointing at.

'Not really,' Rupert confessed. 'It was just that those two are both landscapes, or should I say "seascapes", of the Suffolk coast, are they not?'

'They are indeed. Do you know the artists?'

'Not a clue, I'm afraid, but we know that coast.'

'Yes, of course,' the headmaster mused, 'you would. They are both of the area around Walberswick and Southwold. The one on the right is a Bernard Priestman and the other's a Rowland Suddaby. East Anglia seems to have exerted quite a pull on our artists.'

'*Your* artists, Headmaster?' Perdita asked. 'Are they connected to the school?'

Mr Armitage glanced along the corridor and his eyes flashed in a silent warning that they were being overheard by several sets of juvenile ears working with bat-like precision.

'Sadly no, Miss Browning; I meant "our artists" in the sense that all the paintings hung here are by Yorkshiremen. The next one, that rather surreal daub which looks like a draughts' board someone has taken an axe to, is by Edward Wadsworth. Not to

my taste at all, far too modern, but he was a Yorkshireman –
born in Cleckheaton actually, which is not that far from here
– and he did some sterling work for the navy in the First War
on "dazzle camouflage" on ships. Zigzags and big black and
white stripes, that sort of thing, to break up the outlines and
confuse the enemy.

'And next to that is my personal favourite: a Yorkshire scene
by a Victorian painter of the old school, as it were. That's one of
Atkinson Grimshaw's views of Whitby harbour at evening.
Grimshaw was a Leeds man, but I don't hold that against him.
He's often looked down on as a journeyman painter, slightly
mechanical perhaps, and clearly no Turner.'

'But you know what you like!' Perdita said cheekily.

'We usually do in Yorkshire,' said Mr Armitage stiffly, 'and
being Yorkshiremen we naturally ignore the rather snooty comments
of so-called art critics.'

'Not just those critics based in London and the south?' asked
Rupert gently.

'I thought all critics were based in London,' the headmaster
said casually whilst aiming a steely stare at his goddaughter.
'Especially theatre critics.'

'Well, we certainly don't pay them any heed, do we?' Perdita
bristled.

'We wouldn't give *their* opinions house-room in Yorkshire, my
dear . . . my dear Miss Browning.'

'Good for you, Headmaster, and whatever my hus— Whatever
Mr Campion thinks, I like your Atkinson Grimshaw.'

Rupert, who could not remember passing an opinion on the
painting, bit his tongue and remained silent.

'Thank you. He is an artist who is yet to have his day, I feel.
I bought that canvas ten years ago for seventy pounds and I look
on it as a sound investment. It's going to be worth a pretty penny
one day. But enough of my hobby. The working day of a headmaster extends long after the last day bell has gone and I want
you to meet at least some of the staff before they disappear, so
let us proceed to the Dragons' Den, as the boys call it.'

Mr Armitage indicated they should continue down the
corridor which ended in a small hallway, where a set of incon-
gruously modern stairs rose to the first-floor level providing a
bridge to a more recent extension to the house. As the stairs

were clearly in use by a trickle of departing schoolboys all wearing relieved expressions, it was a safe assumption that they led to a series of classrooms. On the far side of the stairwell was a polished oak door with a shiny brass plate proclaiming: staff room.

In any school, particularly in the early morning before assembly and at going-home time in the afternoon, a headmaster has to take on the role of a traffic policeman on point duty. It was a clearly a role which came naturally to Brigham Armitage, who stepped into the midstream of pupils descending the stairs, one arm raised to halt traffic, the other waving the Campions across the hall to the safety of the staff room.

Their crossing should have been unremarkable and without hazard, despite Perdita having to smother a giggle at the sudden thought of Mr Armitage assuming the responsibilities of the Tufty Club, were it not for a sudden commotion at the top of the stairs just as the Campions were being given right-of-way across the bottom.

'Oh, do get out of my way, you stupid boys! I have a bus to catch.'

The owner of that angry feminine voice appeared through a scrum of startled boys, all of whom melted to the side of the staircase to allow the bustling tornado to pass freely. It was a woman of late middle-age, very tall and very thin, who clearly demonstrated that her elbows were sharp and that she could use them destructively. She wore a double-breasted brown-and-grey check plaid wool coat and a beige hat of plush sheepskin which could only be described as bucket-shaped.

She descended the stairs in a fury, using the handbag she clutched to bat away any boy who might obstruct her progress, and for a second Perdita thought the woman could not have seen them in their little tableau at the foot of the stairs, directly in her path.

'Oh for goodness' sake, move!' the woman snapped at a startled boy who consequently dropped his satchel in panic.

The woman's staring eyes, not softened by an excess of blue eyeshadow, and a large, hooked nose, approaching at speed made Rupert feel grateful he had the protection of the headmaster's authority and military bearing at his side. Yet it seemed as though the woman had not registered the fact that the headmaster was there, even though she was on a collision course.

Only at the last possible moment, as the woman reached the foot of the stairs, did she sidestep rather clumsily, missing the Campions entirely but brushing against the headmaster's shoulder. As she accelerated by and almost sprinted down the corridor, the Campions registered that a vocal exchange had taken place through gritted teeth and tight lips on both sides.

'Brigham.'

'Hilda.'

It was only when his hand was on the handle of the door to the staff room and there was an ebb in the tide of passing school-boys that Mr Armitage offered an explanation of sorts.

'That was Hilda Browne,' he said to Perdita, 'and this was clearly not a good time for introductions, but you will have to meet her at some point. You see, she's your Helen of Troy.'

FIVE

Dragons' Den

Two of the pupils who had taken evasive action to avoid being trampled by the hurtling Hilda Browne watched the door of the staff room close behind the headmaster and his visitors and exchanged knowing looks with the world-weariness only fourteen-year-old boys can conjure at will on the slightest excuse.

'Do you think that's the replacement for Barmy Bertie?' asked the larger of the two in a conspiratorial whisper.

'Could be; how should I know?' replied the other with studied indifference.

'You two should get on well. All you carrot-tops stick together.'

'Don't be a dunce, Andy. Just because we've both got ginger hair doesn't mean we're related and anyway, if he is the stand-in for poor Bertie, you'll see more of him than I will on the rugby field with the under-fifteens.'

The two boys, their school blazers and ties hanging fashionably askew, kept their voices low as they descended the stairs until the satisfying click of the staff room door signalled the all-clear. Only then did the boys' voices resume their normal volume which a casual eavesdropper, had there been one, would have categorized as 'argumentative' given that the boys, as fourteen-year-olds of that sex are prone to do, punctuated their conversation with violent shoulder-to-shoulder nudges as if trying to force each other off a narrow bridge.

'So who d'you reckon the dolly bird is?' murmured Andrew Ramsden suggestively, being a boy who liked to appear older and more worldly than his age, though rarely convincingly. Had he been able to grow a moustache, he would probably have twirled it.

The ginger-haired Roderick Braithwaite refused to engage into the nudge-wink banter his friend favoured. 'I don't know if she's a dolly bird but she looks nice.'

'*Nice?* You fancy her then?' leered his compatriot.

Roderick sighed, ignored the barb and retaliated as only a good friend would, with one of his own. 'You'd better get a move on if you're catching the same bus as Horrible Hilda. I bet she's saved a seat for you. She *likes* you; you're her favourite.'

Despite himself, Andy Ramsden felt himself blushing. 'It's not me, it's my Dad she wants to keep in with!' he protested.

'Got a crush on policemen, has she?'

Young Ramsden began his riposte in the time-honoured way among schoolboys by shoulder-charging his friend. It was a relaxed, almost nonchalant collision of bodies, without significant force or great malice.

'She's always on at Dad about vandalism or littering or Teddy Boys, as she calls them, hanging around the phone box, not to mention speeding cars. She's gone mental about that after what happened to Barmy Bertie. If I catch that bus she'll just start nagging me about how Dad should be doing more about speed limits and road safety.'

'Do you want to come round mine and wait for the next one?' said Roderick, throwing his friend a lifeline, which Andrew grasped with mercenary speed.

'What've you got?'

'Mum's always baking, so there'll be sweetcake of some sort and we've got Black Beer and lemonade.'

'Any Coca-Cola?'

'No, Mum always gets Vimto. You could stay for tea if you wanted to.'

Andrew's head, after a short struggle, got the better of his stomach. 'Better not. My Mum'll kill me if I spoil my dinner.'

His friend did not miss the opportunity and said with fake surprise: 'Oh, I forgot you snobs have *dinner* whereas us poor folk have *tea*.'

'I'm not a snob.' Andrew straightened to his full height (a single, but crucial, inch taller than his companion) and hitched up his haversack by the shoulder straps. 'I can't be, can I, if I talk to you?'

'Don't force yourself. You don't have to come back to mine if you don't want.'

'Can't resist it, really; I've never been in a haunted house before.'

Rupert, when he and Perdita were alone later, reflected that their introduction to the inhabitants of the Dragons' Den had been akin to stumbling into an officers' mess in Poona – or somewhere in the Raj – during the monsoon season, the two main differences being that gin-slings had been replaced by tea in mismatched cups and cracked saucers, and that the temperature was anything but sub-tropical. It had not taken Rupert long to deduce that the school's heating went off precisely as the final bell of the afternoon sounded.

Even though those staff present had only had a few minutes to get themselves settled before Brigham Armitage arrived with his guests, they had already insulated themselves against the falling temperature by boiling kettles and creating an acrid, floating layer of tobacco smoke.

The dragons were in the majority male and seated. The only two females were standing at a small butler's sink in one corner guarding a dreadnought of a kettle balanced precariously on a hissing gas ring. The only face familiar to the Campions was one of the female ones, that of Celia Armitage who had shown them to her husband's study on arrival.

After her offer of tea had been politely declined, Mrs Armitage suggested she 'do the honours', to which the headmaster agreed with a cheerful grunt and a shrug as if to indicate he had little say in the matter. Rupert had heard that an officer's rank cut no ice at all in a sergeants' mess and presumed that the same applied to headmasters in a staff room.

Ladies went first, of course, and the female who was not Celia Armitage was introduced by her as Miss Daphne Cawthorne, who taught mathematics and music, though presumably at different times.

'Actually, it's *Mrs* Cawthorne,' the woman said with a thin smile as she shook Perdita's hand, 'but the tradition of the school is that all females are "Misses". I'm not sure why.'

Daphne Cawthorne was a fair-haired, middle-aged woman wearing a deep pink woollen suit which clung not unfavourably to her not-un-shapely figure. The skirt hung to an inch above the knee – Perdita guessed it would be exactly an inch – displaying legs clad in sheer brown stockings and square-toed shoes with good heels which would give stability whilst bustling up and down a classroom and just a little additional height so that she would not be dominated by the taller boys.

She had, thought Perdita, a stern face though not an unkind one, and the expression of one who had forgotten how to smile, but did not miss the experience much.

'And this is my husband, Stuart,' as a dark-complexioned man whose black, close-cropped curls sat on his head like a knitted swim cap materialized at her side. 'He teaches music and maths in that order, whereas I teach maths and cover for him in music. You might say we're a double act.'

To Rupert, the Cawthornes were the only double act in the den, for all the other dragons, slouched in armchairs strategically placed at angles so they did not have to face each other, were clearly solitary animals.

There was – and his rank was much stressed – Wing Commander Raymond Bland, a wide-shouldered, red-faced man in his fifties with bushy white eyebrows to match a white-clothes-brush moustache. He taught geography, 'Whether they like it or not!' and the fact that he was wearing a leather flying jacket zipped to the throat indicated that he had little time for impromptu staff meetings after school hours.

Next in the receiving line, and clearly responsible for most of the blue layer of tobacco mist in the den, was a pipe-smoking vicar with a round face, small round glasses and a smile which would have been beatific were it not for the pipe stem clenched between yellowing teeth. The Rev. Stanley Huxtable cheerfully announced that he taught physics and, of course, religious education and, as if clarification were necessary, he removed the briar from his mouth and pointed the stem at the dog collar around his neck. He embellished his accomplishments by adding that he tutored 'the brighter boys thinking of trying for Oxford and Cambridge' in Latin and Greek.

Rupert and Perdita exchanged furtive glances, each wondering how much extra work this might realistically entail for the cleric. Perdita framed the question diplomatically by asking cheerfully: 'Does that leave you any time at all for your parishioners in Denby Ash?'

'Good heavens, I am not the vicar of this or any other parish. I do not have a living in the church; I toil at the coalface of education.'

'Stanley was an army chaplain,' Celia Armitage explained as she gently eased Perdita away. 'Rank of captain, I believe.'

'Whereas I was a major,' said the next dragon in line in a strangely measured voice which was high-pitched and slightly feminine.

Physically, this was the smallest and thinnest of the dragons, and though he gave the impression of being a minor civil servant who was bullied at work and brow-beaten at home, Rupert suspected that Major Manfred Poole, the school's senior chemistry master, ruled his science classes with a rod of iron if not tungsten.

'Don't worry, that's the last of the proper officers,' said the next male dragon in the queue, despite the fact that he snapped to attention, his heels almost clicking, in front of Perdita.

This was a dragon of the Campions' generation and though only an inch taller than Perdita and two shorter than Rupert, he was of a muscular bulk which exuded an animal strength and created the impression that here was a man who could expand to fill a room should he so desire. He was dressed in a faded blue tracksuit top-and-bottoms and wore battered white (verging on grey) plimsolls. Celia Armitage introduced him as though she had only just remembered he was on the staff.

'This is Bob Ward.'

'Petty Officer Bob Ward, Miss,' he grinned, offering a meaty hand, 'formerly of the Royal Navy. In fact, the only naval man in the whole Denby Grange crew. I do PE with a vengeance and I also teach French. Could do Russian if there was a call for it.'

'Russian? That's impressive,' said Rupert genuinely.

'There was a course an' I went on it,' said Bob Ward. 'The navy wanted Russian speakers, even ones with a broad Yorkshire accent, so we could listen in to the red menace. Can't say it helped make the world any safer for democracy.'

'But PE probably makes the world fitter,' Perdita said graciously.

'*Mens sano in corpore sano* and all that,' Rupert added affably.

'I wouldn't know about that, I only do Frog and Russki,' the former naval person said with a grimly straight face. 'I leave the Classics to the h'officer clarse, same as I leave them to play their rugby.'

It's a good job you've got muscles, Mr Ward, thought Perdita, *because they've got to support one heck of a big chip on your shoulder.*

'You are not involved in school rugby?'

Ward shook his head as if he had been accused of a crime. 'Not me; never played t'game in me life. Physical fitness, gymnastics and cross-country runs, them's my department. The rugby field was always Bertram's empire.'

'He did play for the Sappers, you know,' interjected Major Poole through tight, thin lips, 'when he was in the Royal Engineers, and for Cambridge. He was quite a talent in his younger days and the boys all looked up to him.'

Whether or not the pupils of Denby Grange viewed Bob Ward with the same respect was left unsaid. It was clear that Major Poole did not.

'Did he take rugby alone?' asked Rupert. 'It must have been quite a burden alongside his teaching duties.'

'He was certainly busy during the winter months, but once the cricket season started he could put his feet up. Bertram wouldn't have had it any other way, he loved his rugby' – Poole checked himself as though the thought had just occurred to him – 'and of course he had Harrop to help him.'

'Harrop?'

'Rufus Harrop,' said Bob Ward, 'is our groundsman, gardener and general handyman. He's not officer class either and not even allowed in the staff room.'

Mrs Armitage, being a headmaster's wife, did what all head-masters' wives did instinctively and intervened as a peace-keeper.

'Manfred, Bob. Permit me to steal Mr and Mrs Campion. I'm sure they want to get settled in their room but they really need to have a word with the wing commander before he goes home, and he's keen to get off.'

'He always is,' said Manfred Poole drily.

'Already got his coat on,' added Bob Ward, and Perdita sensed something of an unlikely alliance between the two of them when it came to the geography master.

Celia Armitage linked arms with the pair to steer them to where the grumpy wing commander was sucking fiercely on an untipped Players' cigarette, speaking quietly as she ushered them over. 'Bob can be a little prickly,' she whispered, 'and Manfred just loves to torment him, so best not to get stuck in the middle. You should have a quick word with Raymond, though.'

'About rugby?' Rupert asked under his breath.

'No,' Celia turned her head into Perdita's, 'about Helen of Troy.'

Before Perdita and Rupert could even exchange befuddled glances, they were presented to Raymond Poole, who made no attempt to rise from the armchair which it seemed would rise with him, so snug was the fit.

'Before you go home, Raymond,' said Mrs Armitage, gently pushing Perdita forward, 'we thought you should have a word with Perdita about Hilda.'

'Hah! Wondered why I was in the official receivin' line.'

Poole crushed his cigarette out in the small glass ashtray he had balanced on the arm of his chair and then flicked along his moustache with a forefinger; a finger and a moustache, Perdita noticed, both stained yellow with nicotine.

'You've known her longer than anyone, Raymond, which makes you the SBO,' said Mrs Armitage diplomatically. Then with a grin added: 'So who better to warn Perdita about what she might expect? Now excuse me whilst I wash up these cups.'

Perdita decided her best strategy was to charm this sulking lion, albeit a lion with a receding mane, and so she ignited her best smile.

'Are you a friend of . . . Hilda, is it? Miss Browne. She passed us in the hallway but she didn't stop to chat; seemed to be running for a bus.'

The balding lion growled softly and eyed Perdita as if she were prey.

'Then you're lucky she didn't trample you to death.'

'As a matter of fact, she almost did.'

'That sounds like Hilda,' acknowledged the wing commander without irony. 'When she wants to go somewhere she just puts her head down and goes full steam ahead. Doesn't matter what's in her way; could be a baby in a pram, could be a blind man with one leg, could be a brick wall – Hilda would go through or over the lot. Bertram always said he could use her on the rugby field if she put on three or four stones. Mind you, she probably will. Spinsters usually do.'

Perdita bit her lip and resisted the urge to reach out and rip off a chunk of those yellowing moustache hairs. 'I'm told that Hilda is to play a part in the production I have . . . inherited.'

'And the best of British luck to you with that, little lady. This damn-fool Christmas show was all Hilda's damn-fool idea from the start, wasn't it?'

'I'm sorry, I don't quite follow, Mr Bland,' said Perdita, conscious of Rupert next to her moving uncomfortably from one foot to the other. He had seen her far from feminine response to being called anyone's 'little lady' before.

'I prefer Wing Commander, if you don't mind,' said the pompous lion. 'That's why Celia calls me the SBO of the staff room – Senior British Officer, don't you know.'

'Oh, I'm sorry,' Perdita said innocently. 'I thought it stood for something else entirely. Could I ask what you mean by the *Faustus* production being Hilda's idea, Wing Commander? I didn't realize she was on the staff.'

'She's not, thank the stars. She haunts the school – on sufferance, mind you – because she was Bertram's sister. No one in Denby Ash, or the adjoining parishes, can stand the woman – me included – but Bertie was a good friend of mine and since he died I seem to have inherited the role of Hilda expert by default.'

The wing commander's expression twisted in on itself as he concentrated silently on picking flecks of tobacco from his pursed lips whilst studiously ignoring the young woman in front of him. Perdita was sure she was not the first of her sex to be so ignored and would not be the last. But as she was determined not to stand for bullying in the classroom, she saw no reason why she should put up with it in the staff room.

'Well?' she said, placing her clenched fists on her hips and leaning over the seated lion.

'Well what?' growled the startled lion, already betrayed by a pink glow blooming in his cheeks.

'Why was doing *Faustus* Hilda's idea? I thought you were about to tell me.'

'Oh, yes . . . Hilda and her *Doctor Faustus* obsession . . .'

Raymond Bland paused as if reluctant to part with information which, Perdita was sure, would have been common gossip in the all-male sanctuary of an officer's mess.

'I must confess,' Perdita admitted with a smile designed, if not to charm, then at least suggest complicity, 'I thought it a distinctly odd choice for a Christmas production when I first heard.'

'Hrrumph!' growled the lion. 'Bloody odd, if you'll pardon my French; we all thought that, but then Hilda is a distinctly odd woman. She took Bertie in, you know, when his wife died. She got killed in a road accident as well, just like Bertie. Funny that; 'cept of course it's not. Bertie was broken up about it and seriously in danger of cracking up, so it was probably for the best that he had Hilda to take care of him. Not that she ever let him forget it. Always on about how she'd given up any hope of bagging a husband to look after him.'

And now the lion snorted.

'Fat chance there was of that happening, mind you, but it had the desired effect on Bertie. Made him feel guilty, so he indulged her; took her to the pictures in Leeds and the theatre in Stratford-on-Avon, of all places.'

'I hardly think it indulgent—' Perdita began to bristle, but her husband intervened soothingly.

'Stratford would be where she saw the RSC doing *Doctor Faustus* last year, wouldn't it? You know, darling, with Eric Porter as Dr F and all the fuss there was about a nude Helen of Troy.'

The wing commander, happier to be talking to a man, purred with enthusiasm. 'Spot on, old chap, and you're dead right: that Helen of Troy was totally nude – completely starkers – not like those gals at The Windmill. I know some of them couldn't muster a fig leaf between them, but at least they didn't move. Hilda was much taken with the production, almost smitten you might say, but then she'd had a thing about *Faustus* since she saw the film the year before. You know, the one with Richard Burton and Liz Taylor. I don't know if Liz was starkers in it. Never saw it meself.'

Bland leaned back in his chair with the air of a man who has put down a heavy suitcase and looked up at Perdita, mildly surprised to see that she was still there.

'You know what women can be like,' he said patronizingly. 'They get totally obsessed by things. Hilda nagged Bertie until he agreed to do the damn play, and once he'd agreed she appropriated the role of Helen for herself. The headmaster laid down the law, though: no nudity, so she won't be starkers, thank God!'

'She wants to go ahead despite her brother's death?' Rupert asked quickly, sensing that the steam valve controlling Perdita's temper was close to bursting.

'More so than ever. I told you, the woman's obsessed. She wants the show dedicated to Bertie's memory. Not much of a legacy if you ask me.'

'I'm sure no one will,' interjected Celia Armitage, riding to the rescue once more. 'Now I really must drag Perdita away as Mr Cawthorne needs a word and you'll be wanting to get off home, Raymond, won't you?'

She emphasized her point by tapping a fingernail against the face of her wristwatch.

'Quite right, Celia,' agreed the wing commander, getting sharply to his feet. 'Mustn't keep the memsahib waiting; always has my tea on the table bang on half-past five.'

Perdita gratefully allowed herself to be pulled out of the wing commander's orbit and she acknowledged Mrs Armitage's gentle squeezing of her arm by leaning even closer into her and whispering, 'I just knew there had to be a memsahib . . .'

Celia Armitage offered a complicit smile and steered her towards the Cawthornes. Rupert said a polite goodbye to the wing commander, who was more interested in delving into his pockets to locate his car keys, and followed his wife, only to have his arm gently touched – blessed, almost – by the Rev. Huxtable.

'Can I have a word, Campion?'

'Of course, as long as it's not about the *Faustus* production or . . .' He had been about to say 'naked spinsters' but checked himself at the sight of a looming dog collar.

'Oh, no, my concerns are not theatrical,' said the beaming dog collar, 'more pastoral, really. I want to give you some advice, or perhaps it is a favour I'm asking.'

'Any and all advice would be gratefully received,' Rupert said politely, though secretly dreading a lecture on schoolboy morals.

'It's about a boy.' The Rev. Huxtable gently tapped his right temple with the stem of his pipe as though dislodging a memory. 'He's in my Form but you'll have him out on the rugby field – his name is Andrew Ramsden and he's pleasant enough and certainly bright enough. I'd like you to keep an eye on him.'

'So what's wrong with him?'

'Nothing at all – he's a fine boy. It could be, though, that he's being . . .'

'Bullied?' suggested Rupert.

'Oh, no, not bullied.' Mr Huxtable now used his pipe, thankfully unlit, as a conductor's baton to make a more emphatic finger-wagging gesture. 'I think the word is "shunned", by the other boys and the villagers and – dare I say? – perhaps by one or two of the more left-wing masters as well.'

Rupert remembered he was supposed to be an actor and managed to suppress his imagination running away with the image of a socialist fifth column inside Ash Grange.

'What has he done?'

'Andrew? Nothing, poor lad. It's his father, who's a policeman, who has been snooping around the village and the school recently, asking a lot of silly questions. People don't like that sort of thing.'

'He's not investigating Bertram Browne's death, is he?'

'What a curious conclusion to jump to,' said the reverend gentleman, his eyes popping behind his spectacles. 'Bertram's death was a road accident pure and simply. Tragic, of course. What they call a hit-and-run, I think. No, Chief Inspector Ramsden is investigating something completely different; something which you might say goes into the very soul of Denby Ash.'

'Really? That sounds quite disturbing.'

'Please don't let it disturb you, my dear chap. It should not concern you, or this school, for that matter.'

Perhaps Huxtable had said too much, in which case Rupert

could not resist teasing him. 'And yet the very soul of the village is at stake?' He feigned surprise. 'That sounds awfully serious, though as we drove in here today we saw you are well supplied with churches of various denominations to cater for any souls in danger.'

The Rev. Stanley Huxtable allowed himself a thin smile. 'You are very observant, young man. We are indeed fortunate here in Denby Ash to have a good, solid parish church, albeit one that is as High as you can go in the Church of England without being Roman, and we are blessed with several versions of Methodism, ranging from the austere to the downright strict. So we have quite a little army of vicars, preachers, lay preachers and missionaries here. But that's not the best of it.'

Huxtable's eyes positively twinkled behind his glasses as he paused for dramatic effect. 'We even have a witch.'

SIX
Eminently Practical

Although a born and bred Yorkshireman of the West Riding, which everyone knows produces the hardiest *genus* of Yorkshire, Detective Chief Inspector Dennis Ramsden had never felt entirely comfortable when his duties had taken him out into the rural mining villages. In his years as a policeman in Huddersfield, he had diligently taken statements from three streets' worth of back-to-back houses where every adult had worked in the same well-insured textile mill which had mysteriously burned to the ground, resolved complicated matters of family honour among proud Indian families, investigated a serious assault on a group of young Pakistani girls almost too frightened to breathe and arrested, single-handed, a gang of flamboyant Polish burglars. Yet despite his experience and proven diplomatic skills, Dennis Ramsden had always felt like, if not a fish out of water, then a fish in a strange river whenever his duties took him into a mining community such as Denby Ash, dominated as it was by the black mountainous spoil heap of the defunct Grange Ash colliery – an ancient society's monument to a forgotten god.

It almost was a foreign country – a ridiculous fancy really as his son was a pupil at Ash Grange School, which should allow him at least proxy visiting rights if not a tourist visa or work permit. He knew that Brigham Armitage's school was tolerated as a curious adjunct rather than an integral part of the village. For the majority of Denby Ash's population, the local school was the small Church of England Primary – invariably known as 'the Infants' – whereas Ash Grange was an isolated example of ancient privilege which just happened to be located nearby. For many it was of no more or no less significance or interest than having a ruined Norman castle in the neighbourhood.

But that was miners for you. They kept themselves to themselves and everyone else at arm's length. If they weren't die-hard members of the National Union of Mineworkers they were die-hard members of the village brass band. More often than not they were both.

The man who Ramsden had come to Denby Ash to interview was both, albeit now retired, and he also had personal reasons for not wanting to talk to policemen.

Ramsden knew enough of the cultural protocols of mining villages not to use the front door of Number 17, Oaker Hill. Front doors were reserved for distant relatives visiting at Christmas or when there had been a death in the house (with the body laid out in the front room) and the undertakers needed a dignified point of entry and exit. Back doors were for family, neighbours, doctors on a house call, meter readers, rag-and-bone men 'on the knock', insurance men, the lad who collected the pools coupons every week, the rent man and, if absolutely necessary, the itinerant policeman.

'Good morning, Mrs Bagley,' he said to the sharp-faced woman who opened the door at his first knock. 'I'd like a word with you and your husband. Is he in?'

'Where else would he be?' the woman snapped as if Ramsden had suggested something outrageous. She turned her back on her visitor and shouted 'Walter!' into the house, then held the door open and flapped a hand, waving Ramsden in. 'Get indoors before the neighbours get to know all our business.'

The policeman felt sure that particular horse had bolted long ago. Gossip spread like a slow incoming tide through these rows of thin-walled terraced houses even without the pull of a three-year-old scandal which everyone in Denby Ash was well aware of.

The back door of Number 17, as in every other 'pit house' on Oaker Hill, opened directly into the kitchen. Ramsden extend his leg to stride over the scoured white edge of the stone doorstep, as a brief glimpse of Mrs Bagley's reddened hands told him that she had only recently completed that particular domestic chore. Putting an inch-wide edge on a slab of stone doorstep with a white, cream or (daringly) brown donkey stone had always seemed a rather pointless cosmetic ritual to Dennis Ramsden, but then he was a man and intelligent enough not to pick a fight with Doreen Bagley in her own domain, or indeed any Yorkshire woman.

'It's that copper from Huddersfield again,' she announced him. 'Likely it'll be about our Haydon.'

There was a grunt of resignation from the corner where Walter Bagley sat in a green upright Parker Knoll armchair which had seen better days, most of them in the previous decade. It was the only armchair in the kitchen and clearly Walter Bagley's throne, drawn up next to the iron fireplace in which a coal fire glowed like lava in a volcano, throwing out enough heat for Walter to be comfortable in shirt-sleeves and braces. At knee-height for the utmost convenience, a metal goblet shape had been welded to the iron fire surround and held a splay of multi-coloured paper spills. Ramsden knew what they were, but had assumed they had become extinct when electricity had removed the need for gas lights and candles. Before he deigned to speak to his visitor, Walter Bagley demonstrated their usefulness by selecting a spill, lighting it from the fire and using it to ignite a cigarette. Only when he had extinguished the spill by knocking it out on the grate and placing the unburned portion – waste not, want not – back in the holder and exhaled a stream of grey smoke did he look up into the face of the policeman.

'If tha's got summat to say, tha'd better get it said, 'cos I've got nowt to tell thee.'

'Now then, Walter, I'm only doing my job.'

'Not much of a job, if you ask me, bothering folk – and it's "Mr Bagley", if you don't mind.'

'Walter! It costs nowt to be civil,' Mrs Bagley chided her husband but left Ramsden under no illusions that he was dealing with two hostile witnesses.

'I was in Denby Ash anyway, so I thought I would call in and ask about Haydon,' the policeman admitted. 'Have you had any contact with him?'

Walter Bagley flicked ash from his cigarette into the fire and his eyes stayed on the burning coals. 'I've not seen Haydon since the trial and I only went to that on sufferance after a lot of nagging from some people.' He did not turn his head from the fire but it was clear where that particular shaft was aimed. 'The wife went to visit him in prison, though I never saw what good that did.'

'The trial was nearly three years ago, Mr Bagley,' said Ramsden. 'I was wondering if he had been in touch in the past two weeks.'

'Since he got out, you mean?'

'Exactly. I presume you were aware he was being released early for good behaviour.'

'Mebbe he was, but I don't see what it's got to do with us.'

'Walter Bagley, how can you say such things?'

Ramsden was surprised by Mrs Bagley's outburst. Her husband had once had a reputation as something of a martinet: as an active union man, as the bandmaster of Denby Ash Brass Band and a staunch Methodist. Those were the three rods of steel running through Walter Bagley until he was diagnosed with 'miner's lung' and forcibly retired from the pit and the band, leaving only a fervent religiosity which had been tested to breaking point by the actions of his son.

'He's no son of mine,' growled Mr Bagley. Mrs Bagley crossed her arms over her bosom and gave him a defiant, though silent, glare.

Feeling himself the reluctant referee in the middle of two boxers who knew each other's best punches far too well, Dennis Ramsden considered the events which had disrupted this household and marvelled, not for the first time, at human reaction to criminal events. He had been roundly abused by an angry mother claiming her thuggish son had been a sheep among wolves and as innocent as a dove, even as she sponged someone else's blood from his shirt. He had been physically assaulted by two brothers who had violently objected to him ending their income from immoral earnings purely on economic grounds rather than the fact that the wage-earner in question was their sister. He had arrested a caring

father so keen for his fifteen-year-old son to pass his driving test
(when old enough) that he had stolen a variety of cars until he
found one that suited. Well, the lad had to get in plenty of practice
because he wasn't the sharpest knife in the drawer and proper
lessons from the BSM were too expensive. And there had been
the young tearaway biker who had cheerfully admitted to driving
over the foot of a uniformed constable on traffic duty, his defence
being that he couldn't have possibly avoided the policeman: 'Not
at the speed I was doing!'

To the crimes of Haydon Bagley, however, the reaction had
been sociological. He had joined the Yorkshire Penny Bank, as it
was then, on leaving school and over fifteen years had progressed
from spotty youth nervously straightening ten shilling notes and
fumbling blue cloth bags of pennies and halfpennies behind a wire
grill to smart-suited junior manager of his own branch: the lord
of all he surveyed, or at least all the overdrafts and mortgages he
surveyed. Having the name Bagley, which came with all the pres-
tige due to a firebrand union official and a stalwart of the brass
band, ensured that there would never be a shortage of clients
seeking chequebooks and savings accounts. In addition, the name
brought Haydon the honourable offices of treasurer for the Denby
Ash band, the Parish Council and the village branch of the Co-Op,
which also put him in charge of numerous Christmas clubs, charity
appeals and holiday funds.

Sadly, Haydon Bagley was not an honourable man.

It was an internal audit by the Yorkshire Bank which raised the
first suspicion, quickly followed, domino-like, by close examination of the financial ledgers of every organization, church, chapel,
charity and savings clubs which had been touched by Haydon
Bagley's sticky fingers. The amounts found to be missing were
never large in themselves and some so small they had easily been
accepted as arithmetical errors, but over the years the syphoned
shillings had provided Haydon with an annual package holiday
from Manchester airport to a destination even more exotic, as well
as a new car every two years. With hindsight, such conspicuous
consumption should have given him away earlier, but it was incon-
ceivable to the inhabitants of Denby Ash that one of their own
could steal from them.

When Haydon Bagley was sentenced to three years' imprison-
ment at Wakefield Crown Court, the inhabitants of Denby Ash

organized a series of jumble sales, flower and vegetable shows, Beetle Drives and bingo nights (thus making allowances for all religious persuasions) to make up the eroded holiday fund to ensure that all children under the age of eleven had their annual coach trips to Flamingo Park zoo and a day at the Scarborough seaside. Yet for all the rally-round enthusiasm generated and the cooperation between bodies who had never cooperated on anything in their history, the prevailing mood in Denby Ash was one of shame.

In the Bagley household, that mood persisted.

'It's no more than God's truth,' Walter Bagley challenged his wife. 'He's not my son just as he's not your son either, Doreen.'

Whilst Mrs Bagley remained, arms folded, as animated as a Mount Rushmore carving, her husband looked up from his chair at the policeman, his eyes steely and biblical.

'Doreen can't have kids but wanted summat to keep her occupied,' he said in a dark monotone, 'so we adopted Haydon as a bairn. If there's bad blood in him, it's not our blood.'

'Mr Bagley,' said Ramsden gently, 'I am only interested in Haydon's movements since his release, and all I need to know is if he has contacted you.'

'That's not likely, is it? I made it very clear to him that this was not a house where sinners could take refuge.'

'Yes, you made that very clear, Walter,' said Mrs Bagley defiantly.

'And he hasn't tried to get in touch; a letter, perhaps, or a phone call? Are you on the phone here?'

'Oh, yes, we had the telephone put in years ago.' At last there was something Mrs Bagley could be proud of.

'There's many a time I wish we hadn't,' sniped her husband. 'Every lazy so-and-so in the row comes traipsing through the 'ouse to use it when it's raining and they can't be bothered to walk to the phone box.'

'Charity, Walter, charity,' his wife soothed; then, remembering the policeman in the room: 'But Haydon hasn't rung. I think he'd know better than to ring here.'

Walter Bagley threw his cigarette end like a dart into the fire, sat back in his chair and closed his eyes, signalling that the interview was at an end.

'Then mebbe he's learned summat in prison.'

*   *   *

Rupert and Perdita had eventually escaped the Dragons' Den to the room they had been allocated in the Lodge, a large redbrick house where the upper floor and the loft space had been converted into a barracks for the thirty boarders, over whom Celia Armitage ruled with a benevolent ruthlessness.

The ground floor had been converted into two self-contained flats, the larger one being the domestic lair of the Armitages, the smaller one reserved for guests, temporary staff or recruited staff new to the area – the Campions qualifying on all three counts. Their flat had a private bathroom but no kitchen facilities beyond an electric kettle on a tray, a bowl of sugar, a jar of teabags and two spoons. Celia Armitage explained that they would be expected to take their meals in the school dining hall in Ash Grange which was always 'something of a maelstrom' at lunchtime but quite civilized at tea time when only the boarders were present. The Campions were, naturally, able to enjoy a cup of tea whenever the need arose and Mrs Armitage promised to send the school cook over with a gill of milk to keep them going.

When they were left alone to their unpacking, Rupert said, 'Did the headmaster's wife just promise to bring us a female ferret?'

'No, my darling idiot, that's jill with a "j". Celia said she would give us a gill, with a "g". That's a measurement of liquid, a quarter of a pint, I believe, though in Yorkshire they call half-pints of milk gills just to confuse southerners.'

'Does it work for half-pints of beer?' Rupert grinned.

'Only if it confuses southerners,' said Perdita, deadpan. 'That seems to be the rule about most things and should you – a full-grown male – ask for anything as dainty as a half-pint of beer round here, I think you deserve everything you get.'

Rupert grasped his wife's hand and clutched it to his manly bosom, striking his most melodramatic pose. 'My dearest, promise me you'll never leave my side whilst we are here, not for a minute. Promise me.'

Perdita laid the back of her spare hand against her forehead as if warding off a swoon. 'I promise, my little turtle dove, but in all honesty I think it's me who might need a bodyguard from all those teenage boys looking at my legs, not to mention Hilda Browne . . .'

'I wasn't thinking of you as a bodyguard, my love,' said Rupert, looking deep into his wife's eyes. 'More as a translator.'

Perdita's retort remained on the tip of her tongue as they both reacted to a discreet knock on their door.

Rupert answered the knock to find a middle-aged woman with sharp but not unattractive features holding a small bottle of milk, much in the pose of a gift-bearing king from the East in a nativity scene.

'Mrs Armitage said you'd be wanting this,' said the woman, making her offering.

'That's very kind of you, but you really shouldn't have troubled . . .'

'No trouble,' said the woman firmly. 'I'm working here tonight, doing the tea for the boys. I should think you'll be at the headmaster's table, won't you?'

'I believe so,' said Rupert, not sure that he wasn't being interrogated.

'Well, I've got some nice neck-end of lamb stewing away already. Slow cooking brings out the flavour, I always say.'

'I'm sure it will be delicious.'

He made to close the door but the woman made no move to go.

'I was hoping,' she said, 'to catch Mrs Campion for a word whilst I was here, if it's not being too forward.'

Rupert, slightly flustered and clutching a milk bottle he felt sure belonged in a dolls' house, turned to his wife for guidance and Perdita, as usual, glided effortlessly to the rescue with her most charming smile.

'Is there anything I can help you with, Mrs . . .?'

'Braithwaite,' said the woman, 'Ada Braithwaite. I work here as the cook, or one of 'em.'

'Nice to meet you, Mrs Braithwaite. I'm Perdita Campion.'

Perdita offered a hand for shaking and Ada took it hesitantly.

'My son Roderick is a pupil here.'

'I'm sure you can be very proud of him.'

'Pride's got nowt to do with it, leastways not with what I've come about.'

'Is there a problem with Roderick? You'll have to forgive me – I haven't actually met any of the boys yet.'

'There's not a problem as such. Roderick's a good lad who

works hard and doesn't lie. If he ever gives you trouble, you let me know and I'll sort him out double quick.'

'So how can I help you?' Perdita asked carefully, recognizing a proud mother when she saw one.

'You're taking on Bertram Browne's production, this *Doctor Faustus* thing.'

'I am indeed,' Perdita said cheerfully, 'and I'm sure it will be wonderful.'

'Well, be that as it may, my boy Roderick was in thrall to Mr Browne and Bertram's death has shaken him up a lot – far more than he lets on. He's taking the main part, I believe, in the production.'

'Your Roderick's playing Faustus?'

'He's learned all his lines. That's not the problem.'

'So what is, Mrs Braithwaite?'

'Hilda Browne, that's what. She's in the show an' all and I don't want her taking it out on Roderick.'

'Taking *what* out on Roderick?'

'Her brother. Roderick and Mr Browne were very close, you see, and I reckon Hilda blames my Roderick for his death.'

Dinner in the long, cold school dining room was a self-service affair, the diners forming a line behind the headmaster, naturally, to shovel food on to plates from a series of metal tureens heated by small spirit burners. Seating around a long refectory table was informal, though the twenty or so boarders (at first sight Perdita had put their number at a round hundred) spaced themselves diplomatically away from the Armitages and the Campions. The food was hearty solid fuel appropriate for a winter evening: a lamb stew with potato and turnips (known in Yorkshire, Rupert learned, as 'swede'), followed by a spotted dick suet pudding and hot custard. Unlike the famous Dickensian scene, when Rupert asked politely if there was any more, Celia Armitage gave him a beatific smile and said he should help himself as he was bound to need all his strength out on the rugby pitch.

It was only when the plates had been cleared that the boarders were despatched to a 'prep room' to which they went, commented Rupert, with an enthusiasm he had not encountered in his own schooldays. This was because, Mr Armitage confided, he had allowed his wife to persuade him to install a television for those pupils who boarded during the week which operated on an honour system and was only turned on once homework had been finished by all the boys.

'All the school's pupils seem remarkably well-behaved for boys of their age,' said Perdita, 'though of course I haven't actually met any to talk to as yet.'

'They're a good crop of lads,' beamed Brigham Armitage, 'and you won't get any trouble from them. If you do, refer them to Celia. They are far more afraid of my wife than they are of me!'

'Actually,' said Rupert, coming in on the cue he and Perdita had agreed upon, 'we have already had a couple of boys referred to us in a manner of speaking, though of course we've no idea who they are.'

'One of them would be Roderick Braithwaite,' said Mrs Armitage to her husband. 'His mother asked permission to have a word with Miss Campion when she took their milk over to the Lodge. I couldn't refuse.'

Mr Armitage patted his wife's hand. 'Of course not. I hope Ada did not upset you, Perdita.'

'Not at all, though I'm not sure I could offer any comfort to her. She was concerned about Roderick's role as Doctor Faustus and Hilda Browne insisting on being Helen of Troy.'

The headmaster nodded solemnly. 'It is a difficult situation, I admit. Hilda is a distinctly odd lady and we have given her an awful lot of leeway because we valued Bertram and his contribution to the school so highly. I am tempted to say that Bertram's death unhinged the poor woman, but frankly she's always been that way. "Mad as a badger", as the wing commander would say.'

'Charity, darling, charity,' Celia reminded him.

'Mrs Braithwaite seems to think that Hilda Browne holds Roderick responsible for Bertram's death,' Perdita pressed.

'Now that's just nonsense, and if Hilda starts acting up, let me know and I'll give her her marching orders. I won't have young Roderick upset. He's a bright lad and he's been through a lot. Lost his father down the pit when he was a nipper, you know, and Ada's done a fine job of bringing him up single-handed. I made sure he got a scholarship to come here and he hasn't let me down academically. He's university material in my opinion, but he took Bertram's death hard so I'd appreciate it if you'd keep an eye on him.'

'I certainly will,' said Perdita. 'After all, he is going to be my leading man.'

'Hmmm,' the headmaster ruminated. 'He insisted on going ahead with the show out of loyalty to Bertram, and of course Hilda sees it as some sort of memorial to her brother.'

'Don't worry, Headmaster,' said Rupert. 'If anyone can handle temperamental actors it's my wife here, and I'm sure she'll look out for young Roderick. Funnily enough, I was asked to keep an eye out for another pupil . . . Andrew Ramsden . . . though I'm not clear why.'

Mr Armitage seemed even more chastened by this news. 'You'll see Andrew out on the rugby field; he's the captain of our under-sixteens and a fine player. He's also best friends with Roderick Braithwaite. Not quite as bright but steady enough. His problem is that his father is a police detective, a chief inspector, and at the moment he's doing his detecting in Denby Ash.'

'And why is that a problem?' Perdita asked innocently.

'He's re-opening some old wounds made by a man called Haydon Bagley, the black sheep of Denby Ash, who, I am sad to say, happens to be an Old Boy of this school. In fact, he was one of our first Old Boys – certainly one of the first of our Bursary Boys.' Armitage saw the flicker of puzzlement on Perdita's face and explained: 'We have always had a policy of providing bursaries for local lads from the village where their families would find it difficult to afford the fees. In Denby Ash that has invariably meant the sons of miners.'

'But not their daughters,' Perdita said sweetly.

'We do what we can,' said the headmaster without embarrassment. 'Not perhaps all we would like to. Haydon Bagley was one of the first of our Bursary Boys, back in 1949. His father was a leading light in the local brass band and taking in young Haydon as a day boy was, I admit, a good piece of public relations for the school – at least at first. Unfortunately, Haydon turned out to be a bad egg. He went to work for the Yorkshire Bank and over the years wormed his way into being treasurer or book-keeper for every organization in the village, volunteering to do the jobs no one else wanted to, from the local Co-Op and the Parochial Church Council to the Pigeon Fanciers' Club and the Mothers' Union. Over the years he stole from all of them, including the brass band

– for which he will never be forgiven. He was caught and sent to prison for fraud and embezzlement.'

'Case closed, then,' said Rupert. 'So why is Andrew Ramsden's dad investigating him?'

Mr Armitage shook his head wearily. 'Haydon finished his sentence and was released some weeks ago. It was thought he might try and return to Denby Ash but he seems to have disappeared. The truth is that so many people here felt betrayed and cheated by him, that if he did show his face he would be greeted with hostility – possibly violence. A mining community can be a very . . . *masculine* . . . entity. Miners have hard lives and when they feel betrayed by one of their own they have been known to deal out their own sort of eminently practical justice.'

'Surely, if he's been in prison, this Haydon Bagley chap has already been punished for what he did?' argued Rupert.

'But judging by local feeling,' said the headmaster, 'not punished enough. Not nearly enough.'

SEVEN

Ghost-hunters of the Upper IV

'**R**ight, boys,' commanded Perdita, 'lay those damned books aside.'

Her command was answered by two rows of silent desks each occupied by a silent, blank-faced boy.

'Oh, *come on*, you guys. It's from the play – just about the first thing the Good Angel tells Faustus to do. Who's playing the Good Angel?'

The classroom remained silent until a nervous ginger-haired lad with an impressive splattering of freckles nervously raised a hand. 'No one is, Miss. He's been cut and so has the Evil Angel. We've also lost the Clown, Robin, a Vintner and a Carter, a Pope, the King of Hungary, the Holy Roman Emperor and five of the seven deadly sins.'

'I see,' said Perdita, disguising the fact that she clearly

did not. 'Can anyone let me have the text we're supposed to be performing?'

The ginger-haired boy offered her a sheaf of Roneo-ed sheets of typed foolscap paper held together by a bootlace toggle in the top left corner. With a sigh she took it, pushing the new Penguin edition of *Christopher Marlowe – The Complete Plays*, on which she had spent ten shillings, into her shoulder bag.

'Mr Browne had to cut quite a lot,' said the boy.

'But not Helen of Troy?'

'Oh no, she stays in.'

Perdita's eyes scanned the classroom but could not find an adolescent gaze willing to meet hers. 'From what I remember it's only a walk-on part,' she said airily. 'We'll just have to hope she walks very quickly.'

An infectious, though barely audible snigger rippled over the bowed heads of Perdita's audience as the boys pretended to concentrate on their scripts and Perdita allowed herself a smile at discovering kindred spirits.

'So who can tell me what's left of what we actors laughingly call "the text"?' she asked, weighing the flimsy sheets of typing in her right hand. 'And please introduce yourselves. You know I'm Miss Browning but I've no idea who you are and we don't have long in which to get to know each other.'

Once again, the red-headed boy in the front row raised his hand. 'I'm Faustus, Miss.'

'So you must be Roderick . . . Braithwaite, isn't it?'

The young man's shoulders straightened with pride at being recognized. 'Yes, Miss.'

'Well, if Mr Browne cast you as Faustus he must have had faith in you and presumably he explained his thinking behind what appears to have been rather major cuts to the play.'

'Bertie – Mr Browne, I mean – had to make way for the music,' said Roderick, his face a study of concentration, as if choosing his words very carefully.

'That's Mr Cawthorne's department, isn't it?'

'He's the music master, Miss, but Mrs Cawthorne won't let him have anything to do with our play,' advised a new, deeper voice, this time from a thick-set youth of dark complexion who, out of school uniform, Perdita felt sure would probably go unchallenged in a public house.

'And you are?'

'Mephistophilis, Miss, second-in-command to Lucifer himself.'

'I know who Mephistophilis is, thank you, but who are you?' Miss Browning asked sternly but politely.

'I'm Banville, Miss. I volunteered to do the music myself but they wouldn't have it. Now we have to put up with the local oompah-band.'

'Excuse me?'

'Don't take any notice of Banville, Miss,' said Roderick, riding to the rescue. 'He's a fan of progressive rock music.'

'You mean like The Moody Blues?'

Perdita spoke before remembering that it was a dangerous thing these days to debate popular music with teenagers, a subject which ignorance of usually resulted in bliss.

The older-than-his-school-uniform-suggested boy snorted loudly in disgust.

'They're hippies! Cream and King Crimson are the future of music!'

'I can't say I appreciate or agree with your taste,' Perdita said with a wry smile, 'but I think Mephistophilis might.'

'Don't take any notice of Banville, Miss Browning,' said her leading man. 'He's just hacked off because he wrote a song for the play and Mr Browne threw it out.'

'You wrote a song? That's quite impressive.'

It was Mephistophilis the prog-rock fan's turn to bristle with pride but Dr Faustus was quick to deflate his nemesis.

'He didn't write anything really, Miss. He just rearranged the last Faustus speech – the "I'll burn my books" one – and set it to a distorted guitar. He wanted to call it *Sixteenth Century Schizoid Man*.'

In case the pretty new drama teacher was unfamiliar with the concept, Mephistophilis rose to his feet and mimed the action of a hyperactive electric guitar player, but fortunately did not burst into song before Perdita waved him back down into his seat.

'Mr Browne said it was a daft idea and told Banville he shouldn't mess with Marlowe's dialogue,' said Roderick, as if summing up for the prosecution.

Perdita adopted what she thought was a judicial pose and addressed the now deflated guitarist. 'I think that's very good advice, Banville. However, I'm still not clear on why the text seems to have been cut to a few sheets of foolscap.' She waved the slight typescript with a flourish.

'Religion, Miss,' said Roderick quietly. 'There's a quite a lot of it in Denby Ash – the church, the Methodist chapels and tabernacles, the Mission – and we also have a vicar as our physics master, so Bertie – Mr Browne – was sure that someone was bound to be offended by a play where somebody conjured up the Devil and traded his soul for earthly knowledge and the sins of the flesh.'

'Not to mention the sins of Helen of Troy – the face that launched a thousand whatsists,' Banville mugged lasciviously, getting in to character.

'Oh, grow up, you great clot!' snapped Roderick, waving a fist at his co-star.

'"Oh, good Faustus, stay thy desperate steps",' Perdita declaimed loudly, only to be met with a surprised and surprisingly vacant set of young faces. '"I shall be the angel hovering over your head ready to pour a vial of precious grace into your soul . . ."'

She paused, knowing from bitter experience that she had lost her audience. 'I suppose that bit's been cut as well,' she sighed. 'Never mind; I'll go through what's left of the text over the weekend and we'll have a proper run through on Monday. *Faustus* really is a very Christian morality play, you know, though that's not all it is, of course. I hadn't anticipated this much bowdlerization.'

In front of her Mephistophilis, assuming a double-entendre, let out a high-pitched giggle but every other young face remained as calmly blank as a mill pond.

'You have heard of Thomas Bowdler, haven't you? Early-nineteenth-century chap who edited the plays of Shakespeare, taking out all the naughty bits and since then anything that has been expurgated has been "bowdlerized". Normally it involves getting rid of anything people find a bit rude.'

Perdita was pleased to see a questioning hand rose from the front desks, though instantly suspicious when she focussed and saw it belonged to Mephistophilis. 'Yes?' she said carefully.

'Did they try and do this boulder thing with that nudey show in London last year, Miss?'

'Do you mean *Hair*?' Perdita realized she had their full attention.

'That had more to with theatre censorship and the abolition of the Lord Chamberlain's office, I think, but speaking personally

. . .' Now her audience was spellbound and, as one, leaning forward in their seats. 'I have never appeared on stage in the . . .'

Perdita extended her comic timing for as long as she dared, even though this was never going to be her toughest audience.

'. . . West End, so I really I can't comment.'

A classroom of youth, as one, deflated around her.

'Now can we get back to my earlier question, please? I'm still not clear exactly whose religious feelings are we likely to upset with our performance of Christopher Marlowe's classic and highly respected tragical history.'

A new hand rose unsteadily. It belonged to an angelic boy with blond curls who looked no more than twelve years old and had a face which, in a previous age, could have advertised Pears soap. Perdita nodded permission for the cherub to speak.

'I'm Lucifer, Miss,' the cherub sang sweetly.

'Oh, I very much doubt that,' Perdita encouraged.

'His name's Philip Watson,' said Mephistophilis helpfully.

Lucifer glared at Mephistophilis briefly, in a most un-angelic way, before continuing.

'They are all a bit bell, book and candle around here, Miss. The vicar, Old Twiggy, doesn't approve of any summoning up the Devil or spirits and things, and all the Methodist ministers and lay preachers don't like the idea of seeing the deadly sins on stage, especially not Lust – which was the first to go. In fact, some of them are opposed to the whole idea of theatre and plays. Mrs Cawthorne is a staunch Methodist, which is why she won't allow Mr Cawthorne to have anything to do with the production, even though he's the music master. The Reverend Stan – that's what we call him – who's our physics teacher and supposed to be a man of science has to disapprove of the show because he still wears the dog collar. We've only got the Denby Ash brass band doing the music because Trotsky is an atheist and he likes upsetting the churches.'

'And just who is Trotsky?' asked Perdita. She quickly added: 'Your brass band one, not the famous one.'

'Arthur Exley, Miss,' said Watson. 'He's bandmaster for Denby Ash and also a militant hothead in the miners' union.'

Perdita was sure that was a phrase young Watson had picked up from his parents at the breakfast table, possibly as Watson *pére* read from the editorial of the *Yorkshire Post*.

'Hence the nickname "Trotsky"?'

Watson, and several of the other boys, nodded in agreement.

'So, to sum up, apart from the late Mr Browne – and, of course, his sister – and, as far as I can gather, a left wing, musical trade unionist, there are very few people in Denby Ash who approve of our show?'

'Even the local witch has come out against it,' said Mephistophilis with a certain amount of glee.

'Ivy Neal is not a witch!' snapped Dr Faustus, gripping the edges of the desk which constrained him. 'She's just an eccentric old gypsy lady.'

'Well, I bet you daren't go down Pinfold Lane after dark!'

'That's enough of that, Banville,' Perdita said sternly, remembering that she had authority and should be asserting it.

'Mind you,' Banville continued with relish, 'you ought to be familiar with ghoulies and ghosties by now, Braithwaite. After all, you're the one who lives in a haunted house.'

Rupert had dismissed the joking suggestions from his family that he invest in thermal underwear for his expedition to Yorkshire and now, in the middle of Ash Grange's rugby field with a shiny referee's whistle bouncing from a cord around his neck and wearing a threadbare purple tracksuit and football boots too big for his feet despite two pairs of socks, he was beginning to wish he had taken the advice seriously.

The temperature was probably not below freezing point and the wind certainly not gale force, but the light rain which had fallen all day seemed – out here, exposed on the playing field – to have the texture of icy needles pricking at his skin. As it would never do for the games master to be seen standing there shivering with only the metal whistle between his lips keeping his teeth from chattering, Rupert decided it was best to keep moving – as much for his circulation as well as his pride – and joined in enthusiastically with 'circuit training' which consisted of running circuits of the field at varying speed in order to 'warm up', an instruction which the boys under his command greeted with a communal and instinctive groan. Their competitiveness soon became clear, however, as one by one they lapped their new coach with relish.

Warmer, but out of breath, Rupert suggested practising scrums – a quick head count assuring him that he had more than enough

bodies on the pitch – and then line-outs as 'set plays' were important. When the boys looked at him in bemusement, he explained
that he had picked up the term whilst at Harvard and observing
that strange illegitimate offspring of rugby, American Football. If
he had suddenly announced the abolition of all homework or the
free distribution of passes to the BBC's Lime Grove Studios for
the recording of *Top of the Pops*, he could not have gained more
instant respect.

The rest of his first training session could easily have been filled
with a question-and-answer session on the topic "What's it like in
America, sir?" but one of the fitter, clearly dominant boys suggested
that they followed Bertram Browne's training regime and split into
teams for a seven-a-side game. As the boy making the suggestion
not only did so politely and turned out to be Andrew Ramsden,
the captain of the school's under-sixteen team, Rupert agreed and
accepted the role of nominal referee, interfering in the game as
little as possible but sprinting in bursts just long enough to keep
his circulation moving.

As the rugby players seemed to know what they were doing
and had no real need of a referee, coach or games master, Rupert
took the opportunity to get his bearings in the local geography.

The playing fields of Ash Grange School occupied an elevated
position overlooking Denby Wood, whilst they in turn were over-
looked by the large black spoil heap of Grange Ash colliery which
rose on the other side of the Huddersfield road like an extinct
Vesuvius. In the distance, through the stinging drizzle, Rupert
could make out the Meccano-like winding towers of two other
collieries, both of which seemed to be in working order judging
by the constant stream of black-dusted lorries trundling from their
direction and straining up the hill through the village.

From his vantage point Rupert reckoned he had a view over
Denby Ash which could only be rivalled from the top of the Grange
Ash muck stack. His eyes followed the descent of the single road
sleeved, or so it appeared to him, by a long, continuous terrace of
redbrick houses, each one with a chimney pluming dark grey
smoke until he was sure he could make out the tower of the church
they had passed on their way into the village the day before.

He shook raindrops from his fringe and realized that the
afternoon was waning quickly. Did dusk fall rapidly in these
northern latitudes, or was that the tropics? Perhaps he should ask

a geography teacher, even one as anti-social and grumpy as Wing Commander Bland. The memory of his encounter with the inhabitants of the 'Dragons' Den' suddenly reminded him that he was now supposed to be a teacher himself and that he had over a dozen increasingly muddy boys in his charge.

Fortunately the boys on the rugby field were clearly capable of managing without adult supervision and were following the instructions being bellowed by the boy Ramsden with the authority of one of Cromwell's field commanders. And following them quite well judging by the applause of the spectators – spectators of which Rupert had been totally unaware until that moment.

Admittedly there were only two spectators, standing at either end of the pitch as far apart as physically possible so they could hardly constitute a crowd. The more vocal of the two, given to shouting clipped instructions such as 'Swerve!' 'Pass it!' and 'Get into 'im!' was a squat, pepper pot of a man wearing a thick donkey jacket with leather shoulder pads, dark trousers tucked into wellington boots and a brown flat cap with its peak pulled over his eyes to deflect the shards of icy rain which Rupert, his teeth chattering, was now sure were falling horizontally.

Jogging across the field as much to keep warm as to have any effect on the game in progress, Rupert paused at the shoulder of a mud-spattered boy down on one knee retying a wayward bootlace. 'Who is that chap over there?'

'That's Rufus, sir,' the boy answered wearily. 'Rufus Harrop, the groundsman. He's always mithering about the way we cut up *his* field.'

'I suppose I'd better go and introduce myself,' Rupert said to the crown of the boy's head, for the boy was concentrating intently on de-knotting his rogue lace.

'Don't be surprised if he swears at you, sir,' the boy advised without looking up. 'He's got a tongue the colour of a dolly blue, or so me Mum says.'

'Thanks for the warning.'

Making a mental note to ask Perdita for translation advice, Rupert loped across the pitch towards the flat-capped figure that seemed to shrink down into his coat as a tortoise would retract into its shell as he approached.

Rupert did not blame him, for had their positions been reversed he knew he would have shrunk from the gangling figure in a soaking tracksuit and mud-encrusted boots which flapped ever closer as if doing a Rag Week impersonation of Joyce Grenfell.

'Hello there. You must be Mr Harrop.'

The flat-capped head tilted upwards just enough to show a grey face displaying badly shaved white stubble, a wide nose that had clearly been broken at least once and small, piggy eyes set into dark sockets.

'No must abaht it, but Harrop I am,' said the smaller man, 'an' you'll be t'new fella replacing Mr Browne.'

Rupert strained an ear in an attempt to tune in to the low, quiet voice which had the timbre of slow-moving gravel.

'Only temporarily, until the end of term, and then there will be a new master starting after Christmas.'

'That'll be a relief, then. Summ'on else can see t'arrangements.'

'Arrangements?' Rupert enquired, latching on to words that he understood clearly.

'Fick-sures.'

'I'm sorry?'

'Games – proper uns – versus other schools,' said the grizzled groundsman with a blatant tone of despair.

'Oh, *fixtures* . . . er . . . yes, I do believe we have some. My name's Campion, by the way.'

''Course it is – I was told as much by t'eadmaster. Any road, I 'ave to tell yer that coach'll be 'ere at nine sharp a week tomorrer to take team to Kwegs.'

Rupert glanced around in dumb desperation but help came there none. All the boys in his charge had found renewed enthusiasm for their wet and muddy practice game and every youthful eye was making sure it did not catch his. Even the only other spectator – a man with his hands deep into the pockets of a gabardine raincoat and a green trilby on his head – seemed to have floated conveniently out of range and was now leaning a shoulder against one leg of the whitewashed H goal post at the other end of the field.

'I'm awfully sorry,' Rupert began apologetically, 'but I'm not exactly following you . . .'

'Well, yer wouldn't, would yer, you bein' a toff from down south, yer mawngy bugger,' growled the gnomic figure under the cap.

Wrong-footed by this unprovoked aggression, if that indeed was what it was, Rupert recalled his father once suggesting that the Campion family motto really should be *Numquam scienter contumeliam* – or 'Never Knowingly Insulted' if he had remembered his Latin correctly (which he doubted). For his current situation, it seemed a good philosophy to adopt.

'You're absolutely correct to assume I am from points south of here,' he said graciously, 'and therefore in need of as much help and guidance as your charity will allow, but please remember to use small, slow words.'

The gaunt, weathered face tilted upwards from under the peak of the flat cap and Harrop's bullet-hole eyes regarded Rupert with the unblinking stare which in Yorkshire passed for curiosity. And then the granite face fissured into a crack of a smile, or perhaps a smirk.

'Aye, well then,' said Rufus Harrop, as if about to announce the state opening of something, 'it's like I said. Coach is booked for nine sharp next Saturday morning.'

'Coach?' said Rupert vaguely.

'Coach – charabanc – bus,' Harrop said slowly, 'to take t'team to Kwegs for t'match.'

'I'm sorry to be southern, but what are Kwegs?'

'Queen Elizabeth's Grammar School – Q-E-G-S – in Wakefield.' Harrop sighed loudly as if in relief at having got the words out.

'Oh, I see!' Rupert exclaimed, a penny having finally dropped. 'We have an away game – a fixture.'

'What I said, weren't it?'

'You probably did,' Rupert admitted. 'And I have to take the boys to Wakefield, do I?'

'Not all of them, just the First XV and any of 'em that's daft enough to say they'll run the lines. Any road, bus driver'll know where to go and the boys'll know what they're doing, even if you don't. That's all I 'ad to say. Tha'd better get them into the showers and off home – it'll be dark before long. It gets dark quicker up here, tha knows.'

Rupert wanted to agree, having felt distinctly in the dark for some time already, but before he could say anything the small man turned on his heels and stomped away, leaving Rupert to decipher the initials 'NCB' in large white letters on the back of his donkey jacket.

*   *   *

'Don't worry about Rufus Harrop – he's got a full bag of chips on his shoulder. Takes against anyone he thinks is posh or votes Conservative or comes from south of Cudworth.'

Rupert had blown two shrill blasts on his whistle, calling a halt to the practice game, and ordered the boys to get showered and changed at the double. It was as he trudged after the column of boys trotting towards the brick pavilion (rugby in winter, cricket in summer), that the spectator in the green trilby strode over the mangled, muddy grass and engaged him in conversation.

'Then I'm probably thrice damned in his eyes, though I'm not awfully sure where Cudworth is,' admitted Rupert.

'I wouldn't lose sleep over that. My name's Ramsden, by the way. That was my boy out there in the ruck – the one doing all the shouting.'

Rupert wiped his hand across the chest of his tracksuit top before shaking the one offered.

'Andrew Ramsden? He's my captain, I think.'

'Well, he was Mr Browne's pick,' said the proud father, 'and the team's done well enough this term.'

'Then I'm certainly not going to change a winning formula,' said Rupert firmly. 'In any case, I'm only a stopgap until the end of term, so if Andrew can put up with me I'll be more than happy to put up with him.'

'So you'll be doing just the two games? Pocklington at home and then QEGS?'

'I believe so,' said Rupert with more certainty than he felt. 'That would be Queen Elizabeth's in Wakefield . . . wouldn't it?' He became aware that Andrew's proud dad was now looking at him with curiosity mixed with sympathy.

'That's right, that's the last fixture of term. Tomorrow Pocklington sends a team here and all you have to worry about there is putting on a sandwich lunch for the visitors; the match itself shouldn't be a problem.' Ramsden paused in his briefing. 'Unlike the one in Wakefield, when QEGS will give us a real run for our money. Could be a tough game.'

'Thanks for the warning.' Rupert grinned. 'Do you get to the matches?'

'Not as often as I'd like.'

'Policeman's lot and all that?'

The policeman in question raised an official eyebrow. 'There are no secrets in Denby Ash, are there? I suppose you got an earful from Rufus Harrop about me. Round here they like bobbies about as much as they like southerners.'

'Or toffs,' said Rupert amiably, 'but our beloved groundsman didn't mention you as such. One of Andrew's masters did.'

'Could I ask in what context?'

Another of Mr Campion Senior's maxims sprang into Campion Junior's mind: that policemen are rarely, if ever, off-duty.

'A pastoral context and done with the best will in the world. It seems your presence here in Denby Ash is not – shall we say – fully appreciated by the locals and their resentment may rub off on Andrew. I have no idea of the details, of course, and naturally I said I would keep an eye on him, though as far as I can make out he seems perfectly able of taking care of himself.'

'Thank you for being so frank,' said Ramsden, 'and you are right, Andrew is a capable boy on and off the rugby field, but I would appreciate it if you would keep an eye on him.'

'Of course I will,' said Rupert, slowing his pace as they neared the pavilion building. 'Your investigation here – it's nothing dangerous, is it?'

'Not at all, just routine checks really, but Andrew lost his mother two years ago.' Ramsden's voice collapsed into a whisper and he turned his head left and right to make sure he would not be over-heard. 'Cancer,' he said, almost mouthing the word, making it an obscenity.

'I'm so sorry,' said Rupert. 'The boy must still be sensitive.'

'Oh, yes, he's sensitive all right, though like most teenage boys he won't show it. That's not what I'm worried about, though; it's Andrew being close to Roderick Braithwaite. They've always been friends and they have a lot in common. Andrew lost his mum and Roderick lost his dad years ago, and he's a credit is the lad.'

'So where's the problem?' Rupert prompted gently.

'It's just things have gotten strange lately, what with all the talk about ghosts and spirits and exorcisms.' The policeman's voice tailed off in embarrassment.

'Is that all to do with the *Doctor Faustus* production? If so, that's my wife's department. I'd be happy to have a word with her if it would put your mind at ease.'

Dennis Ramsden shook his head violently, sending a carousel

of spray from the brim of his hat. 'It's nothing to do with the school play; it's to do with the haunting of Ada Braithwaite's house. Roderick's obsessed with it and he's got our Andrew fixed on it as well.'

'A haunted house? Here in Denby Ash?'

'Bertram Browne believed it, according to the boys, and Ada Braithwaite says he actually witnessed it the night he was killed.'

The word 'killed' instead of 'died' had an immediate sobering effect on Rupert.

'I thought Bertram Browne was the victim of a road accident, a hit-and-run.'

'He was, but it happened no more than half an hour after he experienced a poltergeist. Makes you think.'

'It certainly does, I suppose, but I'm not quite sure why you are telling me this.'

'Thought you'd be curious; thought curiosity ran in the family. Something like this should be right up your street if you're a Campion. You are related to Albert Campion, aren't you?'

'I am, and you were right, Mr Ramsden,' said Rupert thoughtfully, 'there are no secrets in Denby Ash.'

EIGHT
Sit. Rep.

Dear Aged P's, Rupert's letter began, at which Mr Campion huffed 'Cheek!' before continuing to read.

Here, as promised (under duress) is our first Situation Report from the front line in the Frozen North. (Mother was right about the thermals, by the way.)

Ash Grange School, as opposed to Denby Ash the village or Grange Ash the colliery (yes, there is a lot of ash around here), is not the Dickensian nightmare you wanted it to be. The school is not nearly old enough for that, though many of the staff could be.

Perdita tells me not be cruel, so I will say that in the main they are not bad, just odd. Our hosts – bosses, I suppose – the

Armitages are decent people, but I think I must be the only male member of staff of who doesn't go by a commissioned rank. The physics master turns out to be an army chaplain and wears a dog collar, though he's not the local vicar – that's a sour old stick we met yesterday, and the music teacher's wife is a staunch Methodist of one ilk or another, all of which means that nobody seems very keen on this 'Faustus' show that Perdita has been sweet-talked into taking on. They all seem to think that doing a play about conjuring up spirits and demons is the next best thing to actually conjuring them and they're convinced Perdita will be messing about with books, bells, candles, pentacles and a sacrificial cockerel or two.

It does seem, however, that their fears are far from irrational as there is a well-authenticated case of supernatural possession – is that the right word? – not of a person, but of a house where a poltergeist has taken up residence. It's a perfectly ordinary house, one of a row of twenty or more identical ones in a long terrace, built for miners' families by the local mine owner before the Great War. Only the one house seems to have been invaded by the poltergeist and then only at certain times. Thursday evenings seem the most popular time for the spooky curtain to go up and, as far as we've heard, the Noisy Ghost (I think that's the correct translation from the German, but you'd know) doesn't go in for matinees.

This is all quite exciting because the haunted house is the home of a bright lad called Roderick Braithwaite who plays – you've guessed it – Dr Faustus in the production Perdita is struggling to put on. Roderick was also a particular favourite (I suppose I should say 'star pupil') of the late Bertram Browne, whom I have replaced on the rugby field, though not necessarily successfully. Not only that, but Bertram Browne apparently witnessed the poltergeist in action *chez* Braithwaite on the night he was killed in a hit-and-run accident. Spooky, to say the least.

Naturally, polite after-dinner conversation round here (and they really do call lunch 'dinner' and dinner 'tea' and I'm not being a snob, whatever Perdita thinks) turns to exorcism, or how to chuck out the pesky ghost. Despite being rather over-stocked with churches, chapels and clerics of various hues, no one seems keen to volunteer. Our physics master, the Rev. Stanley Huxtable says it's out of his jurisdiction whereas the local incumbent, whom we met at Holy Communion yesterday (all school staff are expected to attend and it's fairly High so they call it 'Mass'), is called Cuthbertson-Twigg and is said to run and hide at the very suggestion.

He is fairly ancient and a dry sort and has been here for ever, I think. I only mention him because one bit of staff-room gossip is that he was once cursed by the local witch!

Now I have your attention(!) I can reveal that Denby Ash has a witch in residence. She doesn't live in a sugar candy house, which would make her popular with the boys here, but a beat-up caravan parked on a piece of common grazing ground known as Pinfold Lane. I have learned that 'Pinfold' is the old term for a village pound or animal enclosure, and the locals seem quite happy for her to be there. At any rate, no one has said anything about an angry mob carrying pitchforks and torches trying to drive her out.

Of course, we haven't actually crossed broomsticks with this witch, who is called Ivy Neal, we're told, as we have yet to venture out of school grounds and into the village proper. However, we will be mounting an expedition tonight so do think of us as we venture forth into enemy territory as Perdita takes me for a night out in the local working men's club.

Actually, it's business rather than pleasure as she has to meet the musicians who will perform in *Faustus*. They're members of the Denby Ash Brass Band and all miners. The bandmaster is a cove called Arthur Exley, a big cheese in the miners' union, whose *nom de guerre* is 'Trotsky', which might give you some idea of his political persuasions. Wish us luck!

One local character we have met has heard of you, though I can't tell if he's a paid-up member of the AC fan club or not as he's a policeman, a DCI called Ramsden. He's hanging around Denby Ash, where he's clearly not appreciated, looking for a con-man recently released from Wakefield Gaol. I think he's worried that this chap, who conned everyone in the village out of their hard-earned apparently, might be in line for some rough vigilante justice should he show his face round here. It seems a bit of a waste of police time if you ask me, as all the local papers and the local television news (a breezy little programme called *Calendar*) are going overboard on the crime wave sweeping the West Riding. It seems there's a highly organized gang operating in the county, robbing mills and factories and department stores by stealing their safes, invariably when they contain the week's wage packets. Not, you'll note, stealing *from* their safes, but taking the entire metal box! Now you have to admit that takes cheek, as well as a fair amount of upper body strength. The press is calling it the biggest, most outrageous act of thievery since Robin Hood rode through these green woods – when there were green woods and not collieries round here.

Funnily enough, legend has it that Robin Hood is buried not that far away at a place called Kirklees. I'm not sure that's true, so perhaps we should ask Lugg as he's bound to be a descendant of one of Robin's Merry Men.

Closing now to catch the post and to get ready for our meeting with militant brass bandsmen down 't'club', as it's known. If Perdita behaves herself and doesn't spark the Revolution, then I'm treating her to a fish supper at Willy Elliff's chip shop, which everyone says is absolutely top-notch and one of the main, if not the only, tourist attractions of Denby Ash.

More anon,

Yours, near Ilkley Moor without a titfer,

Rupert

'Well, Rupert seems to be having a high old time,' said Mr Campion, folding the letter back into its envelope and propping it against the marmalade dish. 'Ghosts, ghoulies, vicars, thieves, policemen and militant trade unionists all on his doorstep.'

'He doesn't say how Perdita's managing amidst all that chaos,' said his wife from behind the pink pages of the *Financial Times*.

'Perdita is perfectly capable of handling a battalion of spotty schoolboys and any amount of Bolshie brass bandsmen, and I'm sure her production of *Faustus* will bring the house down. It's the current West Riding crime wave which interests me.'

'Albert . . .' Lady Amanda's voice was gentle, but the warning it carried was strong enough and the pink screen of newspaper quivered in her grip.

'I was only thinking . . .'

'Please don't think, darling. You know I worry so when you *think*.'

Mr Campion removed his tortoiseshell-framed spectacles and polished the lenses unnecessarily on his perfectly pressed, snow-white napkin.

'It made all the papers, you know. Not the ones you read, my dear, but the comics I glance at down the public library where I often pop in for a bit of a warm or to get out of the rain while I'm waiting for the Darby and Joan Club to open.'

'Don't play the fool,' said Amanda, lowering the paper so that her husband got the full benefit of her admonishing, though slightly twinkly, glare. 'You may be a Darby but I'll be no Joan, and that's a promise.'

'And *that*,' said Mr Campion with a wide grin, 'is almost a quote from *She Stoops To Conquer*, isn't it? Goldsmith in all his glory.'

Amanda nodded her head graciously and Campion, not for the first time (not even the first time that morning) noted with genuine admiration that his wife was still a beguiling beauty even after almost thirty years of married breakfasts.

'In any case,' Amanda said dryly, 'no Darby and Joan Club would have you as a member.'

'Would I join a club who had people like me as a member?'

'Now you are almost quoting Marx – Groucho that is, not the other one that Perdita has to deal with.'

'Rupert said it was Trotsky, not Marx,' said Campion airily. 'I've read about him too: Arthur Exley, the firebrand union activist. He'll be sitting in a smoke-filled room in Downing Street before long, negotiating for a pay rise and shorter hours with the Minister for Power, or whichever minister it is that handles coal. Does that make me sound like a reactionary old fuddy-duddy?'

'It does indeed, darling. The socialists have been in power for five years now and nobody has actually tried to bundle you into a tumbril for the guillotine they have no doubt erected in Parliament Square.'

Mr Campion replaced his glasses and raised himself just enough so that he could peer over the top of his wife's newspaper. 'You always could soothe my nerves when it came to politics,' he said sweetly.

'Politics are not a suitable topic for conversation at the breakfast table,' said Amanda without looking up.

'Absolutely right, darling. Now let me tell you about these robberies . . .'

NINE
Scraps

To Dennis Ramsden it had always seemed unfair that a man should have to go to work in the dark, spend eight hours underground in the pitch-dark and then emerge when a shift ended only to find that the cruelty of winter had brought down its early dark curtain of night. Miners were a strange breed and their closed, tight-lipped communities, not to mention their capacity for large volumes of draught ale, had caused him many a professional problem, but even so he felt that their constant claims for higher wages might be justified. He had seen pit men hand over thin wage packets to their wives on pay days and each time had thought that it would take far more than that to get him underground. At least, though, they had pit-head baths now and the men no longer had to trudge or cycle through the village, their faces black and a fine mist of coal dust floating off their caps and coats, to the prospect of a tin bath in front of the fire and kettles of boiling water.

Ramsden had parked his car in the yard of the Shuttle Eye colliery facing the bath house building and lamp room where the miners collected and deposited their helmet lights and the heavy square batteries which hung from their thick leather belts. The old brass miners' lamps once stored there were now being polished up and turned into bedside lights or ornaments for pubs, for which there seemed to be an insatiable market. Miners' lamps were not, however, the only things going missing from local collieries.

Over the steering wheel of his Triumph Herald, Ramsden watched a steady stream of pink-faced, wet-headed men heading for the gates, some pushing bicycles, a few pulling on leather jackets and crash helmets, all of them carrying the empty 'snap tins' which had held their lunch and with empty thermos flasks tucked under their arms. The men strode past the few cars in the yard – cars were for management and they would leave later when the day's paperwork was done and the night watchmen had clocked on – paying no attention to Ramsden, though his outline in the car was visible in the orange glow of the sodium yard lights.

The chief inspector was beginning to think he had somehow missed the man he had arranged to meet, or the man was deliberately snubbing him. It would not be the first time that Arthur Exley had played ducks and drakes with the police, and Ramsden knew that had he come to the rendezvous in uniform or in a marked police car, Exley would have been waiting with a picket line of union members to greet him, making the point that this pit yard, this colliery and these men were all part of *his* kingdom.

With a rueful smile, he allowed himself the thought that if he had arrived by police car it would have had to be one of the Force's trusted Wolseleys rather than one of their blue-and-white Morris Minors. The Wolseley was too heavy to be picked up and rolled on to its roof by a gang of exuberant miners fuelled by Tetleys bitter after a Rugby League cup final – a fate which had befallen several of the more dainty Panda cars.

His reverie was snapped by the sharp rap of knuckles on his passenger-door window and then the door was pulled open and the car's springs squeaked as a thick-set, meaty figure squeezed into the seat next to him, filling the car with the damp aroma of Lifebuoy soap.

'Mr Ramsden.'

'Mr Exley. Thank you for your time.'

'Y'aven't 'ad any of it yet,' said Arthur Exley brusquely, pushing a damp strand of his thick black hair off his forehead with the heel of his hand. 'And I've not that much to spare tonight if truth were known. Got to get home, get me tea and then I'm out again for a meeting.'

'Union business?'

'Not tonight, it's a band night. Sorting out what the lads'll be playing for this damn silly play up at the posh school.'

Ramsden bridled at Exley's pejorative description of the school where his son was a pupil, but he had a barb of his own in his ammunition locker.

'Yes, I heard the band would be playing in support of the ruling classes. Ada Braithwaite's boy has the main part, hasn't he? I suppose that must have influenced your decision to help out the posh school.'

'Ada's a pit widow,' said Exley with a politician's smoothness, 'and as such is entitled to, and deserves, the full support of the Denby Ash Brass Band, even if it does mean supporting an educational establishment which promotes and supports inequality and privilege.'

'It has nothing to do with you setting your cap at Ada Braithwaite, then?'

Ramsden knew he would have thought twice before saying such a thing in public, especially if any of Exley's union members were in earshot, as it would surely have provoked a physical reaction. Exley would never allow himself to appear in any way weak in front of his men and several years of hard, physical work had left him with muscles itching to be utilized.

'That would be none of your business, Mr Ramsden,' Exley said quietly, 'unless you want to make it such.'

The policeman left the threat hanging in the narrow space between their two faces. He knew via his son's friendship with Ada's boy Roderick that Exley had at least suggested the idea of courting to the widow without, so far, any sign of acceptance.

'You're quite right, Arthur – that's none of my business. I wanted a word about things much less pleasant.'

'The whereabouts of Haydon Bagley, mebbe? That's what you're in Denby for, isn't it?'

Ramsden allowed himself a smile. 'Word gets about fair sharpish round here.'

'You've got to remember, Mr Ramsden, that Walter Bagley was a respected miner, a fine bandsman and a lifelong member of my union. Haydon Bagley's disgrace shouldn't rub off on him, and if I knew where that sly bugger was, I'd as likely be on 'im, smashin' 'is face in until we got back the money he stole from the widows and orphans fund. Then I'd happily ring you up and tell thee which hospital he'd been taken to.'

'I believe you would, Arthur, and I'd probably not blame you,' Ramsden said equably. 'I'm more than happy for folk to think I'm in Denby about Haydon Bagley, but I'm really here to see you.'

'And what have I supposed to have done?'

'Nowt, or nowt I know of. I've come seeking a bit of help.'

Ramsden sensed his passenger bridle in the adjacent car seat and had the distinct feeling that the temperature in the Triumph, already low since he had parked and turned off the heater, had taken a sudden fall.

'Coppers want *my* help? Can't say I saw that coming. Ge'rr'on wi'it, then, it'll be a first,' said Exley, settling back in his seat and folding his arms across his barrel chest.

Ramsden took a deep breath, for he agreed with the solid-framed miner: this was unchartered territory for the pair of them. Ironically, Ramsden knew he would have felt more comfortable if they had been trading insults in front of a picket line.

'The deputy manager here at Shuttle Eye got in touch a little while back . . .'

'Oh aye? What does *he* say I've done?' growled Exley.

'Nothing. Get this through your head, Arthur – nobody's accusing you of anything.'

'But summat's up, that's for sure.'

'We think summat is. There's a goodly chance that quantities of explosives are going walkabout from both Shuttle Eye and Caphouse, blasting charges and detonators.'

'Hell's bells!' Exley breathed. 'Them's not firecrackers, you know.'

'I know that, Arthur, and we don't think it's somebody making jumping jacks for next Bonfire Night.'

'So who'd you reckon? IRA?'

'There's plenty who would point the finger that way. Only natural, given the troubles over there,' said Ramsden resignedly, 'but we've not a shred o'proof one way or t'other.'

'But you're saying it's an inside job?'

Surprise and concern had been replaced by ripples of defensiveness and indignation in Exley's voice. 'Stands to reason, Arthur. We think only small amounts have gone missing but they may have gone missing over a period of time and now it's noticeable.'

'Could it be a case of sloppy book-keeping? Somebody just being careless with the paperwork?'

'Like to think so, Arthur, but we can't take the risk so we've got to face the fact that somebody who has direct access to the explosives has been nicking them. That means somebody on the blasting crews working underground.'

'And that means one of my union members.'

'Almost certainly.'

'So what do you want then, Mr Ramsden? You want to set a union man to catch a union man?'

Ramsden took in another long breath. 'That's exactly what I want, Arthur.'

Roderick Braithwaite and his best friend Andrew Ramsden had allowed their imaginations to run riot on the subject of the status, approachability or employment of witches. How exactly did they earn a living, if indeed they did? Were they eligible for the dole if unemployed? Did they keep regular consulting hours or were they governed by phases of the moon?

Being far too grown-up, in their own objective opinion, to be frightened by myths involving spells, curses, being dive-bombed by low-flying broomsticks and the threat of being roped together and stewed in a cauldron, the boys had set out on their mission with firm strides and stout hearts. Roderick had even voiced aloud the thinking behind his courage, stating that a witch, however hungry, must surely be desperate to conform to that grimmest of fairy-story clichés given that boys were supposed to be made of 'snips and snails and puppy dogs' tails'. And to show that he had researched his decision thoroughly, he had discovered that 'snips' were supposedly tiny eels, which would make the stew of young boys quite unpalatable. His friend Andrew had admired his logic but suggested there were minor flaws in Roderick's argument in that snails were consumed with enthu- siasm in France and the staple diet of cockney Londoners was surely eel pie and mash, whatever that was. Andrew did admit that he could not think of a primitive culture, not even one as far south as London, where puppy dogs' tails were regarded as a delicacy.

Nervous frivolity aside, they had resolved to call on Ivy Neal, Denby Ash's local (and possibly only) witch with a business proposition. It was a proposition to which they had given serious consideration and it was one which, by their boyish logic, she could not conceivably refuse. They had not, however, counted on the obstinacy of adults in general and witches in particular.

'We should have brought a torch,' said Andrew, his voice muffled by the thick woollen scarf wrapped around his neck and mouth against the rain.

'Don't be daft. It's only just across the Green – you can see her caravan from here,' chided Roderick, then he sniffed loudly. 'Fancy a bag of chips on the way back? My treat.'

They were standing opposite the church of St James the Great at the bottom of Oaker Hill where it joined Pinfold Lane and curved around what the residents of Denby Ash called the Green, a lozenge-shaped piece of rough grazing that had been known to previous generations as the Pinfold, a secure area where straying animals were penned or 'pinned' until reclaimed by their owners on payment of a fine to the local pinder. About the size of one of Ash Grange's rugby fields, the Green was best known to the boys as the site for the annual visit of the 'Feast', a travelling funfair which had once boasted a dancing bear on a chain but nowadays brought the delights of toffee apples, candy floss, rickety rounda-bouts seemingly powered by loud pop music, and the opportunity to win a goldfish or a cuddly toy by means of air rifle shooting or the throwing of round hoops over square objects, or darts at playing cards.

At his friend's offer, Andrew turned his head towards the nearest building, the rectangular redbrick shed known to all despite the absence of signage as Willy Elliff's Fish Shop, and he too sniffed loudly.

'He's started frying,' Andrew confirmed. 'I'll get some chips for the bus home if he does bits.'

''Course he does,' said his friend and founder of the feast to come.

The very mention of 'bits' pricked a nerve in Roderick, for he remembered his mother's furious edict that he should never be seen in Willy Elliff's ordering 'bits' – the crunchy scraps or excess batter from the fish which floated to the surface of the deep fryers and which would be skimmed off and sold for tuppence rather than the sixpence charged for a bag of chips. 'Asking for bits instead of proper chips makes it look like we can't make ends meet,' the formidable Ada Braithwaite had told her son. It was clearly a stigma to be avoided, and a stigma which the various members of the Elliff family serving behind their chrome-and-Formica counter were maliciously keen to propagate. A bag of chips *with* bits was, however, perfectly acceptable so long as Willy Elliff, who was notoriously keen when it came to his profit margins, did not charge extra.

Their supper arrangements settled, the boys stepped off the road and on to the Green towards the only habited dwelling in Denby Ash not illuminated by the yellow glare of the street lights. Even so, the domed outline of a small caravan was clearly visible at the far end of the field where, the boys knew, the Oaker Beck formed a natural boundary with the pitch-dark Denby Wood.

They squelched through the cold wet grass and mud with determined steps, hands in pockets to hug their winter coats closer, using the glow from a light behind a red curtain at one of the caravan's windows as a homing beacon.

Close to, the caravan loomed like an ancient earthwork or prehistoric barrow; silent except for the rain bouncing off its metal roof. It was with some trepidation that Roderick placed one foot on the two metal-framed steps, raised a fist and rapped on the door set off-centre towards the rear end of the vehicle.

When there was no response, Roderick knocked again and said 'Hello?' in a voice which came out a higher pitch than he had planned.

Now there was a response, of sorts. The red curtain at the window to the left of the door definitely twitched, the boys heard a distinct creak of movements from inside the van and then more lights came on, illuminating the bulbous front end.

'Come in, then, if tha's coming, and put t'wood in t'hole to keep rain out.'

The voice was of indeterminate age and sex but had undoubted authority and the boys did as they were instructed, climbing into the caravan and pulling the door closed behind them.

They found themselves confined in what was clearly a kitchen area, a tight mesh of folding Formica surfaces surrounding a gas hob on which was balanced two unwashed metal saucepans and a battered kettle which looked as though it had been used for target practice. From the ceiling, hung from a latticework arrangement of lengths of clothes line were bunches of dried flowers, herbs and sprigs of mistletoe.

So far, so odd, if not exactly *witchy*, but then the boys' heads turned in unison to face the front end of the caravan where three hissing gas lights provided a focussed pool of bright light in one corner, casting the rest of the van into dingy shadow. The effect was theatrical, as if an overhead spotlight had been shone down only to illuminate upper stage left – and the actors who were there waiting for their cue.

'You're not the ones I expected,' said the woman. The large, long-haired tabby cat resting across her knees opened its mouth and showed its teeth, but said nothing.

The woman wore a wool wrap or blanket around her shoulders and a headscarf tied in a big knot under her chin. Her face was long, thin and white and her lips pursed as if permanently puckered. She was sat on one of the corner bench seats which all caravan enthusiasts knew converted into a bed. Behind her head were long dark drapes and though she could not have been, given the dimensions of the van, more than twelve feet from the boys (who had stayed close together and within leaping distance of the door), she seemed to be far more distant and, when she spoke, her voice was strangely disembodied.

'Well, then. What's Old Ivy done to deserve this, then? It's a mucky old night to go visiting.'

Roderick felt a friendly nudge in the small of his back and, thus prompted, found his voice. 'Mrs Neal,' he began politely, 'I'm Roderick Braithwaite.'

'Ada's lad, aye, I know that,' said the woman, who remained strangely inert even whilst smoothing the cat on her lap with long, exaggerated strokes. 'An' you'll have come to Ivy about your haunting, I'll bet.'

'It's actually a poltergeist,' said Roderick with the seriousness of a train-spotter, 'and we want it gone. We thought you might help us.'

The woman inclined her head slightly but her face remained expressionless, staring not quite at the intruders but off to the side.

'You'll have tried our spineless vicar, I suppose?'

'Yes,' Roderick said quietly, but saw no reason to add that they had also tried three Methodist ministers and a lay preacher.

'Just what d'you think Ivy can do?'

'Perform an exorcism. I'm willing to pay. I've got over twenty-five pounds in my Post Office savings,' Roderick pleaded. 'I just want it gone, for my mum's sake.'

'Keep your money, lad and stop roaring . . .'

'I'm not crying!' said the boy defiantly.

'You're close to it,' said the witch harshly. 'But tears won't help anybody; they never did. Now I don't know what you think or what folks have told you I am . . .'

'Everyone says you've got powers,' said Andrew in support of his friend's plea.

'I don't do exorcisms – that's priest work,' snapped the woman, 'so you'd be throwing your money away. Now get yourself home before your mother starts to fret. If I could help Ada Braithwaite, I would. She's a good woman and she's never done me harm or called me bad behind my back, but my powers don't run that way. Tell her she won't have to put up with it much longer, that's all I'm saying. Now go and leave me in peace.'

'I could get more money . . .' started Roderick.

'I said go!'

The witch woman known as Ivy Neal slowly rose to her feet and it seemed, under the peculiar light thrown out by the popping gas mantles, as if she was not only standing up but growing taller as she did. She had gathered the cat in her arms and, clearly displeased, the beast showed its teeth again and hissed at the two boys.

Then Ivy Neal took one step towards them and totally disappeared.

Roderick and Andrew looked at the empty interior of the caravan, then at each other, and then scrambled for the door.

Being the rugby player of the two, Andrew easily outstripped Roderick as they beat a very hasty retreat away from the caravan across the Green, aiming for the sanctuary offered by the street lights on Oaker Hill. Through their noses they were able to judge their proximity to safety by the smell of frying fish and chips which hung in the air like the scent of a night-blooming tropical plant.

They stumbled on to the road almost opposite the Green Dragon pub and turned right, slowing their pace to a purposeful stride, towards Elliff's fish shop and the long hill up through the village.

'She really is a witch,' said Roderick, catching his breath, 'if she can disappear like that right in front of us.'

'That was a trick and a half, all right,' agreed Andrew, looking over his shoulder to make sure no one had seen their undignified flight across the Green, 'and it must be a trick. If she had any real magic she'd have turned us into frogs, or would that be toads?'

Roderick giggled nervously. 'Warty toads in your case,' he said, then squealed as Andrew punched him on the arm. 'Ow! Gerroff! Seriously, I reckon it's best we don't mention our little meeting with Ivy to anyone.'

'I'm with you there. We'd be laughing stocks. I won't say a word to anyone, not that anyone's likely to ask.'

But within less than a half a minute, Andrew Ramsden was proved painfully wrong and if their experience in Ivy Neal's caravan had startled them, the two black-clad figures looming out of the shadows down the side of the fish-and-chip shop terrified them.

'Just what d'yer think you've been up to, young 'uns?'

The voice which stopped the boys in their tracks was pitched low and carried menace, but its owner and his companion were little more than half-a-dozen years older than the youngsters they confronted. They were, however, bigger and more muscular. Dressed in dark jeans, leather jackets and crash helmets, and blocking the pavement, their intentions were clearly hostile.

'Cat got your tongue, then?' snarled one biker, grabbing the front of Roderick's coat. 'Ivy Neal's cat got your tongue, p'rhaps?'

'Hey, take your hands off my—' Andrew began, only to find a leather gauntlet, slick with rain, at his throat, and then his legs kicked from under him by a steel-capped boot.

Roderick, eyes bulging in fright, clawed at the hands that had grabbed him and which were lifting him until he stood precariously on his tiptoes.

'What were you up to at Ivy Neal's?' his attacker barked into the boy's face, so close that Roderick recoiled at the stench of fried fish and vinegar coming from behind a row of tombstone teeth. 'What she say to you? You'd better tell me or it'll be the worst for you.'

'None of your business, you dozy prat!' Roderick said with a bravado he did not feel as he caught sight of Andrew landing heavily on the edge of the pavement and rolling into a large puddle in the gutter as a biker's boot descended on his chest.

'If you won't let on then mebbe you'll learn,' said his own attacker. 'You stay clear of Ivy Neal or we'll come after you again. And this is to make sure you remember the lesson.'

Roderick felt the breath leave his body and his legs buckle before he registered that he had been punched savagely in the stomach. Disorientated, he saw a yellow street lamp, the night sky, the road, the shiny wet concrete kerb and the pavement, which looked very hard indeed. And then he took a blow to the side of his head and a knee came up to meet his face. As he tripped over and on to his prostrate friend, he saw a slash of white light from the open door of the chip shop.

'Oi!' came a shrill but authoritative voice, 'leave my Faustus alone!'

TEN

Men Only

'Is it for a lady?'

'I beg your pardon?'

'The half of bitter; if it's for a lady, it needs a lady's glass,' the matronly barmaid explained patiently, but Rupert looked no wiser.

'Of course I'm a lady,' chirped Perdita, 'and so I should have lady's glass.'

The barmaid, who was more than old enough to be Perdita's mother, adopted the expression of a mildly shocked maiden aunt, but said nothing and busied herself filling a small dimple jug with a handle from an electric beer tap which seemed to know by magic when to stop dispensing beer and leave a half-inch of foamy 'head' atop the brown liquid.

'That'll be two-and-fourpence.'

'Good heavens! Is that all?' Rupert blurted out.

'Tha' can pay more if tha' wants but nobody'll thank you for it,' snapped the barmaid. Then she flicked a tea towel at an imaginary spillage on the bar and flounced away.

'I don't think that lady approves of me,' said Perdita quietly. 'I should have demanded a pint. I bet that would have put a twist in her girdle.'

'Don't be so sensitive, darling,' Rupert soothed. 'I'm sure all the women in here drink the beer . . . when there are women in here, that is.'

Perdita lowered her voice to a whisper as she glanced around. 'So you finally noticed I'm the only one in here not working, have you? We're probably committing some terrible social faux pas.'

Rupert grinned mischievously and whispered back: 'I think saying "faux pas" is probably making a faux pas in this neck of the woods, but from what I've seen of the locals, they won't be reluctant to point it out.'

They stood facing each other, toe-to-toe, their heads almost touching, bent down concentrating on their drinks, resembling naughty children awaiting an inevitable and properly justified scolding, glancing around to take in their surroundings in short, sharp, furtive glances. The décor of the main room of the Denby Ash Working Men's Club ('and Institute') was predominantly of varnished pinewood, tables, chairs and the bar itself all stained to make them look older, although the design was spare, functional and modern. There was a small stage – a platform really – at one end with a metal stand which seemed to be buckling under the weight of a large square microphone which had probably, Rupert thought, been declared surplus to requirements by the BBC around the time of the Abdication. At the other end of the room was a raging coal fire and between that and the stage were lines of tables, each with six chairs and two large green ashtrays, arranged with almost military precision.

The tables nearest the stage were fully occupied by groups of men, almost all wearing flat caps, with pints of foaming beer in straight glasses in front of them and the majority puffing on untipped cigarettes so that a blue haze formed above their heads but a foot or so below the nicotine-stained ceiling. The tables and chairs nearest the coal fire were conspicuously empty and the only sound was the *tap-tap* of dominoes being laid.

'I wonder why nobody sits near the fire,' said Rupert, partly to engage his wife in conversation and partly to break the uncomfortable silence.

No one in the club had protested at their arrival and none of the inhabitants were actually staring at them, but even so, the atmosphere was a nervous one.

'They don't want their beer to get warm,' intruded an unfamiliar Yorkshire voice.

The Campions had not been aware of his approach, so quietly did he move across the carpeted floor for a broad, muscular man.

'Oh, I see,' said Rupert. 'It just seemed strange to us as in our part of the world a coal fire in a country pub would act like a magnet in winter and you wouldn't be able to get near it. You must be Mr Exley.'

'That I am,' said the short, bulky man, offering neither a hand-shake nor a smile, 'and I bet it's not the only thing you find strange round here. F'r a start this in't a country pub, it's a working men's club. If tha' wants a pub, we've got two: Green Dragon and t'Sun at either end of the village; take yer pick. Mebbe better suit the lady. We don't get many in here unless it's a bingo night or a Saturday when they put on a turn.'

Exley nodded his square-shaped head towards the far stage as if to clarify what 'turn' meant.

'This lady,' said Perdita brightly, 'is perfectly happy here. Your beer is tasty and remarkably cheap and I'm dying to know what sort of turns you put on here.'

Exley eyed her suspiciously, but Perdita's face shone with honest curiosity.

'We have singers – proper singers, none of them rubbishy pop groups – the odd impressionist and even a magician on occasion, but most popular are the comedians. Some of 'em might be a bit blue for you, though.'

'I doubt that,' said Rupert, and was secretly pleased that Exley looked slightly shocked.

'So there's no proper music here?' Perdita asked with the briefest flutter of eyelash. 'I mean brass band music. I thought that was why you asked to meet us here.'

Mr Exley now looked mildly embarrassed and it was his eyes which flashed furtively around the room to see if his encounter with the two strangers, especially the pretty female one wearing the Mary Quant pink alligator cape coat and the soft brown leather boots, was being noticed. It was, Rupert estimated, by at least ninety per cent of the drinkers.

'I thought here would be convenient for you after school, like,' said Arthur Exley. 'Band practice is in the parish room down the hill a-ways, by the junior school and the church.'

It had nothing to do with convenience, Rupert thought. The Campions had been told by all the dragons in the Ash Grange staff room that Arthur Exley would rather be seen dead than crossing the threshold of 'the posh school' and that he would insist on meeting in a place he considered more proletarian. In the club, he would have all the advantages as his 'toff' southern visitors would be like fish out of water. Yet this brace of fish appeared to be quite relaxed, particularly the girl, who insisted on standing at the bar rather than taking a seat as most females were expected to, and supping bitter instead of gin-and-orange or a Babycham.

'Well, as you're the bandmaster, can I at least pick your brains about the musical element of our end-of-term show?' Perdita smiled sweetly and then played her masterstroke, producing a purse from the folds of her coat. 'And you *must* allow me buy you a drink, Mr Exley.'

She had raised her voice enough to make sure she was heard by their unofficial audience, over which a hush had descended. Even the dominoes were being laid more quietly.

Exley cleared his throat loudly before declaiming: 'I don't drink, Mrs Campion, but I don't begrudge others the pleasure if that's what they see it as.'

Marxism or Methodism? Rupert wondered, for he had been warned to expect both dogmas, but Arthur Exley preferred to play the host and guide rather than the soap-box evangelist.

'I thought I'd take you down to the parish room so you can meet the lads who'll be playing in your show. They're practising tonight,' he said, then pointed a finger at Perdita's glass. 'When you've supped up, that is, but don't swig it down on my account.'

Perdita nursed her glass in front of her face to show she had no intention of being hurried and tried to ignore Rupert taking large, rapid swallows to lower the level of his pint.

'I hope you haven't put the band to any trouble on my account,' she said sweetly.

Exley stuffed his hands in his trouser pockets and rocked back on the heels of his boots before answering. 'Band has to practice, otherwise it won't be right on t'night, will it?'

'I'm sure the musical contribution will be the one thing that does go right on the night, though I'm afraid I have absolutely no idea what the music content is going to be or how it fits with the play. Mr Cawthorne, the music master, seems to know very little about it.'

Exley twisted his head as if exercising the muscles in his thick neck.

'He's been warned off by Mrs Cawthorne, hasn't he? Mustn't have owt to do with a play about conjuring up Old Nick, not with her being a devout churchgoer.'

'Didn't Mr Browne leave any instructions?' asked Rupert between rapid sips from his glass.

'Mr Browne was in no position to give the band instructions,' said Exley stiffly. 'The committee instructs the band on matters of policy and the bandmaster, reporting to the committee, chooses the music. In any case, Bertie Browne didn't dare stand up to his sister. *She* wanted to swan on stage to Offenbach!'

'Not *La Belle Hélène*?' Perdita spluttered into her beer.

'Aye, the same.'

'Did you tell her it wasn't in your repertoire?' grinned Rupert, then wiped the grin away when he saw Exley's stony face.

'Of course it's in our repertoire; it's a recognized test piece in competitions along with "Poet and Peasant" and the "Zampa" overture, but they're all a bit too happy-go-lucky for your play, I'd've thought.'

'Oh, you're absolutely right,' Rupert said, making hurried amends. 'Those would remind people of cartoons – Bugs Bunny and Woody Woodpecker and such – not conjure up the Devil.'

'That's the way I figured it, so we've gone for the overture from *Rienzi*. There's a fanfare leitmotif suitable for when the Pope and the King of Hungary and the Holy Roman Emperor appear, and it speeds up nicely for when the devils come and get Faustus to drag him down to hell.'

'Richard Wagner,' said Perdita. 'Good choice.'

'Wasn't he a favourite of Hitler?' said Rupert casually.

'Yes, he was; and Hitler was a teetotaller as well, if you want to make anything of it.'

'Please ignore my husband, Mr Exley,' Perdita jumped in quickly. 'He is well known for speaking when his foot is only halfway to his brain. Now, is it far to this band room of yours?'

'It's the parish room and it's tacked on to the village school down the 'ill a step, next to the church. The band rents it off the Parochial Church Council and I reckon what we pay keeps old Twiggy in Bourbon biscuits for 'is coffee mornings.'

'Twiggy?'

'The Reverend Cuthbertson-Twigg,' said Exley, curling a lip as if the words tasted bitter, 'vicar of this parish for longer than anyone cares to remember and no earthly good to man nor beast. He's about as much use as a chocolate teapot.'

'Isn't that a bit harsh?' said Rupert. 'I'm sure he means well. Country vicars usually do.'

'Singing hymns, smelling of incense and consorting with the landed gentry isn't my idea of looking after the needs of this community, but I'm an atheist so it's none of my business what he does. For them that wants religion, we've no shortage of chapels in Denby Ash.'

'We've noticed that you seem well served by all the known branches of Methodism,' said Perdita.

'Aye, and I bet there's a few branches you've not heard of. It's all the same to me, but Old Twiggy 'asn't got much of a flock left.'

Exley looked at his wristwatch, then at Rupert's pint glass, then back at his watch. 'We'd best get a move on, otherwise they'll have finished their practice afore we get there.'

'Well then,' Perdita beamed, 'let us make haste to Wittenberg.'

'Nay,' said Exley, smiling for the first time, 'we're not goin' that far. It's nobbut a step down Oaker Hill.'

The Campions deposited their empty glasses on the bar, thanked and wished the surly barmaid a good night, which she acknowledged with a nod but no change of expression. As they followed Arthur Exley across the bar towards the small entrance lobby, they felt all the silent eyes in the room tracking them but their escape was delayed as Exley held open the door to allow a small, shambling figure to enter.

It was an older man who walked with a pronounced stoop. He wore a dark suit with a scarf knotted around his throat in lieu of a tie and was vigorously shaking a flat cap. The cap and his suit jacket were shadowed with wet stains.

''Evening, Tom,' Exley greeted the newcomer. 'Is it raining?'

'Just now started spittin', Arthur,' came the answer as the man wiped a hand down his face and strode firmly towards the bar where the barmaid was already pulling the pint with Tom's name on it.

Perdita peered out of the open door and into a night curtain heavy with rain, through which the street lights shimmered weakly.

'I'd hardly call this a few spits of rain,' she said, pulling a tightly folded polka-dot plastic rain hood from the folds of her coat. 'It looks positively torrential. Does it always rain this much here, Mr Exley?'

'Might do; couldn't really say. It's difficult to know if it's raining when you're seven hundred feet below ground.'

Arthur Exley did not seem to mind the rain; in fact, he seemed impervious to it and as they trooped and splashed their way down Oaker Hill he played the role of tour guide as if escorting visiting dignitaries around a county show. He pointed out the 'pit house' he had been born in, though even with the street lighting is was difficult to pinpoint exactly which part of the terrace would one day be adorned with a commemorative plaque. On the nearside of the road – Perdita remembering the road safety adage to always 'walk on the right, especially at night' – Exley indicated a new road leading to a new housing estate, an area called with a breath-taking lack of imagination 'the New Houses'. And then another, older road where there were no street lights, which ended, their guide assured them, in not one but two dissenting chapels: the Zion Methodists and The Mission.

'To be honest,' Exley said, 'the Mission is little more than a glorified garden shed rented from the Zion Chapel and it probably has less of a congregation than St James', but most folk of that persuasion go to the Primitive Methodists up the other end of the village near the Co-Op.'

Perdita noticed that once outside the working men's club, Exley's Yorkshire accent had almost disappeared.

'You seem well provided here with the opiate of the people,' she said, but Exley did not break stride.

'I wondered when you would start to quote Marx at me but it doesn't worry me. It's you that should be worried because all the God-botherers we have in Denby – whatever they call themselves – are all dead against your *Doctor Faustus*, and have been from the start.'

'Do you know the play, Mr Exley? You picked up on my refer-ence to Wittenberg back at the club.'

'I've read it.'

'Did you have to do it at school . . . or university?' Rupert asked.

'No. It might surprise you to learn that I did go to university but I didn't do literature – I did politics at Manchester. I read the Marlowe play for . . . personal reasons, and so I knew what I was getting the band into.'

'Sensible chap,' said Rupert, then stopped dead in his tracks and loudly sniffed the wet night air. 'I say, what is that delicious smell?'

'That's Willy Elliff's chip shop and he's frying tonight,' said Exley. 'He uses proper lard – none of that oil muck. Can't beat it for frying.'

All three of them paused outside the dark stone frontage of the village school to take in the aroma wafting through the steadily pouring rain.

'And what's that sound?' asked Perdita.

Exley cocked his head to one side as if his ears were direction-finders. 'That would be the tenor horns.'

Perdita would later think of her first encounter with a brass band as diving into a pool of warm tonal mellowness. That feeling was encouraged by the fact the she and Rupert were sitting on low, fat iron radiators, their wet clothes steaming faintly to demonstrate that unlike Ash Grange School there seemed to be no curfew for central heating in the parish room.

Arthur Exley had explained that the full band would not be providing the music for *Doctor Faustus* for the simple reason that the school hall was not big enough to accommodate band, play and an audience. The music would therefore be provided by a select unit of younger members of the band: four cornets, a soprano cornet, three tenor horns and one euphonium.

The bandsmen – no bands*women*, Perdita noted – sat on folding wooden chairs in a circle almost, she thought fancifully, like garden gnomes arranged around an ornamental pond, though these gnomes did not hold fishing poles but brass instruments to which were attached ornate clips holding a musical score written in minute calligraphy on postcard-sized sheets.

When Exley entered the band fell silent as if a teacher had entered a classroom earlier than expected and nine red faces turned towards him. But these boys displayed neither fear nor guilty conscience. They were eager for instruction – a situation any teacher in any school would have been jealous of.

'Good work, lads,' said Exley. 'We're almost there. Now I want you to run through the whole piece for Mrs Campion here, who'll be producing the show. So we'll go from the top when you're ready, Neil.'

The soprano cornet player licked his lips and nodded acknow-ledgement.

'And Kevin . . .' he turned to the euphonium player, '. . . just keep in mind we've got neither tuba nor percussion for this, so you're our bass line. Don't be frightened to show it. Right, keep it crisp and put a drop of devilry into it. After all, that's what it's all about.'

Although neither of the Campions professed to be fans of Wagner, they had to admit that the arrangement performed for them was a subtle one and certainly well-executed. Perdita also recognized it as a clever choice to accompany the Faustus story as it had a long, single-note motif introducing a baleful fanfare of cornets; there was a section of an almost pompous march and even a 'gallop' before a dramatic finale, all of which she could relate to scenes in the play even though she had as yet no idea how they might be welded to the text.

She and Rupert started to clap as the piece finished but Exley waved a finger at them.

'Steady on, we don't want them getting swell-headed,' he admonished, which raised a nervous titter from the band members.

'Well, I thought that an exemplary performance,' said Perdita. 'Who did the arrangement?'

'That'd be me,' said Exley rather coyly.

'And they follow the score from those little cards? The notation is so small I'm surprised they're not all wearing glasses.'

'You've got be able to read spider shit if you want to be in this band,' offered the soprano cornet player, a tousle-headed young man not long out of his teens.

'Language, Neil,' warned Exley.

'Oh, sorry, Arthur, forgot teacher were int' room. Is she going to give me lines, then? Bin a long time since I 'ad to stay behind after school . . .'

The band began to laugh and Neil played to his audience with a wide grin.

'You'll have to forgive Neil, Mrs Campion,' Exley apologised. 'He's a bit rough round the edges but he means well.'

'Well, his playing certainly isn't rough,' said Perdita graciously. 'I thought it as smooth as silk and his triple-tongue technique is amazing.'

She eased herself away from the radiator and walked slowly

towards the circle of players, the clicking of the heels of her boots acting like a metronome on the eyes of the bandsmen. As she approached the cornetist, she lowered her voice and spoke with a stage-vamp breathlessness as she looked down at young Neil, whose cheeks were starting to glow pink though not from musical exertion.

'It must be true when they say that the cornet is a divine instrument,' she purred. 'Man blows into it but God only knows what comes out of it.'

There was a pin-drop silence and then the room exploded into laughter.

'Good one, lass,' said Exley, moving to stand behind the blushing Neil and gently patting him on the top of his head. 'In Yorkshire we always ask why are cornets smaller than trumpets?'

Perdita knew a vaudeville cue when one was being offered. 'I don't know,' she mugged. 'Why are cornets smaller than trumpets?'

'They're not,' said the bandmaster, deadpan. 'It's just that cornet players have bigger heads. Now I know some of you lads are on earlies tomorrow, so let's get packed away and leave it tidy so Old Twiggy has no cause to bash my lugholes or put the rent up.'

There was a ripple of good-natured grumbling from the bandsmen as they got their feet, packed away their instruments and folded and stacked their chairs.

'Be thee up at t'club later on, Arthur?' asked one of the horn players.

'Not me, Jim. I've shown me face in there already,' said Exley, 'and though I'd take a lemonade shandy off you any day if you're offering, I'll be looking after our visitors from . . .' Exley paused and nodded towards the Campions, '. . . down south.'

'So you'll be going somewhere posh then?' asked the second, or possibly third cornetist.

'Oh, yes.'

'The Green Dragon, mebbe?'

Exley, still with a granite face, shook his head. 'Better than that. Willy Elliff's.'

'Fish and chips! How perfectly splendid!' Rupert gushed with boyish excitement. 'That smell has been driving my stomach crazy. Come on, darling, I'm starving!'

Rupert looped an arm around his wife's waist and propelled her at speed towards the door. As he did so, he pulled Perdita close so that he could whisper in her ear. 'Where did you learn about brass bands and triple-tonguing, whatever that is?'

'I asked Stuart Cawthorne, the music master, for some tips,' hissed Perdita, 'so we might blend in a bit more with the locals.'

'Is it working?'

'Well, it can't do any harm, and it's better than your Bertie Wooster enthusiasm for the quaint local cuisine.'

'They're never going to let us forget we're from the south, you know,' said Rupert, opening the parish room door and easing his wife outside.

Perdita looked out at the wet darkness and pulled on her plastic rain hood. As she tied it under her chin, she whispered, 'You're right, but if we act nicely they might forget to remind us.'

'Hurry up and get in t'queue before this lot get a fancy for six penneth o'chips,' said Exley from behind them.

The Campions, arm in arm and heads down, splashed across the road with Exley at their side but were only halfway across when a caped figure on a bicycle appeared out of the rain right in front of them, so close that Rupert felt the end of the handlebars raked across his stomach. Automatically he tugged Perdita back a step but by then the cyclist was beyond them and tackling, with a concerted effort, the slope of Oaker Hill; a hunched, demonic figure clearly visible under the street lights. Even though the rider had passed within inches of his nose, Rupert had no idea of its sex, age or identity, only the very strong memory of the smell of fried food mixed with tobacco.

Arthur Exley, however, had no such doubts when it came to identification. 'Adrian Elliff! You clumsy bugger!' he yelled after the retreating bicycle. 'Are ye blind as well as daft? You coulda killed somebody!'

'One of your bandmen?' Rupert asked as they resumed their progress.

'Not flamin' likely,' said Exley. 'He's a bit slow is young Adrian.'

'Not on a bike he's not.'

'Aye, well, 'e's late for work – again, isn't he?'

'He'll be even later if he has an accident,' Rupert observed rather primly.

'I think he already has,' said Perdita suddenly. 'Look over there. Somebody's lying in the road.'

Rupert shook his head to clear raindrops from his eyes and followed his wife's stare to the dark curve of road beyond the chip shop. There was indeed a supine figure lying half on the pavement, half in the road. No, there were two prostrate bodies and two upright ones clearly intent on doing them harm.

'That's not a road accident,' said Rupert, 'that's a fight!'

'And that's Ada's boy, Roderick,' said Exley as all three broke into a run.

They were level with the fish-and-chip shop when the door opened, releasing a fug of steam carrying the scent of warm malt vinegar and a beam of white light which illuminated the shadowy figures struggling in the rain.

It was Perdita who gave the rescuers their battle cry: 'Oi! Leave my Faustus alone!'

ELEVEN

Platelayers' Interlude (Off-Duty)

'Well, Charlie, do I congratulates yer or do I salutes yer? I fort commanders came with boats or perhaps submarines. Did you tie yours up to Tower Bridge now they've closed the docks?'

'Promotion comes with many a stress and strain, you old codger, but they don't give you a boat unless you're River Police. It's frowned upon if you splash muddy Thames water over the smart new uniform.'

The recently anointed Commander Charles Luke of the Metropolitan Police shrugged his oak-beam shoulders inside the folds of a damp raincoat and squeezed his bulk fluidly around the sharp corner of a table. He settled into a bench seat and accepted the pint glass of beer being slid carefully towards him by a pink hand which could have been mistaken for a pound of unwrapped sausages.

The Platelayers' Arms, as it seemed with all of London's pubs, was undergoing a facelift; or as Luke thought of it, suffering improvements. Previously small, dark but snug and intensely private areas had been collapsed into one large, open plan and brightly lit area and on the single extended bar the brass and wood beer pumps which had once stood proudly to attention had been displaced by an implacable army of garishly-coloured 'dispense points'. Everything seemed to be painted red. In a shadowy corner to the right of the bar which had once housed a battered upright piano, a shiny chrome jukebox as big as a Sherman tank sat glowering at customers but remained blissfully silent.

Luke's off-duty drinking companion, however, had resisted both facelifts and improvements quite majestically.

'Have to say you're looking well on it. This commander-ing seems to agree with you. Must be the sea air.' Magersfontein Lugg raised his own glass towards thick, expectant lips. 'Down the 'atch then, as you nautical types say.'

Charles Luke sighed in resignation, drank, replaced his glass on the table and sighed again.

'I might have known I'd get your end-of-the-pier act,' he said without malice, 'and I'm just glad I'm off-duty and didn't come in my uniform or you'd have piped me aboard as I came through the door.'

'They really 'ave put you back in uniform, 'ave they?' Lugg applied his glass to his face again, his eyes twinkling over the rim.

'The perils of promotion: you get a smart new uniform and a desk big enough to take a double mattress. Trouble is it doesn't come with a mattress, just enough paperwork to stuff one, if you like a firm kip, that is.'

Lugg lowered his glass and raised his eyebrows, doing neither with conviction. 'Charlie Luke stuck behind a desk all day instead of running down footpads and hooligans? Perish the thort! You'll be puttin' on weight, my lad.'

By no means a small man, Luke cast a jaundiced eye over the spherical proportions of his companion which strained the buttons of hunting green wool waistcoat to popping point.

'And you, me old china, have absolutely no room to talk,' said the policeman, doing a fair impersonation of a reproving judge.

His fellow imbiber recoiled as if electrified, though by a very mild voltage. 'I'll have you know I'm a shadder – a perfect shadder – of me former self. I believe in keeping meself nimble, I do. Before the war my reg'lar fighting weight was eighteen-and-a-half stone.'

'Which particular war are we talking about?' Luke asked gently.

'What cheek!' blustered Lugg. 'Still, it's true that time flies when you can only remember you once 'ad fun. But I like to keeps nimble, that's my secret. How old's that girl of yours now? I bet she's at the 'andful stage.'

Luke's face softened – a sight never enjoyed by unrepentant members of the criminal class – as into his memory floated a picture of his daughter and, inevitably, the face of Prunella, far too briefly his wife, who had died giving birth to her.

'Hattie?' he said with genuine warmth. 'She's a seven-year-old bundle of tricks and no mistake. Don't know where she gets the energy. She's like a wind-up toy that doesn't need winding. Same principle as a self-winding watch, I suppose: the more she moves the longer she keeps going. Runs my poor old mum ragged. Even infants' school doesn't seem to tire her out. My mum says she's going to get her a treadmill for Christmas, or maybe a giant hamster wheel.'

'We're none of us getting any younger,' Lugg observed rather primly.

Before he could stop it, Luke's left hand twitched towards his head where his black curls, although flecked with grey, were still thick. The waywardly vain hand came under control and was returned to the table to nurse his glass.

'But some of us still have to patronize a barber now and then,' the policeman growled, casting a disparaging eye over his companion's shining expanse of bald pate which glowed like a full moon under the pub's neon lighting.

'No need to get personal,' said Lugg, gathering his mental skirts about him. 'I was finking of yer muvver.'

Commander Luke conceded the point with a brief nod. 'I know what you're getting at and you're right. Mrs Luke should be putting her feet up at her age, not running round after a seven-year-old, and seven isn't that far off teenage these days. Don't think it's not a worry, though she won't have it, of course. "She's no trouble," she insists and says "Kids will be kids" even when a bit of her prize china goes for a Burton.'

'What you need,' said Lugg imperiously, 'is another Mrs Luke – the wife kind, not another mother.'

When his suggestion provoked only a drooping of the eyelids rather than a clenching of fists, Lugg pressed his luck. 'Do I take

it that as you 'aven't told me to mind my own flippin' business
or planted a bunch of fives on me, that you have somebody in
your sights?'

'You're right,' said Luke sternly, 'that it's none of your business,
but as it happens there is someone I might have my eye on – a
young detective inspector, if you must know.'

'A lady policeman?'

'We do have 'em, you old dinosaur. We've had them in the
Flying Squad for ten years and this summer we had our first woman
to make Commander – made it before I did.'

Lugg's eyes narrowed to slits. 'Is that entirely kosher – wiv the
hierarchy. I mean? You know, fraternization among the troops, bit
dodgy for morale, that sort of thing . . .'

Charlie Luke conceded the point with a seismic shrug of his
shoulders. 'It's early days and we're taking it quietly, but if we
think there's a future for us then Kathleen will resign from the
Force and go back to her first career.'

'You mean that to play lovebirds she'd 'ave to get an honest job
of work?' Lugg's eyes widened now, the malicious imp replaced
by the astonished innocent child.

'You probably wouldn't call it that, but Kathleen always fancied
training as a barrister,' said Luke, allowing himself a brief smile.

'Blimey!' snorted Lugg. 'That's frying pans and fires any way
you cut it. Still, you're over twenty-one and of sound mind, I
reckon. Would you 'appen to 'ave told Mr C. about this paramour
of yours?'

Luke sipped beer before answering. 'Campion? No, I haven't
mentioned anything about Kathleen to Albert,' he said soberly.
'Nothing's certain yet and, in any case, Albert's never thought
much of my choice of women.' He held up a hand to stifle Lugg's
protest. 'Oh, I know he didn't approve of Prunella and I but he
was too nice to say anything. That's his trouble – he's always been
far too nice for his own good.'

'Don't, for Gawd's sake, let 'im hear you say that. Make 'im
really swell-headed, that would. Positively unbearable in my
'umble h'opinion.'

'To be honest,' said Luke with pleasure, 'I've never found your
opinions humble, though they're often amusing, and since you
brought up the subject of Mr Campion, would you have an opinion
on what he's up to at the moment?'

'Just as I suspected,' said Lugg, pushing an empty glass across the table, 'there's a h'ulterior motive to you inviting me here above and beyond the sheer pleasure of my company.'

'I'm not asking for State Secrets,' said Luke, easing himself out of his seat and scooping up the pair of glasses. 'Same again?'

'If they've nothing better,' breathed Lugg.

When Luke returned with refilled glasses, Lugg sat up straight, covered his heart with his right hand and placed the palm of his left over his beer. 'I promise to tell the truth, the 'hole truth and very little but the truth, so 'elp me Gawd.'

'You can knock that off right now,' said Luke. 'I was just curious as to why Campion was up in Yorkshire. It's not his usual hunting ground.'

'I don't think he's gone a-hunting for anything. He's retired from all that malarkey. He's doin' no more than presenting prizes at a school Speech Day. In fact, he's probably not even doin' that, just holding Lady A's coat whilst she does the 'onours. Where could be the 'arm in that?'

'Campion could find some if anyone could.'

'Now then, Charlie, draw it mild. I'm telling you straight – he's retired. He's too old for private narking, which in most people's opinion is rather low anyway. I told him so thirty years ago and I think it's finally sunk in. There's to be no more adventuring for his nibs – he's been clear on that. "No more hopping about pulling guns and shooting lines," he said and I heard that with my very own ears. Of course, Lady Amanda was standing over him with a metaphysical rolling pin while he said it, but there were witnesses, not just me.' He leaned forward conspiratorially. '*Reliable* witnesses.'

'Is it his health?' Luke asked with concern.

'Nah,' said the fat man, 'he's fit as a fiddle for 'is age. Always believed in keeping hisself nimble, just like what I do.'

Luke bit his lower lip to suffocate a laugh. That Lugg clearly did not know the meaning of 'metaphysical' was one thing, but any comparisons between his planetary girth and Albert Campion's slim silhouette of a figure raised the possibility that he had not fully grasped the concept of the word 'nimble'.

'So what's he doing in the frozen north?'

'I've told you, he's at a school – a proper school, for young gentlemen – not like the Reform Schools you and me attended,' said Lugg, his eyes twinkling.

'You speak for yourself,' bridled Luke. 'This school, it wouldn't be in a place called Denby Ash, would it?'

'Might be,' said Lugg suspiciously. 'What's your interest? Is this a professional sniffing around or just social nosiness?'

'You know me, Maggers, never nosey just for the sake of it.' Luke spoke in a voice not even Lugg would take issue with. 'Not like some. Call it professional curiosity. Does the name Malcolm Maud mean anything to you?'

'Now we gets to our muttons.' Lugg grinned. 'I knew you didn't invite me 'ere just for the pleasure of me company and my insights into the social calendar of Campions large and small.' Lugg saw a flicker of surprise in Luke's expression.

'Oh, yes, the junior branch of the family's up in Yorkshire as well – the lad Rupert and his missus, the lovely Perdita. Staying with Perdita's godfather, as I understand it.'

'That should mean Campion will be behaving himself.'

'You know his nibs better than that, but what's any of it got to do with Malkey Maud?'

'So the name does ring a bell, eh?'

'I'll say. He's from my old stompin' ground – Canning Town. Different generation, o'course, and I can't say we was ever bosom buddies, but I knew 'im when he was starting to move up in the world, just after the war. Went from burglary and petty thieving to the finer points of safe-breaking; became quite a cracksman, Malkey did. Got himself the nickname "Banger" because he always liked to blow the bloody doors off, as they say these days.'

'That's the feller: Malkey Banger Maud. Not one you'd give a character reference for, then?'

Lugg crumpled his face into a scowl. 'Wouldn't even make me Christmas card list,' he growled. 'Far too cack-handed for my liking; no finesse. You've got to 'ave finesse when you're dealing with explosives. I've known cracksmen – "Petermen" we used to call them – who could blow a safe without disturbing a spider in its web in the skirting board. Then there's them like Malkey Maud, who used enough Composition C to blow up that bridge over the River Kwai. Not exactly subtle was Banger Maud, an' I suppose that's how your lot nabbed him. Not before time in my not-so-humble. There were some London streets where he did more damage than the Luftwaffe. Was he one of your collars?'

Luke nodded modestly in professional agreement. 'Yes, Banger Maud did leave quite a trail of destruction behind him and his hauls were never much to write home about. The judge gave him ten years not so much for his thieving as for his "reckless and dangerous disregard for public safety and private property".'

'Well, I never thought I'd live long enough to find myself agreeing with a judge,' said Lugg ruefully, 'but I reckon His Honour called it just about right for once. I don't think nobody was upset to see Malkey go down, not even his dear old mum, God rest her soul. At least she got a few years of peace with him out the way. Is he still doin' his bird?'

Luke dug a packet of Gold Bond cigarettes and a Cricket disposable lighter out of a deep raincoat pocket and Lugg nudged a triangular red plastic ashtray across the table towards him with a faintly disguised look of disdain.

'Them things'll stunt yer growth, yer know,' he said without conviction.

'Too late to worry about that,' said Luke, lighting up, 'but I'm cutting down with a view to giving up completely. It could be my New Year's Resolution this year.'

'Girlfriend don't approve, is that it?'

'Kathleen's not keen, she's made that plain; but then, she's worth the sacrifice. Six months, by the way.'

'I beg yours?'

'Malkey Maud – you asked if he was still enjoying bed and breakfast at Her Majesty's pleasure. He got out six months ago.' Luke was matter-of-fact and coolly professional. 'And nobody's seen him since.'

'You think I might have?' Lugg feigned horror the way a maiden aunt might suddenly discover dirt under a fingernail. 'If I 'ad, I'd tell yer in a heartbeat, Charlie, Scouts' honour. I never had no time for that toerag. Banger Maud was a menace to the dregs of society, let alone the decent half.'

Luke hid a smile at Lugg's outrage. 'So, no whispers on the Canning Town grapevine, then?'

'Well, I might not be completely up-to-date, what wiv me moving in more refined circles these days, but I haven't heard of anyone laying eyes on Malkey since he was sent down. Like I said, nobody was sorry to see him go. Was he expected back in the Smoke?'

'He had a travel warrant for London with his release papers but he never used it.'

'Where was he in jug?'

'For the last two years of his sentence he was in Wakefield,' said Luke, averting his eyes from the face he knew his fellow drinker would be pulling.

'I gets it now,' murmured the older man. 'Wakefield and the Campions, they're all in Yorkshire, aren't they?'

'Probably coincidence, just me clutching at straws,' said Luke, stubbing out his cigarette with such force that the ashtray squealed across the tabletop.

Lugg pulled back his massive head as if dodging an incoming right cross. 'Show me a policeman who believes in coincidence an' I'll give you change from a nine-bob note! Come on, Charlie, you know me an' I knows you. That's too thin to get your juices going, there's got to be something else.'

'There is,' said Luke, flexing his arms and shoulders like a weight-lifter, his raincoat straining at the seams, 'but that's thin too. For the last year of his sentence, Malcolm Maud shared a cell in Wakefield with a chap called Haydon Bagley. The name won't mean anything to you; it didn't to me until recently, 'cos Bagley was a local boy made bad. He never visited London as far as we know, so he never blipped on my radar and he was pretty much second division as a villain.'

'Don't sound as if he'd be of much interest to Mr C., even if he wasn't retired, which of course, as we all know, he is.' As he spoke, Lugg looked flamboyantly around all points of the compass to make sure he was not being overheard.

Luke began to button his raincoat. 'Haydon Bagley wouldn't mean a thing to Campion even if he knew he'd been a cell mate of Malkey Maud. It's just that Bagley was born and bred in a place called Denby Ash, where Albert and company seem to have pitched their tent.'

'So how's that related to the price of fish?' asked Lugg, extending a pugnacious lower lip.

'Bagley finished his sentence and was released two weeks ago and was supposed to be heading home to Denby Ash. He hasn't been seen or heard of since.'

'Just like Banger Maud,' said Lugg.

'Exactly,' said Luke, rising to his feet like a Titan emerging from the sea, 'and you're right, I don't like coincidences.'

TWELVE
Prep

'**M**y dear boy, I came with all haste as soon as I heard you'd been arrested,' said Mr Campion pleasantly, and the staff room fell ominously silent.

Rupert, conscious that he had an audience, stifled any emotions he had about being confronted by twin figures of authority – his father and a headmaster – and replied coolly: 'Nothing so dramatic, I'm afraid. I was merely helping them with their enquiries.'

'But there were fisticuffs, or so I hear,' said Campion with a twinkle in his smile, 'so it was a good thing you had Perdita there to protect you . . .'

'Steady on, Campion,' said Brigham Armitage, 'that's my goddaughter you're talking about.'

'And my daughter-in-law; a most welcome addition to the family.'

'The girl showed spunk,' growled Raymond Bland from his chair where he sheltered behind an open copy of the *Yorkshire Post.* 'Should get credit for standing up to those hooligans just hanging around looking for trouble – there's few around here who would do that. They turn a blind eye when it's their own that are involved.'

'Actually,' said Rupert, 'I was rather glad Arthur Exley was with us as he set about them with a will and chased them off pretty quickly.'

'That's a nice twist.' Campion, who was good with names when he wanted to be, identified the speaker as Bob Ward, the PE master. 'Students and staff from the privileged posh school being rescued by a militant class warrior. A bit ironic, eh?'

'Keep those opinions to yourself, Mr Ward,' the headmaster snapped, 'and just remember that it was two of our pupils that were set upon. They did not go looking for trouble.'

'Where exactly is the lovely Perdita?' Campion asked calmly.

'She's in the middle of a *Doctor Faustus* rehearsal,' said Rupert, 'with a dozen adolescent boys, which could go on all afternoon.'

'In comparison,' Campion observed thoughtfully, 'a bit of street-fighting probably came as light relief.'

When Brigham Armitage had telephoned Mr Campion to tell him of the fracas in which Perdita and Rupert had become involved, he apologised for having few factual details to hand except that they were mostly unharmed, that they appeared to have been going to the rescue of two Ash Grange pupils who had been set upon by local thugs who had escaped apprehension on motorcycles and that the police had been involved because one of the boys was the son of a police inspector. To Mr Campion, it seemed a fairly thorough report, given in that regretful tone of a headmaster telephoning a parent to inform them of their offspring's bad behaviour and, having assured Amanda that no serious harm had come to Perdita or their 'son-and-heir-to-not-very-much', he announced that he would go to Yorkshire more than a week before they were expected.

Lady Amanda objected on the grounds that she had business commitments which would keep her in London, that they would not be expecting him at Ash Grange, that it was a long drive and that the weather in the north would be bad because it always was at this time of year – in fact, Yorkshire was probably already cut off by snowdrifts. Mr Campion countered with the argument that as she would be busy he would have many lonely hours to fill: the George Hotel in Huddersfield had perfectly suitable accommodation available (he had checked); his car had recently been tuned and serviced and would eat up the miles with the speed and grace of the jaguar it was named after; and the BBC's trusty shipping forecast had assured him that snow ploughs were not yet needed in the West Riding, though for the unknown territory that was the North Riding he could not speak.

When she realized that her objections were being rapidly overruled, Amanda tried one last time. 'Exactly what use do you think you will be up in Yorkshire?' she had asked bluntly.

'Absolutely none,' Mr Campion had replied with a beatific smile, 'other than perhaps offering moral support.'

Lady Amanda's beautiful eyes had narrowed. 'You're bored, darling, aren't you?'

'Nonsense. OAPs – that's Over Active Pensioners – such as myself and the dreaded Lugg couldn't have more on our jolly old plates. Lugg has his Beadle duties at Brewers' Hall; I have a library full of books which need reading, a posse of charities are chasing me for my patronage, I've been meaning to get down to falsifying the family history for years and then, of course, there's my stamp collection to sort out – and where exactly *is* Bechuanaland these days? So you see, my dear, I am so overworked I am desperately in need of a holiday.'

Amanda tried one final parting shot before surrendering to the inevitable. 'Who on earth goes on holiday to Yorkshire in December?'

'The Easter bunny?' Mr Campion had replied hopefully.

Brigham and Celia Armitage had professed delight at Campion's arrival at Ash Grange, having quickly ascertained that he was not an early substitute for Lady Amanda, whose presence at the end of term Speech Day had already been widely advertised. Once reassured that he was merely acting as advance reconnaissance for the guest of honour, the headmaster had shown Campion in to the Dragons' Den and introduced those members of staff currently off-duty and enjoying a mid-afternoon tea break.

There were only two dragons present and they had staked out their territory at either end of the den. Both were nursing cups and saucers close to their chins, giving them plausible excuses for not talking to each other until politeness and the presence of the headmaster and his guest forced them to break their silence. It did not take Mr Campion more than a minute to understand the icy atmosphere he had entered, for though he had never set eyes on Wing Commander Raymond Bland or PE teacher Bob Ward in his life, he knew the types of men they were, or at least the image they chose to project to the outside world. He was confident that somewhere between the blustering of the wing commander, the sarcasm of the PE teacher and the diplomatic interventions of Brigham Armitage, he would get a good sense of the state of affairs in the castle of Ash Grange School, if not in the surrounding kingdom of Denby Ash.

He asked few questions, no more than two or three, and then did what he did best: he listened, his face a picture of bemused innocence. By the time Rupert appeared wearing a tracksuit and carrying a pair of football boots coated in dried mud, Mr Campion felt himself fully briefed on who-was-who even if not what-was-what. For that, he would interrogate Rupert in private and so offered to accompany him towards his obvious destination – the playing fields.

With his Crombie coat done up tightly, a green wool fedora firmly screwed in to place and brown leather gloves buttoned at the wrist, Mr Campion felt if not equal to the Yorkshire weather then at least prepared for it. On the drive north the rain had been persistent though at times hardly heavy enough to trouble his Jaguar's very efficient windscreen wipers, but out on the exposed rugby field he was sure he felt the prick of sharp raindrops needling their way through his protective layers of wool, cashmere and leather. The wind, he decided – simply because the fancy took him – was deliberately sweeping towards him, personally, across the frozen slopes of the black mountain that was the muck stack of Grange Ash colliery.

A dozen gangling figures in damp rugby kit awaited Rupert's arrival and with a collective groan obeyed his command that they should run three laps of the field in order to warm up, Mr Campion marvelling at the sullenness of eleven-year-old boys who would rather stand and shiver than get their circulation moving enough so they could feel their extremities. How little the young knew of the simple pleasures of life.

Rupert had explained that the training session he was super-vising that afternoon was little more than an exercise in keeping part of the Lower Fourth occupied, the object being to tire them out before teatime. Much more would be expected of Rupert's coaching of the First XV for their final competitive match of the term, a match they would somehow have to play without their inspirational captain – and, in truth, only decent player – Andrew Ramsden.

It had, he explained, been Andrew Ramsden and his friend Roderick Braithwaite – of particular interest to Perdita in the leading man stakes – who had been involved in the fracas outside the fish-and-chip shop, assaulted by persons unknown and for reasons unknown, although neither of those things were strictly true. Rupert felt sure that Arthur Exley had a shrewd idea of the identity of the boys' attackers, though was saying nothing, and the boys themselves had been evasive to say the least on what they had been up to that evening or why they might have been attacked.

When Exley and the Campions had charged to the rescue, the two leather-jacketed hooligans had broken off their attack on the boys and fled towards the car park of the Green Dragon, from where they had emerged almost instantaneously astride large motorbikes, roared off down the Wakefield road and into the night.

The two Ash Grange boys, bloodied and bruised at the fists and boots of their attackers, seemed at first more surprised at the sight of Perdita's pretty face framed by a dripping plastic rain hood looking down at them rather than in pain. When their administering angel and her assistant, the temporary games master, attempted to get them up and off the wet pavement, however, they gave vent to howls of agony: Andrew clutching his right wrist to his chest and Roderick failing to stand as his left ankle gave way under him. Both boys were bloodied, muddy and their coats were soaked, giving them the appearance of bedraggled dogs that had been ordered, shame-faced, out of a particularly murky river.

Rupert had half-expected Exley, whom he had pegged as a fearless man of action when defending his own territory, to go charging after the assailants but instead he remained solicitously at Roderick's side, offering a strong broad shoulder for the boy to lean on. With Perdita putting a comforting arm around Andrew (who would later boast that he had received the better treatment by far), the sad little group decided as if by osmosis to seek safety from footpads and the weather in the nearest, warmest and best-lit sanctuary available.

The warm fug and neon strip lights of Willy Elliff's offered a comforting welcome to the refugees even if the humans inside the chip shop greeted them in shocked and complete silence. It was, Rupert had told his father, as if they had burst into a church at the moment the congregation was receiving the blessing, except that in this church the worshippers were all busy eating rather than praying and the vicar officiating was a tall, thin, cadaverous man with a gaunt face and a toothbrush moustache, who wore a white coat rather than a dog collar and the altar he stood in front of was a range of stainless-steel deep fryers and glass-fronted

hot cupboards. Any further spurious similarities to the interior
of a church were belied by the arrangements of the pews. There
were in fact only two; they were made of wooden planking and
they ran along the long sides of the establishment. They were
occupied by two couples who were busy eating from newspaper
parcels and concentrating on not engaging in conversation. On
the north wall of the shop sat an elderly pair, cocooned in damp
overcoats and scarves, whilst on the southern bench a brace of
teenage girls wearing matching shiny red plastic raincoats over
short skirts and knee-length white PVC boots had their heads
together so they could whisper confidences as they ate chips with
one hand and delicately raised bottles of Vimto to their lips with
the other.

The only sound to mark the arrival of the walking wounded
was the crackle and hiss coming from the deep fat fryers until
Arthur Exley gruffly ordered the two girls to 'budge up' and settled
the limping Roderick on to the bench seat next to them. He then
turned towards the counter where the white-coated chef de cuisine
was standing, open-mouthed, holding an empty wire basket.

'Has tha' got a phone in here, Willy?'

The tall stick of a man, who was hardly a potent advertisement
for his trade, shook his head. 'There's a phone box up by t'club,
Arthur, as you well know,' he said severely. 'Or there's one in the
public bar of the Green Dragon if it's urgent.'

'It's not a social call,' snapped Exley. 'These lads need a doctor,
mebbe an ambulance, mebbe the police.'

Perdita, having sat Andrew down next to his friend, was
conscious that the shop's customers – or should that be diners?
– were following this exchange with their eyes and heads like a
crowd at a tennis match.

'Nothing to do with our Adrian, is it?'

'For once, it's not, Willy. Mind you, the daft beggar almost ran
us over on that bone-shaker of a bicycle of his five minutes since.
Late for work again, I see.'

'You see a lot round here, Arthur Exley, and not all of it's your
business.'

'And you can't see what's under your nose, Willy Elliff, unless
it's fish or spuds or batter.'

Exley scowled at the proprietor but it seemed to have more
effect on the two girl diners, who edged nervously further along

the bench, than it did on Mr Elliff. The scowl slipped from his face when he turned back to Roderick and said calmly that he would go to the pub and telephone for an ambulance and, whilst that was coming, he would go fetch the boy's mother if the Campions would stand guard in the meantime.

Not quite sure what he was 'guarding', Rupert naturally agreed but pointed out as delicately as possible that Andrew, his star rugby player, was also injured. Exley cleared his throat – and was the man blushing? – and said that he would naturally make a call to Andrew's father, Chief Inspector Ramsden, whose number he seemed to know. Perdita's offer to run all the way back to the school to fetch her car was instantly dismissed by both men and, to Rupert's amazement, Perdita did not argue.

As Arthur Exley charged out into the night, the hiss of wet, battered fish submerging in hot fat came from behind the counter as Willy Elliff played his range of fryers and hot cabinets with the dexterity of a concert organist piloting his Wurlitzer.

Rupert sniffed the air and asked if anyone else fancied something to eat while they were waiting.

'Am I reading this menu correctly?' asked Mr Campion. 'Does it actually say *whole* chicken and chips in the basket?'

He had insisted that Rupert and Perdita join him for dinner at a suitable 'local watering hole' and had selected the Green Dragon on the recommendation of Brigham Armitage, not at all because it was near 'the scene of the crime'.

'It wasn't much of a crime,' said Perdita as she closed her faux-leather bound menu, 'and yes, they really do give you a whole chicken, though it's quite a small one, more of a *poussin*, really.'

'Now don't be modest, my dear,' said her father-in-law. 'I've being doing my prep all afternoon. Rupert briefed me on the basic facts and Mrs Armitage added much useful background, both medical and sociological, with the various denizens of the staff room contributing amusing, if unnecessary, local colour.'

'Perdita's right, Pa,' said Rupert. 'There really wasn't much to it, just a bit of old-fashioned bullying.'

'Didn't the choice of victims strike you as suspicious: the son of a policeman and the victim of a poltergeist? Even as a complete outsider, knowing only the very little I have gleaned so far, that strikes me as a touch odd.'

'"Odd" being your stock in trade?' Perdita asked with a grin.

'A lifelong pastime, I admit, but no more than a minor hobby. Other gentlemen of my advancing years revert to their potting sheds or their rose gardens, but I have always preferred a different form of pottering – one that involves less compost.'

'So you're exchanging compost for coal dust?' Rupert closed his menu decisively. 'Well, you'll find plenty of that round here. I'm having the chicken, by the way, and we have to order at the bar.'

'Scampi in the basket for me,' said Perdita.

'That sounds good,' said Mr Campion. 'I don't think I could manage a whole fowl unless I could devour it Henry VIII style, tossing bones over my shoulder to the wolfhounds.'

'They do have table manners here,' chided Perdita.

'Of course they do, my dear. I was implying that it was I who was lacking them. Do we go for white wine?'

'Best stick to the ale,' whispered Rupert. 'I've already discovered the wine list here comprises a Barsac and Sparkling Blue Nun.'

'Useful local intelligence, my boy. You can never have too much, and I intend to add to our stock of it by pottering around and meeting some of the fascinating inhabitants of Denby Ash you have told me about.'

'You mean you're going snooping,' grinned Rupert.

'Pray, do not call it that,' said Mr Campion, feigning outrage. 'I am a retired gentleman of leisure. I potter, I ramble, I rove, I may even loiter, but I no longer "snoop". That is an activity dear old Lugg always regarded as "common" and I'm surprised he let me get away with it for so long.'

THIRTEEN
Flockton Thick, Flockton Thin

Mr Campion had never put much faith in the saying 'Know Your Enemy'. He remembered fondly a post-prandial discussion with a military historian of some repute who had told him that while the popular story that

Montgomery won at El Alamein because he had a photograph
of Rommel above his bed was an excellent piece of morale-
boosting propaganda, his victory in the battle was more probably
due to his extra six hundred tanks. If anything, Campion had
always found it more useful to adopt the maxim 'Know Your
Friends' and he was hoping to find a new one in Huddersfield's
new police headquarters, even though his hopes were pinned
on a second-hand conversation between his son and a stranger on
the edge of a windswept rugby pitch.

Rupert had not played him false. Detective Chief Inspector
Ramsden, it turned out, would be delighted to see Mr Campion
even though he had not been expecting him.

'To what do we owe the honour?' the policeman asked warmly
as Campion was ushered into the offices of Huddersfield CID.

'Far from an honour, more a nuisance really,' said his visitor as
they shook hands. 'I see from this morning's *Yorkshire Post* that
your local plague of robberies continues, which means your plate
must be almost as full as mine was at breakfast.'

'I cannot discuss ongoing investigations, I'm afraid, not
with . . .'

'Mere members of the public, like little old me,' said Campion
with a broad grin. 'Quite right too, Chief Inspector. I am little
more than a tourist and my nose has no business in your business.
As it happens, I am staying at the George and cheekily thought
I would pop in to ask how your son Andrew was.'

Ramsden took a moment to consider not the question but why
it was being asked. 'His wrist was broken but he's recovering
well. He's young and fit; and the hospital says he'll be wearing
a plaster cast for six weeks or so but he's back at school, though
not on the rugby pitch.'

'Much to my son's dismay,' said Mr Campion. 'It sounds to
have been a very nasty incident.'

'Nasty, vicious and unprovoked but not exactly uncommon –
young bikers out looking for trouble after a pint or two . . . Andrew
and his friend were simply in the wrong place at the wrong time.'

'And you are happy that is all it was?'

'Do you know any reason why it was more than that, Mr
Campion?'

'I know very little about anything, Chief Inspector,' said
Campion affably, 'but I suffer from incurable, possibly terminal,

curiosity. I am the cat that curiosity will undoubtedly do for one day, but my enquiry about the health of your son is a genuine one for *my* son tells me Andrew is a key part of the school rugby team. I would go so far as to say vital.'

Ramsden's shoulders straightened as he failed to contain his obvious paternal pride. 'Kind of you – and the other Mr Campion – to say so; are you a rugby man yourself?'

Mr Campion pressed a forefinger to his chin as if a momentous decision was required. 'I realize that in this part of the world my answer may contribute to the schism that some say has ruined the beautiful game of rugby, but I will be honest and declare that though I believe the schism resulted in *two* great games – Union and League – my allegiance has always been to Rugby Union. My experience, in a long-forgotten youth as a school and varsity winger, could best be described as over-enthusiastic amateur but my fondest memory was as a spectator, not a player, watching England beat the All Blacks at Twickenham in 1936.'

'You were there? You saw the Flying Slav's try?' There was undisguised admiration in Ramsden's voice.

Mr Campion smiled demurely. 'Yes, I saw everyone's favourite Russian émigré Prince Obolensky score that famous try, but it was the England Captain, Bernard Gadney, who started the move and dominated the whole show. It might have been Obolensky's try but it was Gadney's game.' His smile turned into a wicked grin. 'But isn't it high treason or something to even have heard of such things in these parts?'

'You are not wrong there, Mr Campion,' Ramsden agreed. 'This is League country and if you don't follow Fartown then it has to be Wakefield Trinity or, at a pinch, Featherstone Rovers.'

'I promise to do my best not to show my ignorance and embarrass my Yorkshire hosts,' said Campion.

'I doubt you ever show your ignorance, Mr Campion, unless you've got a damn good reason for doing so,' Ramsden said in a voice which reminded Mr Campion that he was in the presence of a policeman.

'I shall take that as a compliment, Chief Inspector, and will answer your next question before you ask it, if that does not sound presumptuous.'

'It sounds like what we call straight talking in Yorkshire.'

'I hope it is. You were about to ask me what I am doing here – not just in your office, but in the West Riding.'

'If that hadn't been my next question it would have been the one after. This is not your usual stomping ground, is it, Mr Campion?'

Campion held up the palm of his hand, slightly self-conscious that he appeared to be impersonating a traffic policeman making a 'Stop' sign. 'I like to think I rarely stomp anywhere, but in essence you are correct; I cannot say that I know the lie of the land here, at least not yet.'

'And what's the answer to my question? The one I haven't asked yet.' Ramsden spoke firmly but politely, giving Mr Campion a clear signal that their verbal sparring should reach a conclusion.

'What am I doing here? I take it that is the question,' said Campion, 'and it is one I asked myself on the drive up here. By the way, should I give you a sensible answer, would you be good enough to pass it on to my wife and son? They also seek enlightenment on the matter.'

Ramsden smiled broadly at that then rummaged around the papers on his desk until he located a packet of cigarettes, which he opened and offered to his guest.

'No, thank you,' said Campion. 'Not allowed anymore, but let me give you a light.'

He reached into his jacket pocket, produced a silver Ibelo Monopol lighter and flicked it into life.

'Nice lighter,' said the policeman with the standard policeman's eye usually reserved for stolen goods.

'A present from my dear wife,' said Mr Campion, holding it so that Ramsden could see the engraved inscription. 'It says *To A from A, Polite Use Only*, which reminds me I can offer to light the cigarettes of others but not one of my own.

'Now, back to my interrogation as to what I am doing hereabouts. The truth is I am not sure, Chief Inspector. I can only refer you to my previous answer: curiosity, the nemesis of our feline friends. As a man with copious amounts of time on his hands these days, almost anything sends sparks between the old curiosity antennae and when two or three sparks follow in quick succession the static electricity produced raises a full pelt of hairs on the back of my neck. Not exactly what you would call hard evidence for anything, I know, and perhaps no more than an old man's affectation.'

Ramsden kept his eyes on his guest, inviting him to say more.

'The death of Bertram Browne raised the first hair.' Mr Campion patted the air in front of him with the palms of his hands as if quashing a rising hope. 'I know, I know, it was a road accident, but as I understand it the vehicle involved has not been identified and no driver charged.'

'That is not uncommon – sadly,' Ramsden admitted. 'Mr Browne died instantly and the driver kept going; the very definition of a hit-and-run.'

'Quite, but why didn't Bertram Browne run?'

Ramsden's brow furrowed and he leaned forward in his seat. 'I don't follow.'

'I have done a bit of checking up on him with his old army unit. He was in the Royal Engineers, a Sapper, as I'm sure you know, and he had a very good war record. Highly thought of, decorated, bravery under fire and all that. Plus we know he played rugby, so one presumes he kept himself fit. Why didn't he get out of the way?'

'It was dark,' said the chief inspector. 'Perhaps the whole thing happened too fast for him.'

'Which raises a second hair. Browne doesn't sound to have been the sort who was scared of the dark and he was indeed walking on a stretch of road which was dark. I drove down that road last evening. The stretch between the school and that stone bridge just before the Sun Inn seems to be just about the only piece of road in the West Riding which isn't festooned with street lights. The rest of the village is lit up like an airport runway at night; goodness knows how many sixpences the local council has to put in the meter every day . . .'

'Yes, it was dark and the road was unlit. What's your point?'

'Why didn't Browne see any headlights coming towards him? And did he not hear an engine, which would have given him some warning? That road runs alongside the school playing fields, which he knew well, and not along the edge of a precipice or anything. He could easily have got out of the way.'

'Perhaps he was distracted, his mind elsewhere,' countered Ramsden.

'It almost certainly was,' said Campion with relish. 'I believe he had just come from witnessing the effects of a poltergeist haunting when the . . . accident . . . happened. I must say, that alone would cause a third hair to stand to attention. And when I heard that a certain policeman was investigating the black sheep of Denby Ash . . .' Mr Campion removed his large, round tortoise-shell spectacles, produced a white handkerchief square and began to polish the lenses, '. . . and that the son of that policeman and the son of the woman visited by the noisy Germanic ghost had been jointly assaulted by vicious, unknown thugs – well, by that time the back of my jolly old neck felt in need of a crewcut.'

Mr Campion replaced his spectacles and slowly twisted his neck and head to emphasize his point.

Ramsden smiled weakly across the desk. 'Mr Campion, I am a policeman, not your barber. The death of Mr Browne was a road traffic accident, on that the coroner has pronounced in the absence of any concrete evidence to the contrary. The police do not, as a rule, investigate a supernatural phenomenon, especially where none has been reported to us, and the thugs who assaulted my son and Roderick Braithwaite are not necessarily unknown to us. We have, as you might say, our suspicions, although no proof.'

'Local lads, are they?' tempted Campion.

'Not as we would call 'em. A pair of tearaway cousins called Booth, from a place called Cudworth which you've probably never heard of, but round here that's not a thing to be proud of. Both the Booth boys have records for minor bits of villainy and they've done a spell in New Hall Camp – that's our local detention centre for young offenders. They now work at one of the pits in Denby Ash and are supposedly going straight, but an eye is being kept on them.'

'Do I get the feeling that justice may be meted out vigilante-style?'

'I could never condone that.' Ramsden was emphatic and then he raised his eyebrows. 'If I knew about it, that is. Stranger things have been known to happen in Denby Ash, though, which is a consideration you should bear in mind, Mr Campion.'

'I should? What exactly is it that my tiny and already overstuffed mind should take on board?'

'That you are not from around here; you are stranger, a foreigner, an incomer to Denby Ash,' Ramsden said seriously. 'You are from a different place, a different class and possibly a different time.'

'Oh, come now, Chief Inspector, I may be a pampered southerner and here as no more than a tourist, but I am hardly an alien invader from outer space.'

'In Denby Ash, you might as well be, unless you can prove your father was a miner.'

'That,' said Campion softly, 'is not remotely possible, I'm afraid.'

'Don't worry, neither was mine, which gives them another reason to steer well clear of me, as well as being a bobby. Did you know that on the census forms they used to put "Hewer-of-coal (underground)" as the occupation for a miner? They're proud of that description in Denby Ash – fiercely proud. And they take care of their own. Denby Ash does not like outsiders, Mr Campion, and whatever you're fishing for you won't get anything out of the locals because as far as they're concerned, it's none of your business – whatever "it" is.'

'You mean no one in the village will talk to me?' Campion asked innocently.

'I shouldn't think so. Good Lord, they hardly speak to me, even when it's official police business. Oh, they'll be friendly enough and they'll talk, they just won't tell you anything.'

'Even the local witch?' Campion feigned surprise. 'How disappointing; I've always wanted to meet one and I'd hate to think I had driven all this way for nothing. You see, I had an uncle who always claimed to have met three witches one night on Salisbury Plain and they assured him that he was going to go far in his chosen profession. Of course, we all told him that someone who was already the Bishop of Devizes shouldn't really go around saying such things, but I don't think – deep down – anyone really believed him.'

The chief inspector shook his head slowly. 'Mr Campion, are you serious?'

'As rarely as possible,' replied Mr Campion. 'Now, tell me all about your witch.'

Chief Inspector Ramsden had not been the first and would not be the last to advise Mr Campion that his natural charm might not be enough to enable him to integrate fully into the community of Denby Ash. Whilst waiting for Rupert and Perdita to wash and change before taking them out to dinner the previous evening, Campion had been escorted by Brigham Armitage on a guided tour of his personal Vasari corridor of paintings, all linked by a proud Yorkshire provenance if not subject matter. In between admiring glances and appreciative murmurings, Mr Campion had gently steered the conversation to include the history and sociology of Denby Ash.

It had been, the headmaster had informed him, a pet theory of the late Bertram Browne that the people of Denby Ash were inextricably linked, economically and philosophically, to the seams of coal which ran under the village. With his background as a Sapper, the late Mr Browne had naturally taken an interest in matters geological and the 'black gold' on which the prosperity of the local population depended and whose bounty had been, in a way, responsible for the existence of Ash Grange School. There were those who found it whimsical that the long, subterranean solid rivers of coal were known as 'Flockton Thick' and 'Flockton Thin'. Indeed, certain habitués of the staff room, who really should have known better, used the expression to describe formal gatherings of the Mothers' Union, but not Bertram. He knew that Flockton Thick referred to twin seams each two-feet thick, whilst Flockton Thin was a fifteen-inch layer of coal of the very highest quality. Neither were laughing matters, for down there, six hundred feet underground, the men of Denby Ash (and, a century ago, not a few women and children) had lost their lives harvesting them.

Bertram Browne had taken a keen interest in the history of mining in Denby Ash and would frequently expound – too frequently, many said – on how the Flockton seams had been mined since 1770, the coal being transported far and wide first by turnpike and tollgate, then by canal and then railway before the modern era and the convoys of heavy lorries which pounded the road through the village, leaving a fine sheen of black dust on everything they passed. Bertram had also delighted in springing on the unsuspecting his patent lecture on the various products of mining – gas coal, coking coal, manufacturing coal and fire clay used in firebricks, pottery and ceramics – or alternatively, his potted history of the Denby Ash Brass Band and the concomitant rise of Methodism locally.

If all that made it sound as if Bertram Browne would be an unlikely guest to be asked back to a second dinner party (and Mr Campion admitted to himself that it possibly did), then the headmaster was, he insisted, doing his former colleague a disservice. When not on his hobby horse, Browne had been a delightful chap; an intelligent conversationalist and a dedicated and much-liked teacher. His interest in coal mining had resulted in friendships struck with numerous pit deputies and colliery managers as well as miners and their wives, who all acknowledged him in the street just as their husbands acknowledged him, albeit less chattily, should he visit the public bar of one of the village pubs. He was a popular and respected figure in Denby Ash, something which could not, sadly, be said of the majority of school staff, and had even formed what Raymond Bland, the geography master, called 'an unholy alliance' with the firebrand trade unionist, Arthur Exley.

'Ahh yes, Trotsky . . .' Mr Campion had breathed softly. 'Him I must meet.'

'I would be surprised if he gave you the time of day,' Armitage had said with genuine regret. 'You, I and this school represent everything Exley despises and wants to tear down. He is dangerous because he combines the energy of youth with the conviction of the zealot. Wing Commander Bland, of course, blames it all on the fact that he never did National Service.'

Mr Campion had commented that he had noted the political divide between Bland and Bob Ward in the school's own staff room.

'Oh, you'll find it much worse down in the village,' Armitage had said ruefully. 'In fact, most places in the West Riding are staunch socialist and they say that, come election time, you could put up a pig wearing a red rosette and it would get elected.'

Mr Campion had smiled broadly at that and said that he had, so far in his brief acquaintance with Denby Ash, not observed any demonstrations by Red Guards or mobs of angry students storming the police barricades, and most lampposts seemed mercifully unadorned with hanging aristocrats. Nonetheless, on his meanderings around the village – for he certainly intended to explore the area – he would make sure to avoid the topic of politics.

'Well, don't expect too much,' the headmaster had warned. 'They don't take kindly to strangers if they don't earn their living on their hands and knees underground. Oh, the women may seem motherly enough but they'll gossip about you as soon as they've passed you on the street, and you'll find the men doffing their flat caps to you in the most sarcastic way. The truth is they are very class conscious round here and the likes of you and I, Campion, they regard as toffs. Denby Ash doesn't have much time for toffs.'

'But I hear it is happy to tolerate a witch,' Mr Campion had replied quietly. 'Do tell how the village acquired her.'

FOURTEEN
Man on a Mission

With the warnings and caveats of both Brigham Armitage and, that morning, DCI Ramsden, rattling inside his head, Mr Campion had collected his Jaguar from outside the George Hotel and taken the Wakefield Road towards Denby Ash. He had no clear plan or timetable, other than if he took lunch today it would be a late one, for the full Yorkshire breakfast provided at The George had consisted of enough bacon, eggs, black pudding, mushrooms (tinned), tomatoes (likewise) and fried bread to keep a sergeants' mess quiet for an hour – even though he had politely declined the baked beans, the stack of slightly toasted, still foldable sliced white bread and an aperitif of either Cornflakes or porridge, or possibly both.

A military maxim – time spent in reconnaissance is seldom wasted – sprang to mind, though he was not sure whether it had been prompted by actual circumstances or by the fact that he was, at that moment, driving through the Huddersfield suburb of Waterloo, where the main attraction appeared to be a square buttress of a grey-brick building called The Waterloo, a cinema built in the 1930s heyday of modernist functionality but now awaiting its inevitable fate as a bingo hall.

The road became rural rather than urban and turned into a series of long, steep hills where Campion's Jaguar had to slow down in the wake of lorries bellowing black clouds of coal dust, almost as if the cargo they were carrying was boiling and giving off steam. The fields at either side of the road were shared equally by cows and marching armies of electricity pylons and, on the higher ground, outcrops of bare rock were guarded by ferocious-looking sheep.

He could see the black mountain that was the spoil heap of the exhausted Grange Ash colliery for many minutes before he passed the Urban District Council sign telling him he was in Denby Ash and then he was turning left, following a far more ornate wooden sign with gold lettering announcing that he was once more on the premises of Ash Grange School for Boys.

Brigham Armitage had given Mr Campion permission to park at the school whenever the need arose and even extended an invitation to visit the school's classrooms whilst they were in action. Campion had hastily declined the offer whilst admitting that he had promised Perdita that he would look in on her rehearsals at some point, at which the headmaster had raised his eyebrows, shaken his head slowly and changed the subject.

Campion took his coat, hat, gloves and scarf from the back seat and locked the Jaguar. Suitably wrapped, for although it was not raining there was a stiff mid-morning breeze, he put one sturdy brogue in front of the other and set off back down the driveway to conduct his reconnaissance on foot and, with luck, mingle with the natives whom he was sure could not possibly be as unfriendly as had been suggested to him.

From the tree-lined driveway of Ash Grange, he turned left and marched down the Huddersfield Road. To his right was the unavoidable looming presence of the giant Grange Ash muck stack, and as he progressed he could see, peeping from behind the pyramid, the metal tower and wheels of the pit's winding gear which had lowered cages of men deep into the dark earth.

He passed the slip road, no wide or better surfaced than a country lane, which had given access to the pit if the faded wooden sign saying 'NCB Grange Ash' was to be believed, but which now was being reclaimed by weeds, grass and brambles spreading from the hedgerows lining it. That particular colliery may have been retired, but others nearby were still of working age judging by the number of lorries passing Campion – fully-loaded and deep-throated when travelling towards Huddersfield and rattling empty when speeding towards Denby Ash and the two still working collieries on its eastern border.

A stone bridge came into sight and Campion realized he was nearing the spot where Bertram Browne had died, though of course there was no trace of the incident. Still, Campion mused, wincing as more trucks thundered by, even at full dark night, Browne *must* have heard the engine or seen the lights of the vehicle which hit him and, if he had, why had he not taken evasive action? On one side of the road there was ditch; not deep, but no set of wheels would have followed him in there. The other side ran adjacent to an open field dotted with rocky outcrops and, again, would have provided sanctuary from homicidal traffic on the road. Indeed, Campion felt confident he could himself make it to safety should the need arise and surely the younger, fitter Browne would at least have tried.

He crossed the stone bridge over the Oaker Beck, marvelling at the size and solidity of the structure needed to cross such a tiny stream; an indication that things in Yorkshire were built to last. The fast-flowing stream was no more than four feet wide and the water was a bright rust colour, almost the shade of light ale, which suggested the presence of iron as well as coal in the local geology. It was possible, Campion mused, that the Oaker Beck had got its name from a corruption of 'ochre'.

Once over the bridge he felt that he was in Denby Ash proper. There was the Sun Inn guarding the western entrance, but this long, low stone built, slate-tiled pub had an unassuming air about it, at least compared to its brighter, brasher competitor the Green Dragon at the eastern edge of the village. This establishment, Mr Campion noted, did not make any claims to being famous for basket meals or indeed anything else.

Beyond the pub the road, now called Oaker Hill, began a steep descent and the views over the playing fields of Ash Grange school – blissfully, as far as Rupert was concerned that morning, deserted – and of Denby Wood were blocked by the stone and brick of human occupation.

Campion strode on purposefully, hands thrust into the pockets of his Crombie, content in the knowledge that the walk back up the hill might be just the thing to restore his appetite following his Yorkshire breakfast. Initially, though, Denby Ash seemed more concerned with providing for Mr Campion's soul rather than his body, for the first building he encountered was the large but impressively plain frontage of the Primitive Methodist Chapel which squatted like a silent grey toad overlooking the village. As he strolled past it, Campion noted that from the reverse angle the chapel itself was dominated by the Grange Ash muck stack. The Methodists might have fine views over their earthly kingdom but demand for picture postcards of their chapel would be small.

God was soon followed by Mammon, albeit a lukewarm incarnation in the shape of the Co-Operative store, divided by large picture windows displaying its wares, into two halves: Grocery and Drapery. For the first time that morning, Mr Campion encountered the native population of the village and determined to discover whether they were friendly at the earliest opportunity. They appeared to be entirely female.

The Co-Op appeared to act as a hive, attracting a steady stream of middle-aged women clutching shopping bags but clearly intent on making withdrawals rather than deposits of honey. Through the main window of the grocery department, Campion could see the open racks of vegetables being examined by a swarm of headscarves and pointing fingers. Although he could not hear what was being said, he felt sure that the portly, white-haired man in the brown coat behind the counter was unlikely to get the best of whatever argument over quality and price was raging.

If commerce in the grocery department resembled that of a souk then the drapery department, as seen through the next window, suggested the interior of a *duomo*. There were fewer women here and they were politely waiting their turn as the first customer perused a bolt of brightly coloured curtain material. This gave them the opportunity to look sceptically through boxes of buttons, ribbons and streams of lace whilst keeping one watchful eye on the street outside. To those ladies who thus spotted him, Mr Campion smiled and raised his hat, to be rewarded, through the glass, by several silent mouths in various diameters of openness.

He hurried on down the hill, confident that news of his presence would reach the bottom before he did.

To his left, a long row of uniform terraced houses wound down Oaker Hill like a snake resting on the edge of a crag, although Campion quickly realized it was not one continuous terrace but several blocks of identical houses separated by narrow alleyways not wide enough to drive through. Campion had seen from the bridge across Oaker Beck that access by vehicle was via an unmade road running behind the houses which serviced the low brick coalhouses and a large area of ground (albeit north-facing) subdivided into gardening allotments.

Across the road he noted the low single-storey building of dark stone which proclaimed itself the Hill Top Wesleyan Church – somewhat presumptuously, Campion felt, as technically the Primitive Methodists had already claimed the high ground, at least geographically.

The next detached building, its stones stained with coal dust from the passing haulage trade, was twice the size of the Wesleyan chapel and just as functional, if only marginally more welcoming to the casual passer-by – the Denby Ash Working Men's Club – and the sign outside proudly added in brackets that it was 'Affiliated', though to what was a mystery to the casual passer-by. Its front door was propped open with a large iron cobbler's last but the sound of aggressive hoovering coming from its unlit interior suggested that it was not yet open for business.

Mr Campion stretched his legs and continued on his downward path on the pavement which ran parallel to the row of 'pit houses' and, across the road, he ticked off on his mental guide book a small development of new housing before he found himself opposite yet another religious house. Or to be accurate, two, for the Zion United Reform Church – once clearly a substantial detached house dating from the 1920s – was next-door neighbour to the much smaller (a converted garage or stable?) Denby Gospel Mission, which Campion guessed was a much more recent invention. The Zionists had a sturdy wooden sign with faded gold lettering, whereas the Gospel Mission had a crudely painted board nailed to a short stake in the ground to announce its presence.

He was almost at the bottom of Oaker Hill now, opposite the small primary school protected from the threat of Methodists sliding down the slope by a thick dry stone wall, and its more modern extension which, from Rupert's description, was the parish room as used for band practice. Beyond that, the village church and what looked to be the vicarage stood in splendid defiance, and then the road forked at the Green Dragon.

Mr Campion thought it somehow symmetrical that on entering Denby Ash he had been greeted by a pub and then a chapel and, on leaving, he would wave farewell to a church and then a pub. He had, however, no intention of leaving the village until he had made some human contact other than nodding at a speeding lorry driver, and for the first time since he had passed the Co-Op store he spotted a fellow pedestrian stepping out from the lychgate of the churchyard.

It was a thin, very elderly, bird-like figure of a man with long white hair flowing in the breeze like seaweed on an outgoing tide. He wore a dark blue gabardine raincoat with the top buttons undone to allow his dog collar badge of office to be displayed.

'Good morning,' said Campion from across the road. 'Brisk, isn't it?'

'What they call a good drying day around here,' answered the reverend gentleman and then added, rather enigmatically: 'Pity it's not a Monday.'

'I beg your pardon?'

Campion crossed the road, having first convinced himself that there was a safe lull in the lorry traffic, almost because he could not help himself. Country parsons had always intrigued him; not necessarily for what they knew about their parishioners but what they did not.

'Monday is wash day in Denby Ash and as immovable as the Sabbath. If it rains on a Monday washing cannot be pegged out until Tuesday, to the consternation of all. If it continues to rain on the Tuesday there is great wailing and gnashing of teeth. Peter Cuthbertson-Twigg. I'm the vicar of St James' here. Would you like to see the church?'

'I seem to be seeing churches everywhere,' said Campion lightly, 'or chapels.'

'Yes,' agreed the vicar, as if considering the point for the first time, 'we are rather well-equipped in that department, possibly because there were once no fewer than twenty-one pubs and beer-houses in the village. Religion always followed the brewers' dray and I am delighted to say has more staying power. Now there are only two pubs and the club, so they find themselves outnumbered.'

'And do you form, dare I say, a holy alliance against the demon drink?' Campion spoke with a smile which was not returned.

'Oh, that's hardly necessary these days.'

The Rev Cuthbertson-Twigg seemed suddenly distracted, as though he had forgotten why he was speaking to this stranger.

'So you co-exist with your competitors?' Campion persisted gently and was rewarded by regaining the vicar's full attention.

'The Methodists? Oh, they're fine fellows and we do have the same boss in the end. There's not really any competition; in fact, they're quite accommodating and they've always held their services at different times from St James'. Well, at least the *established* ones have. I cannot speak for the latest church to pitch its tent here.'

'Would that be the Gospel Mission? I passed a rather temporary sign on my way down the hill.'

'You are observant, sir.' The vicar's brow furrowed as he remembered something. 'Yet I do not know your name. Was I expecting you? Am I to show you round St James'? Or are you seeking spiritual guidance?'

'Forgive me, I did not introduce myself. My name is Campion and I am an all-too-brief visitor to your parish. I would indeed like a tour of your church, but not just at the moment and, as for my spiritual welfare, I feel I am fully accommodated. The prevalence of places of worship here is, I find, most interesting though. You say this Mission place is a new arrival?'

It took the vicar almost a minute to digest Campion's response and for half of that Mr Campion feared that Cuthbertson-Twigg had 'switched off' again. It was a trait, he felt, which must prove very annoying for his congregation during sermons.

'The Mission? Oh, yes, that's a recent innovation. A one-man mission, or that's how it started. Chap turned up with a soap box six months ago and started demanding to know who wanted to "see the light".'

'Did anyone?' asked Campion.

'A few, and oddly enough they were mostly young miners who wouldn't come through the doors of St James' unless I was marrying them or burying them. They must have heard something they liked from Preacher Chubb, though, because he gathered enough of a congregation to rent a building from the Zion Chapel and set up shop, so to speak.'

'This Preacher Chubb . . .'

'Robin Chubb, that's his name,' said the vicar, as if in thanks.

'. . . Isn't attracting customers with bingo and beetle drives, is he?'

'I very much doubt it. They don't approve of bingo and whist drives and raffles – that's where we have the advantage. They class it as gambling. Well, the Methodists do and I assume Preacher Chubb's Mission is of a similar ilk.'

'He must be a forceful preacher, this Mr Chubb – quite a character.'

Campion left the sentence hanging until Cuthbertson-Twigg took his cue. 'Oh, yes, quite a character, I'd certainly say that.'

'I hear you have a few here in Denby Ash,' nudged Campion.

Cuthbertson-Twigg recoiled as if struck. 'I hope you're not a newspaper man snooping after that blackguard Haydon Bagley, because if you are then I cannot help you. I take a very unchristian attitude to that . . . that . . . person. In my opinion, he should still be rotting in jail.'

'Please, let me reassure you, Vicar,' Campion soothed, 'I have no interest in the whereabouts of Haydon Bagley.'

'Good, because no one knows where he is and his poor mother and father have been pestered enough.'

'I was merely commenting,' Campion said quickly whilst he still retained the older man's attention, 'that among the many colourful characters in Denby Ash, I hear you boast a witch.'

'Ivy Neal?' The vicar seemed only mildly surprised. 'Oh, some say she's a witch and has the second sight: tells fortunes, predicts the future, that sort of thing. She's not missing, though. She hardly goes anywhere.'

Mr Campion feared the vicar had drifted again but then he rallied.

'She lives just over there.' He pointed with a long, bony finger. 'Beyond the chip shop, turn left on to Pinfold Lane and cut across the Common. She has a caravan there and I'm told she doesn't mind company.'

'Oh, good,' Campion smiled inanely, 'and if she really does have the second sight, she'll be expecting me. She might even have the kettle on.'

FIFTEEN
The Feast Witch

Mr Campion, by no stretch of the imagination a serious student of the occult, had nevertheless been intrigued by Rupert's early report of the presence of both a poltergeist and a witch in Denby Ash. Deciding, rather arbitrarily in the opinion of his wife, that he had nothing better to do, he had spent a morning in the London Library immersing himself in folklore, myth and dubious social history, enthusiastically collecting trivia whenever it referred to the county of Yorkshire.

He became familiar with the legend of the Simmerdale Witch from Wensleydale and the more famous 'Mother Shipton' of Knaresborough, universally and probably unfairly described as 'fantastically ugly'. Then there were the real life, or rather real death, cases of 'Old Wife Green', said to have the distinction of being the last witch to be burned in England – in Pocklington in 1630 – and Mary Bateman from Thirsk, who combined the careers of prophetess and poisoner until she was hanged as a murderess in 1809 and strips of her skin were sold as souvenirs. Before her arrest and trial – events which, oddly for a prophetess, she did not see coming – Mary Bateman's credentials as a confidence trickster had been established by the 'Prophet Hen of Leeds' which she claimed laid eggs engraved with religious messages. Mr Campion could not, however, discover whether a Leeds cockerel was complicit in the hoaxing. Denby Ash had not featured in his researches; indeed, it was the North rather than the West Riding which seemed to have taken to the dark arts. Perhaps Ivy Neal was a white witch, no more daunting than an eccentric herbalist and tolerated, even liked, by a local population which clearly took its religion seriously.

Mr Campion's immediate concern was crossing the road in safety, and he took more care doing so than he would have done in Piccadilly Circus, fearing a speeding coal truck far more than a horn-honking London cabby. With a large exhaling of breath he reached the safety of the opposite pavement outside Elliff's chip shop where a printed cardboard sign complete with a clock with plastic moveable hands informed him that the establishment would be open for Wet Fish Sales at 1 p.m. and then Frying Tonight from 5 p.m.

He turned down Pinfold Lane where the lorries serving the Shuttle Eye and Caphouse pits seemed to move with greater velocity than they did coming down Oaker Hill. It was with some relief that he stepped off the pavement and on to the greasy grass of the Common, although there was no evidence that the residents of Denby Ash had exercised their ancient rights to graze livestock there recently. But perhaps he was mistaken in that for he sensed, and then saw, that he was being stalked – he rather hoped not hunted – by something on four legs moving quietly through the damp bracken and dead brambles.

Ignoring the fact that the bottoms of his trousers were soaking up water as effectively as a syphon, he pressed on in the general direction of Denby Wood where he estimated, if he had judged the topography correctly, he would find the Oaker Beck. He kept an amused eye on the rustling in the underbrush to his right whilst carefully observing the only other sign of habitation on the Common – a much-weathered blue caravan. As he altered direction to move nearer, his bestial shadow broke cover and shot across his line of march.

'Hecate! Stop pestering the gentleman!'

Both Mr Campion and the large, long-haired tabby cat froze in their tracks and looked towards the shrill commanding voice coming from the open door of the caravan. Then they looked at each other and Campion bent over and reached out a gloved hand, intending no more than a friendly stroke. The gesture may have been misinterpreted but it was emphatically rejected by the cat who responded with a swipe of paw and claw, causing Campion to rapidly reclaim his hand.

'Did she catch yer?' the caravan voice enquired as Mr Campion peeled off a brown leather glove to discover four red needle pricks in the heel of his hand. By the time he had replaced the glove the cat had joined the voice and was not so much nestling as hanging over the edge of a hammock formed by the folded arms of a formidable woman of indeterminate age.

'A glancing blow,' Campion said cheerfully, starting towards her. 'Not even a proper flesh wound. She's a fine animal and aptly named for a witch's familiar.'

The woman tilted her sharp face to one side and scrutinized her visitor. 'Hecate – aye, goddess of magic. Not that many round here would cotton to that. You must be from t'school; posh school up the 'ill, not the infants.'

Mr Campion raised his hat politely. 'Only indirectly, I'm afraid,' he said. 'My son is teaching there temporarily but I am only visiting, no more than a tourist.'

'We don't get many of them, so I suppose we should be grateful. Got a question for the Feast Witch, have you?'

'Oh, nothing so formal,' said Campion lightly. 'The fact is I'm just being nosey.'

'Now "nosey" is summat we've got plenty of round here, so you'd best come in and satisfy your curiosity. You don't have to cross me palm with silver or owt like that, just make sure to clean your boots first.'

It was an offer Mr Campion could not refuse, despite the fact that this was no quaintly painted, hoop-roofed horse-drawn gypsy caravan but a rusting 1957 Eccles Aristocrat, its tow bar propped up on a pile of house bricks and its tyres so fat that its wheel rims rested in the muddy ground. A fine patina of green mould encrusted the door and window frames and the whole structure creaked and swayed as Campion followed the woman inside.

He took off his hat and stooped as he found himself in the van's galley, an area festooned with hanging bunches of dried herbs and flowers and, on every flat surface, precariously stacked jam jars, many with white labels in spidery ink secured by strips of sticky tape.

'You have quite the apothecary's shop here,' said Campion, surveying the display. 'Liquorice I recognize and is it that pickled rhubarb? And coltsfoot . . . I ought to know what that's for but I'm getting very old. Do you have anything for memory loss?'

The woman had sat down on the bench seat at the window end of the caravan, facing her visitor. Hecate the cat had settled on her knee and also kept her eyes firmly on Mr Campion.

'You might know coltsfoot as coughwort and as you'd guess, it's good for coughs. The liquorice and the rhubarb – well, I'm sure you know what they're for.'

Campion held up a jar containing a swirling black sludge of vegetation and examined the label.

'*Pis-en-lit*,' he read. 'I see you prefer the French terminology. It does sound more exotic than dandelion, I admit.'

'Very good for them with high blood pressure,' said his hostess, 'especially men, and they wouldn't pay for summat they give to their rabbits.'

'I think you are absolutely spot-on there,' smiled Campion, 'but I am being rude. My name is Albert Campion and you must be Mrs Neal.'

'I was never a "Mrs" anybody. My name's Ivy Neal, plain and simple, though there's plenty call me the Feast Witch.'

Campion had not been offered a seat, not that there was one to offer, and so he leaned his long, slim frame gently against a cupboard unit which rattled with the sound of shifting crockery.

'I am unfamiliar with that expression,' he said, then checked himself. 'Goodness, that sounds pompous. I didn't mean it to.'

Ivy Neal's sharp face remained sharp. The cat on her knee yawned, showing white teeth and the inside of a salmon-coloured mouth.

'They call me the Feast Witch because I came here with the Denby Feast; years ago, that was, before I got too old for touring and decided to settle down. Thought I'd come back here.'

'Denby Feast . . .' Campion said quietly, almost to himself. 'I haven't heard that expression for years. Are the old touring fairs still going? I thought everyone was watching the goggle-box these days.'

'Plenty are,' said Ivy Neal with a sniff of disapproval, 'but the Feast still comes to the Common every year and pitches the vans and the rides right here outside my front door. It's not the same, mind you. When me mother travelled with the Feast they had a dancing bear on a chain; nowadays it's all fast roundabouts with loud pop music and flashing lights.'

'I used to know a chap,' said Campion rather dreamily, 'who gave up a steady office job in London and took to the road, following the northern Feasts round places such as Hunslet, Hull, Whitby and the Nottingham Goose Fair. Fancied himself a grafter as he called it, doing card tricks and a bit of fortune telling, feeding off the gullible.'

'Fortune telling and horoscopes – that was my first racket. They used to call me Madame Francesca afore I switched to love potions and remedies. You sound like you didn't approve of your grafter friend.'

'Oh, he was harmless enough,' Campion replied, 'but this was in the Thirties, during the Depression. He had a regular income and a family to fall back on, yet he was taking sixpences and shillings from people who could ill afford it.'

'If he brought a bit of pleasure into folks' lives, where's the harm? I could do your horoscope for you, if you like.'

The old woman picked up the tabby cat with both her bony hands around its chest and held the beast up until its face was at her ear.

'What's that, Hecate? You reckon he's a Taurus? Looks more of a Libran to me.'

'Hecate got it in one,' said Campion, 'but I like the double act with your familiar, which immediately shortens the odds on you guessing the right star sign and impressing the customers. However, I'm more interested in the past than the future.'

If Ivy Neal was disappointed at the loss of new business, her sharp face did not show it. Hecate the cat, settling herself back on her lap, however, glared at Mr Campion, opened her mouth wide and issued a long, mewling howl.

'Hecate says you won't learn much from the past – you should look to the future,' said the woman.

'Forgive me,' said Campion, 'but I long ago stopped believing anything I was told by a cat. Have you observed that cats only talk to people? When they meet each other they are quite silent – no conversation at all. Perhaps they just like giving orders to humans. I mean, they would know that there's little point trying to tell a cat what to do. In any case, I am of such a venerable age now that the future cannot possibly hold any surprises, so please indulge an old man's curiosity in the recent past – an old man who is not averse to crossing a palm, or a paw, with silver if that proves necessary.'

'I can't tell if you're a clever man or a daft apeth, Mr Campion, if that's your name,' said Ivy Neal, and Hecate squawked again as if in echo.

'It's certainly the name that I go by,' said her guest, 'and I suspect I lean more towards the daft apeth than the clever, though I am not terribly sure what an apeth is. Something simian, perhaps?'

'Oh, stop your blathering!' she snapped. 'Say what you want or take yourself elsewhere.'

Hecate opened her mouth wide again but made no comment this time.

'I was interested – purely out of nosiness, you understand – in why those two boys from the posh school came to see you the other night.'

'What's it to you?'

'They are both star pupils of my son and his wife at Ash Grange School and both got rather badly beaten up after you scared them off.'

'That wasn't owt to do with me. There's always hooligans hanging around looking for trouble.'

As the woman snarled at him, so too did the cat, and Mr Campion suspected that the Feast Witch was using a long fingernail to prompt Hecate into responding on cue.

'I'm not saying it was, but you did scare them off, didn't you? I've talked to the father of one of the boys and by all accounts you disappeared in front of their very eyes. That's quite a trick in a van this size. When you were touring on the feast circuit did you count magician's assistant among your achievements, as well as fortune telling and potion peddling?'

'I don't know what you're on about, I really don't.' The woman's hands cradled the head of the cat on her lap, making sure that Hecate's eyes were pointed at Campion. 'As for them lads – well, they wanted me to do an exorcism, if you can credit it, on Ada Braithwaite's house.'

'Ah, yes, the home of the famous Denby Ash poltergeist,' said Campion. 'I take it you couldn't offer any remedy?'

'Told them they should ask the vicar or one of the lay preachers – Lord knows we've got plenty of them on hand – and then sent them on their way.'

'By disappearing before their very eyes! I do hope you've nothing similar planned for me; I'm not sure my old ticker could stand it!' Campion's face became a picture of innocence. 'But of course, you really need it to be dark to do the trick properly.'

'Don't know what you mean,' said Ivy Neal sulkily, turning her head away and staring out of the caravan's bow window.

Hecate let out a loud, moaning mewl.

Mr Campion was dismissed.

From the window of the preparation room of Willy Elliff's, where he had been cranking the handle on an industrial potato peeler, Adrian Elliff watched the thin man climb down from Ivy Neal's caravan just as he had earlier watched him cross the Common and be invited in by the old witch.

He was too smartly dressed to be a policeman – in any case, Adrian knew most of them, just as they knew him, by sight. He was not a rent collector, as Ivy Neal didn't pay rent to anyone and unlikely to be from the council as they knew better than to tangle with her. It was unlikely to be a doctor, as Ivy did her own doctoring, so perhaps he was a solicitor – but then he was not carrying a briefcase and in Adrian's experience (which was considerable for one of his age), solicitors always had paperwork – usually paperwork which prevented you from doing things or which demanded the payment of a substantial fine.

As he got nearer, Adrian could see that the man was older than his bearing and languid movement suggested, though to Adrian, anyone over thirty was 'old'. In fact, he must be a pensioner, but he was unlike the retired miners he knew who shuffled about the allotments or sat in the club making a half-pint of top mild last all evening. Those old men seemed tired, somehow finished. This one still had life and energy, a bounce in his step, probably due to never having done a hard day's work in his life. Probably a rich old sod judging by the car he'd been driving yesterday, and definitely not from round here.

The boss man had told him to watch out for strangers and for anyone visiting that crazy witch, who was probably a gypsy if truth were known. Here was a stranger *and* he'd been to see Ivy Neal.

The boss man would be very interested indeed.

When her visitor had left, Ivy Neal sat immobile for almost an hour. Only when Hecate the cat was finally bored with being stroked and jumped off her lap, demanding loudly to be released on to the Common, did the woman stir herself.

As she waited for her battered kettle to boil to make a pot of tea – she might sell 'herbal infusions' to her customers but a brace of Tetley's tea bags was always her preference – she thought long and hard about what she should do.

The tall, thin-as-a-streak-of-water old man, a proper toffee-nose if she ever saw one, was nowhere near as daft as he liked to let on and unlike anyone she had come across in her colourful lifetime. Her skills at fortune telling and horoscopes had been earned over the years in her dealings with paying, and usually complicit, customers. She did not fool herself that she really had any psychic powers or sixth sense. Spotting him as a Taurus had been no more than a good guess and he had known that.

Yet there was something not right about the old gentleman's presence in Denby Ash. He simply did not fit, but then in many ways, neither did Ivy Neal.

As the kettle whistled, she made up her mind. She would report to the preacher; he would know what to do.

But she would have to wait until dark.

Still determined to walk off his breakfast, Mr Campion strode fitfully up Oaker Hill taking in the smell of coal fires with every breath of cold, damp air. It was a scent which reminded him of a London which had disappeared.

Halfway up the hill, near the working men's club, he stepped aside to allow a young woman, a headscarf protecting a huge beehive hairdo, pushing a pram the size of a pocket battleship the full use of the pavement and as she nodded a polite thank you, he took the opportunity to ask if by any chance she knew where Mrs Braithwaite lived.

'Looking for the 'aunted 'ouse then? It's number eleven but Ada won't be there – she'll be up at the big school now doing the dinners. Shocking what happened to her Roderick, wasn't it? Shocking. You talk nice, don't you? Got to go. See you later, alligator.'

Mr Campion watched the woman continue downhill, holding the heavy pram back rather than pushing it, and shook his head in amused wonderment. Both DCI Ramsden and Brigham Armitage had said that the people of Denby Ash might talk to him but not tell him anything.

Campion rather felt that what they didn't say might tell him quite a lot.

*   *   *

He reached Ash Grange just as a bell was ringing to signal the end of lunchtime and the first lessons of the afternoon. Celia Armitage met him at the school entrance and apologised profusely for the fact that Campion had missed the school dinner they had been keeping for him, though she was sure it could be warmed up.

Mr Campion politely, but equally profusely, insisted that he was, despite tramping the length and depth of the village, still sated, though he could be easily pushed in the direction of a cup of tea as well as whichever classroom Perdita was rehearsing in.

Mrs Armitage said both things were possible, though perhaps he would prefer a drop of something 'stronger than tea' in his tea.

When Campion looked suitably confused, she explained thus: 'Hilda Browne has invited herself along to poor Perdita's rehearsal and I find her a lot easier to deal with if I've had a stiffener beforehand.'

Mr Campion declined the offer, insisting that tea would be sufficient. It was a decision he was to regret within three minutes of meeting Helen of Troy.

The rehearsal space occupied by the cast of *Doctor Faustus – A Morality Tale With Music for Speech Day* (Mr Campion had seen a Roneo-ed poster on the school notice board) was a first-floor classroom where all the desks and chairs had been pushed against the walls. A dozen or so boys in school uniform stood to one side, shuffling their feet as they studied texts, whispering to each other and pointing out of the window, doing everything possible to avoid looking directly across the room at the tall, plain and very angular middle-aged woman sitting primly on a chair, hands folded in her lap, her knees precisely together. She wore something long, opaque and diaphanous in a vivid shade of lime green.

In the middle, Perdita stood as a Berlin Wall keeping the two warring cultures apart. She was wearing a crisp, very masculine white shirt and shiny blue trousers with wide bell-bottoms (which Mr Campion had been told by his wife were not 'loon pants') and her Cuban heels made sure she was not looked down upon by her more gangling pupils. She was holding a paperback edition of *Christopher Marlowe: The Complete Plays* and she had adopted her best 'governess' voice, as Rupert called it.

Celia Armitage showed Mr Campion in, pulled out a chair for

him and closed the door quietly as she withdrew. Mr Campion was left balancing a cup and saucer and trying not to look like a school inspector or a drama critic.

'All right, let's have Faustus out here, centre stage,' Perdita ordered. 'Come on, Roderick, I promise not to tell you to break a leg until opening night.'

The boys laughed and the reason for their amusement became clear as Roderick Braithwaite limped towards Perdita with the aid of a black, silver-topped cane.

'Now I need my Mephistophilis – come on, Banville, stand to – and also the Old Man.' Perdita looked up from her text. 'Who's playing the Old Man?'

A short boy with bright red hair raised a hand. 'Atkinson, Miss,' he said in a surprisingly deep voice, 'but I'm not terribly sure who the Old Man's supposed to be. He just seems to come and go without rhyme or reason.'

'It's a crucial role, Atkinson,' said Perdita gently. 'Earlier in the play we have the Good and the Evil Angels, which are sort of the two halves of Faustus' conscience. I think they've been cut from our version, which makes the Old Man even more important, because when Faustus is tempted by Helen of Troy it's the Old Man – an allegorical figure – who begs him to give up "this damned art" because he will lose his soul. The Old Man is the voice of Christianity. He's the one who believes in God's grace – that God will save even the worst sinners, but Faustus rejects him and the Old Man gets chased away by devils.'

The ginger-haired Atkinson looked far from convinced but stepped forward anyway.

'And I need my two Scholars. I know it says three in the text, but we've only got room for two. Right, we'll go from where Mephistophilis escorts Helen across the stage.'

'Do I have to, Miss?' Banville whined.

'Yes, you jolly well do!' hissed Perdita.

Campion's eyes flashed towards the woman opposite but her expression and demeanour had not flickered.

'Now there will be music throughout this part of the scene, so it's rather like a beauty pageant where the contestants walk down the cat walk,' she continued in directorial mode. 'As long as nobody trips over their own feet, this should go quite smoothly. So, Faustus is here with the two Scholars, Mephistophilis brings Helen from

Stage Right to Stage Left and then the Old Man comes in
from Stage Right. Got that?'

The boys around her nodded as one but Perdita had to jerk
her head dramatically towards the woman in green to prompt
Mephistophilis into action.

The boy's movements reminded Mr Campion of another Tudor
dramatist's description of an unwilling schoolboy creeping like
a snail. His lack of enthusiasm seemed to go unnoticed by his
acting partner, who rose to her feet – rather large feet, Campion
noticed – with imperious grace. Even in flat-heeled shoes, she
towered over the quivering Mephistophilis who nervously
extended an arm to help guide her.

Regally, she placed the flat of her right hand on the offered
forearm and began to slide in stately fashion across the classroom
floor at iceberg pace, dragging the reluctant servant of Lucifer
with her.

'Now imagine music playing as Helen passes over the stage,'
Perdita directed the rest of the cast who were watching the
lime-green apparition wide-eyed. 'Music, music, music . . .
Faustus, imagine you're showing off to the two Scholars. You're
saying "Look what I can do" and the Scholars are impressed,
but the Old Man – that's you, Atkinson – you see this is all
going to end in tears and you plead with Faustus to "leave this
damned art".'

Perdita looked up from her text to see that the lime-green galleon
was still proceeding at funereal pace, clearly considerably behind
her directorial timetable.

'Music . . . music . . . music . . .' vamped Perdita, 'and then
Helen is offstage but Mephistophilis comes back centre.'

From the back of the room, Mr Campion heard his daughter-
in-law's slow exhalation and saw her knuckles whiten as she
gripped her copy of the text until Helen finally made it to her
appointed destination. (She could almost have made it to Troy by
now, Campion thought.)

Perdita, like all good field commanders, improvised. 'Tell
you what, chaps, let's skip to the end of the scene and Helen's
second appearance – the famous one. That way we won't have
to delay anyone who might want to get away. So I need
Mephistophilis and Faustus front and centre and halfway
through, as Faustus says "all is dross that is not Helena", that's

the cue for the Old Man to come in with an expression of sadness and disapproval. Can you manage that, Atkinson?'

'Yes, Miss,' said the red-haired boy, mugging an expression which resembled gastric pain.

'Are you sure you can manage to look old, Old Man?'

'Oh, yes, Miss, my mother's going to put talcum powder in my hair.'

'That should do it,' Perdita said cheerfully. 'Now, places. Miss Browne, your cue is Mephistophilis here saying "twinkling of an eye" then you progress across the stage as Faustus admires "the face that launched a thousand ships". But remember, Helen, you have to clear stage right before Faustus gets to "thou shalt be my paramour".'

A barely suppressed giggle ran through the boys and was curtailed by a severe look from Perdita, who then said, with a deep sigh of resignation 'Right then, in your own time, Miss Browne . . .'

SIXTEEN
All is Dross

'It's awfully kind of you to give me a lift home and in such a nice car,' said Helen of Troy, settling herself and a large black patent leather handbag in the Jaguar's passenger seat. 'I hope I'm not taking you out of your way.'

Mr Campion was driving in exactly the opposite direction to the one he would have taken to return to his hotel in Huddersfield, but he reasoned that a few shillings' worth of petrol and an hour of his time were worth their weight in gold when it came to purchasing Perdita's peace of mind.

'Not at all,' he lied smoothly, 'but you'll have to act as navigator as I don't know the roads hereabouts. We are pointed towards Wakefield, which I believe is the right direction.'

'Oh, you can't go wrong, this is the main road. We live in Lupset, which is just before you get to Wakefield.'

Campion guessed that his passenger had trouble saying the

word 'suburb' but was far from reluctant to volunteer other information.

'When I say "we" I of course mean my late brother, Bertram,' said Hilda Browne. 'He left me the house, though it's probably too big for a single lady and it is very inconvenient without Bertie's car. I had to sell it. I don't drive, you see, and the cash came in useful when I had to cover his funeral expenses. I may have to sell the house as well, but goodness knows what I'll do with all Bertie's books and papers. He was a big collector of old maps and plans, you know.'

'His death must have come as a terrible shock,' said Mr Campion sympathetically.

'Well of course it was. Bertie was no age. I mean, forty-five is no age, is it? He was my *older* brother, of course, and I always thought he would be the first of us to go, but not run over like that by a drunk driver – well, he must have been drunk, mustn't he? If he'd fallen down a mineshaft I wouldn't have been at all surprised, but a road accident . . .'

'What an ex—' Campion checked himself and then finessed his thought, 'extremely imaginative concept. Was that a premonition? About the mineshaft, I mean.'

'Premonition? You mean like in a dream? No, nothing like that, it was just that Bertie was always rummaging around the pits. Fascinated by them he was, and if he'd fallen down one of the old shafts and broken his neck I wouldn't have turned a hair.'

'I'm sorry,' said Campion gently, braking to allow a Yorkshire Traction double-decker to pull out into the road ahead, 'I must have fortune telling on the brain. You see, I visited the local witch this morning.'

'Ivy Neal? That old hag?'

'Oh, I don't think she's that old.'

Campion kept his eyes on the twisting road, though he could feel the heat of Hilda Browne's stare. She may not have had a face to launch ships but he suspected her glare to be as powerful as a laser beam.

'Nowadays, compared to myself, everyone seems so very young,' he said, and the atmosphere in the Jaguar softened. 'I suspect Ivy has an interesting history. Do you know her well?'

'Good heavens, no!' snorted Hilda. 'I wouldn't like it thought I was socially acquainted with a woman like Ivy Neal! I only spoke to her once – to be polite, you understand – and that was when she took me by surprise when I ran into her at my charity work in Wakefield. I never expected to see her there, doing good works like decent people.'

Mr Campion gently bit his bottom lip to prevent the outburst of anger he felt rising inside him like hot lava. 'I think Ivy has had a bit of a harsh life,' he said eventually.

'Yes, well, it's different for men,' said Hilda, changing tack, now with a coy, little girl voice. 'Men get more distinguished as they age but women have to struggle or they just *fade*. It is very easy just to fade away, especially when they live alone.'

Mr Campion was shrewd enough to realize that Miss Browne was no longer talking about Ivy Neal and he felt guilty at finding the woman's simpering as repellent as her snobbery. He brusquely changed the subject. 'I understand that Bertram was a Sapper, so I suppose his interest in mines and engineering was perfectly logical.'

'Oh he was very proud of his time in the Royal Engineers.' Campion winced at the emphasis the woman put on 'Royal'. 'I wish he'd stayed in the army in many ways as he could have risen to great heights, but he met this girl near the end of the war. Hungarian *and* Jewish, can you believe? It didn't come to anything, though I'm sure she'd have wanted it to, but she got killed just like he did, in a road accident. Of course, hers was years ago.'

'How terrible for the poor chap. But surely an experience like that would have made him more careful when walking along an unlit road at night . . .?' Campion suggested.

'You clearly didn't know Bertie. If he had something on his mind he might as well have been away with the fairies. He'd get an idea in his head about a bit of pit history and then he'd spend hours in that *working men's club*.' Once again there was disdain in the woman's voice and Campion marvelled at the amount of spite which could be contained in such a frail shell. 'He used to hang around with the colliery men and not care who saw him. He even' – she lowered her voice as if in a confessional – 'climbed to the top of that awful Grange Ash muck stack with the dreadful Arthur Exley. Acting like a pair of Boy Scouts going mountaineering they were, in full view of everybody and anybody. Goodness knows what the school thought of it.'

'Why should the school object to a bit of extra-curricular

mountaineering?' Campion asked, secretly thinking it sounded quite a jape.

'Being seen with somebody like Exley couldn't be good for Bertie's position. I mean, what would the other staff think – or the parents of the boys?'

'I'm not sure I follow.'

'Arthur Exley is nothing short of a communist, dedicated to destroying everything Ash Grange teaches and stands for!' growled Hilda.

Campion glanced at the profile of that sharp and snarling face. She was staring straight ahead through the Jaguar's windscreen as if trying to spot Red Guards waiting in ambush.

'Oh, I hardly think climbing the north face of a muck stack together is a treasonable offence or be seen as immoral,' said Campion. 'Unless, of course, it was the devilish Exley taking your brother up to a high place in order to tempt him into selling his soul to socialism. I don't believe that for a minute, though such a scenario might have led to a discussion on the plot of *Doctor Faustus*.'

Campion had not intended to switch the conversation away from Hilda's social and political hobby-horses, at least not quite so abruptly, but he had inadvertently stumbled upon the one topic which was guaranteed to light the woman's blue – and very short – touch paper.

'Hah!' snorted Hilda, so violently that Campion tightened his grip on the wood-rimmed steering wheel. 'Even putting that little Hitler Exley in charge of the music is not going to stop the production! Bertie promised me I could play Helen and despite their attempts at sabotage, I will. I insist on performing as a tribute to Bertie's vision. I will not betray his memory!'

Mr Campion drew in a deep breath through his nose, then smiled beatifically at his passenger, who had taken a handkerchief from the handbag balanced on her bony lap and proceeded to strangle it. 'Are we nearly there yet?' he asked innocently.

Perdita decided she owed her father-in-law a great big kiss, her undying love and her unwavering devotion for so tactfully removing Hilda Browne from the rehearsal. The mood in the room had lightened instantly and the boys had settled down and concentrated on the task in hand. The cherubic Watson was doing his best to look fearsome as Lucifer demanding Faustus' soul; Banville was actually rather good as a sneering Mephistophilis, especially when pointing out that fools who laugh on earth are destined to weep in hell; and young Atkinson was making a good fist of displaying despair.

Even though she later said it herself, Perdita was the best actor in that room by a country mile for her performance as a drama teacher determined not to be derailed from her appointed task by a deranged Helen of Troy who was making such a meal of a non-speaking part which consisted of a couple of promenades across the stage.

In her directorial role, Perdita put the boys through their paces and reassured herself that they at least knew their lines, even if two of them seemed unsure of when to deliver them and one felt confident enough to try and improve on them. All in all, she felt pleased with the performance of her little troupe and morale was high now that Hilda had gone. She felt confident that her 'show' – she was loathe to call it a play – would amuse if not enlighten its intended audience, for even though the text had been violently pruned, the music of the Denby Ash brass band contingent would plaster over the many cracks.

'Before you shoot off, we ought to talk about costumes,' she said as the boys were collecting their bags and coats in anticipation of the school bell. 'What did Mr Browne have in mind?'

'He always left all that to Daffers,' said Roderick, leaning two-handed on his walking cane as if he was about to break into 'Puttin' On The Ritz'. When he saw the look of confusion on Perdita's face, he added: 'Oh, sorry Miss, I meant Miss Cawthorne. She always does costumes and make-up for school productions.'

'I see,' said Perdita, thinking that if the boys called Daphne 'Daffers', what did they call her? 'And what has she suggested?'

'That I should have horns!' Mephistophilis yelped enthusiastically. 'Not big ones like a cow or a water buffalo but small, nubby ones, and they should be red so they look really evil.'

'Don't listen to Banville, Miss,' Roderick intervened diplomatically, 'he's having you on. Miss Cawthorne said no such thing because she won't have anything to do with this play.'

'She thinks it's evil,' said her baby-faced Lucifer knowingly. 'She's very religious.'

'So we've got just over a week to go and nobody has a costume?'

'Only Helen of Troy,' said Roderick without a trace of irony. 'She has very firm ideas on what she'll be wearing.'

'I was afraid of that,' Perdita muttered under her breath, but to her cast she only showed a smiling, confident face.

'Right then, we improvise. Atkinson, as you're the Old Man, you'll dress as an old man – big overcoat, scarf and a flat cap. Have you got a grandfather you can borrow from?'

The very young old man said that he had.

'Good, now the rest of you will all be scholars.'

'Scholars, Miss?'

'I know it's casting against type in your case, Banville,' said Perdita coolly, 'but this is a play about a scholar who gets above himself, so I'm going to ask the headmaster if we can borrow the gowns your teachers wear. Underneath I want grey pullovers, dark trousers and your school shoes, but make sure they're polished. And yes, Mephistophilis, I'm looking at you.'

She had not been looking at Banville, but that was the sort of thing teachers said, wasn't it?

'Right then, chaps, well done so far. We'll have another run-through tomorrow, last period, in the school hall, and Mr Exley will be joining us to get some idea of the timings for the music.'

A low murmur rippled around the classroom.

'Excuse me,' said Perdita, 'but what's the problem?'

'My father says Arthur Exley is more of a devil than anything Faustus meets,' said Banville with pugnacious glee.

'You shut your mouth!' snapped Roderick, rapping his walking stick on the floor and shooting a withering glance at his fellow pupil.

'That's enough!' commanded Perdita. 'We should count ourselves lucky to have the village band. Their playing will add hugely to the atmosphere and drama.' Hopefully distracting the audience, she thought. 'I won't have any rudeness or discourtesy shown to Mr Exley, is that understood?'

It appeared that Perdita had made her point and, as the school bell sounded, the boys trooped out in best order. Perdita tapped Roderick gently on the shoulder and indicated he should stay behind.

'How's the ankle? Are you going to be able to go through with the performance?' she asked when they were alone.

'I'll manage, Miss, if I can use the cane.'

'Absolutely. I think it adds to the character, makes you look rather distinguished and slightly sinister.' She leaned her head towards the boy's and lowered her voice. 'Now tell me, what is Helen of Troy planning on wearing?'

Of all the Campions in Denby Ash, Rupert had had the least stressful afternoon, supervising a game of touch rugby (thus avoiding broken bones and muddied kit) for the youngest, first-year boys. There had been no injuries and no tears and, even when complaining about his refereeing decisions, the boys had all called him 'Mr Campion, sir' so, all in all, he had counted the afternoon a success even if it had been a damp and chilly one. He had timed the end of the games period carefully so that the boys were showered and changed and back in the school before the end-of-the-day bell. He had made his by now regular offer to groundsman Rufus Harrop to help with the packing away of the corner flags and rugby balls and had, as he'd expected, been impolitely told that Mr Harrop was perfectly capable of managing without the help of a 'new boy'. He made no second offer and, having changed muddy boots for shoes and assessed that his tracksuit was roughly presentable, he hurried to the school to check that Perdita had survived her rehearsal.

At the entrance to the school he noticed that his father's Jaguar had gone and a Triumph Herald was now parked on the spot it had occupied. The car looked vaguely familiar but he could not put a staff member's face to it. All became clear as he entered the hallway, for there stood DCI Dennis Ramsden with a square, grey plastic case at his feet, deep in whispered conversation with none other than Arthur Exley. Two boys caught sharing a cigarette behind the cricket pavilion could not have looked guiltier to have been discovered thus.

'Chief Inspector, Mr Exley,' said Rupert, nodding to each then glancing around the empty hallway. 'Is somebody seeing to you? Can I help at all?'

'No need, Mr Campion,' said the policeman. 'I'm here to see Roderick Braithwaite.'

Exley looked at Ramsden in surprise and said, 'So am I.'

'During rehearsals for *Doctor Faustus* I think my wife has first dibs on him but they should be out any second now. How's Andrew, by the way?'

'Really cut up that he'll be missing the last game of the season,' said Ramsden with a hint of pride, 'and, of course, he's missing his mates, but the doctor says he can come back to lessons next week.'

'I'm sure that news delighted him,' Rupert laughed, 'if I remember what I was like at his age.'

Ramsden smiled and gently kicked the box-like case with the toe of his shoe.

'He wanted Roderick to have the loan of this. It's his pride and joy.'

'What is it?'

'It's a tape recorder. Got it for Christmas last year so he could record 'Pick of the Pops' off the radio. He said Roderick had a use for it tonight.'

Arthur Exley reached down and picked up the clearly heavy case by its carrying handle. 'I'll carry it for him. I promised his mother I'd walk him home as it's getting dark and the lad's got his ankle to contend with.'

Rupert made no comment but Exley took umbrage at the startled look he was being given by DCI Ramsden.

'What? What's wrong with me seeing the lad home?'

'Nothing, nothing at all,' said Ramsden, oddly defensive for a policeman.

'His mother's worried about him after what happened the other night – only natural. And she couldn't come herself as she's baking.'

'Now then, Arthur, nobody's suggesting anything untoward.'

'They'd better not be.'

The uncomfortable trio were saved by the school bell and after the daily stampede of boys, complete with flying bags and scarves, Perdita and Roderick appeared in the hall.

The boy made a beeline for Ramsden and the tape recorder.

'Hello, Mr Ramsden. Thanks for bringing the recorder. Did Andrew put in a blank tape for me?'

'He wiped one clean specially for you,' said Ramsden. 'Told me to tell you it was a *Kenney Everett Show* so it'd better be worth it.'

'Lots of actors tape-record their lines to help learn them,' said Perdita, clearly impressed. 'I think that's a jolly good idea.'

'Oh, it's not for the play, Miss Campion,' said Roderick, his face flushed and his eyes wide. 'I'm going to record our poltergeist tonight.'

The four adults were temporarily struck dumb until Rupert said: 'Do you think that's . . . er . . . sensible, Roderick?'

'Oh, it's perfectly safe, as long as you know when to duck,' said the boy cheerfully, 'and Mum always packs away the breakable things on Thursdays. You can come and watch if you want. It would be good to have some witnesses to prove I'm not imagining things.'

The boy looked at each of their faces in turn.

'Honest, it would be really useful if you could. It usually comes around ten o'clock and Mum wouldn't mind at all. If you're interested that is.'

'I know someone who would be very interested,' said Rupert.

SEVENTEEN
The Noisy Ghost

Ada Braithwaite tied the strings of a clean pinafore behind her back, smoothed down the front of the garment across her dress, consulted a small mirror on the mantelpiece to make sure her hair was in place and opened the back door to admit her four guests.

''Evening, Ada.'

'Arthur. You'd best come in before you give the neighbours summat to gossip about, visiting this time of night.'

Arthur Exley stepped inside the kitchen of Number 11 Oaker Hill, followed by Rupert and Perdita and then Mr Campion carrying two items wrapped in tissue paper. Once inside the four newcomers shuffled until they were standing around the small square kitchen table, Exley taking up position with his back to the glowing coal fire.

'I do hope you'll forgive this invasion, Mrs Braithwaite,' said Campion, removing his hat, at which point Exley whipped the cap from his own head and held it behind his back. 'My name is Albert Campion. I believe you have already met the other members of the Campion clan, my son and daughter-in-law.'

Ada nodded her acknowledgement of the junior Campions.

'Our Roderick said you'd be coming. He's in his bedroom finishing his homework – he'll be down in a minute. Let's go through to the front room; might as well get comfortable until the trouble starts.'

'I am impressed with the way you are handling all this, Mrs Braithwaite,' said Campion. 'From what I hear it must be quite a strain and having a house full of gawking strangers can't possibly help. In fact, we feel so guilty about intruding that we have brought you small gifts, or bribes if you prefer, which we hope you'll accept.'

Campion held out the tissue-wrapped packages and Ada took them nervously.

'There was no need . . .'

'Oh, please, it's nothing much, but I did some rapid research on you courtesy of Celia Armitage. She told me you were a first-rate cook and always provided the school with their Christmas puddings. If my calculations are correct, your mixture will be coming up for a stirring sometime soon and I thought this would be a useful ingredient.'

Ada unwrapped the smaller package to reveal a quarter bottle of brandy.

'Very kind of you,' she said. 'I'll pop that somewhere safe so it won't get broken when we have our visitation.'

Mr Campion, admiring her phlegmatic approach to the expected 'visitation', handed over the second, rectangular parcel.

'And Mrs Armitage is entirely to blame if she has given me a false steer, but it seems that your son did let it slip that you have something of a sweet tooth, so I hope these will satisfy it.'

Ada tugged at the tissue paper and uncovered a pound box of Black Magic chocolates.

'The cheeky little devil! These are Roderick's favourites, though he only gets them at Christmas. I prefer Milk Tray.'

'Oh, I'm sorry,' said Mr Campion, 'I should have known the lady loves Milk Tray. That's what the adverts say, isn't it? Can I exchange them for you?'

'No need for that – I'm sure they'll find a good home. It was kind of you to bother. Now let's go through and I'll put the kettle on for some tea – or cocoa, if you prefer.'

'Tea will be fine, thank you. Cocoa may well send me to sleep and I feel I might need my wits about me.'

'Can I help at all, Mrs Braithwaite?' Perdita asked.

'No, you go and sit yourself down with the men, dear, and keep an eye on Roderick for me.'

As they squeezed into the small front lounge, a room already bursting with a three-piece suite and a television on a lacquered coffee table, Rupert deliberately rubbed shoulders with Arthur Exley and whispered in his ear, 'I hope you've made a note that the lady loves Milk Tray.'

Exley said nothing but the look he gave Rupert suggested there might be more than one angry spirit visiting the house that night.

Just before ten o'clock, Roderick took charge of proceedings by setting up Andrew's Elizabethan reel-to-reel tape recorder on the kitchen table. He threaded the brown tape through the magnetic heads and wound it on to the receiving spool with a forefinger, then placed the black plastic microphone on a folded tea towel on a chair and plugged in the connecting wire. To test the mechanism, he held the 'record' knob with his left thumb and pushed the 'play' tab upwards, an operation which made Rupert think of a clutch-and-gearstick manoeuvre in a car. He did all this with his tongue protruding from between his teeth, his face a study of concentration which would have warmed the heart of any schoolteacher.

'Testing, testing,' said Roderick, then flicked the machine's gear lever down and to the left to rewind. On 'play' again, his voice boomed out into the hushed room.

'All systems go, it seems,' said Mr Campion. 'I take it we should try and restrain ourselves if something happens, should we? Or would you like us to add sound effects?'

'I think a few screams and perhaps some swearing might add to the effect,' said the boy calmly, avoiding the eyes of his mother.

'There will be no swearing in this house,' said Ada sternly.

'You mind your mother, lad,' said Arthur in support.

'I am in your home, Mrs Braithwaite, therefore I will try to restrain myself,' said Mr Campion. 'But tell me, Roderick, to whom do you intend to play any recording?'

'To the vicar and to Stan the Man and to the Methodist ministers and to the circuit ministers and even the preacher man.'

'That's quite a list,' said Perdita gently.

'And maybe one of them will believe me now and do us an exorcism.'

'Now then, Roderick, we've talked about this and you know it's all superstitious nonsense, that stuff,' Exley said gently.

'You think that, but it'll make Mum feel better.'

Ada clenched her hands in front of her and lowered her head, saying quietly, 'We've got to try, Arthur.'

'Let's see if we get anything on tape, shall we?' Campion intervened. 'A few rattles and shakes and things going bump in the night ought to impress your vicar if we play them back loud enough. I've met him, though, and I think you might have more luck with one of the Methodists. Who is "Stan the Man", by the way?'

'Mr Huxtable,' said Roderick.

'The Rev. Stanley Huxtable,' added Rupert, 'who teaches physics at the school, an ex-army chaplain.'

'I asked them all if they'd do an exorcism but none of them would. Stan said it wasn't his parish or something. Mr Cuthbertson-Twigg didn't seem to understand what I was asking and the Methodists weren't keen because we're not Methodists. Only Mr Chubb took me seriously and then said not to worry because the poltergeist would go away soon.'

'Interesting,' said Mr Campion. 'Who is this Chubb? I seem to have heard that name and quite recently.'

'He's a lay preacher or a circuit preacher or whatever they call them,' Exley offered. 'Turned up in the village a few months back breathing fire and brimstone, determined to set up the Mission, as he called it, and rented a place off the Zionists. Doubt if he has enough of a congregation to make up a cricket team.'

'Now, Arthur, we all know your views on religion,' said Ada.

'Actually, I don't,' said Mr Campion, 'as I only met Mr Exley on the way here this evening. We must have a chat sometime. I had an uncle who was a cleric. He used to say that when his congregation dropped down to three, he would cut his sermon short and make up a fourth at bridge. You asked all of them, Roderick, and then you asked Ivy Neal as well, didn't you?'

'She wouldn't help either,' the boy said angrily, 'even though I offered to pay.'

'You offered Ivy Neal money?' his mother gasped, open-mouthed.

'I believe it is traditional to cross a palm with silver now and then,' said Campion lightly, 'but Ivy's powers, or perhaps I should say skills, don't run to exorcisms and she has the sense not to pretend they do.'

'It's all superstitious rubbish, anyway,' said Exley. 'I don't know why we're even talking about such things. This isn't the Dark Ages—'

At that precise point a tremor ran through the house and the television set in the front room fell on to the floor with a crash which startled the entire company.

Ada Braithwaite had, quite sensibly, taken precautions. Having a good idea of what was coming, she had moved virtually everything moveable to a lower level or a cushioned location. Even so, there was an impressive rattling of crockery and metal pans, a loud clatter as a set of fire irons toppled against a coal scuttle, the chairs and table shook and a solid-looking washing machine shuffled a good two inches across the stone floor to bang unceremoniously into the sink in the corner. The central light swung on its flex from the kitchen ceiling and snowflakes of emulsion paint floated down on to startled, upturned faces.

Rupert's hand found Perdita's as if by osmosis and Arthur Exley stretched out an arm to comfort Ada, although its protection hung ignored as Mrs Braithwaite leaned forward instead to protect her son. Mr Campion, his hands gripping the back of a chair, felt the tremor shudder through his wrists and forearms and silently counted off the seconds.

'Got it!' yelled Roderick, snapping back the gear-lever control to stop the spools recording.

'Nine seconds,' Campion said to him. 'Is that normal?'

'It varies, sir – anywhere between eight and twelve usually. Mr Browne asked about that several times. Must have thought it important, so I thought I'd make a recording even though Bertie's not around any more . . .'

The boy's voice trailed away, but Campion continued to address him as if the two of them were alone in the room.

'You told Mr Browne all about your noisy ghost, did you?'

'Yes, *he* was interested; *he* didn't think I was being stupid or childish. He said he had some theories about it but he wanted to see a visitation for himself.'

'Which he did, did he not?'

Roderick nodded sadly. 'Mum agreed eventually but she said I couldn't be there, so I had to spend the night at the school with the boarders. I waited up for Mr Browne – he'd left his car up at the school – but he never came back. That was the night he had his accident.'

'Now then, Roderick,' said his mother, 'I've told you umpteen times: you can't go blaming yourself for that.'

'Of course you can't,' Perdita added supportively. 'Nobody thinks that, do they, Mr Exley?'

'Nobody in their right minds,' said Exley in a voice which did not allow for disagreement.

'You said Mr Browne had a theory . . .?' Mr Campion persisted gently.

'So he said, but he wanted to see for himself. He didn't tell me what his theory was, said he wouldn't until he had some evidence. Then I never got to ask him.'

There was a catch in the boy's voice and Mr Campion moved on swiftly. 'Well, we've got some evidence now, haven't we? Could we play the tape back?'

Roderick moved the gears on the recorder and they listened in rapt silence to the short symphony of disconnected sounds – tinklings, thumps, rattles and clatterings – all without any human intervention and in isolation of context, a strange mix of the domestic and the ethereal.

'Pity we missed the television falling over,' said Rupert. 'That was quite dramatic.'

'Perhaps that's not all we missed,' said Campion, 'but our poltergeist wasn't considerate enough to give us a precise arrival time. We should, however, acknowledge his presence in some formal way. Is your microphone still connected, Roderick? Then be so good as to take a witness statement from me.'

Roderick set the recorder then picked up the microphone and held it below Mr Campion's chin, his face as expectant as the keenest trainee radio reporter.

'My name is Albert Campion of Bottle Street, Piccadilly, London. I am here at Number Eleven, Oaker Hill, Denby Ash and it is Thursday the fourth of December 1969. I am in the presence of other witnesses, whose names and particulars can be supplied, and we swear that this tape recording is an accurate, unadulterated record of the physical phenomena we have experienced tonight and for which we have, at present, no rational explanation.'

Mr Campion looked up and discovered he had an audience. He beamed at them and said, 'That should do it. Now keep that tape safe, young Braithwaite. It might be needed in evidence, you never know.'

'What for?' blurted Arthur Exley, moving closer, protectively, towards Ada. 'There's not been a crime here.'

'Oh, not here,' said Mr Campion, 'but I'm sure there's been one somewhere and probably more than one.'

The three Campions took their leave of Mrs Braithwaite and were followed out of the back door by Arthur Exley, who then muttered that he would just 'Make sure Roderick's all right' and turned back into the house.

'Do I detect that Mr Exley's presence tonight was not in the role of trade union official or social revolutionary?' asked Mr Campion.

'Much more basic,' said Perdita, linking arms with Mr Campion as they negotiated the dark ginnel at the end of the row of houses. 'I think Arthur has what's known hereabouts as set his cap at Ada.'

'She's a fair bit older than he is,' said Rupert, walking behind them.

'And I am considerably older than your mother,' Campion replied over his shoulder, 'but I never held her immaturity against her. Ada will be just as tolerant; she seems a sensible woman. But please don't tell your mother I said that, and another thing: around here they *throw* their caps, they don't set them.'

'At each other?' Perdita smiled in the darkness.

'I believe the suitor – the gentleman – signals his intentions to the lady by throwing his flat cap into her house through the back door. If she throws it back out his suit is rejected. If the door closes with said cap still inside, a match is made. It's really quite charming.'

Perdita squeezed Campion's arm. 'So are you,' she said, her face nuzzling his shoulder.

They emerged on to Oaker Hill and after the warmth of Ada's house and the shelter of the ginnel the damp night air cut into them as they crossed the road to where Campion's Jaguar and Perdita's Mini were parked.

As Campion reached his car, he looked back across the road and satisfied himself that he had parked exactly opposite Number Eleven.

'Now let's see if my experiment worked,' he said, leaning over the bonnet which shone in the reflected yellow glow of the nearest sodium street light.

'What experiment?' Rupert asked, his gaze following his father's pointing finger towards the windscreen and the wiper blades, against which rested an odd assortment of objects.

'While you were buying the wrong sort of chocolates for Mrs Braithwaite,' said Campion, 'I did a little shopping of my own.'

On the bonnet, lying on their sides were a packet of twenty Embassy cigarettes, a tub of Ski yogurt and a bottle of aspirins.

'You will note, my pair of young Watsons, that I have parked parallel to our haunted house. I balanced my few groceries carefully, all the right way up as if still on the shelves of a shop, having waited until a lorry or two thundered by, to make sure that they would not be disturbed by slipstream or vibration. Now look at them: all tipped over as if they've been disturbed by some supernatural force.'

'I'm surprised they weren't pinched by a passing pedestrian,' said Rupert.

'Ah, my boy, there I trusted to the basic honesty of the Yorkshireman, although I could have had the bad luck to attract the one petty thief in the West Riding who smoked, had a headache and a weakness for fruit-flavoured yoghurt.'

'Is that who the police are after down there?' said Perdita, her outstretched arm pointing down Oaker Hill to where the road bisected around the Green Dragon pub and a number of vehicles with flashing blue lights were beginning to swarm.

'Interesting,' said Campion. 'I wonder what's going on down there. Drunken shenanigans in the pub or yet more fisticuffs outside the fish shop? And here come reinforcements.'

Another flashing blue light appeared coming down the hill from the Huddersfield road. It was attached to a Morris Minor in blue-and-white police livery which slowed as it approached then parked opposite Campion's Jaguar to allow a dishevelled DCI Ramsden to climb out of the passenger-side door and wade across the road through the beams of the headlights. Ramsden did not speak until he was within touching distance and several times glanced over his shoulder at the terrace of houses, checking for twitching curtains.

'Have you been here all evening?' the policeman asked without preliminaries.

'Pretty much,' said Campion. 'The three of us plus Mr Exley imposed ourselves on Mrs Braithwaite at Number Eleven. In fact, Mr Exley's still in there.'

'That's useful to know, but it was you I was hoping to catch. Did you go and visit Ivy Neal after our little chat this morning?'

'Yes, I did, and it was a most interesting experience.'

'Then we'll be needing your fingerprints.'

Rupert and Perdita gasped loudly in synchronized shock, but Mr Campion's face remained impassive.

'What's happened, Chief Inspector?' he asked quietly.

'I can't say for sure just yet and I'd like young Mr Campion and his good lady to go back to Ash Grange and go to bed. You're staying at The George?'

Campion nodded.

'Then please go to your room there and speak to no one. I will be in touch as soon as I can. I've got to get down to the Common. There's a body been found in Ivy Neal's caravan. Most likely it's hers and it doesn't sound as if she went quietly.'

EIGHTEEN

Investigations

As neither Rupert nor Perdita had scheduled commitments on the games field or in the rehearsal room the following morning, they embarked on the task Mr Campion had set them before he had driven back to his hotel where he would remain, as he put it, in 'police purdah'.

They had gone to bed with something of a sense of disappointment, a feeling that they should have been more impressed, or frightened, by Ada Braithwaite's poltergeist, coupled with the unease any normal person would feel when told by a policeman that something nasty had happened but not exactly what. They assumed that they would hear no further details of the previous night's police action until Mr Campion reappeared in Denby Ash. In that, they were completely mistaken.

Given that there were no more than half-a-dozen telephones in private homes in the whole village, the jungle drums of Denby Ash must have been busy overnight. Certainly by the time breakfast was being served in the school dining room, the two kitchen ladies, the Armitages and the still sleepy, tousle-headed boarders all seemed to have inside knowledge, and numerous theories, on what had happened on the Common the previous night.

First reports had filtered out from the men changing shifts at the Shuttle Eye and Caphouse pits who passed the Common on their way to or from work and had seen the improvised police cordon around Ivy Neal's caravan. Then Mrs Somebody-or-other, who cleaned at the Green Dragon, and Mrs So-and-so, who 'did for' the vicar and his wife, had compared notes on what they had seen, which was little, and on what they had surmised, which was quite a lot. It was theorized that Ivy Neal had been attacked by burglars (though surely she had little worth stealing); murdered by a spurned lover (although no one could actually remember seeing her with a likely male candidate for that office); had been asphyxiated by a faulty Calor Gas cylinder; had been smothered in her sleep by her vicious cat; that she had been casting a spell – even communing with a minor devil or two – which had somehow rebounded.

The latter theory, thought Perdita, would inevitably be expanded in local gossip to be directly connected with the godless production of *Doctor Faustus* at the school.

When asked for their own observations on the terrible rumours by Celia Armitage, Rupert and Perdita limited their answers strictly to the facts. They had seen police cars and flashing lights but from a distance at night and had no idea what they had been investigating.

They had exchanged a look as if to say 'Talking of investigating . . .' and excused themselves on the grounds that they had errands to run. Fortunately, their first port of call was the staff room where the first dragon to arrive in the den was, as usual, the Rev. Stanley Huxtable, who liked to compose himself in solitude before officiating at each morning's school assembly.

'Forgive the interruption, Mr Huxtable,' said Perdita, 'and we don't want to break your concentration, but could we have a quick word?'

'Of course, my dear Mrs Campion. Isn't it absolutely shocking?'

'Is it?' said a startled Perdita.

'Of course it is – poor Ivy Neal murdered. Not the most popular person in the village but nobody deserves to have their head bashed in like that.'

The reverend gentleman managed to appear both concerned and slightly smug at the same time.

'We know nothing of that,' said Rupert, 'terrible though it sounds. Has it been on the radio?'

'I have no idea,' said Huxtable carelessly. 'Old Twiggy – the Reverend Cuthbertson-Twigg down at St James' – flagged down my car on the way here and told me about it. Poor chap's been up most of the night with all the commotion on the Common.'

'Actually, we wanted to talk about something completely different,' said Perdita, noting the look of disappointment on the cleric's face. 'Roderick Braithwaite asked you to perform an exorcism in his mother's house, didn't he?'

'Ah, your Faustus . . . I think he might have been taking his role in your little show far too seriously.'

'Is that why you refused?'

'Not at all, though it is not my area of expertise and I would certainly have thought twice about pandering to the whims of a hysterical teenager.'

'Roderick is the least hysterical teenager I've ever known,' bridled Perdita, 'and I'm counting myself!'

'Be that as it may, my dear, diocesan protocol had to be observed. Peter Cuthbertson-Twigg is the vicar of Denby Ash, not I.'

'And if he wouldn't help?'

'Well, as I told the lad, he could always try the Methodists.'

Mr Campion was drinking tea and eating toast – and absolutely nothing else, despite the persistent lobbying of several matronly waitresses – in the dining room of the George Hotel, when a rumpled and unshaven Chief Inspector Ramsden apologised for disturbing him.

'Hate to say this, Chief Inspector, but you look like hell,' Campion greeted him as he folded away his copy of the *Yorkshire Post*.

'Didn't get much sleep,' Ramsden mumbled in reply. 'Bit of a hectic night.'

'Is there anything I can do to lighten your burden? I would suggest a large intake of coffee but frankly the tea here is far stronger.'

'Nothing for me, thanks, but you could assist by popping round to the station and allowing us to take your fingerprints – purely for elimination purposes, of course.'

'Happy to oblige; in fact, I'm quite excited about the idea as it would be a novel experience for me. Does that sound heartless? What exactly am I being eliminated from?'

Though there were only two other diners in the breakfast room – a young woman wearing a pink two-piece suit, her hair and make-up immaculate (job interview, perhaps?) and a beefy, red-faced man reading *Exchange & Mart* whilst worrying the end of the sausage impaled on his fork (travelling salesman?) – Ramsden lowered his voice to a whisper.

'Ivy Neal was murdered sometime yesterday evening. She was strangled and her caravan was ripped apart as if whoever did it was looking for something. We're asking around but at the moment it seems like you could be the last person to see her alive.'

'Apart from the murderer,' said Mr Campion reasonably.

Ramsden's face gave nothing away. 'I have to follow procedure.'

'Of course you do, Chief Inspector. I will come very quietly and very willingly. You will need me to give a statement, I take it.'

'We will, in due course, but the priority is your fingerprints. I have a car outside and we can have you back here in fifteen minutes. I hate to rush you but my fingerprint chaps are waiting to go out on another job.'

'That would be the latest payroll robbery, would it?'

Campion had posed the question casually but he watched closely for a reaction. Ramsden's face remained police-issue deadpan, which impressed the older man.

'What makes you say that, sir?'

'Oh, very good, Chief Inspector, a lesser mortal would have said "How did you know that?" thus admitting that there had been another robbery. Forgive me, I am not playing games.' Campion tapped the folded newspaper on the table with a forefinger. 'It made the Stop Press in the *Yorkshire Post*; their Barnsley stringer was on the ball and earning his corn last night.'

'Bloody tuppence-a-line reporters,' sighed Ramsden, 'but you'll hear soon enough, I expect. Yes, there was another robbery last night, a light engineering company in Barnsley. That makes eight in the series so far.'

'I was aware you were suffering something of a spate of them. A similar M.O. each time, I presume?'

'Every time. They pick small firms, all within a radius of twenty miles or so, and they hit them on a Thursday when the office safe has all the cash for the pay packets they make up on the Friday. They seem to know exactly where to go and they're in and out quick. Cheeky blighters don't try to open the safe – they steal the whole flamin' thing and cart it off. They must have a trolley to move it and a big van to get it away. Then they disappear, safe and all.'

'Any similarities to connect the victims?'

'All small to medium firms, all local: a dye works, a furnishings and furniture manufacturer, a plumbers' merchant and a small wool mill, but nothing in common.'

'Except they all had a safe and they were all robbed,' said Campion. 'Has any of the money surfaced?'

'Difficult to say. The notes were not marked and the rest was a mixture of ones, fives, tens and ten shilling, plus a fair chunk of silver change, which could all be spent in dribs and drabs without anyone noticing. But all in all, whoever's doing this has got away with getting on for forty thousand pounds and we've no idea what they're doing with it.'

'More to the point,' said Campion thoughtfully, 'what are they doing with all those safes?'

Just as Mr Campion was helping the police with their enquiries, Rupert and Perdita were helping him with his.

They left Ash Grange just as the bulk of day boys were being disgorged at bus stops on the main road or tumbling from cars turning into and out of the driveway with Grand Prix aplomb – the drivers, invariably fathers now late for work, chiding their offspring with dire warnings not to miss the so-and-so bus again.

It was a cold, damp and dark morning, only just worthy of the designation daylight, and the junior Campions had dressed accordingly as they now considered themselves Old Yorkshire Hands, if not entirely acclimatized. To supplement the warmest clothing they had brought with them, Celia Armitage had taken pity on them and added (from the school's Lost Property cache) woollen gloves, scarves and a knitted Beanie hat for Perdita. Rupert had declined the offer of a dark green Balaclava and opted, sensibly, for a multi-coloured ski hat with a bobble on top. He would not, Perdita had observed, be lost in a snow drift, and Rupert had replied that was just as well as it was indeed cold enough for snow.

Rupert set a brisk, circulation-boosting pace despite repeated punches on Rupert's shoulder as they marched down to the village, in the shadow – had there been any sun – of the Grange Ash muck stack.

'It looks like a pyramid,' Rupert had said. 'I wonder if it conceals a pharaoh's tomb stuffed with wonderful things?'

'I very much doubt that,' said Perdita through chattering teeth.

'Still, I wouldn't mind a run up to the peak. Good fitness training and the view from there would be pretty good.'

'A view of low cloud and chimney smoke if you ask me, but if you fancy yourself as Edmund Hillary, go ahead, or I could make you run up and down as punishment like Sean Connery was made to do in that film.'

'You mean *The Hill*?'

'That's the one. Probably a better title than *The Muck Stack*.'

On that they both agreed and pressed on, careful to cross the bridge over the Oaker Dyke when there was a lull in the thundering lorry traffic, until they arrived at their first destination, the Primitive Methodist chapel. The sign outside indicated that whilst the congregation was clearly devout and enthusiastic in the act of regular worship, they were not so keen that they demanded services at nine in the morning. An additional piece of information was that the 'Circuit Minister' was a Mr Henry J. Bamforth, BA (Hons), but there was no indication as to where he could be contacted other than at the specified times of service.

'Do Methodists have vicarages?' asked Perdita.

'I'm afraid I don't know,' replied Rupert, casting around. 'I suppose we could ask a passing primitive. Primitive Methodist, that is.'

'But there's never one around when you want one, is there, darling? Why not pop into the Co-Op, buy a newspaper or something and work your natural charm?'

Rupert smiled at his wife. 'But you outclass me hugely when it comes to natural charm.'

'I know that,' said Perdita gaily,' but the shop will be full of Denby women and they'll only want to gossip. You're a man and you can pretend to be dim, so they'll take pity on you.'

Rupert never confirmed whether Perdita's prognosis was correct but he was in and out of the Co-Op in less than two minutes, emerging with a red face and a large bottle of Ben Shaw's Dandelion and Burdock.

When Perdita looked askance at the bottle, Rupert said: 'Don't ask. I panicked a bit and this was the first thing I grabbed, but I did find out that the minister here lives in Barnsley and is only here when he's preaching on Sunday evening. However, we might have better luck at the next one.'

As they set off down Oaker Hill, Perdita could not resist asking if Rupert actually liked Dandelion and Burdock.

'I've no idea,' said Rupert with the air of a man who no longer wished to discuss the matter, preferring to share the intelligence he had collected on the religious hierarchy of Denby Ash.

The incumbent at their next port of call, the Hill Top Wesleyan Church, did live in the village in the development of newer houses beyond the working men's club. The noticeboard there gave the times of meetings and the information that Circuit Steward Miss Jessica Haigh lived at 2, Lilac Close, which was easy enough to find, between Primrose Close and Rose Terrace.

As she knocked on the door of the modern, red-brick bungalow, Perdita realized she had no idea what a circuit steward did, or what one might look like. In fact, Miss Jessica Haigh looked like any middle-aged woman caught in the middle of housework, and politely hoped that her visitors would forgive her for answering the door wearing a pinafore and pink rubber gloves.

Perdita naturally excused the older woman and introduced herself and Rupert as teachers from Ash Grange School calling on a pastoral mission involving one of their pupils.

Miss Haigh insisted that if that were the case they should come in, sit down in the spotlessly neat front room and make themselves comfortable whilst she put the kettle on. Rupert protested politely, saying the she should go to no trouble on their behalf. Miss Haigh replied, with astonishment, that making tea was no trouble at all and what was the latest news on the horrible murder of Ivy Neal?

The speed with which their hostess had changed subjects took the Campions by surprise. Perdita recovered first and decided to press their business before the kettle boiled, telling Miss Haigh that they knew nothing whatsoever of such things and were instead anxious to learn whether her church had been approached to perform an exorcism by a boy called Roderick Braithwaite.

On any other day, Perdita felt sure that would have been an irresistible topic of conversation but Miss Haigh, clearly anxious for the latest gossip, seemed most disappointed.

Yes, she had been approached by young Roderick, though what he thought he was doing even thinking about such things she would never know. It was not a matter for her, of course, but she did put it to the circuit preacher, Reverend Archibald, who quite rightly judged that the boy should look to a minister who perhaps knew the family and its circumstances better. The Zionists, perhaps.

As they carried no news of value to her, Miss Haigh was not distressed when, after two or three gulps of scalding sweet tea, the Campions took their leave, though not before she had helpfully pointed out that Deacon Horwood of the Zion United Reform Church, now more or less retired, lived only just around the corner at 6, Primrose Close.

As the Zion chapel had been their next port of call anyway, the Campions set off with a will, only to be called back when no more than thirty feet from the doorstep by Miss Haigh.

'Yoo-hoo, Mr Campion! You've forgotten your Dandelion and Burdock!'

In Huddersfield, the elder Mr Campion was leaving police head-quarters with something of a spring in his step. Although his fingerprints had been on official record for many years as a matter of national security which need not concern the West Riding Constabulary, he had found the inky ritual rather exhilarating.

Chief Inspector Ramsden had witnessed hundreds of examples of the process in his career and seen every sort of reaction on the part of those being printed, from blustering outrage to resigned acceptance. Yet he could never remember anyone quite so cheer-fully relaxed and cooperative as Mr Campion and as, from his office window, he watched Campion saunter back towards the George having refused a lift in squad car (he had no desire to waste any more police time), Ramsden was sure he could detect a spring in the old man's step.

Exactly how old was Campion? He was certainly well into his sixties and had made numerous off-the-cuff remarks about being 'a disreputable pensioner' and that his fingerprints, as they were being taken, might be found to match those on several exhibits in the Natural History Museum. Yet Ramsden could see the man was physically fit – fitter than some of his plainclothesmen at least twenty years younger – and in that slim frame was a spine of steel. The over-polite, self-effacing, sometimes rather fey manner he had perfected would certainly wow the ladies and easily fool the pompous or the criminally inclined who had him down as an easy mark. He had, Ramsden knew, a reputation for helping with police enquiries, though not in Yorkshire. Here he was out of his natural habitat. Could he possibly be useful? There was no doubt he had intelligence – he had been frighteningly well-informed about the spate of payroll robberies – resources and contacts, and a man like that would surely not be interested in a place like Denby Ash unless there was a good reason.

Perhaps it would be worth telephoning that Commander Luke down in London.

Deacon David Horwood was delighted to receive visitors – any visitors, at any time. Being retired he had only his books for company and in one sense he could be said to have three thousand friends permanently visiting, though admittedly quite a few were still strangers.

Perdita and Rupert smiled and chuckled in all the appropriate places, tried and failed to refuse another cup of tea and settled down on a sofa where a third of the space was already taken by a pile of hardback books which gave off a pungent odour of must and damp tobacco.

Deacon Horwood, a wizened old man, almost completely bald, whose skin on his face, neck and hands resembled the patina on a walnut, was more than happy to answer questions about Roderick Braithwaite's request for an exorcism. Prayer was, of course, powerful enough to defeat even the most pugnacious poltergeist, but the concentrated effort to perform an exorcism was often overwhelming for young and immature minds. If Ada Braithwaite, whom the deacon knew to be a good and charitable soul, had come to him for help it might have been different, but then Ada had been brought up attending St James' and surely that was where the Braithwaites should turn first.

In any case, he was now a *retired* deacon and certainly should not be considering anything as dramatic as an exorcism, even if he could remember exactly how one should be conducted. After all, he was a pensioner these days and all pensioners had to do was keep the fire in the grate and their allotment tended – wasn't that the case?

Rupert and Perdita exchanged knowing looks, then thanked Mr Horwood and took their leave. Once again, they were almost clear of the house and its small untidy front garden when a voice in pulpit mode called after them.

'Thank you for the gift, by the way. Naughty of you to hide it behind the hymnals. How did you know Dandelion and Burdock was my favourite?'

'So he really is just a retired old gent with time on his hands who likes reading about crimes in the newspapers as a pastime?'

'I wouldn't put it *quite* like that,' said Commander Charles Luke down the line, 'but he is supposed to be retired. There again, does a cat ever retire from hunting mice? Even if he's too old and slow to catch them, he'll still take an interest.'

'Does he have a personal stake or professional interest in our current epidemic of robberies?' asked Chief Inspector Ramsden.

'I can't think of any. You're a long way off Campion's patch up there.'

'In more ways than one. A toff like him sticks out like a sore thumb in a mining village like Denby Ash.'

'Don't judge a book by its cover, Chief Inspector. It's hardly Campion's fault that he is always underestimated by his enemies – you might say it's his greatest asset – and surprisingly for a chap of his education and breeding, not to mention his sense of humour, he can fit in just about anywhere and everywhere. I always thought there was a bit of the chameleon about Mr Campion. If you lose sight of him for an hour, don't be surprised if he pops up in a Mothers' Union meeting or playing the sousaphone in one of your brass bands, and everyone around him will swear he's been there for years.'

Ramsden could not tell, over the long-distance wire, whether Commander Luke was smiling as he spoke. In his experience, the real 'top cops', as the newspapers called them, rarely did.

'Has Campion ever been involved with our particular type of crime: robberies involving safe-cracking, that is?' Ramsden asked patiently.

'But that's not what you've got on your hands, as I understand,' Luke replied with an air of omniscience. 'You've got some bright spark who's stealing the whole safe and having it away on his toes. I've not come across that before and neither, probably, has Campion. That would intrigue him, though – get his juices flowing. I remember him following the case of one of our local villains, a safe-cracker of the old school who preferred gelignite to all that messing about with stethoscopes and tumblers. Famous for making a lot of noise and even more mess was Banger Maud, before I put him down for a ten-stretch, that is.'

There was silence and for a moment, in London, Luke thought the line had gone dead, but in Huddersfield Ramsden gripped the receiver tightly and took a deep breath before he spoke.

'Would that be Joseph Malcolm "Banger" Maud, by any chance?'

NINETEEN
Prisoner's Friend

To make Rupert and Perdita's quest easier, the vicar of Denby Ash not only lived in a conventional Victorian vicarage, conventionally located next to the church of St James the Great, but was at home when they called.

'You're the chap who wanted to see around the church yesterday,' announced the Rev. Peter Cuthbertson-Twigg as he opened the door to Rupert.

'I think that might have been my father,' said Rupert apologetically.

'Ah, yes, I see now. You did look older yesterday. But would you like to see the church anyway? It has a famous window painted by Burn Jones, you know. Sadly, he seems to have painted Saint James the Less rather than James the Great, but nobody really minds.'

Rupert declined the offer whilst trying to ignore the silent giggles which wracked his wife's body as she struggled to keep a straight face. He explained that they had already seen the St James' window, had attended Communion there with the Armitages from Ash Grange School and the purpose of their visit was to see him rather than his splendid church.

'So you've come to tell me what happened to poor Ivy Neal,

have you? I saw the police cars and the ambulance from our bedroom window.'

The abrupt change of subject took Rupert by surprise. Perdita, however, recovered quickest.

'I'm afraid we know nothing about Ivy Neal,' she said in a tone which suggested that follow-up questions would not be allowed. 'We are here on behalf of one of the pupils of Ash Grange.'

After a full minute of open-mouthed hesitation whilst Cuthbertson-Twigg absorbed this information, and after issuing the rather curious warning that his wife was out shopping, they followed the vicar into his study, a room knee-deep in piles of parish magazines which the visitor had to negotiate like a maze. There was only one chair in the room, a striped deck-chair bearing, in faded stencil, the legend that it had once been the property of an Urban District Council.

'This is where I write my sermons,' said the vicar, making himself comfortable. 'Now remind me, what was it I promised to do for you?'

For fifteen minutes Rupert stoically kept the conversation on the subject of Roderick Braithwaite and his request for an exorcism. The cleric admitted that he had never performed such a ritual and was far too old a dog to be taught new tricks, especially a trick which required the permission of his bishop. For a start that would have required contacting the bishop, something he had managed not to do for several years.

Eventually after many diversions, mostly down cul-de-sacs of logic, the Campions deduced that Cuthbertson-Twigg had dismissed Roderick's request primarily on the basis that a teenage boy brought up without a father was bound to be highly sensitive if he perceived his mother was being threatened. His demand for an exorcism was surely no more than attention-seeking and a hysterical overreaction to whatever had upset his mother. As to what that might possibly be, the reverend gentleman had absolutely no idea.

'So you were not willing to help Roderick?' Perdita asked through gritted teeth.

'Oh, yes, I helped him,' said Cuthbertson-Twigg without hesitation. 'I advised him to go and see Mr Chubb at the Mission, which is just up the road by the Zion Chapel. He's only been in the village a few months and I suspect his congregation is very small. I thought Mr Chubb might be grateful for some business coming his way.'

Once they had escaped from the vicarage – Perdita breathing deeply while clenching and unclenching her fists – they turned back up Oaker Hill to retrace their steps to the Denby Gospel Mission which they had blithely passed on the way down.

'What a perfectly awful man,' Perdita fumed. 'Stark raving bonkers, if you ask me.'

'No wonder there are so many chapels in Denby if that's the best the C of E can manage. Do we know anything about this Chubb chap?'

'Roderick said something about him, didn't he? Something like Preacher Chubb being the only one to take him seriously about the poltergeist?'

'You're right, and didn't he also say that Chubb had told him the hauntings would end soon?'

'Probably just to reassure the poor boy. It was more sympathy than he got from that crusty old vicar who really is a disgrace to the dog coll— Oh! Hello!'

Perdita's train of thought was broken by three short blasts on a car horn directly behind them. A grey Jaguar whipped passed and continued up the hill without slowing, only a blurred arm seen waving through the windows indicating that the driver had toot-tooted in greeting rather than warning or anger.

'That was Pop,' said Rupert. 'I wonder where he's off to?'

His fingertips still damp from the soap and nailbrush provided at police headquarters for the removal of ink, Mr Campion had collected his car from the George Hotel and once again taken the Wakefield road out of Huddersfield. He had no intention of calling in at Denby Ash just yet, though he did note the presence of police vehicles on the Common around Ivy Neal's caravan and when he spotted familiar figures of Rupert and Perdita, muffled against the weather, he thought them worth a friendly honk on the Jaguar's horn.

He drove on through the village following the route he had taken the day before, but then he had been performing a rescue mission of sorts: rescuing Perdita by driving Hilda Browne away. Now it was perfectly possible that he would be the one in need of rescue.

Hilda Browne, no slouch when it came to twitching a curtain, opened her front door before Campion had a chance to knock. 'Why Mr Campion, I thought I recognized that lovely car,' she cooed.

'Is it all right to park it there?' Campion asked, knowing the answer.

'Of course it is; it will be perfectly safe there.'

And all the neighbours will get a good look at it, thought Campion, just as they were probably scrutinizing him at this very moment.

'I wasn't expecting you, Mr Campion, was I? I must look a mess. What on earth must you think of me? Where are my manners? What can I do for you? Please do come in.'

Campion concluded that the woman had allowed her neighbours sufficient time to complete their observations, clearly anticipating with relish the erroneous conclusions they might draw.

'Please forgive my dropping in without warning, but there was something you said yesterday when I drove you home . . .'

'There was?' Hilda Browne made a valiant attempt at an expression of girlish innocence, complete with fluttering eyelashes. A look, thought Campion, which had failed her at least twenty-five years earlier but for some reason she persisted in keeping it in her locker.

'You mentioned that your brother had a collection of papers and maps relating to the local collieries. I wondered if I could see them – if it is not an imposition, that is.'

'Bertram's books? Well, his things are in a bit of a mess, just as he left them really.'

'That may actually be a help,' said Campion hopefully. 'If you are sure I'm not interrupting anything or preventing you from the daily round or the common task?'

'No, not at all, I was merely doing some sewing on my costume for the school play.'

'Ah, yes,' breathed Campion, displaying no enthusiasm to pursue that subject. 'Well, if you're sure . . .'

'Upstairs,' said the woman, 'in the back bedroom. We have three bedrooms, you see, so Bertie used one as his study. Promise me you'll excuse the mess in there. I simply haven't had the time since the funeral . . .'

'Please don't worry about such things, and I would not ask if I did not think it important.'

'Important?'

'I think Bertram may have had a theory about the Denby Ash poltergeist.'

'Pah!' snorted Bertram's sister. 'I won't have all that superstitious rubbish discussed in this house! Ghosts and poltergeists? Ridiculous. I refused to be interested and I told him not to get involved. It was messing about at Ada Braithwaite's that got him killed that night.'

'I am sure your brother was only trying to help – help young Roderick, who seems a sensible lad. I understand he hasn't had an easy life.'

'Who has?' snapped Hilda.

Campion remained blank-faced and outwardly calm. 'May I see Bertram's study, please? I am only interested in things concerned with Denby Ash and I assure you I will not be snooping among any private or personal documents.'

'You won't find anything like that!' she said haughtily. 'Bertram did not have a private life.'

That you knew about, Campion said to himself as he followed the woman upstairs, noting that Hilda Browne had ankles almost as thick as her skin.

She showed him into a small room with a window which looked out over a small, neat back garden, a creosoted fence, another back garden and the identical window of the identical neighbouring house. It was not an inspiring view but that was exactly what one needed in a study and, judging from the books on the shelves there, Bertram Browne's reading habits provided plenty of distractions.

It was an eclectic library split evenly between literature and local history. There were Shakespeare, Marlowe and Webster texts in numerous editions and novels by Tolstoy, Hardy, Dickens, Waugh, Amis, Powell, John Braine and Stan Barstow. The remainder were titles which meant little to Campion, although he recognized some of the places they referred to and could not resist flicking through a slim commemorative volume bound in green leather: *Denby Ash Brass Band 1838–1938, The First 100 Years.*

The desk in front of the window was likely to be a more fruitful hunting ground. It was covered with papers, contour maps of the local area, schematics of mineshafts and diagrams illustrating how coal seams were undercut or collapsed using explosive charges. There was clearly a pattern to it all but it required an engineer's mind to see it. Campion's brain, he felt, would be more engaged by the nine Anthony Powell volumes on the shelf and his soul more nourished by the Tolstoy.

Two documents among the loose papers took his eye. One was an Ordnance Survey map of the Denby Ash area on which a circle and radiating lines, along with several question marks, had been drawn around the defunct Grange Ash colliery. The pencilled doodles could, of course, simply be doodles, but Campion thought it well worth getting a second opinion.

The second document was in careful schoolboy 'best hand-writing' on four pages of lined paper torn from an exercise book. Campion settled himself on the edge of the desk and read what transpired to be a naïve but very moving short story about a boy who lived in a haunted house. The ghost in residence was that of his dead father and whilst not violent, its presence was disrup-tive and upsetting to his mother, who had loved his father very much. Saving up his pocket money, the boy buys a spell from a local witch, guaranteed to rid the house of its ghost. The spell is a single magic word, but after much heart-searching, the boy decides not to utter it when the ghost appears. He does not banish the ghost because he knows his mother is not yet ready to say goodbye to it.

Campion removed his spectacles and pinched the bridge of his nose with forefinger and thumb. He had no need to read the very last line, which gave the name of the young author.

'It seems anyone can rent a garden shed and call it a chapel round here,' Rupert observed.

'It's hardly a shed, darling,' Perdita corrected, 'probably a coach house. Literally, a house for a coach or rather a small buggy or trap, and it was built just as the motor car arrived. When it turned out it wasn't suitable as a garage it was used for other purposes.'

'Such as being a shed,' her husband persisted.

'Whatever it was, it's now the Denby Gospel Mission.'

'And it's nothing to do with the Zion Reform Church?'

It was a question which had no doubt been asked many times,

with good reason. The Campions had walked up the overgrown driveway to the Zion United Reform Church, taking the long view of a grey brick building built in unconvincing neo-Classical style with a stone portico guarding a brass-studded oak door and leaded windows which, even that far set back from the road, were begrimed with coal dust. Perhaps its stark lines had once impressed the faithful Zion Reformers as they dutifully trudged up the drive, but now everything about it said that few trudged there any longer.

In contrast, the smaller building to the left of the main building at least looked lived in, if not the obvious choice for a building to worship in – if only in groups of less than a dozen at a time.

There was a maroon-coloured Austin A40 parked carelessly outside the Mission, partly obscuring the open doorway.

'At least somebody's home,' said Rupert before calling out, 'Hello there! Good Morning!'

A figure appeared between the door and the rear of the car; a middle-aged man with thinning mousey hair and a darker Van Dyke beard putting a point on a pale and wan face which clearly did not belong to a sun-worshipper. Rupert was by now familiar with the bone white complexion of the miners of Denby Ash, though this one had clearly changed professions for the day. He wore a set of brown overalls and from the pockets protruded a pencil, a screwdriver, a folding wooden ruler and the triangular end of a set square. In one hand he held an old wooden box plane and, as he moved, sawdust and wood shavings drifted off him.

'I'm sorry,' said Rupert genially, 'are we interrupting a bit of DIY?'

'Our Lord was a carpenter,' said the man, 'and there can be no better example to follow in life, especially when you have to make-do-and-mend. What can I do for you good folk?'

'It's Mr Chubb, isn't it? Our name is Campion – this is my wife Perdita. We're both temporary teachers at Ash Grange School and we'd like to talk about one of our pupils who may have called on you recently.'

The sallow-faced man shook his head as if weighed down by a great sadness. 'They that sit in the gate speak against me and I am the song of drunkards.'

'I beg your pardon?'

'Mr Chubb is, I think, quoting from Psalms,' said Perdita, 'about the dangers of listening to village gossips.'

Robin Chubb gave her a thin smile, showing just enough teeth to suggest that a visit to the dentist was overdue.

'More or less,' he admitted. 'It'll be about Roderick Braithwaite. You'd better come inside.'

The Campion jury may have been undecided on his proficiency as a preacher but there was little doubt from the evidence of the interior of his Mission that Mr Chubb was an excellent carpenter. It was not a large Mission, though neither Rupert nor Perdita had any real idea of the average size of Missions, with wooden benches still smelling of fresh pine to seat no more than eight in comfort, ten at a squeeze. There was a varnished wooden table where an altar would have been expected and on it, a foot-high Calvary crucifix on a stepped base in sombre dark oak.

The Mission was essentially one room, but a portion of it had been clearly reserved for the preacher's personal needs, an area delineated by what looked suspiciously like an old fire curtain from a theatre hung on a rail from the ceiling. Robin Chubb indicated that the Campions should 'take a pew' whilst he drew the curtain along its track, but not before his visitors had observed the outline of a sturdy pine bed.

'Do you live here, Mr Chubb?' Perdita asked.

Chubb completed drawing the heavy red curtain then turned to face the Campions, his hands down by his sides, palms outwards.

'No, I live in Cudworth but occasionally feel the need to rest between meetings. Spreading the fragrance of the knowledge of the Lord can be an exhausting business and I have several missions to visit on my little circuit. That's enough of me; you'll be wanting to know about Master Braithwaite and his exorcism, I suppose.'

'If you don't mind,' said Perdita. 'We are rather concerned for the boy.'

'There's not much to tell,' said Chubb, his pale, deep-set grey eyes never leaving her face. 'He asked me if I could perform an exorcism to get rid of a poltergeist. I told him to go home and look after his mother and wait for things to sort themselves out.'

'I think he came to you because he was worried about his mother,' Perdita said, returning Chubb's stare.

'I'm sure he was, but if the mother was troubled she could have come here and been saved through prayer. Prayer is the only way to defeat real evil; I'll have no truck with the magic tricks brigade where they spray incense like mustard gas. You can't just put on a show when you think you need one – you have to work hard at prayer. There's plenty in this village, when they go to a church, can only think about getting home and putting the meat on.'

'We have no opinion on the various brands of religious faith on offer in Denby Ash,' said Perdita firmly, 'or whether exorcisms work or cause more problems than they solve. We are only concerned about Roderick.'

'I don't rightly understand why,' said Chubb. 'I mean, you're newcomers, aren't you, from down south?'

'We were told there were no secrets in Denby Ash,' Perdita began lightly before turning serious, 'but Roderick is a pupil at Ash Grange and he had already approached the school for help.'

'Had he now?' Chubb seemed surprised but so did Rupert, who wondered where his wife was steering the conversation.

'Roderick confided in his English master, Mr Browne . . .'

'The chap that got run over?' Chubb's grey piggy eyes flashed.

'That's right. We think he was trying to find ways to help Roderick, but then he had his accident. We don't want the boy to think he has been abandoned.'

Chubb raised his hand to chest height and made a tent with his fingertips. 'It's comforting to see you have such concern for the lad,' he said, 'but he's young and probably going through a phase. I'm sorry I couldn't help him.'

'Yet you told him the poltergeist would go away soon, didn't you?'

'I could have. It's a phase he's goin' through and phases pass, don't they?'

'Is it all right if I steal these, Miss Browne?' Campion called out as he descended the stairs. 'It's a map of the area which is quite interesting and an essay from one of his pupils, which I can easily drop off at the school.'

'I'm in here, Mr Campion.'

Mr Campion followed the voice into the front room of the house and stopped dead in the doorway at the sight of Hilda Browne kneeling before a full-sized mannequin, her mouth full of pins, the hem of a garment in one hand, a needle and thread in the other. She had pushed all the furniture in the room back to the walls to give her space. It had the effect of turning the room into a small amphitheatre with her posing as the defeated gladiator and the mannequin as the imperious victor.

'May I borrow these?' Campion held up the map and the essay. 'I will make sure they are returned.'

Hilda chewed on a pin and screwed up her eyes to focus on the papers. 'Please take the map. It's only clutter and you'd better let the Braithwaite boy have his stupid story back. I ask you, poltergeist and witches! And him supposed to be a star pupil. Hah! I never understood why he was such a favourite of Bertram's. The boy's addled. I wouldn't be surprised if Ivy Neal didn't put him up to it!'

'Why would Ivy Neal do anything of the sort?' said Campion severely.

'Because she puts herself about as a white witch, a wise woman, the healer of the tribe, but some of us see through her.'

Campion controlled his breathing and his temper. 'Did you know her well?' he asked, watching for a reaction to his use of the past tense, but none came.

'I wouldn't let anyone think I associated with the likes of Ivy Neal. She's no better than the gypsies who come with the Feast every year.'

Campion wondered if the woman had any idea what she looked like, speaking with those pins between her lips as if they were the points on the words she was spitting.

'Mind you,' she continued unabated, 'I only spoke to her the once and then because I couldn't really avoid it. I mean, she took me by surprise. I never expected to see her there and certainly not doing good works like I was.'

'Where was this?' Campion asked gently.

'Wakefield Prison. Could have knocked me down with a feather when she turned up one afternoon and I asked her, straight out, "What are you doing here?" Bold as brass, she said, "Same as you."'

'And what were you doing – the two of you?'

'Visiting. I've been a prisoner's friend for years; it's my charity work, bringing a bit of cheer to those miserable sinners. I had no idea Ivy Neal was doing good works as well.'

'Very commendable,' said Mr Campion. 'Was this recently – when you ran into Ivy Neal, that is?'

Hilda frowned, remembering, and her mouth turned upwards, the pins in it taking on the menace of a boar's tusks. 'Earlier this year, perhaps three months ago.'

'It must be interesting and rewarding work,' said Campion. 'Do you visit anyone in particular?'

'No. Any lost soul who needs comfort.'

'I hope they appreciate your dedication,' said Campion, and then, because he could not put it off any longer, he added, 'I'm sorry, I should have asked earlier: is there a happy event in the offing?'

Hilda, still on her knees, followed his gaze to the mannequin towering above her and reacted as if she was seeing the garment she was working on for the first time.

'What? This?' She giggled girlishly. 'This is my Helen costume for *Doctor Faustus*.'

Fitted snugly over the mannequin was an ivory satin Empire wedding dress with a lace collar embedded with fake pearls and flared sleeves.

To Mr Campion's undiscerning and masculine eye, it was not a wedding dress which had seen active service, but that was a matter he had no wish to pursue.

He made his excuses and almost ran for the safety of his car.

It began to rain as Rupert and Perdita trudged back up Oaker Hill, but it did nothing to cool her temper.

'What an awful man!'

'Which one?' asked Rupert.

'All of them – well, the last two anyway. Cuthbertson-Twigg is senile and Chubb is . . . is just . . . weird.'

Rupert put an arm around his wife's damp shoulders. 'Weird in what way?'

'His accent, for one thing. Didn't you notice it? He doesn't sound like a local.'

'Well, he's not, is he? He said he came from Cudworth.'

'Cudworth's not that far away – it's still in Yorkshire. It's not like Cudworth is the home of lost causes.'

'My father always said that was Oxford,' grinned Rupert, then recoiled as Perdita shrugged off his arm.

'Be serious. Chubb didn't have a Yorkshire accent – well, not a proper one. It sort of came and went, like he only did it when he remembered to.'

'That's hardly a crime, darling. Not even terribly suspicious.'

'I tell you what is suspicious,' said Perdita, poking Rupert in the chest with a stiff finger. 'Chubb didn't once ask us about Ivy Neal. Everybody else did – everybody except Chubb. In a place that thrives on gossip, that's suspicious.'

TWENTY
Love Lane

For no good reason he could put a finger on, Mr Campion always expected prison governors to remind him of either a supercilious Greek master from his schooldays or the sarcastic sergeant-major who had instructed him in parachute jumping at Ringway during the war. Not once had his misgivings been justified, but he still lived in dread until he actually met Mr George Dennison, Governor of Her Majesty's Prison Love Lane, Wakefield, and once again all his fears proved groundless.

'Mr Campion, what a pleasure to greet you. We rarely get such distinguished visitors so highly vouched for and at such short notice.' Governor Dennison greeted him with a smile and a handshake.

'I do apologise for me popping up on your doorstep like a jack-in-the-box, Governor, and I am suitably embarrassed to have had to resort to pulling a few strings to get an interview with you.'

'Think nothing of it.' Dennison waved away Campion's apology. 'It's always a pleasure to get a personal phone call from Commander Luke at Scotland Yard. After all, he does provide us with a steady stream of customers.'

Campion smiled. 'He said he would give me a good reference, however much he might perjure himself. It was a rather sudden decision to try and visit you without notice, but I was in the neigh-bourhood and couldn't resist. I phoned Charlie Luke from a call box at the station just round the corner. Cost me a fortune in sixpences, but I was lucky and caught him between promotions. He said he would phone ahead on my behalf and clear the way for me.'

'He did so very graciously, speaking very highly of you,' said Dennison, smiling also, 'and he told me to point out that while his request was to welcome you *in*, he left the matter of letting you *out* entirely to my discretion.'

Now Campion laughed; not too nervously, he hoped.

'Good old Charlie. He will have his little joke. He was joking, I take it? Good, well, I won't take up too much of your time, Governor.'

'Did you wish to inspect our facilities?' Dennison offered.

Campion had no desire to inconvenience the governor more than was necessary and the inmates not at all. From outside the grim sooty walls he had deduced that the establishment dated from the early part of Victoria's reign when there had been a burst of new prison building as the traditional transportation of convicts went out of fashion, or perhaps because Australia was deemed full. The Love Lane site had probably been chosen by that eminent Victorian Joseph Jebb, a noted expert on prisons and, coincidentally like the late Bertram Browne, an officer of the Royal Engineers.

'I require a few moments of your time, on a trivial matter,' said Campion.

'Then you had better come into my office after you've signed in.'

Campion's eyes twinkled behind the round lenses of his spectacles. 'Can I take it that signing out will be as swift and painless?'

'We'll see,' said Governor Dennison.

Campion followed Mr Dennison up an echoing iron staircase and along a corridor, passing through two grilled doors which were unlocked by a prison officer with sound effects supplied by Hammer films. Once seated on opposite sides of the governor's leather-topped desk and once tea had been provided in solid, plain white china cups of impressive capacity, Mr Campion got down to business.

'I am curious,' he said, 'about one of your female prison visitors.'

'Not Hilda Browne, I hope. Not again.'

'Not directly,' said Campion suppressing his surprise, 'although it was something she said which brought me to your door.'

'You know the woman, then? You have my sympathy. Miss Browne tries hard to do good works . . . very hard. She sees her visits as comforting and uplifting for lonely prisoners, those who have no relatives to visit them. Yet very few, if any, of our loneliest, most abandoned, most depressed inmates have ever requested a second visit from her.'

'That must put you in a difficult position,' Campion sympathized.

'It does, it does. I can't very well turn down offers of Christian charity and I have no wish to deny our inmates the comfort of occasional contact with the outside world. But when prison visits appear to be adding to the punishment handed down by the courts rather than aiding or encouraging reform and a return to society, then . . .'

'Quite,' said Mr Campion, 'but it was another of your prison visitors I was interested in, one whom Hilda Browne ran into here whilst she was doing her . . . social work . . . a Mrs Neal, Ivy Neal.'

Governor Dennison looked into his teacup as if seeking inspiration.

'The name doesn't ring any bells, I'm afraid. Did she come with Hilda?'

'I got the impression that she was quite surprised to see her here. She knew her from the village of Denby Ash. Would you have a record of Hilda's visits so I could check a few dates?'

'Of course we have,' said Dennison. 'I'll have them sent up from the front gate. Just a minute, though – you did say Denby Ash?'

'That's right. Ivy Neal lived there and Hilda is connected to Ash Grange School where her late brother taught.'

'Then you mean Doreen Bagley.'

'I'm sorry?'

'Denby Ash, that's the connection. Perhaps you don't understand, Mr Campion, but the most notorious prisoner at Love Lane was not a mass murderer or a gangster or a train robber, but an embezzler. A nasty petty crook called Haydon Bagley who stole from charities, schools and churches by cooking the books. He was famous, or rather infamous, locally, and he was from Denby Ash.'

'And he received visits from . . . Doreen Bagley . . . a relative?'

'His mother. She was the only visitor he ever had and she was from Denby Ash, I remember that. In fact, I remember her very well. Quite a card she was, offered to do the horoscopes of the guards and the other prisoners, tell their fortunes, that sort of thing. She would put on an act like she was at a fairground.'

'Or a Feast,' Campion said quietly. 'And this was definitely Doreen Bagley?'

'So she said, and to be honest, no one would own up to being Haydon Bagley's mother if they weren't. They'd get lynched, such was the bad feeling about Haydon locally.'

'Was she a prisoner's friend in the sense that Hilda Browne is?'

Mr Dennison leaned back in his chair. 'You won't find many within these walls who would call Hilda Browne a friend, but I know what you mean. And the answer to your question is "no". Doreen Bagley only came to see Haydon Bagley, a personal, one-on-one visit.'

'Often?'

'No, two or three times during his sentence perhaps. I can check if it's important.'

'I understand that this local criminal mastermind, Bagley, was released not long ago,' said Campion thoughtfully.

'That is correct and there are concerns – we are all concerned – that he hasn't been seen since he walked out of these gates.'

'That concerns you?'

'Of course. Any prisoner released from here who reoffends is a black mark against us all. It means we have failed that individual and failed society Of course, there are habitual criminals. In fact, Commander Luke said on the telephone that you were actually acquainted with several—'

'I simply cannot imagine what he must be thinking of,' Campion said innocently.

'He mentioned,' the governor said slyly, 'something about a butler you had in your employ, an ex-cat burglar called Lugg . . .'

'Good grief! Lugg would throw a fit if anyone called him a butler. He was, as he put it so succinctly, a "gent's gent", and as for cat-burgling, he hasn't done any of that since he was a kitten and he certainly doesn't have the girth or the flexibility for it any more. I'm surprised the newly promoted Commander Luke has not got more and better things on his mind than to think of old cons we have known and loved.'

'Actually, when he was Detective Chief Inspector Luke, he used to check up quite regularly on certain inmates, ones he had been personally responsible for ensuring they enjoyed our hospitality here in Wakefield. In fact, he mentioned one of them on the telephone when he rang and even asked if your visit was connected in some way, as the name would be familiar to you.'

'Whose name?' Campion could not help but be intrigued.

'A chap called Malcolm Maud. Does it mean anything? He was from down south.'

'Quite a few of us are, I'm afraid,' said Campion smoothly, 'and yes, the name rings a distant bell. "Banger Maud" he was known as on the lawless streets of Canning Town. A safe-cracker, or to be accurate, a safe-blower who didn't care how much damage he caused. He was one of Charlie Luke's collars; got quite a hefty sentence, as I recall.'

'Ten years and did them all, the last three of them here, but he was released six months ago.'

'Charlie would have known that, surely?'

'I would think so.'

'So why mention him?'

'I get the impression that Mr Luke, being a very professional policeman, doesn't like loose ends.'

'And you think he has unfinished business with Banger Maud?'

Dennison nodded. 'I suspect he thinks Maud is unlikely to have been reformed by his incarceration and is quite likely to re-offend, although to be perfectly honest, he behaved himself well enough when he was one of our . . . er . . . guests. I remember he took to our carpentry classes like a duck to water. He spent hours in our woodwork room under very close supervision, given the sharp tools there and the obvious temptation to build a glider in the roof.'

Mr Campion grinned politely to show he had understood the Colditz reference. 'Wouldn't Luke be in a better position to know that rather than you whether Maud had relapsed into his old ways,' he said, 'if he was released six months ago?'

'That's the really curious thing, you see.' Mr Dennison leaned forward, his elbows anchoring to the desk. 'Malcolm Maud was supposed to be heading back to London on his release but he never did and nobody seems to know where he is. Just like Haydon Bagley.'

'I'm sorry . . .?'

'Haydon Bagley, Doreen Bagley's son. He did the very same thing – just disappeared. I presume Mrs Bagley knows where he is.'

'I don't think so,' said Campion doubtfully. 'As far as I know he hasn't shown up in Denby Ash.'

'How odd. It's not unusual to lose track of ex-prisoners and, of course, they have done their time, paid their debt to society and all that. Still, two cell mates both dropping out of sight on release like . . .'

'Cell mates?' Campion interrupted.

'Oh, yes, didn't I say? Maude and Bagley shared a cell for nearly two years up until Maud got his release. Thick as thieves they were, if you'll pardon the expression.'

'So they got on well together?'

'Splendidly as far as I could see, even after Maud got into religion in a big way. That happens in prison, you know: a prisoner sees the light and starts preaching to the other inmates. It can sometimes lead to ugly scenes when men are confined in a small cell, but Bagley seemed happy to go along with Maud's Bible bashing. My officers nicknamed him the Disciple – and they called Maud the Preacher.'

As Mr Campion drove into Denby Ash that afternoon, the dark outline of the Grange Ash muck stack was fading into the glowering, darker sky, even though the illuminated dashboard clock told Campion that he would be at Ash Grange before school was out for the day.

Celia Armitage met him in the entrance hall and offered to show him to the room Perdita was using for her rehearsals. Rupert had, she reported, come in from his afternoon training session with the First XV and retreated to his rooms in the Lodge in search of a hot bath and dry clothing. Mr Campion tut-tutted sympathetically and said he would be fascinated to see Perdita putting her cast through its paces.

As she escorted Campion along corridors and up a flight of stairs, Celia urged him to hurry as the bell was about to go and, this being Friday, they could well be engulfed in a tidal wave of boys hurrying home for the weekend. Campion, who had no wish to become a piece of flotsam battered by satchels and prodded by adolescent elbows, kept pace with the headmaster's wife and reached the appropriate door with seconds to spare.

'And so Faustus gets dragged down to Hell by all you lot,' Perdita was saying. 'And you'll all be wearing teachers' gowns, so I want them flapping. It should look as if you're a swarm of bats – or whatever the collective noun for bats is – descending on Faustus and carrying him off, but for goodness' sake remember that Faustus has a poorly foot, so please be gentle with him, but make it look as vicious as possible. It's called acting. Please remember that.'

She clapped her hands just as the school bell sounded.

'That's all for today, lads. Well done. Now put the chairs and desks back before you go.'

Amidst the crash of furniture and bustle of scrabbling boys eager to depart, Perdita sidled over to Mr Campion's side and put a hand on his arm. 'What do you think of my little company?'

'You seem to have them well drilled,' said her father-in-law, 'though I didn't see much. You seem to have the knack for teaching and the boys certainly approve of you. I suspect' – Campion lowered his voice – 'half of them are madly in love with you.'

'How can you tell that? You've only been in the room thirty seconds,' protested Perdita quietly.

'I know teenage boys. I'm pretty sure I was one myself once. Oh, and by the way, it's a colony.'

'What is?'

'The collective noun for a group of bats.'

'Show off! What have you been up to today?'

'Nothing much,' Campion said lightly. 'Had me dabs taken by the rozzers, so I did, cor blimey and luv a duck. Then I called on yer actual 'Elen of Troy, so I did and – stone the crows – ended up in chokey. God's honest, I ended up in the nick.'

Perdita made a fist and punched Mr Campion lightly on the shoulder. 'Now you're setting a bad example for the boys, cheeking the teacher like that. I don't know how Amanda puts up with you.'

Campion peered over the tops of his spectacles. 'Now that is a genuine mystery, but one for another time. At the moment I'm hoping young Roderick can help clear up a different one.'

Roderick Braithwaite's ears pricked up at the mention of his name. He had been quietly straightening the desks and chairs to their proper classroom order and collecting dropped books, pencils and sweet wrappers – the sort of jetsam which follows in the wake of teenage boys.

'You don't have to do that, Roderick,' said Perdita, 'though it is kind of you.'

The boy blushed, his cheeks pink. 'It's no bother, Miss. I've got to wait for me Mum anyway.' He turned his face to the floor in shame. 'She's insisted on walking me home,' he added quietly.

'Let me pick your brains, young feller, and I'll run you and your dear mother home in my car,' said Mr Campion.

'The Jaguar?' The boy's head snapped upright and on his face, enthusiasm having banished embarrassment.

'Can't have you limping down the road on that bad ankle of yours, can we?' beamed Campion. 'In fact, let us both take the weight off our legs and sit for a minute, if Miss Browning does not mind, that is. I want to ask your opinion on something.' He removed a sheaf of papers from the 'poacher's pocket' of his overcoat and laid them on a desk top. 'But first, can I ask you about your visit to Ivy Neal on the night you and Andrew Ramsden were attacked?'

'She's dead, isn't she?' the boy said gravely. 'Everybody was talking about it at break. It wasn't anything we did, was it?'

'Good gracious me! The very idea! You should put that idea right out of your mind this minute, my lad,' said Campion.

'And if anyone suggests that, they'll have me to deal with,' Perdita offered in stout support.

'There's some that blame me for Mr Browne's accident as well,' Roderick added in sepulchral tones.

'That sounds just as ridiculous,' said Mr Campion. 'What sort of a petty, small-minded busybody would—?'

'Hilda Browne,' said Perdita.

'Well that explains it perfectly,' said Campion, delighted to see a smile flicker across the boy's face. '"Come Faustus, why so glum?" Is that a quote, Miss Browning? If it isn't it should be.'

'If it is, we've probably cut it,' sighed his daughter-in-law.

'Not to worry. What I wanted to hear more of was this disappearing trick that Ivy pulled on you. Andrew's father told me about it but I wanted to hear first-hand.'

Roderick shrugged his shoulders. 'Well, clearly, it was a trick of some sort, though it fair made us jump at the time. I've not said much about it in case people thought we were making it up and they'd say we were scared of the witch. She just disappeared in front of our very eyes, better than anything on David Nixon, it was. One minute she was sitting there, stroking her cat and the next she was gone and so was the cat.'

'Ah, yes,' said Campion, 'the cat. Every witch has a familiar, or so they say. But it was a trick, you think, not magic?'

'Well, there were no magic spells or puffs of smoke. It was just like someone had turned the lights off and back on really quickly. Blink and she'd gone; just disappeared. It was impossible, really, in a caravan that size. There was nowhere she could have gone . . . Not that we hung around to find out.'

'Very wise; I'm sure I would have scooted out of there toot-sweet, but I am delighted you realized it was a trick and not witchcraft or jiggery-pokery.' The boy returned Campion's broad grin. 'Now turn your agile and youthful brain – adjectives I use with a fair amount of jealousy – to this map, if you wouldn't mind. But first, I believe this is yours.'

Campion handed Roderick the handwritten essay which, after a quick glance of recognition, the boy slid off the desktop and on to his knees. As he did so, he exhaled a sigh of relief and shuffled his chair closer under the desk. His 'essay' was now out of sight, literally off the table, and would not be mentioned again. Campion knew he had forged an instant bond with Roderick and calmly unfolded the map so that it spilled over the edges of the desk like a tablecloth.

'It's one of Mr Browne's, isn't it?' said Roderick, leaning forward. 'That looks like his scribble there in the margin and those blue pencil lines . . . he was always doing those on maps. He called it doing "overlays" when he used red pencil. And "underlays" when he used blue.'

'So these lines he drew,' Campion smoothed the map flat with the palm of his hand, 'they're all underlays, indicating something underground, because they're in blue?'

Roderick nodded enthusiastically.

'They all come from the two collieries,' observed Perdita, leaning over the two male heads to get a good look at the map. It was a standard Ordnance Survey map of Denby Ash but solid blue lines had been added stretching from the Caphouse and Shuttle Eye pits at the eastern end of the village. From Caphouse, two blue lines ran in a 'V' roughly westwards into, or rather under, Denby Wood whilst the Shuttle Eye sprouted three lines like a trident to points south and west, the central prong running in a line over the OS symbols for a public house and a church.

'Not all of them,' said Campion. 'Look at these faint ones . . . dotted lines. What would that mean, Roderick?'

'Those would be his best guesses. He would make the lines solid when he was sure they were accurate.'

'But the dotted lines come out of the Grange Ash colliery,' Perdita pointed at the map, 'and that pit's been shut down. So what's the point of knowing where the mineshaft was?'

'I don't think they are mineshafts, my dear. Those go from the pit head straight down. At first I thought they might be fault lines in the local geology but they look more as if they are the galleries or tunnels – I'm sure there's a very earthy technical term for them in this part of the world – which run along the seams of coal as it is extracted. And look at this one . . .'

Roderick's eyes widened as they followed the line of Campion's jabbing finger.

'It comes right into the village and cuts across Oaker Hill.'

'Right *under* the village to be precise, and if Mr Browne's line is accurate, I'll bet it crosses Oaker Hill somewhere between Numbers Nine and Thirteen.'

'Number Eleven!' said Roderick excitedly. 'Our house!'

'You're suggesting this map has something to do with Roderick's poltergeist?' asked Perdita sharply. 'How can you be sure?'

'I found it in Bertram Browne's study, at his home. It had . . .' He caught Roderick's eye and winked conspiratorially, '. . . other papers with it which suggested they were linked. You told him about the poltergeist some time before his accident, didn't you?'

Roderick nodded. 'Two months ago. He said he would look into it and then he would come and see the effects for himself.'

'We'll never know what Mr Browne actually concluded, but I think he was a thorough man and used his training with the Royal Engineers. He did his research – his reconnaissance, if you like – and then went to observe the front line, so to speak, before he made his mind up. I have a feeling, though, that he had formed a theory.'

'So what was it? Man-made subsidence along a fault line or because of mining rather than a poltergeist?' Perdita's voice was tinged with hope and relief.

'Well, I'm pretty sure it isn't a poltergeist,' said Mr Campion, 'and it's not subsidence. Subsidence doesn't happen regularly on Thursday evenings, but man-made? Oh, yes, quite definitely.'

'Is that you being enigmatic or just baffled?' Perdita asked with a look of mock disapproval.

Mr Campion glanced up at her with his most beatific expression. 'My dear, you should know by now that I am rarely enigmatic and almost always baffled. I would like to speak to Mr Exley again, in order to clarify my thoughts.'

'He'll be in the club tonight,' said Roderick, drawing surprised looks from the two adults. 'Always is, Friday night,' the boy explained. 'He has his tea with me and Mum and then goes across to the working men's to collect union dues and pay out Christmas Club money, stuff like that, as it's pay day.'

'Of course it is,' said Campion. 'I'll let you have your tea in peace and I'll catch him in the club – if they'll let me in, that is.'

'You won't have any trouble if you're with Arthur Exley,' said Roderick with confidence. 'He even managed to get them to let Miss Browning in there.'

'Mmmm . . . yes,' murmured Mr Campion. 'Mr Exley did strike me as having true Yorkshire Grit. I'm very glad he's on our side.'

'He is?' Perdita said in a high-pitched squeak.

'Of course he is. I would have thought that was obvious. Oh, by the way, have you seen the costume Hilda Browne will be wearing as Helen of Troy?'

'No,' said Perdita, momentarily confused by Campion changing the subject.

'I have,' said Mr Campion with a broad grin.

TWENTY-ONE
Pepper's Ghost

All three Campions ate with the Armitages in the Lodge, along with the few boarders who were 'full-timers' due to their parents being abroad; the 'part-timers', who boarded during week days only, having already achieved their release. The headmaster attempted to cheer them up by pointing out that term would end the following week and Rupert by reminding them they were all expected to support the rugby team the next day in the away match against the old enemy, Queen Elizabeth's, Wakefield. Perdita attempted to cheer herself up by reminding everyone that the following Saturday would be Speech Day and two unforgettable performances of *Doctor Faustus* – a matinee for visiting parents and an evening show for local friends of the school, if, she thought, the school still had friends after the matinee. Mr Campion, as a guest, scored highest in the cheering-up stakes by announcing that Christmas was coming and that he had already written to Santa twice, recorded delivery. It was, however, Celia Armitage who lit up the boys' faces by serving, as it was Friday after all, fish and chips which she had personally fetched from Willy Elliff's chip shop, each portion insulated by what seemed like an entire edition of the previous week's *Wakefield Express*.

'You must try these, Campion,' urged Brigham Armitage. 'A local delicacy and a treat for all concerned. They boys love 'em, the cook gets a night off and look, you even get a little wooden fork so there's no washing up. Only drawback is that the car tends to smell a bit for a few days afterwards.'

'They are truly delicious,' said Campion, spearing a chip. 'I believe the secret is in the fat they use for the frying.'

Mr Armitage, his mouth full, nodded in agreement. 'You won't get fish and chips like this down in London, I'll bet.'

'No, indeed,' Mr Campion said graciously. 'It was the sole reason I came here in advance of my wife, so I could indulge in the local cuisine. I've had black pudding for breakfast and am looking forward to roast beef and Yorkshire pudding for Sunday lunch. I also intend to make room for a Barnsley chop and possibly tripe at some point, and I intend to smuggle several Wensleydale cheeses about my person for the return trip down south.'

The headmaster gave Campion the sort of sideways glance in which headmasters specialize, unsure how seriously to take the older man. He decided, as headmasters often do unwisely, to opt for humour.

'It had not occurred to me before,' he said rather ponderously, 'that there may be a business opportunity in sending food hampers from Yorkshire to the deprived south.'

'What a splendid idea,' said Campion, straight-faced. 'I'm sure there will be a ready market. Fleet Street is almost entirely staffed by Yorkshiremen these days and I'm sure they're missing their home comforts. Strangely, the longer they stay down south, the more Yorkshire they seem to become. Absence really must make the heart fonder.'

'Yorkshire has that effect on her sons and daughters,' said Mr Armitage.

'Mostly her sons,' observed his wife softly.

'I understand you are seeing Arthur Exley at the club this evening,' Armitage continued, and when Campion nodded, he said: 'Then you will be treated to a taste of *serious* Yorkshire.'

Mr Campion had seen the scene in dozens of cowboy films but had never envisaged himself taking a role centre stage, and until now he had never really thought the scene remotely realistic. There were, of course, no swinging saloon bar half doors, but as he entered the Denby Ash Working Men's Club and peered through rapidly misting spectacles at the patrons, the whole bar definitely went quiet, as if a central volume knob had been turned down.

It was not a total silence – several pins could have been dropped and not easily gone unnoticed – and there were none of the accompanying western sound effects: the metallic cocking of a revolver, the bell-like clang of a spittoon receiving a hole-in-one or the rasp of the bottle of some fiery spirit being slid the length of the bar counter. It was still possible to hear the clack of dominoes and the whine of an electric beer engine filling another foaming pint glass, but all conversation had stopped momentarily and dozens of pairs of eyes had narrowed on the well-dressed, elderly gentleman standing calmly in the doorway wiping the condensation from a pair of large, round tortoiseshell glasses with a handkerchief which could, as one voice murmured through the fug of tobacco smoke, 'come in useful as a white flag'.

Mr Campion heard and for a moment seriously considered that anonymous suggestion, but then he replaced his spectacles, straightened his shoulders and marched through the maze of tables towards the bar with what army drill sergeants, possibly mis-remembering their Kipling, used to call 'bags of swank'.

Gradually, as he passed them by, conversation returned to each table in a growing but indistinct rumble, giving Campion the feeling that he was wading through an ebb tide of faces, most of which were upturned to observe rather than welcome his progress. The faces were all male and in the main pink and freshly scrubbed and shaved. In years they ranged from early twenties to middle age, with no more than three or four of Campion's vintage. The standard form of dress appeared to be a plain dark suit, shiny with wear but still pressed regularly, a collarless shirt and a thin wool or silk scarf worn as a cravat instead of a tie. Apart from one or two of the younger ones the men, some fifty to sixty in all, wore flat caps, which made Mr Campion wish he had left his fedora in the Jaguar. Without it, he cynically reassured himself, he would have fitted right in.

One of the flat-capped figures standing at the bar turned and offered the first words of welcome. 'By heck, Mr Campion, this i'nt tha usual sort of club, I'll bet!'

For a split second Campion was startled to hear that Arthur Exley's Yorkshire accent had thickened considerably overnight, but then this was Exley's constituency and he had to play to his electorate.

'It certainly is not, Mr Exley,' Campion replied loud and cheerful, 'but I am told the beer here is considerably superior.'

'Cheaper too, I'll bet.'

A growling chuckle rippled across the room, even causing the darts players over by the glowing coal fire to pause briefly – very briefly – between throws and exchange nods of agreement.

'In that case,' said Campion, playing to the audience, 'allow me to buy you a pint.'

Now there was another surge of supressed mirth – not, this time, at Campion's expense but rather at Exley's.

'I don't drink, Mr Campion, at least not alcohol. I would not put an enemy in my mouth to steal my brains,' said Exley.

'That's almost *Othello* if memory serves, another play which doesn't end well. Still, you'll join me in something whilst I sample the ale, won't you?'

Exley indicated a wine glass half full of a greyish liquid on the bar. 'I'll take another Bitter Lemon from you.'

Campion felt a sense of disapproval in the hot, smoky air, which suggested that his fellow club members felt that Exley's temperance was somehow letting the side down.

'Certainly,' said Campion, catching the eye of the barmaid, 'and I'll have a shandy made with your best bitter and Ben Shaw's lemonade.'

He handed over a pound note and as their drinks arrived he moved in next to Exley so the two of them were shoulder-to-shoulder at the bar.

'I hope I'm not embarrassing you by being here,' Campion said, keeping his voice low, 'but I need to pick your brains.'

'No embarrassment on my part, Mr Campion. A bit of a surprise mind you; you wandering into the lion's den.'

Campion turned his head and surveyed the drinkers, the darts players, the games of dominoes and the bent heads studying the racing pages of newspapers. 'They don't look very fierce lions.'

'Don't be fooled – some are barely house-trained. A posh toff from down south is like raw meat to them.'

'I'm not really one for oppressing the downtrodden workers, you know,' said Campion. 'Really I'm not.'

'I suppose you treat all your staff with respect, paying them a fair wage and a bonus at Christmas?'

'My dear chap, I freed all my serfs years ago and I answer to only one feudal lord, or rather lady, and that is my wife. I have had a privileged upbringing, which I cannot and will not deny. My accent may sound ridiculously upper class to you but I assure you in some circles it is regarded as quite rough and ready.'

'I find that hard to credit, Mr Campion.'

'Please, call me Albert.'

''Rather not. Folks might think we're friendly.'

Campion pursed his lips, conceding the point. 'Are you sure I'm not embarrassing you, Mr Exley? You don't mind being seen with me?'

'Know your class enemy is my maxim, Mr Campion,' Exley said, loud enough to make sure his constituents at the bar heard clearly.

'Maxims are useful things,' Campion said after a moment's thought. 'They were very useful machine guns, of course, back in the days of Empire, but I am also informed, by an old and distinguished friend of mine, that Maxim is also the name of a rather nourishing stout brewed in Sunderland.'

Exley eyed him suspiciously. 'Mebbe I should be worried about being seen with you.'

Campion seemed to consider the point carefully. 'On the whole, you may be right to be worried, though I assure you I am quite harmless, and I would dare to suggest that you had no qualms about being seen with Bertram Browne.'

'Bertie Browne was a gentleman,' said Exley sharply.

'Then he clearly had the advantage over me,' Campion replied. 'All I can say is that I am a man, and I am generally thought of as being gentle. But I think Bertram Browne was that also, especially when it came to young Roderick Braithwaite.'

'He treated the lad well, I'll give him that. He was a very fair man.' Exley's voice suggested there was no room for dissent. 'Took an interest in life down the pit; in the community, in us . . .'

He waved his glass in a small circular movement, indicating the clientele of the club.

'It's about Mr Browne's interest in local mines that I wanted to talk to you and, I hope, enlist your aid as I think it will be invaluable.'

Exley looked politely curious. 'You're asking me for help?'

'Just as Bertram Browne did, I believe. I would be very grateful if you would teach me what you taught him.'

Slowly, Arthur Exley turned until he was face-to-face with Mr Campion. Although not as tall, he was broader and more muscular and with his chest out and shoulders back, the two men, their eyes locked, assumed the pose of unevenly matched boxers at a weigh-in.

'You fancy working down the pit then, Mr Campion?' Exley's voice was quizzical rather than sneering, but there was no doubt that the tone met with the approval of the men crowded at the bar, their ears pricked in anticipation of the bell to start round one. 'It's a mucky job, tha' knows, that'll take the shine off them fancy brogues you're wearing. Pit work's not a hobby for bored toffs with time on their hands.'

'I couldn't agree more, Mr Exley.' Campion's eyes never wavered or blinked. 'Working down a mine is a dirty and dangerous job, probably the most dangerous job in the world in a country not fighting a war, and I wouldn't last two minutes at it. Even were I your age and not so ancient and decrepit, I would scream like a baby if sent down a mine. Going underground to hew coal takes more guts than I've ever had.'

Exley stared at Campion's face for half a minute before he spoke, softly and deliberately. 'Are you taking the mickey? No, I don't believe you are.' He paused and looked at Campion as if the older man had suddenly materialized in front of him. 'Fair enough, then. How can I help you?'

Mr Campion stifled the urge to let out an obvious sigh of relief. 'You took Bertie Browne up the Grange Ash muck stack, I believe.'

'Yes, I did. He wanted to climb to the top for a bird's-eye view of the village, he said.'

'Was he looking for anything in particular?'

'If he was he didn't say. Got to the top and took out a compass, like he was taking a bearing. Seemed satisfied and we came down again.'

'Would you take me up there?'

Exley's eyes dipped to the floor. 'You'll need proper boots,' he said, as if it was a regular request, 'and you'd better leave that fancy hat behind or the wind'll have it, but tomorrow's Saturday, so we could go in the morning.'

'That would be perfect. I promise to bring only the minimum number of Sherpas and my own ice pick.'

'Bring what you like – just remember to do as I tell you. It's not a playground up there. Men have got injured, even killed, on that stack.' Exley lowered his voice and leaned in closer to Campion. 'This is more than just sight-seeing, isn't it?'

'I hope so,' Campion replied softly.

'Right then, tomorrow morning, about ten o'clock? Meet you at the school?'

'Excellent. It really is kind of . . .' Campion broke off, conscious that the room had suddenly fallen silent again.

'More bloody strangers,' someone muttered as Chief Inspector Ramsden entered and strode across the bar.

'Would you come with me, please, Mr Campion, I've a car outside,' said the policeman in his best official voice.

'Oh dear,' said Campion, 'it looks like I've been rumbled.'

'Would you join us as well, Mr Exley? It shouldn't take long.'

'We appear to be partners in crime, Arthur,' said Mr Campion cheerfully. 'Shall we go quietly?'

*   *   *

Once outside on Oaker Hill, with collars turned up against a misty rain and flinching as coal trucks thundered up and down the road, the three men gathered in the lee of the police car parked behind Campion's Jaguar.

'I apologise, Mr Campion,' said Ramsden, 'but I've used you as a bit of a decoy. I needed a word with Arthur in private, not in front of his men.'

'No need to apologise, my dear chap – at my age being a distraction is all I'm good for. Shall I be on my way, leave you to your confab?'

'That's not necessary, because I've got something I want you to take a look at in Ivy Neal's caravan. Tell you what, you take Arthur in your car and follow my driver.' Ramsden turned his head and squinted through the glare of the street lights. 'There are too many twitching curtains around here.'

'Right-ho,' said Campion. 'Come on, Mr Exley, let me be your chauffeur for the evening.'

If Campion had expected a Marxist diatribe about bloated capitalists driving luxury limousines, he was disappointed. Arthur Exley settled himself in the Jaguar's passenger seat as if in a favourite fireside armchair and pronounced it a 'really comfy' vehicle.

The police car pulled away and Campion followed it down the hill and into the car park in front of the Green Dragon from where Ramsden and his uniformed driver, both carrying powerful torches, lead the way across the road and on to the Common.

Mr Campion sniffed the air, picking up the scent of frying from Willy Elliff's shop at the bottom of the hill, where the lights were on and customers were hurrying in and out.

'They do fry a good piece of haddock there,' said Campion. 'Had some for my tea tonight. No wonder business is good and it must be a prime location when the Feast comes to town as well, so near the Common.'

'That's true enough,' said Ramsden, ploughing through the damp grass. 'The preparation room of the chip shop, round the back, looks out directly on to Ivy's caravan.'

'Is that important?' asked Campion, matching the policeman's stride.

'Adrian,' said Exley without warning.

'I'm sorry?'

'Adrian Elliff, the dopey son of Willy. Mr Ramsden has his eye on him, or at least I hope he has. He may be one of us but he's a wrong 'un.'

'Excuse me, gentlemen,' said Campion, stopping dead in his tracks. 'I know full well that I am on a piece of common ground in the middle of the West Riding on a dark and stormy night, but I have to say I am totally lost.'

Ramsden and Exley, realizing Campion was no longer in step, stopped and turned.

'Go and get the ropes down, Lumley,' Ramsden ordered the uniformed constable who strode off, his torch beam dancing in the dark.

The chief inspector pointed his own torch at the ground and the three men gathered around the pool of light.

'Adrian is a person of interest, as we say, because he hangs around with a couple of reprobates from Cudworth – two cousins called Frederick and Colin Booth. Now we suspect it was the Booth boys who attacked the two lads from Ash Grange – and I'm pretty sure Arthur thinks so too.'

Ramsden paused and his torch beam wavered slightly towards Exley.

'Trouble is,' he continued, 'Arthur wouldn't ever say so in court, them being miners and part of the union.'

'You can't ask a man to betray his comrades,' Exley said sullenly.

'Not even when they hurt someone important to you?' suggested Campion.

'That'd be my business, not yours.'

'Well, now it's police business,' Ramsden intervened, 'though to be honest we're not that interested in the Booth Boys as street brawlers. There's no harm in Mr Campion knowing – that is, according to a very senior policeman at Scotland Yard – but the Booths are among our prime suspects in the theft of small quantities of explosives from the pits round the corner here. Fred works at Caphouse and Colin at Shuttle Eye.'

'Have you caught 'em at it?' asked Exley.

'No, we haven't, but they're well-known to our blokes in Cudworth, and the gossip there is that they have both applied for passports. I checked with the passport office in Liverpool and it's true, they have.'

'Is that unusual – or incriminating?' Campion said meekly.

'The Booth boys don't stray far from home,' said Exley. 'They went to Manchester once but didn't take their coats off 'cos they weren't stopping. I reckon that's the only time they've been outside Yorkshire. Can't think why they need passports unless they're doing a runner to somewhere abroad.'

'Which takes cash money,' said Ramsden.

'Cash money which might be from the proceeds of your spate of payroll thefts?'

'Charlie Luke said you cottoned on quick, Mr Campion.'

'Hang on,' said Exley, 'you don't think the Booths have the brains to do the robberies what have been in the papers, do you? They're a pair of proper loons, them two; good for brawn but well short on brains.'

'I can't argue with that, Arthur. That's why we're keeping an eye on them, but it seems they were keeping an eye on somebody themselves.' Ramsden flicked the torch beam over his shoulder to where Constable Lumley was removing iron stakes and winding up the rope that had cordoned off the crime scene that had been Ivy Neal's caravan. 'The landlord of the Green Dragon tells me that Fred and Colin had started coming in of an evening and sitting where they could see out across the Common. They'd never been regulars until a fortnight ago and they always had something to say about the beer and the prices. They used the pay phone a few times but otherwise kept themselves to themselves. Only person they spoke to was Adrian Elliff who popped in once or twice, had a word then popped off.'

'And you said the fish shop also had a good view of Ivy's caravan,' said Campion.

'Correct. That's why I want you both to have a look inside the van. Our fingerprint chaps have finished and the council will probably need to shift it next week. Between you, you might spot something I've missed.'

'So we really are helping the police with their enquiries. How exciting!' exclaimed Campion, and then almost immediately his face fell and he was glad the darkness hid his blushes. 'Oh, I do apologise, gentlemen, that must have sounded terribly heartless, which it was. I should have asked about the poor victim. Has Ivy . . .?'

'She's been taken away to await a post-mortem, but cause of death was fairly obvious – strangulation. We're trying to trace relatives for a positive identification but that could take some time. Her background is a bit hazy to say the least.' Ramsden paused and sighed loudly. 'There's not many in Denby Ash that seem to know much about her, which is sad considering she's been a fixture for many a year.'

'Bloody amazing,' growled Exley, 'considering what a nosey bunch of buggers they are round here.'

'You can say that, Arthur; I can't. Now, can I ask both of you to come and have a look around the crime scene, please? Two pairs of fresh eyes can't hurt, because as far as I can tell there was nothing taken, not that Ivy had much to take.'

'So the motive was personal,' said Campion. 'She was murdered – why? To keep her quiet for some reason, or out of revenge or some long-held grudge?'

'Don't know yet, Mr Campion. In my experience as a policeman, the motive usually surfaces later when we've got a suspect more or less bang to rights. Nine times out of ten murders are spur-of-the-moment jobs and it's usually a member of the family, though in this case that seems to be ruled out as Ivy didn't have any family that we know of.'

Constable Lumley had cleared the way for them, removing the cordon ropes and the police seal on the caravan door – even venturing inside to light the gas lights.

'When I was a kid,' said Ramsden as the three men crowded into the kitchen area, 'the hiss of a gas mantle in a caravan was one of my favourite sounds. It meant we were on holiday and it was the last sound I heard before going to sleep, and that never took long after a long day on the beach at Bridlington. Now, though, it's a bit scary.'

'That's because you know what happened here,' said Campion. 'Violence always leaves a trace in the air, like a whiff of sulphur after the Devil has come to call.'

The three men stood shoulder-to-shoulder in the cramped space, so close together they could feel each other breathing as they surveyed the damage which had been visited on the caravan's interior. It seemed as if only the gas mantles and their shades had been left untouched. The folding Formica table had been ripped from its hinges, the mattress cushions had been slit open and disembowelled to reveal white fluffy stuffing material, and the contents of the storage drawers beneath them, mixed with large shards of glass and ripped curtains, covered every square inch of floor space.

'The windows aren't smashed in, so where did all this glass come from?' Exley asked.

'That would be Pepper's Ghost,' said Campion, a remark greeted with total silence.

'Any chance you could explain that, Mr Campion?' said Ramsden patiently.

'It's a trick – the trick she played on Roderick Braithwaite and your son, Andrew – and, I suspect, on any other unexpected or unwanted visitors. It's an old fairground favourite, though it was first used in theatres and said to have been invented by a chap called Henry Dirks, when it was known as the Dirksian Phantasmagoria, but it was improved by John Pepper in the nineteenth century and became known as Pepper's Ghost.

'Piece those bits together and you'll find a large sheet of unsilvered glass. By playing with the lighting levels and using the reflection you can create the illusion of a ghost suddenly appearing; alternatively, a figure suddenly *dis*appearing. What Roderick and Andrew were looking at and talking to was not Ivy Neal, sitting on the right-hand bench seat, but a reflection of her sitting behind a curtain or something on the left-hand bench. She would have had some mechanism for suddenly dousing the light where she was and her reflection would then disappear like a puff of ghostly smoke. If the boys had taken just a few steps forward they could have reached out and touched her, but like any normal person after seeing something impossible, they got out of it as fast as they could.'

'Sergeant Pepper and his ghost didn't help get rid of her last visitor,' Ramsden said grimly.

'Unfortunately not,' said Campion, 'and whatever he was after, I don't think it was a piece of music hall magic or one of Ivy's dubious herbal remedies. Did you find any fingerprints?'

'Only yours; he must have been wearing gloves.' The chief inspector turned his head. 'You see anything odd, Arthur?'

'Well, none of it is normal, is it? I can't see anything here that would cause Fred and Colin Booth to be interested in the old witch,' said Exley. 'Can we go? This place gives me the creeps.'

'What if the Booth boys weren't watching Ivy per se,' said Campion slowly, 'but if they were watching out for who *visited* Ivy?'

Ramsden considered the idea. 'It would make sense if they were in cahoots with Adrian Elliff. He could keep an eye on her from his dad's chip shop during the day – he works nights, doesn't he, Arthur?'

'That gormless so-and-so doesn't work very hard any time,' snorted Exley, 'but he's supposed to be a watchman at Grange Ash – does split shifts with old Tom Townsend. But why would they be interested in who visited the old crone? She never had any visitors as far as I know.'

At that moment there was a gentle knock on the door of the van and the face of Constable Lumley appeared. 'Excuse me, sir, but you've got a visitor.'

Ramsden squeezed out of the caravan and turned on his torch, training its beam in line with that of his constable's. Campion and Exley followed and saw illuminated the rather shapeless figure of a woman wearing large Wellington boots, a plastic raincoat and a headscarf knotted under the chin. She clutched a shopping bag to her chest with both hands and was shivering violently.

'Doreen?' said Ramsden gently. 'What are you doing here?'

Exley leaned into Campion's shoulder and whispered in his ear. 'Doreen Bagley. She lives up the road. Her husband Walter's on disability.'

Mr Campion consumed this information in silence.

'It's all right, Doreen,' coaxed Ramsden, 'you can talk in front of these two as I doubt you've done owt wrong. You know Arthur, anyway, and the elderly gentleman is called Campion. He's with me.'

'I think I might have done summat wrong, Mr Ramsden,' the woman said nervously. 'That's why I came down here across the allotments, so as not to be seen.'

'Now, lass, don't say owt you'd regret,' said Exley, moving forward as though to protect her. 'Does Walter know you're here?'

Mrs Bagley held up her shopping bag as if to ward off Exley. 'No, he doesn't, and I don't want it getting back to him, Arthur Exley. Walter's gone across to the club and I'd better be back to have a bit of supper waiting for him when he gets in. So let me say what I've got to say.'

'Go on then, Doreen, get it off your chest. Whatever it is, it's probably not as bad as you think,' urged Ramsden.

'My Walter wouldn't say that if he found out,' said the woman.
'That's why I thought you'd better have them. By rights they
belong to Ivy anyway.'

'What do?'

'These.'

The woman plunged a hand into her shopping bag and
produced a small brown paper parcel which she offered to the
chief inspector. Campion stepped up to his side and offered
to hold Ramsden's torch as he accepted the package.

It was a brown paper bag, the sort a greengrocer would use
for fruit or vegetables, folded over and around its contents. As
he took hold of it, Ramsden rubbed his fingers together and held
them under the torch. The tips of his fingers were smeared black
as if he had just fingerprinted himself.

'Sorry if they're a bit mucky,' said Doreen Bagley. 'I have to
hide them in the coalhouse in case Walter finds them.'

Ramsden unfolded the bag and from it took a wedge of small,
formal, buff-coloured envelopes covered in spidery writing about
an inch thick and held together by a rubber band. Even in the
watery light of the torch, both Campion and Ramsden knew
exactly what they were, for they had seen the like before.

'Letters from prison,' said Campion.

'They're addressed to you, Doreen,' said Ramsden, 'so I'm
guessing they're from Haydon.'

'They're from him but they're not to me, they're to his mother,'
said Mrs Bagley.

The chief inspector placed the bundle of letters back in the bag
and tucked them inside his raincoat. 'I can't read these here and
now, Doreen, but they'll have to be read. You'll get a receipt for
them.'

'I don't want one. They're not mine. I told you, they're addressed
to me but they were always for Ivy.'

'Hold on a minute, Doreen . . .' Exley spoke as if he had just
woken up from a bad dream. 'Are you telling us that your Haydon
was really . . .?'

'The son of Ivy Neal,' said Campion, 'and she visited him
several times in Wakefield Prison, passing herself off as Mrs Bagley,
which would be easy enough to do if she was able to use the real
Mrs Bagley's address.'

'We might not have broadcast it, but we never made any secret of the fact that Haydon was adopted,' protested the woman. 'Not that it was anybody's business but our own. It was during the war, nobody asked too many questions and the hospital was very happy to have a good home already lined up for an unwanted baby.'

'Did you meet Ivy at the annual Feast?' asked Mr Campion, and Doreen Bagley gave him a long, steady look before answering.

'Yes, as it happens. Right here on the Common, that last summer before the war. She had a tent and called herself Madame Francesca and was telling my fortune, reading my palm, that sort of nonsense. Said I would make a good mother and I said chance would be a fine thing as me and Walter had been trying for two years without result. Walter was sure there was nowt wrong with him, so it must be me. Ivy said she could fix me up with a baby as long as I never let on who the mother was. There wouldn't be a problem with the father as Ivy didn't know who that was. They were a bit loose when it came to morals, them fairground folk.'

'What did Walter say to all this?' interrupted Exley, as if a defence counsel was needed for his fellow miner.

'He didn't know about Ivy. Still doesn't. All he knew was we were adopting and he was pleased enough to leave it all to me. He had his work down the pit – reserved occupation during the war – and the brass band and the club. The baby made me happy and Walter was happy to let me get on with it.'

'When did you tell Haydon?' asked Ramsden.

'The last time I saw him before your lot took him off to jail. I thought he ought to know and I wouldn't see him again. After what he'd done, stealing from all those charities, I knew Walter would never allow it. Least I could do was give the lad a chance to contact his real mother.'

'And Ivy was happy with that?' said Campion.

'Oh aye, she always had a soft spot for Haydon. Called him "My little Orlando" – said it was her gypsy name for him – and I'm sure that's why she parked her caravan here in Denby after she'd finished touring with the Feast, so she could keep an eye on him. She didn't see him going bad the way he did – that really upset her – but in his letters he said he would make it all up to her.'

'Ivy let you read the letters?' pressed Ramsden.

'Once she had, yes. With Walter on the sick, he never gets out of bed until I take him his morning tea, so I'm up first to light the fire and . . .'

'Head-off the postman,' Campion finished for her.

She pointed a finger at Ramsden but looked at Campion when she said: 'He ought to be doing your job, Mr Ramsden.'

'You won't be the first to say that, Doreen, and I'm sure Mr Campion is dying to know how come you've got these letters now.'

'I never opened them, I passed 'em on to Ivy and then she'd give 'em back when she'd read them. Said I could keep them to remind me of the son that we shared, which was right Christian of her.'

'Can I be rude and ask what the letters contained, Mrs Bagley?' said Campion.

'Nowt you wouldn't expect from a son to a mother, even to one he didn't know he had. Memories of school days – he went to Ash Grange, you know. They were very kind to him there. And times he'd been to the Feast and seen the Madame Francesca sign for fortune telling. All nice, loving stuff, and sorry for the trouble he's caused, but he would see her right in the end. Oh, and how much he appreciated Ivy going to visit him in Wakefield.'

'Did he ever mention his cell mate in Wakefield?'

Now Chief Inspector Ramsden seemed to be more interested in Mr Campion than in Mrs Bagley.

'Malcolm?' said the woman, unconcerned. 'Yes, he mentioned Malcolm. Ivy must have met him during visiting times 'cos Haydon always said things like "Malcolm sends his love" or "Malcolm hopes you're looking after yourself" – that sort of thing.'

'Are those *all* Haydon's letters?'

'All except the last one that came about a week before he was due to be released. I passed it on as always, but Ivy never let me see that one, said she wanted to keep it until . . .' Her voice faltered and faded away.

'Until Haydon came home to Denby Ash?' said Ramsden. 'Except that he didn't, did he? At least that's what you told me.'

'I've not seen him and that's the truth.' The woman tightened her grip on her shopping bag, twisting it out of shape, and her mouth opened and closed like a goldfish. 'You don't think Haydon had anything to do with Ivy dying, do you?'

'I'm sure the police think nothing of the sort,' Campion said quickly. 'Now why don't we ask Constable Lumley to escort you back home?'

'Don't be so bloody daft,' Mrs Bagley said with scorn, clearly revising her opinion of Mr Campion. 'What would the neighbours think if they saw me frog-marched home by some clod-hopping bobby? I'll go back up the allotments, thank you very much.'

'You'll let me know if Haydon does get in touch, won't you, Doreen?' said Ramsden as the woman turned on her heels and shuffled off through the wet grass.

'I'm not expecting to see Haydon,' she said without turning around, and then added mournfully, 'ever.'

When Mrs Bagley had disappeared into the darkness, Ramsden turned on Campion.

'You seem very sure of what the police thinking is on this case, Mr Campion.'

'I do apologise for my presumption, Chief Inspector, but surely you don't suspect Haydon Bagley, do you? A man who could have easily refused to see Ivy when she visited him in prison . . .'

'You were going to mention that at some point, were you?'

'Ah, yes, perhaps that was remiss of me. Do forgive me. However, if Bagley was happy to have his secret mother visit him and to write to her with love and contrition, or so we're told, why would he wait two weeks after he got out to suddenly decide to kill her?'

'Haydon Bagley would have been spotted the minute he turned up in Denby Ash,' said Exley. 'There's no secrets in this village.'

'I'm afraid you're wrong there, Arthur, judging by what we've heard tonight,' said Campion.

'I'll tell you what I'd like,' said Ramsden with exasperation, 'and that's a witness; just one flamin' witness who actually *saw* something and who is willing to tell the police.'

As Chief Inspector Ramsden's outburst faded into the night air, there was an audible *thump* as something struck the caravan. All three men turned their heads as one and Campion trained the torch he was still holding to sweep the curving roof, where the beam reflected the gleaming white eyes of a crouching cat.

'Hecate,' said Campion quietly, 'I wondered where you'd got to. You wanted a witness to the murder, Chief Inspector? There she is.'

TWENTY-TWO
The High Place

The following morning Mr Campion parked his car in front of Ash Grange School in what resembled a staging area for a major military operation. Cars were arriving, disgorging the troops – boys with their kit bags – who then formed ranks and awaited their embarkation orders before climbing on board one of the three charabancs which would transport them to the battlefield, or rather the rugby field of their arch enemies, Queen Elizabeth's in Wakefield. Directing operations was their general, Brigham Armitage, his wife clearly having volunteered for the post of quartermaster. There were masters filling non-commissioned roles checking lists of boys and directing them to their allocated coaches, and even Rupert and Perdita had been dragooned as temporary corporals conducting vital equipment checks to make sure that rugby players had the correct number of boots, the right shirt and shorts, and that those boys going along as supporters had a regulation school scarf to wave. This latter duty involving the confiscation of numerous blue-and-white Huddersfield Town scarfs as being non-school regulation and, indeed, the wrong sport entirely.

'Quite a turnout,' Campion said as Rupert and Perdita greeted him. 'Plenty of supporters for the big game, I see.'

'Last match of the term and a bit of a grudge match against Queen Elizabeth's,' said Rupert. 'There's no love lost between the two schools, but if you're a betting man your money might be better put on the home team rather than us. I'm afraid our record against them isn't good. In fact, it's pretty pathetic, and without Andrew Ramsden I don't rate our chances.'

'Still, you're taking quite a crowd to cheer you on. Good for morale and all that.'

'Don't be fooled,' said Perdita. 'Most of the day boys have been sent by their parents so they can go Christmas shopping and quite a few of the staff here will be sneaking off to the shops in Wakefield to do exactly the same.'

'You're welcome to come along,' said Rupert, 'and watch us be gracious in defeat.'

'A much undervalued attribute, I always thought,' said Campion, 'but I must decline. I have an expedition planned for this morning.'

'Expedition? Nothing dangerous, I hope.'

'Not at all, just a walk in the local countryside,' said Mr Campion, turning his back on the Grange Ash muck stack in order not to unconsciously reveal his intentions.

'Is that why you've gone native?' Rupert's eyes flashed to the top of his father's head on which proudly sat a flat cap, so clean and new that Rupert half expected to see a price tag dangling from the back.

'Oh, this?' Campion's fingers fluttered to the brim of the cap. 'Well, when in Rome, you know. Bought it this morning, first thing, in Huddersfield indoor market. I believe it's called a "Garforth" but I can't quite work out the pattern of the weave. I want to call it a Tattershall check, but there's a dark red stripe in there. Rather fetching, eh? And we're not *that* far from Ilkley Moor and I couldn't possibly be seen without a hat, could I?'

'Quite sure that's all you're up to?' Perdita chirped with a coy smile as she linked arms with him. 'I promised Amanda I would ring her tonight to tell her how *Doctor Faustus* was going. I could tell her you'd been out taking the air if you'd like me . . .'

'That's exactly what you should report, my dear. No more, and preferably a lot less. However, you could tell my lovely wife that I will be joined, nay guided, on my perambulations by Mr Exley in order to give him a chance to convert me to dialectical materialism, and by this evening I will probably be answering only to the title of "Commissar", though she of course may call me "Comrade" as a term of endearment.'

Perdita butted her forehead gently against Mr Campion's shoulder. 'I will tell her that, word-for-word. It's so ridiculous she will know you are full of beans.'

Campion patted his stomach. 'I'm certainly full of a hearty Yorkshire breakfast, hence my need to go for an invigorating walk. Now you get on and marshal your troops and make sure they are in good voice on the touchline. Play up, play up and all that sort of stuff.'

When the last of the parents' cars had departed and Mr and Mrs Armitage, in a Standard Ensign which still bore its RAF paintwork, had lead off the convoy of charabancs, Mr Campion was left alone outside the front doors of the school. The morning was cold and grey but at least it wasn't raining and a weak sun was straining through the clouds. For the first time Campion had a good view of the top of the Grange Ash muck stack which suddenly seemed nearer and larger than he had anticipated. From the glove compartment of the Jaguar, he took a pair of Zeiss miniature binoculars and focussed them on the summit. From that angle he could make out an arrangement of ironwork protruding from the point of the peak, which he reasoned must be the buffers of the railway tracks which carried a single truck of waste 'muck' on a pulley system to the top of the long incline before tipping, allowing its contents to slide and skitter down the slope. Thus would the black mountain have risen over the years until the pit ceased to be profitable – or 'economic', as one was supposed to say these days – but now the pit was closed and the stack would grow no more. This pyramid, thought Campion, was finished and ready for its pharaoh.

Before his fantasy could go any further, Campion's concentration was broken by the sound of an approaching engine and a light blue Hillman Imp drew up alongside the Jaguar. Arthur Exley levered his bulk out of the car, stretched his shoulders and twisted his upper body as though uncoiling his spine. He was a naturally muscular man and seemed even bulkier by virtue of the thick donkey jacket he was wearing along with, Campion noted with a smile, a flat cap identical to his own. Exley walked around the rear of the Hillman and flipped open the boot.

'"Morning, Albert," he said as he reached down into the small luggage space.

'Hope you don't mind first-name terms, now there's nobody around.'

'Not at all Arthur, I'm rather flattered,' said Campion, 'and very grateful that you are allowing me to monopolize your weekend.'

'I see you got yourself some new boots,' said Exley, glancing down at Campion's feet and the shiny black leather army boots which had replaced his brogues. 'They've not got hobnails, have they?'

'Heaven forbid! I borrowed them from Chief Inspector Ramsden and they're almost the right size. Police-issue thick rubber soles but no hobnails. Don't worry, I got the full safety lecture on why you don't wear hobnails in a colliery. If I were tempted to do my famous soft-shoe shuffle the sparks from my boots could have explosive results.'

'Then all you need is one of these,' said Exley, pulling another donkey jacket from the boot of the Hillman. On the back, beneath the leather shoulder patches, in white lettering four inches high was the legend: NCB.

As he removed his Crombie and pulled the donkey jacket on over his sports jacket, Campion chuckled with boyish glee.

'I'd love to buy one of these. I'd wear it to all the poshest parties in London and tell everyone my name was Nicholas Charles Bonkerstein!'

'And down in London, they'd believe you,' said Exley. 'Nice 'at, by the way.'

In deference to Campion's age, even though he was unsure exactly what it was – pensionable certainly, but physically fit with less fat on him than a butcher's pencil – Arthur set a leisurely pace as the two of them marched out of the school grounds, across the road and into the fields and rough ground which lay in the shadow of the mountainous muck stack. It was the route a crow would have flown, though a pair of sensible pedestrians would have stuck to the drier roads, but more importantly it was exactly the route he had taken with Bertram Browne, something on which Mr Campion had insisted.

Outwardly cheery and energetic, Mr Campion was secretly daunted by the size and scale of the muck stack as it loomed nearer. Its steep sides, so much steeper close to, appeared to have a sheen of slime so slick that it resembled the skin of snake. Campion dismissed the thought as childish, for snakes were not slimy to the touch, yet there was something about this great black mass of dust and shale and coal which, when wet, did indeed resemble the scales of a reptile. If this mountain of spoil came to life it would be as a dragon, Campion fantasized, though with the rivulets of water pouring down its sides from days of persistent rain, he knew the reality would be that any movement would be more likely to be that of a slowly deflating balloon, spreading thick and unyielding black mud like lava from a volcano. Fortunately the Grange Ash pit stood in splendid isolation away from any habitation and if the stack ever should collapse and slide it would be unlikely to claim human life, except perhaps the lives of any human foolish enough to try and climb it.

Exley guided Campion around the western side of the black pyramid and, after climbing over a single strand of drooping barbed wire, they entered the pit yard. Until that moment they had been tramping through a rural landscape of grass and bracken but suddenly they were in an industrial setting, with concrete underfoot and brick and metal all around.

Whatever function the various buildings had served when the pit was a working entity, they were now no more than forlorn, empty shells. Windows had smashed panes, doors hung off their hinges and coils of telephone or electric cable drooped from insulator brackets in roof corners. The largest of the buildings was a row of three corrugated-iron hangars with curved roofs. Although brown with rust, they seemed sturdy enough and undamaged by weather or vandalism, but the dominant feature was the metal winding rig with its huge wheels and thick cables which would have lowered men down and raised coal up in small wheeled tubs. As they crossed the pit yard, stepping over the railways lines on which the tubs had run, empty cans, broken bottles, large lumps of shiny black coal and unidentifiable pieces of twisted brown metal, Exley explained that only the old colliery office and the winding room were maintained in any sense; the office as a place for the night watchman to have his 'snap' and maybe take in a crafty forty winks, and the winding room because the cage which went down the main shaft had to be kept in working order in case the Coal Board geologists needed to inspect things underground.

They followed the grooved railway tracks to the base of the pyramid of spoil where two lines became three as a chain cable ran up the middle providing the mechanism by which full tubs were hauled to the buffers at the top of the slope. Planting his feet either side of the chain, Exley began the ascent with Campion close behind.

'We can take it easy,' he advised the older man. 'It isn't a race. If you want a breather just say so and don't be afraid to grab on to me if you slip.'

Campion looked at Exley's broad back and said, 'I will be hanging on to your NCB coattails, have no fear.'

If the angle of the slope was not quite that of one of the Great

Pyramids, it was steep enough and Campion was grateful when
Exley suggested they rest and get their breath back. Though they
were still less than halfway to the summit, Campion's thigh muscles
burned and his ankles ached due to the unnatural side-footed gait
he had adopted to stop his unforgiving police boots from sliding
in the loose grey shale.

They were high enough already to get a view eastwards over
Denby Ash and the trees of Denby Wood and back down the slope
– which did seem dauntingly steep. The old buildings around the
pit yard were already taking on the proportions of a scale model.

'When was it you brought Mr Browne up here?' asked Campion
when he got his breath back.

'Be over a month ago now,' Exley replied.

'So, after the poltergeist had started visiting, but before Haydon
Bagley was released . . .'

'Eh? I'm not followin' you.'

'Of course you're not. I barely am myself, old chap. Now let
us crack on to the summit. We're doing this because it's . . . well,
because it's here, I suppose. I say, you don't have a spare oxygen
mask about you, do you?'

'Are you all right?' asked Exley, sincerely concerned. 'I don't
want you to conk out on me 'cos I don't want to have to carry
you down.'

'I'm perfectly fine, just feeling my age, that's all. But if I do
conk out you have my permission to give my lifeless corpse a
good kick and let gravity roll it down the hill.'

'I shan't need to be asked twice,' growled Exley, and Campion
reassured himself that the gruff Yorkshire sense of humour was
indeed an acquired taste.

It took another quarter of an hour for them to reach the summit,
Campion conscious that his methodical sideways plodding had
slowed Exley to the equivalent of a crawl, but once he had his
breathing under control he forgot everything except the three-
hundred-and-sixty-degree view.

From the peak, where the buffers for the rails jutted out into
space, Campion could see the outline of Ash Grange school and
its playing fields and then, turning to the east, the haul road
which had provided access to the pit, the stone bridge over
Oaker Beck by the Sun Inn and then length of the village running
down Oaker Hill. Using the working men's club as a reference

point, Campion estimated which of the rooftops belonged to Number Eleven, just as, he guessed, Bertram Browne had checked a compass bearing. With his small Zeiss binoculars he could make out the winding wheels of the Caphouse and Shuttle Eye pits on the far side of the village on the Wakefield road. Below him, back down the slope he had just climbed, the pit yard and buildings looked even more like toy buildings from a model railway set and strangely, looking through his binoculars, negated the feeling of vertigo he feared.

It was as Mr Campion was completing his circular sweep through the Zeiss lenses – his own spectacles pushed up on to his forehead – that he caught a glimpse of movement at the far end of the pit yard. Around the corner of one of the derelict buildings, a figure moved furtively, a figure larger than a dog but smaller than a man, and seemingly walking on three legs.

Campion turned the focus dial and the figure became Roderick Braithwaite, limping across the yard with the aid of a walking stick.

'How did you know he'd be here, Albert?' said Exley from somewhere behind him, his voice low and serious.

'I'm sorry, how did I know what?' Campion replied absently, the binoculars still at his eye. 'I didn't know he'd come here but I suppose I should have expected it, boys being boys and all that.'

'Not down there, Albert. Here! Look here, over the edge.'

Campion responded to the urgency in Exley's tone and turned quickly – too quickly for an elderly gentleman on top of a wet and far-from-solid mountain, and he felt Exley grab his arm to steady him.

'What are you talking about, Arthur?'

'I'm asking how you knew Haydon Bagley was up here.'

'What? Where?'

Campion took a nervous step forward towards the very tip of the stack where Exley stood, feet apart, pointing over the edge through the frame of the metal tracks which protruded ominously out into open space.

He felt Exley's right hand tighten on his left arm and he looked the younger man full in the face. 'I didn't know I had vertigo until I came up here,' he said, his lips suddenly dry. 'You won't let go, will you, Arthur? I'm too old to learn how to ski.'

'Just look over the edge and don't worry, I've got you. Take it easy, there's no rush. He's not going anywhere.'

Campion took a deep breath and shuffled forward until the toes of his borrowed police boots – which felt more like the shoes of a circus clown – were level with Exley's feet and he leaned gently forward, grateful now for his companion's anchoring grip, and looked out and down into the void.

Except it was not a void – it was almost a mirror image of the slope he had just walked up but the absence of the iron rails removed any sense of perspective and safety. When climbing Campion had had the upward slope under his boots – those boots again! – and the solid mass of the spoil heap in his eye-line. Now he was peering over the edge and staring at a precipice of black rock, scree and mud, a vista of desolation where no plants grew and the rivulets of water run-off resembled bleeding wounds.

'There,' said Exley, 'about forty feet down. All the rain we've had these past two weeks has moved the muck.'

What the rain, or gravity or that unnatural state where solids turn unexpectedly to liquids had done was to expose a hand and an arm. The body to which it was attached remained mercifully hidden, its outline a shapeless black lump.

'My goodness,' said Campion. 'How do you know that's Haydon Bagley?'

'There's nobody else missing, is there?' said Exley with a gruff logic which defied rebuttal.

'If it is, the question is how did he get there?'

'Either he walked up here and threw himself off, which I don't put much credence in, or he was killed down below some-where, brought up in one of the tubs and tipped over the edge. Chap with a shovel could have climbed down there and covered the body.'

'Is that likely? I mean, it would take some nerve to slide down there and start digging virtually in mid-air.'

'Happens all the time on muck stacks when fires break out; men climb up with shovels and put the fires out. What's not very likely is how you knew he'd be here.'

'But I didn't,' pleaded Campion. 'Honestly, I had no idea.'

'But you just said . . .'

'I said I should have expected it, but I was referring to young Master Braithwaite, who is down there in the pit yard doing a bit of detective work off his own bat as we speak.'

'Roderick? Bloody hell! Can't let him see any of this.'

'I quite agree. Haydon Bagley, if that is he, isn't going anywhere, at least not until we get the police here.'

Exley pulled Campion away from the edge and made sure he was steady on his feet by placing a hand on each shoulder and pressing down, as if planting him.

'Can you make it down by yourself, Albert?'

'I'm sure I can,' said Campion. 'It won't be quick and it probably won't be dignified, but I'll make it.'

Exley looked down the slope towards the pit yard.

'You're sure you saw Roderick down there?'

'Yes, by one of those iron-framed hangar-like buildings. Can't see him now, though. Try these.' Campion offered the binoculars which Exley barely glanced at.

'I don't need opera glasses,' he said gruffly. 'I'll find him. Pit yard's not safe for a young lad. You come down at your own pace.'

They exchanged silent nods as two men do when neither is prepared to show weakness or sentiment, and Exley launched himself into a sliding run down the hill, his hips at right angles to the slope.

Campion geared himself to follow with much more care over his footing and far less speed. One foot in front of the other and lean backwards not forwards. If anything goes wrong, it is better to reach the pit yard on one's backside than on one's head. *Albert and Arthur went up the hill . . . to find a dead body . . . Arthur ran down like a gazelle while poor old Albert came tumbling after . . .* No. Don't think like that. Go down on your hands and knees if need be; there's no one around to see you make a fool of yourself.

Except there was somebody around – somebody coming up the haul road to the colliery. Campion did not need the binoculars to see them as he could hear the sound of their motorbike engines quite clearly.

Arthur Exley did not look behind him until he careered off the muck stack, stumbled into the pit yard and paused, doubled-over, to catch his breath. Only then did he check on how his unlikely ally and implausible friend was managing his descent. To be fair, the old boy was game enough going up there in the first place. Exley was half Campion's age, and had been forged (he considered) from much stronger metal, but even he was feeling the strain on his thighs and calves. Still two-thirds back up the slope the mild-mannered southern toff was making a brave fist of it, coming down in a staggering side-to-side motion, arms flapping and hair flying and mouthing something Exley could not hear. Was he cursing? Shouting a warning? Or singing *Jerusalem*?

Exley shook his head. The old man had to look after himself; Roderick was his priority now, and when the blood stopped pounding in his ears he heard the noise of motorbike engines echoing off buildings and then cut out. He began to run.

Campion had lost sight of the motorbikes approaching the pit on the haul road, being far more concerned to keep his balance. He had tried to shout a warning but realized that it must have sounded like a drunken hunt master shouting 'View-halloo!' and possibly in Romanian.

He decided to concentrate on getting down the slope in one piece. With a broken leg or a twisted ankle he would be no good to Roderick or Exley, and with a broken neck no good to anyone.

Below him – still a long way below – he saw Exley bend over and turn his face up towards him. He shouted breathlessly 'Go, just go!' but had no idea whether he was heard or understood. Clearly Exley had no intention of waiting for him as he set off diagonally across the yard towards the desolate office buildings and the metal hangars. Exley was strong, he was fit and, more to the point, knew his way around a colliery. If young Roderick needed protecting from anything he was the man to do it and he had a personal stake in doing so. What could Campion do but limp along bringing up the rear too late to do any good, providing only tea and sympathy?

Perhaps that was all he had to offer now.

Exley paused at the corner of the building that had once served as the lamp room, where miners coming off shift had checked in their lights and batteries before getting undressed in the attached shower block, which had been thoroughly stripped of all its useful fitments and copper piping.

There was no sign of any motorbikes or of Roderick. Had Campion imagined seeing him?

He jogged along the front of the Manager's Office, noting that at least one door seemed to be still in place and properly locked, and hurried in the direction of the winding rig over the main shaft. That shaft, which went down at least eight hundred feet, was surely the most dangerous place in a landscape of dangers. A waist-high square skirt of iron panels formed a protective fence around the shaft, one side of which was split in two as a gate to allow access to the cage which used to lower men into the bowels of the earth and bring the coal they ripped, hacked and shovelled up to the sunlight. The cage was in place and the iron gates guarding it secured with a hasp and heavy padlock, which ruled out the possibility that Roderick had accidentally plunged to his death. The knowledge gave him some comfort. The pit had already taken one Braithwaite; he would not allow it another.

He ran on across the yard to the large corrugated-iron sheds which had acted as garages and workshops, one of which had been equipped as a blacksmith's shop, something Exley remembered fondly as every child in Denby Ash had probably had a snow sledge made there as a Christmas present; their runners forged from off-cuts of sheet metal courtesy of the National Coal Board.

The sliding door of the nearest shed was half open and Exley could see the dim outline of a coal lorry inside – one of the smaller ones, a low-sided Atkinson four-wheeler. More disturbing were the two BSA Bantam motorbikes parked outside the shed, each with a black crash helmet resting on the seat.

There was no sign of the riders of the bikes and, more to the point, there was no sign of the duty watchman. Arthur knew that the watchman's duties were rarely onerous, especially during daylight, being on hand basically to deter kids from vandalizing the place even more and the scrap dealers from helping themselves to copper wiring and piping and any old iron that had been deemed surplus to requirements by the NCB. Yet neither old Tom Townsend nor that idiot Adrian Elliff, who alternated the day and night shifts, seemed to be on hand, and even if they were sleeping off a hangover they would surely have heard the bikers arrive. They had no right to be there and, come to think of it, neither had that lorry. As a union official, Exley reasoned, he had every right to know what was going on and he did not falter or break stride, but continued running full pelt into the shadows of the shed's interior.

His vision had not even begun to adjust to the gloom of the shed when a pick-axe handle was swung into his stomach with considerable force.

TWENTY-THREE
The Dark Place

Campion reached the bottom of the stack and hobbled into the pit yard. His lungs as well as his leg muscles burned and his ankles felt like bags of marbles. There was no sign of Exley or Roderick Braithwaite and no sound of motorbike engines. He felt totally alone, though he knew he was not for he was conscious that behind and above him was a dead body, most likely that of Haydon Bagley, and he could not help but wonder why whoever had killed him had gone to the trouble of carting the body up to the top of the muck stack for a burial of sorts when there was a perfectly good mineshaft nearby.

Such things were matters for the police and if Campion could somehow summon them, he would be making a useful contribution to events. If Roderick was in danger, Arthur Exley was more than capable of protecting him; of that Mr Campion was certain. Exley was younger, stronger and clearly passionate about the boy's well-being. Roderick could not have wished for a more ferociously loyal surrogate father.

Discovering that he was sweating profusely, he unbuttoned the NCB donkey jacket, reached into his trouser pocket for his handkerchief and mopped his face. His great white flag of a handkerchief came back streaked with black, sooty smears. He risked wiping the lenses of his glasses and was relieved to find that his vision improved marginally, though he was convinced he was shedding a fine mist of coal dust with every movement and that he could taste it on the back of his tongue. He felt extremely old, filthy, exhausted and lame, and desperately in need of a hot bath or an ice-cold gin-and-tonic – preferably both – but they would have to wait.

Campion raised his head and looked around until he located an intact wire hanging at roof height. If there was a watchman to watch over the premises, surely they would have supplied him with a telephone.

He sighed and said aloud, 'Come on, old bones, no peace for the wicked' and followed the line of the wire across the yard to where it disappeared into the Manager's Office.

Only when he was a yard away from it did Campion realize that the upper half of the office door comprised six square panes of glass so coated with black dust that they looked like solid mahogany. Using his sleeve, Campion cleaned one of the panes and peered in. He could make out a desk and a captain's swivel chair and – yes – a telephone. All he had to do was get through the door which was secured with a Yale lock.

Had there been a time when a more dashing, confident Campion would have picked that lock in three seconds with a borrowed hairpin? Perhaps, but this was no time to dwell on the past.

There were large lumps of coal dotted around the yard, several of which he had stumbled over. He picked up the nearest, a piece as big as a small loaf of bread, smashed in the glass pane nearest the lock and then reached in and turned the knob on the lock.

The telephone, an ancient black Bakelite affair, offered a reassuring dialling tone and Campion dialled the number he had memorized early that morning, though in truth he had not the faintest idea where Cudworth was. He spoke briefly and clearly then replaced the receiver and went to find Exley.

The first blow made Arthur Exley double over; the second landed across his shoulders and propelled him into an enforced forward roll across the oily concrete floor which ended as he collided painfully with the front offside wheel of the lorry.

'Tha'd no need to belt 'im like that!'

'The booger come chargin' in like a bull in a china shop. What else was there to do?'

''E was allus trouble, that one.'

As Exley's head cleared he discerned three distinct voices and recognized them all.

'You bunch of bastards!' he spat, tasting blood from where he had bitten his tongue and oil from where his face had met the floor of the hangar. 'I'd say you were keeping bad company Adrian, but I reckon you and the Booths deserve each other. Now just what the bloody hell are you up to?'

Of the three men standing over him, only the spindly Adrian Elliff, hopping lightly from foot to foot, seemed disturbed by Exley's outrage. The two men in biker leathers, the cousins Fred and Colin Booth, remained confident and menacing as each held a pick-axe handle in their right hands which they slapped in unison into the palms of their left.

'Didn't know you couldn't count, Arthur,' said Fred, the elder Booth. 'There's three of us 'n' just the one of you, so you tell us what you're doin' here.'

'And stay down there,' snarled Colin Booth, jabbing Arthur with his wooden baton as Exley moved to stand up. 'You're not speakin' at a union meeting now, Arthur. Any road, tha'd be out-voted, three-on-one.'

But Arthur Exley had participated in much tougher negotiating situations than this in his career and was not to be cowed.

'Now listen here, Fred Booth, as area convenor I've got every right to be here, which is more than I can say for you.' Exley spoke slowly and deliberately, with an authority which hardly fitted his ungainly position. 'I'm checking up on this daft so-and-so' – he nodded towards Adrian Elliff – 'and it seems it's about time somebody did. You're in trouble, lad, big trouble. There's more than muck out on that muck heap.'

The Booth cousins flashed urgent, rodent looks at each other. Adrian Elliff continued to quiver nervously, his thin legs clearly shaking through his greasy blue jeans.

'What's he talking about, Colin?' Adrian squawked in a high-pitched voice.

'No idea, Adrian, no idea,' Fred Booth answered.

'So they haven't told you, have they, Adrian?' said Exley, taking his chance. 'Haven't told you about Haydon Bagley lying dead up there on top of the stack. How long since you put him there? Didn't count on it raining so much recently, did you? If it hadn't he might have stayed up there until spring. As it is, he's come back to haunt you, lads, so you might as well give it up now.'

'What's he talking about, Colin?' Adrian squealed again.

'Oh, change the record, will yer?' snapped the younger Booth, lunging with the axe handle at Exley, stabbing as if with a foil or an épée.

'You said you were just here to get rid of the lorry.'

'Well, they would, wouldn't they,' Exley blustered, 'because it's evidence. Are you really that stupid, Adrian?'

'You can shut your mouth, Mr High-and-Mighty Exley!' Fred Booth shouted.

'Let's shut it for him!' Colin joined in and the pair raised their wooden clubs and lunged at Exley.

Arthur instinctively protected his head with his arms and brought his knees up to his stomach, at the same time attempting to press himself backwards under the wheel arch of the lorry so that the first strikes by the Booths clanged off metal rather than thudded into his body. But then the pair doing the beating adjusted their aim and the blows began to count. With a loud, hysterical giggle, Adrian Elliff joined in with some wild and mostly ineffective kicks at Exley's legs.

Then, above the grunting and the yelps of pain, a new voice rang out inside the hangar. 'Leave him alone, you big bullies!'

And Roderick Braithwaite, covered from head-to-toe in coal dust, rolled and then fell over the side gate and out of the back of the lorry.

Campion saw the motorbikes outside the hangar-like shed and immediately changed direction across the yard so that he could approach it from an angle out of sight of whoever was inside. When he reached the shed, he pressed his shoulders against the corrugated-iron frame and edged sideways towards the open sliding door.

When he was level with the two bikes he could hear the unmistakeable sounds of violence coming from within and he inched closer to the edge of the door, straining without success to make sense of the babel of voices. He knew he had to risk a look inside so about-faced and inched towards the open door, his face pressed into the rusty troughs of the corrugated iron.

It took him several seconds for his brain to work out the choreography of the disturbing drama on a stage he was now, as it were, observing from the wings. Arthur Exley was on the ground in a foetal position being beaten by two figures in leather trousers and jackets wielding clubs of some sort. At first, Campion thought Arthur was trying to edge himself under the lorry parked there to protect himself from the blows raining down on him, but then Campion felt his heart in his throat as he realized that Arthur was crawling, or trying to crawl, not to safety but to help Roderick Braithwaite, who lay face down on the concrete three long yards away. Roderick was pinned by virtue of the thin, gangly youth kneeling on his back and repeatedly slapping him on the back of the head. Everyone – the hitters and the ones being hit – were howling in anger and pain.

Campion had to help; he knew that instantly, just as he knew he was old and slow and weak. He could not do much but he must try and whatever he did he had to do it quickly. He looked around frantically for a distraction or a weapon and found both.

The two BSA Bantam bikes were almost within arms' reach and, uncaring whether he was seen or not, Campion grabbed the crash helmet balanced on the seat of the nearest and placed it near the door. Then he turned back to the bike, twisted off the petrol cap on the top of the tank and gently pushed the machine back and forth on its stand until he heard the gratifying slosh of petrol.

Tearing at the buttons, he pulled open his donkey jacket and took his handkerchief from his trouser pocket, feeding it into the tank then extracting it halfway, draping it, soaked and stinking, along the tank. He fumbled his cigarette lighter from his blazer pocket, flicked it into life and touched the flame to the edge of the handkerchief.

He picked up the crash helmet and swung a practice swing holding it by the chinstrap, then with a deep breath he summoned up the last dregs of his energy, raised a leg and kicked out to knock the first bike off its stand and into its companion, sending both machines crashing noisily to the ground.

He was back, flattened against the corrugated-iron shed when he heard the first angry shout from inside, and then the Bantam's tank exploded with a whoosh rather than a bang, making him think of a wet firework in the rain.

It wasn't much of a diversion or a rescue, he thought, but it was the best he could do.

Colin Booth was a rebellious youth, or so he liked to think, who had never seen the need to respect person or property unless, of course, they were his. When he heard, and then saw, his precious BSA lying on the ground in a heap, flames and smoke licking from it and embracing its twin, he let out a howling obscenity, flung down the axe handle and raced towards the hangar door.

He reached the entrance in four or five rapid strides and then his face met the crash helmet swung at precisely the optimum height and with all the strength Mr Campion could muster, who suddenly appreciated the expression 'stopped in his tracks' as Colin Booth came to an abrupt halt and sank to the ground as his legs crumpled beneath him.

Unbalanced from the effort of launching the ambush, Campion staggered and almost fell over his victim. He was breathing heavily, his heart pounding, his head swimming and he desperately wanted to sit down and rest for just a minute, but he forced himself to enter the shed where there were two more opponents to deal with, though he doubted he would be able to present much of a threat. Campion's actions, however, had sown confusion among his enemies and given inspiration to his allies.

Fred Booth's brain did not work quickly enough to take in exactly what had happened to his cousin. He could see Colin laid out on the pit yard and what appeared to be a frantic old man in a flapping coat standing over him. Beyond, he noted that their precious bikes had been pushed over and seemed to be on fire, black smoke starting to billow from them. The absorption of all these facts made him stop beating on the cowering Arthur Exley, turn and take a hesitant but threatening step towards the old man in the shed doorway.

It was all the respite Exley needed. He uncoiled his bruised and aching body and, on his knees, wrapped his arms around Fred's shins from behind and pulled. With a crack, Booth's forehead hit the concrete floor before any other part of his anatomy could cushion the impact.

As Fred Booth yelped in surprise and toppled over, Adrian Elliff – whose rat-like cunning had always put a premium on self-preservation – assessed the situation with surprising speed. He removed himself from Roderick Braithwaite's back, jumped to his feet and ran, wild-eyed, towards the door. He had no intention of helping either of the Booths, on whom the tables seemed to have been comprehensively turned. His sole motivation was to escape.

Campion saw the skinny youth charging towards him and knew that he did not have the physical strength to stop him and so resorted to offering some helpful advice.

'Quick, get down!' he shouted, gesturing to the burning bikes. 'They're going to blow!'

In a panic, Adrian Elliff did exactly as he was told and threw himself down, covering his head with his arms. Mr Campion casually stepped over his prone figure and said, 'Everything under control here, Arthur? The police should be with us momentarily.'

Exley was already on his feet and helping Roderick on to his with a protective arm around the boy's shoulders. 'Police, did you say?'

'I've already telephoned for them.'

'Well then,' said Exley, unbuttoning his donkey jacket, 'I'd better get my retaliation in now.'

He shrugged off the jacket and handed it to Roderick, then he unbuckled the wide leather belt he was wearing, pulled it through the loops on the waistband of his trousers and wound it tightly around his right fist.

With two paces he was standing over Adrian Elliff, who was still face down, his body shaking in anticipation of an explosion.

'Get up, Adrian, and pick on someone your own size,' said Exley grimly.

Mr Campion held out his hand to Roderick. 'Let's step outside for a minute.'

'They killed him, you know; those Booths, the ones who beat up me and Andrew. I heard them say it. I got in the back of that lorry when I heard their bikes coming and I kept my head down.'

'Sensible lad,' said DCI Ramsden. 'You did the right thing. Was Adrian Elliff with them?'

'Not then, not when they were talking – and laughing – about it. He came a few minutes later and asked what they were doing as he hadn't been expecting them.'

The pit yard was filling up with police cars and policemen. Fred and Colin Booth, both bloodied and dazed, had been handcuffed and placed in one car. Adrian Elliff had followed suit in another, but only after receiving a considerable amount of first aid roughly applied by an unsympathetic police sergeant.

Roderick sat on the rear seat of Ramsden's Wolseley, the door open wide with Campion, Exley and Ramsden gathered in a semicircle to hear his story.

'They thought it was funny,' the boy continued with a sob, 'to run him over like that. Funny. They *laughed*. Said he looked like a frightened rabbit.'

'They didn't mean Haydon Bagley, did they?' asked Campion quietly.

Roderick stared up at him, puzzled. 'Who? No, they were talking about Mr Browne – Bertie. They called him "that snooping teacher who was getting too close" and how he "never saw it coming" in the dark and now they were going to get rid of the lorry there would be nothing to link them to it. They were going to put their bikes in the back, drive the lorry to Manchester, dump it and ride back. I was sure they were going to find me, but then Arthur turned up.'

Campion and Exley exchanged a knowing glance, then Campion turned to Ramsden.

'Chief Inspector, I'd like to share a theory with you,' he said. 'It's not my theory in the sense that I can claim credit for it, but I think it was Bertram Browne's and I am sure young Roderick here has worked it out for himself by now.' He smiled down at the boy. 'Otherwise he wouldn't have come up here this morning to play at being a detective which, and I speak from bitter experience, is admittedly a young man's game but not, perhaps, *too* young.'

'I'm all ears, Mr Campion,' said Ramsden. 'We haven't got a peep out of the Booth boys and on past form we're not likely to. Typical Cudworth yobboes, they'll keep their mouths shut, though we've got them on suspicion of pinching detonators from the NCB, that lorry is almost certainly stolen and they'll be in the frame for the hit-and-run on Mr Browne now. We haven't even got to Haydon Bagley yet.' He paused as if reconsidering. 'When we've thrown all that at them, they'll talk eventually. In the meantime, given that Adrian Elliff seems to have had a minor nervous breakdown' – he glanced at Exley who stared back blankly – 'I would appreciate any theory you'd like to pass on.'

'I think,' Campion began, 'and I hope Roderick will back me up here, that Bertram Browne was convinced that the poltergeist visitations to the Braithwaite house were a result of underground seismic activity – shockwaves running along the fault line of a seam of coal which was mined out years ago, a seam which had at one time run right underneath Eleven Oaker Hill.

'What he did not know – or he would surely have gone to the police, being as far as I can tell a straightforward, law-abiding chap – was that the seismic activity was man-made and the direct result of criminal activity, your recent epidemic of rather cheeky robberies by the gang who doesn't just steal payrolls but steals the safes in which the payrolls are kept.'

'And then they blow the safes with the detonators stolen from the pits,' said Ramsden. 'We guessed that was what was going on. The question was where on earth were they doing it?'

Mr Campion extended a forefinger and pointed it downwards.

'Not where *on* earth, Chief Inspector, but where *under* the earth . . .'

The cage door rattled shut, a winding engine hummed, a cable twanged taut and the metal plates underfoot shuddered; then their stomachs flipped as the floor fell away and they dropped into the void. The daylight disappeared with frightening speed and their field of vision was limited to the dank, black wall of the shaft speeding upwards as they sped downwards.

DCI Ramsden had summoned reinforcements to Grange Ash and deployed them as quickly and efficiently as a good battlefield general. As well as policemen, he had also enlisted the expert help and equipment of the National Coal Board's emergency rescue team of miners trained in handling pit accidents. They set about their task of recovering the body of Haydon Bagley with grim dedication and quiet professionalism, although Campion noticed that the rescue team members automatically looked to Arthur Exley for confirmation whenever Ramsden issued an order.

It had been Exley who had insisted on a safety check on the winding gear so that they could descend into the old pit workings, and Exley who had borrowed helmets and torches from the rescue team for Ramsden, two constables and Campion. They would be guided underground by two of the team who had first-hand experience of the Grange Ash shaft and tunnels.

'You are not coming with us?' Campion had asked him. 'Not at all curious as to what's down there?'

Exley shook his head. He was filthy; his clothes smelled of oil and dust. There was dried blood on his shirt collar and a large purple bruise was blooming on one cheek. Campion guessed that he himself looked even worse.

'My concern was first and last seeing young Roderick safe,'

Exley said without embarrassment. 'All else is your business, not mine. If one of Mr Ramsden's bobbies'll run me round to the school, I'll get me car and take Roderick home to his mother. She'll be expecting him for his dinner.'

Campion automatically thought 'lunch' and chided himself for doing so.

'That's a very good idea, Arthur – the boy's seen things he shouldn't have.'

'Don't worry about the lad. He's Yorkshire and so are we. He'll be looked after.'

'Of that,' said Campion with a smile, 'I have absolutely no fear – something I wish I could say about the prospect of going down into the bowels of this pit without my faithful Sherpa and bodyguard.'

'Seems to me you did most of the body-guarding. You weren't bad for . . .'

'I know, I know,' Campion interrupted, 'for a man of my age . . . my great age . . . my advancing years . . . my decrepitude . . . my . . .'

'I was going to say for a southerner,' grinned Exley.

After firmly placing a miner's helmet on Campion's head, attaching the light to it and then clipping the heavy battery which powered it to Campion's belt, Exley accompanied the expedition party to the lift cage over the main shaft.

'Just keep your extremities inside the cage and swallow as much as you can when your ears pop,' he advised and then held out a hand to Campion as though to receive something rather than shake.

'Oh, you want your coat back,' said Campion, misunderstanding. 'I really should have it cleaned – it's quite filthy.'

'Nay, you can keep that and a bit of muck never hurt anybody anyway. It's that lighter of yours I'm after. Safety procedure. We're a bit keen on that and I've seen the damage you can do with that thing.'

Campion fumbled the lighter out of his blazer pocket and handed it over. 'Keep it,' he said, 'as a souvenir. It's already engraved from A to A – from Albert to Arthur if anyone asks.'

The cage landed at the bottom of the shaft with a thump which reverberated through the feet and legs of Campion and the policemen but which went unnoticed by the miners accompanying them. The chamber-like area at the bottom of the shaft was much larger than Campion had imagined and more claustrophobic than an Underground station; in fact, the dust, the cables crudely fixed to the brick walls, the rusted railway tracks and the sheets from a newspaper wafting in the downdraft from the shaft all conjured images of a chilly evening on any one of a number of stations on the Northern Line.

One of the rescue-team miners announced in sepulchral tones that there were two tunnels leading off the chamber, the larger being the Grange Ash end of the Flockton Thick seam. That, he was pleased to say, was perfectly comfortable for a man to walk down without 'bashing 'is 'ead' as long as he wasn't over five-foot-six tall, at least for the first three-quarters of a mile. After that, he added with just a hint of malice, they would have to get down on their knees and crawl.

In fact, having travelled eight hundred feet vertically, the expedition had to make their way no more than thirty yards horizontally before they discovered buried treasure – or rather the chests which had once contained treasure.

Their helmet lights illuminated a row of eight similar-sized office safes littered along the rail lines on which had once been pushed trucks of finest Flockton Thick coal, freshly hewn. The safes lay on their sides or backs, as though they had been rolled like dice by some giant subterranean hand, their doors clearly and conspicuously having been opened by force.

'No sign of £40,000 or thereabouts, is there?'

The voice of Dennis Ramsden, echoing in the tunnel, snapped Campion out of a minor reverie. He had been focussed on the way the light from his helmet lamp was so quickly swallowed by the dark maw of the tunnel which stretched ahead into infinity.

'They wouldn't stash the loot here, Chief Inspector. It would be far too difficult to get at in a hurry if the gang needed to make themselves scarce.'

'Well, the Booth boys certainly seemed to be planning to do a runner,' said Ramsden. 'Applying for passports and getting rid of that lorry points that way.'

'It does,' replied Campion, 'and it ties in with something Roderick said – or rather something somebody said to him – about the poltergeist; about its visits coming to an end soon.'

'So you reckon the gang's called it a day?'

'I think so. It doesn't answer your question about where the money is, though.'

'But you have an idea, don't you, Mr Campion?'

'That's very flattering, Chief Inspector, but I would put it no higher than a notion if that – it's probably only half a guess.'

'Go on. I'm not proud, Campion, I don't mind asking for help now I've got three murders on my books as well as the robberies.'

'Well, then, for what it's worth, you'd agree that the gang who did the robberies was highly organized?'

'Certainly, and somebody far cleverer than the Booth boys was giving the orders.'

'Working with some degree of insider knowledge, perhaps?'

'Naturally we thought of that and we looked into it long and hard, checking all the usual suspects: disgruntled employees, ex-employees, managing directors with debt problems or gambling habits. We found a couple of shady individuals but nothing to connect them to any other of the eight companies that got robbed.'

Campion turned to Ramsden and then rapidly turned away, redirecting the light on his helmet from the policeman's eyes.

'Perhaps there was someone who could have inside knowledge on all eight firms, and I mean "inside" quite literally.'

Now it was Ramsden's turn to blind Campion with the beam from his lamp. 'Haydon Bagley.'

'I would suggest it as a distinct possibility. He was, I believe, a local bank manager before his arrest. You might find all those robbed firms were clients of his, in which case he would know what sort of safe they had and how much money was likely to be in it at any one time.'

'That certainly needs checking,' said Ramsden with energy. 'In fact, we should have done that but it never occurred to us. I mean, why would it? The robberies started months back but Haydon Bagley was in Wakefield Prison until two weeks ago.'

'But his cell mate wasn't. Malcolm "Malkey" Maude, or "Banger" as he was known, due to his liking for explosives when it came to opening safes. Not that we were on nickname terms, of course. I've never met the fellow, though I know a man who has.'

'Malkey Maude? He was one of Commander Luke's Greatest Hits, wasn't he?'

'I doubt that Charlie Luke would put it that way,' said Campion, 'but Maude was certainly a person of interest. I take it he's not on your Most Wanted list here in Yorkshire.'

'I shouldn't think so. As far as I know we've not even got a photograph of him or his prints, let alone an outstanding warrant. We wouldn't have if he hasn't done a crime in the West Riding.'

'I think he has made up for that oversight in his curriculum vitae in recent months. I suspect Malkey Maude and Haydon Bagley whiled away the long winter nights in their cell. Bagley had the targets, Maude had the expertise. He was released first, recruited his gang and went on a spree. The mining industry provided him with a pair of young thugs with access to explosives and a disused pit as a base. It began to fall into place when Arthur and I found that body on top of the muck stack. Why bury a body on top of a hill when you have a very large hole at your disposal?' Campion turned his head so that his head torch shone around the tunnel. 'Unless,' he continued, 'you were using the very large hole for some other purpose?'

'So Bagley and Maude plan the robberies when they're in jail and when Bagley gets out he comes straight here to get his cut of the loot?'

'Something like that, or perhaps it was the classic "thieves fall out" scenario. Bagley had had six months alone to think things over and maybe decide he wanted a bigger share.'

'So Maude topped him?'

'He would be my odds-on favourite,' Campion agreed, 'and he probably gave the order for the Booths to arrange a road accident for poor Bertie Browne who was getting close to tracking the source of the noisy poltergeist. By the way, if you check the dates, I'll lay even money this time that the poltergeist manifested itself only in the immediate aftermath of one of the robberies.'

'They'd have brought the safes down here when that idiot Elliff was night watchman,' said Ramsden.

'That was how he earned his cut, but I suspect his slice was a thin one. He didn't strike me as being over-blessed in the brains department.'

'You can say that again. He'll talk right enough; all I have to do is threaten him with another lathering from Arthur.'

'Hardly proper police procedure, Chief Inspector, but I won't tell on you and you might try asking who told him to watch Ivy Neal – and Ivy's visitors. The problem is I'll lay odds – my

goodness, I'm beginning to sound like a betting office, aren't I?
– that he doesn't know. I think it is perfectly possible that Adrian
never met our Mr Big. He was recruited by the Booths.'

'And this Mr Big killed Ivy Neal?'

'I can't prove it but I'm sure of it.'

'Why?'

'If our Mr Big is Malkey Maud, Ivy Neal was the one person
in Denby Ash who could identify him. She'd met him when visiting
Haydon in prison and he'd mentioned a "Malcolm" in his letters.
Perhaps he said something in that last letter . . .'

'The one we can't find.'

Campion nodded, his helmet torch beam slashing the musty air,
which made him feel rather ridiculous.

'The one he *did* find, when he killed her? Haydon could have
been telling her things were going to look up and life get better
now he was coming out. Didn't Mrs Bagley – the real Mrs Bagley
– say as much last night?'

'Maybe the old witch was trying to negotiate a bigger share for
her son,' said Ramsden.

'Could have been, though I've a feeling she was a loose end
which needed tying off. Eight jobs, eight safes. Perhaps Bagley
only knew of eight suitable targets. The job was done and he
was dead; so was Bertie Browne. The gang were pulling out,
intending to disappear. Ivy Neal was the last link in a very nasty
chain.'

'Let's go topside,' said Ramsden wearily. 'I must have a cigarette
before I take a look at that body on the stack.'

They walked back down the tunnel to where the track ended at
the cage and one of the rescue team miners made sure they were
secure before starting them on their ascent.

As the cage started to rise, both men turned off their headlamps,
the darkness of the shaft holding fewer fears for them now they
were heading for that grey lozenge of daylight which marked the
surface.

'So how do we flush out this Malkey Maude when we don't
even know what he looks like?' asked Ramsden.

'I might be able to help you there,' said Campion lightly,
swallowing hard to relieve the pressure in his ear. 'You see, I
may not have the resources of a modern police force but I do
have a Lugg.'

TWENTY-FOUR
A Very Important Person
Travels North

Mr Magersfontein Lugg had performed many unusual tasks for Mr Albert Campion over the years, several of them perfectly legal and none of them at all 'common'.

His current task was to catch an early morning train heading north, take a first-class seat, equip himself with all the more outrageous Sunday newspapers and avail himself of any breakfast facilities on offer as frequently as he so desired. In case of a sudden alteration to Campion's plans, it might be wise to bring an overnight bag of essentials such as pyjamas and toothbrush. It would not be necessary to pack knuckle-dusters, wigs, false moustaches or any form of firearm. He would be met at Wakefield Westgate station (the one nearest the prison as Campion was sure he knew) and taken to a rural location for a few minutes' work, after which he would be able to sample the local ale to his liver's content and at Mr Campion's expense. He was not, on any account, to scream, sulk or throw a fit when he was met at the station by a police car.

As he sat in the back of a black cab en route to King's Cross, Mr Lugg allowed himself to release a stream of quiet invective, the content of which ranged widely over numerous subjects yet always returned to the iniquity of liberties being taken on loyal retainers who really should be allowed a lie-in on a Sunday morning and not be turned out of a warm bed before the pigeons had rubbed the sleep from their eyes.

By Peterborough he was somewhat mollified by several cups of British Rail tea and distracted by the misfortunes of the high and mighty as chronicled in the salacious British press, and by Grantham had summoned up enough enthusiasm to devour a pair of kippers and half a loaf of toast in the dining car. At Doncaster, the sky darkened as though the morning had had enough and given up, and the rain rained. By Wakefield, the rain had eased to a light drizzle but the sky and his mood were in perfect harmony; both were glowering.

He stepped from the train on to the platform, sniffed loudly and planted his large, highly polished black brogues on either side of a Gladstone bag which could have been a Victorian doctor's holdall or an exhibit in a particularly gruesome murder trial. He buttoned up his dark blue overcoat, unfurled his umbrella and held it high above his bowler-hatted head.

In that position he remained as immobile as a sentry at Buckingham Palace despite the curious stares of the few other passengers who came and went about their business. Eventually a uniformed policeman appeared at the ticket barrier, exchanged words and gestures with the inspector there then marched down the platform towards him.

Lugg took a mischievous delight in the fact that the policeman had been forced to buy a platform ticket.

The bell of St James' the Great was tolling over Denby Ash as the Campions gathered in the car park of the Green Dragon. Mr Campion's car was the only vehicle there, there still being a godly hour and more to go before opening time, and he was behind the wheel concentrating on the Common across the road through his Zeiss 'opera glasses' as Perdita parked her Mini Cooper parallel to the Jaguar.

'Bird-watching?' Rupert asked as he opened the car door for his father.

'Cat-watching, actually,' Mr Campion replied, offering Rupert the binoculars. 'Over there, on the roof of Ivy Neal's caravan.'

Rupert raised the glasses, following the direction of his father's pointing finger. 'That shaggy beast is a cat? Are you sure? It looks more like a lynx.'

'That's Hecate and I do hope someone is feeding her, though I am sure she can forage for herself. How did the big match go yesterday?'

'Predictably,' sighed Rupert. 'With Andy Ramsden out injured we were bound to lose, but I didn't expect by quite so many points.'

'Best not to ask for any details,' said Perdita, winding an Ash Grange school scarf around her throat. 'The match report in the school mag will make pretty depressing reading. We hear you had a far more successful day. A quiet stroll in the countryside indeed! Amanda always said you were a big fibber!'

Perdita cosied up to Campion, stood on tiptoe and planted a chilly kiss on his cheek.

'The village grapevine again?' he asked with a smile.

'And the jungle drums and the smoke signals. Fun and games up at Grange Ash: police called, bodies found – two thugs from somewhere called Cudworth, a place I'm sure I've heard of before – laid out, motorbikes exploding and goodness knows what else.'

'I think that just about covers my day,' Campion said smoothly. 'How was yours?'

'Nightmare-ish,' said Perdita. 'Oh, not having to watch my darling husband tear his hair out on the touchline. That was quite fun. It was having to put up with Hilda Browne for three hours, though it seemed a lot, lot longer.'

'I didn't have Miss Browne pegged as a rugby fan.'

'She's not. I'm sure she didn't have a clue what was going on on the pitch. That wasn't the point. She *had* to be there to represent her brother and had to be seen doing it in front of the local gentry. She's a terrible snob and quite mad, and of course I got lumbered with her because of *Faustus*, which I am truly dreading.'

'I'm sure it will be all right on the night,' Campion beamed. 'But to take your mind off things, I have a surprise for you both.'

He nodded towards the police car which had just pulled off the Wakefield road and into the car park. It stopped a few yards from their vehicles and a policeman got out, scurried round to the passenger-side door and opened it. With some ceremony and a fair portion of dignity, a large bowler-hatted figure emerged and looked around as if waiting for applause.

'Lugg!' cried the junior Campions together. 'What are you doing here?'

'I was told there would be ale!' boomed Lugg, opening his arms to embrace them both.

'Not just yet, old fruit,' said Mr Campion as the bell of St James' struck again. 'First we have to go to church.'

He comes! He comes! The judge severe.

'What sort of an 'im is this?' hissed Lugg. 'There's no tune to it.'

'It's one of Wesley's and I think it rather apposite,' whispered

Campion. 'And there's no music because there clearly isn't room for a harmonium in here.'

The three Campions and Lugg had almost doubled the size of the congregation in the Mission hut, the other participants being half-a-dozen elderly women in headscarves, though Preacher Robin Chubb seemed unaware of his sudden popularity and went about his business of leading the faithful in prayer.

There was another hymn and then a psalm, all spoken not sung, and prayers which Chubb declaimed, with convincing sincerity, whilst standing on a solid pine stool. In one hand he held a leather-bound Bible and with the other he would casually stroke his pointed beard as though a philosopher composing his next great thought.

Lugg, squeezed uncomfortably into one of the pews between Mr Campion and Perdita, kept his head bowed and concentrated on the bowler hat perched on his knees. He could not resist, as Chubb commenced another prayer, to say to Perdita out of the corner of his mouth: 'They don't go in for bells 'n smells 'ere, do they?' and Perdita choked back a giggle.

As the prayer ended, Chubb opened his Bible and addressed the congregation. His eyes widened as if he had only just discovered there were other people in the building.

'Dear brothers and sisters,' he began, 'I take Matthew chapter twenty-four, verse thirty-six as the inspiration for my sermon today.'

Campion nudged Lugg with an elbow – an elbow which made only a minimal indentation in the combined padding of overcoat and fatty tissue which acted as a natural defence mechanism against such warranted intrusions.

'Get ready, you couldn't have a better cue,' whispered Campion.

'We must all be ready at all times,' said Chubb in a conversational rather than preachy tone, 'for the Son of Man is coming at an unexpected hour.'

Mr Campion's elbow bounced off Lugg's torso a second time. 'That's delicious. You're on, old son.'

Mr Lugg rose ponderously to his feet with all the grace of a walrus mounting a bicycle, settled his feet a comfortable distance apart and slapped his bowler hat to his chest roughly where his heart should be.

'Malkey Maude,' he declaimed in a booming baritone, 'as I live and breathe! You are Malkey Maude and I claim my five pounds.

I bring greetings from your nearest and dearest in Canning Town, though in truth they ain't what yer might call well-wishers. Still, they'll be pleased to hear you've seen the light, though I almost didn't recognize you, me old china, what with that Bible in yer 'and an' that poncey beard. Not sure the face fungus suits you, Malkey . . .'

Preacher Chubb abandoned any pretence of preaching, his face a mixture of shocked recognition and sheer panic. Dropping his Bible as though it burned, he jumped down from his small podium and raced through the startled congregation towards the door of the Mission.

Rupert struggled to his feet and made a grab for him, but Chubb was too quick. He made the door of the hut, ripped it open and continued running straight into the arms of Chief Inspector Ramsden and three constables waiting outside.

'*Now* is it time for ale?' asked Lugg, to no one in particular.

'So what have you been up to?' Lady Amanda asked gently, then her voice hardened. 'And please don't try your usual flannel. You know I know what a terrible liar you are, plus I have spies everywhere.'

'You are omnipotent and omnipresent, my darling, and I would not dare to deceive,' said Mr Campion. 'I have spent the last few days driving up into the beautiful Dales, where I acquired a Wensleydale cheese which probably does not meet health regulations but I am sure will be delicious. It appears to have been made in a lady's nylon stocking, though I couldn't identify the denier.'

'Albert!'

'I do not lie, darling – I really did buy a cheese, which the hotel is kindly keeping for me in a refrigerator, and I really have been seeing the sights: the parsonage at Haworth, Fountains Abbey, Rievaulx Abbey, Jervaulx Abbey and I even discovered a magical little place called Masham. It's spelled with a "sh" but it's pronounced "Massam". There's a brewery there where they brew a beer called Old Peculier and that's "peculier" with an "e" not "peculiar" with an "a", which is in itself peculiar.'

'Albert, I won't tell you again.'

'That sounds a very Yorkshire thing to say, my dear.'

'It is. Perdita taught me it. She said all the mothers here use it on husbands and naughty children alike.'

Campion put down the knife and fork he had been using to dissect a perfectly delicious Barnsley chop and poured some more wine into his wife's glass. They were dining at the George Hotel, Amanda having arrived by train in Huddersfield that evening prior to her starring role at the Ash Grange Speech Day and end of term celebrations.

'My dear, I swear on everything I hold dear – which is to say you – that since Monday I have been doing nothing more strenuous than a crossword puzzle.'

'And prior to Monday?' Amanda asked, her eyes cold but still beautiful.

'Mingling with the locals, studying the flora and fauna . . . the usual . . .'

'Bringing Lugg up north is not "usual", Albert. I don't know who to feel more sorry for – Lugg or Yorkshire.'

'It was a flying visit and he thoroughly enjoyed himself,' said Campion stoutly.

'He had a terrible hangover when I saw him on Monday evening,' countered his wife.

'Ah, yes,' said Campion meekly. 'He was taken on a tour of the flesh pots of Huddersfield by some grateful policemen. Apparently there are flesh pots in Huddersfield and they are open on Sundays.'

'The pair of you! You are incorrigible, untrustworthy and possibly insane. You clearly deserve each other and I don't know why I worry so much.'

'Oh, yes you do,' said Mr Campion softly, reaching out to take his wife's hand, 'but there really is no need. I have been exploring, broadening my horizons and meeting some fascinating people. I've been made an honorary member of a working men's club and even bought myself a rather stylish flat cap to go with my new donkey jacket. I have walked uphill and down dale and even been down a coal mine. That was quite scary, I admit, but perfectly safe.'

'And that's all you've been up to?' Lady Amanda put her head on one side and narrowed her eyes. Even when highly suspicious, Mr Campion still felt hers was the most beautiful face he had seen.

He was stroking his wife's hand and considering the magnitude and whiteness of the lie he was about to tell when a welcome distraction arrived. Their waitress, a homely middle-aged woman wearing a smart black dress with white apron, collar and cuffs approached their table and waited politely before speaking in a hushed tone so that fellow diners could not overhear.

'There's a gentleman in Reception, sir – says he would like a word with you if it's convenient, that is. He said the last thing he wanted to do was spoil your dinner but he had a bit of news for you.' The waitress leaned in closer as if to impart a vital secret. 'He's a policeman,' she said knowingly.

Lady Amanda slipped her hand from underneath Mr Campion's and raised a quizzical eyebrow. 'How interesting and yet somehow unsurprising,' she murmured before turning her face to the waitress. 'Do ask him to join us.'

If Chief Inspector Ramsden noticed the slightly cool atmosphere at the table or the fading blushes on Mr Campion's cheeks as the introductions were made, he was professional enough, and well-mannered enough, not to mention it.

'I'm so sorry to intrude,' he said, shaking Amanda's hand, 'but I'm going off-duty and thought I'd catch you tonight before the fun and games at the school tomorrow.'

'You will be present, I assume,' said Mr Campion.

'Absolutely. Andrew's getting a prize for his rugby and of course we're all keen to hear Lady Amanda's address.'

'So is Lady Amanda,' said Amanda. 'Do you have official business with my husband, Chief Inspector? Should I avert my ears?'

'No need for that, Lady Amanda,' he said apologetically. 'I just wanted to update your husband on a couple of things. It is sort of official, but not confidential or sensitive.'

'Then please, update away,' Amanda said with a flourish of her hand before settling down to study Mr Campion's face intently as Ramsden spoke.

'Well, I'm really here to thank you, Mr Campion. You gave us a few ideas which were very, very helpful.'

'Guesses,' said Campion. 'No more than shots in the dark.'

'Let's call them educated guesses, then, but you were right about that last letter from Bagley before he got out of prison. It told Ivy Neal that she could always rely on the new preacher in Denby Ash and though it didn't name him, it was clear that she should go to him if money was tight. It's circumstantial, of course, but it sounds to me that Bagley was setting up a bit of an insurance policy for his dear old mum. Chubb, or Maude as I should say, didn't want to take the risk that his former cell mate hadn't named him. So he—'

Campion saw one of his wife's eyebrows rise and quickly intervened.

'So the letter turned up? Did Maude find it?'

'No, he missed it completely. Mind you, it was well-hidden, in a box with a load of dry cat food.'

'Then it would have been well-guarded by Hecate,' said Mr Campion. 'Did you check Maude for claw marks, say, on the back of his hands? Like my own war wounds.' He held up the back of his own right hand, which still showed four tiny spots of dried blood.

'I hadn't noticed, but we're certain he wore gloves when he . . .'

'Gloves would not have deterred Hecate, as I know to my cost,' said Campion quickly. 'Hecate is a cat, my dear – hopefully one being well-cared-for.'

'Rest assured on that one. Mr and Mrs Armitage have offered her a good home at the school so you may well see her tomorrow.'

'We are looking forward to the occasion, aren't we, darling?'

Amanda smiled thinly and asked the policeman: 'Has my husband had any other good ideas lately, Chief Inspector?'

'Oh he's been very helpful, Lady Amanda, very helpful indeed. So was your Mr Lugg. Very popular with some of my lads down at the station is your Mr Lugg. And young Mr Rupert – he came up with a good 'un as well, he did.'

'I'm delighted to say that Mr Lugg isn't one of mine in any sense, but I do proudly admit to Rupert. Pray tell, what was his particular eureka moment?'

'We took a statement from him about when he met Maude – of course, he didn't know he was Maude then – and he mentioned all the wood-working tools Maude was messing around with and how good he seemed to be at carpentry. He said he'd noticed a bed in the Mission hut, behind the side curtain, and it looked as if Maude had made it himself. That got us thinking so we tore the thing apart. He'd hollowed out the legs and made four perfect hiding places for rolls of bank notes. We recovered nearly £20,000 from that and then found near enough another twenty thousand hidden behind some new skirting boards in the place he was living in over in Cudworth.'

'So a good result for the forces of law and order all round, then?' asked Campion.

'Pretty much,' said Ramsden. 'The Booth boys are starting to come clean. They're claiming Bertie Browne's death was an accident and they're blaming Maude fair and square for Bagley and Ivy Neal.'

Campion was aware that Amanda's eyes were slowly widening.

'Well, that's all jolly good, Chief Inspector,' he said hurriedly. 'Will you join us for coffee?'

'No, thank you very much; I'll leave you to finish your dinner in peace. I'll say good night and wish you luck for tomorrow, Lady Amanda.'

Ramsden stood up and left the table in a silence which continued for a full two minutes before Amanda spoke.

'Are you sure there's nothing you've forgotten to tell me, Albert?'

It was part of Ash Grange lore that Speech Day was the favourite day of the school year for its misanthropic groundsman, Rufus Harrop, as he was put in sole charge of car parking which thus gave him ample opportunity to continue his own class war against the richer parents and take revenge for personal sleights both real and imagined. He had, though it rankled, been told to be on his best behaviour when supervising the arrival of the guest of honour, Lady Amanda, though he could not for the life of him see what a posh southern woman with a fancy title could possibly have to say to interest the folk of Denby Ash.

He waved Campion's Jaguar into a reserved parking space and, as he had been rehearsed by Celia Armitage, opened the passenger door for Amanda. As he had been strictly rehearsed by Brigham Armitage, on pain of instant dismissal, he welcomed her to the school grounds in stony silence.

Amanda, as she did with any public engagement she undertook, had done her research and as she got out of the car she offered a hand. 'You must be Mr Harrop,' she said graciously. 'My son has told me what an absolutely splendid job you do on the school grounds and the playing fields. I doubt the school knows how lucky it is to have you.'

Rufus said nothing, merely stood open-mouthed, though he did weakly shake Amanda's hand. Long after the event he would say, to anyone who would listen, that it had been 'like meeting royalty' and that 'them Campions aren't such a bad lot and not at all stuck up'.

Rupert, who had observed the encounter from the steps of the school, had been impressed and told his mother so as he greeted her with a kiss.

'You seem to have tamed our ferocious groundsman,' he said, 'and if you can do that, you'll absolutely wow the boys and the staff here. Let me take you in, they're all gathering in the Dragons' Den . . . that's the staff room. All except Perdita, who's giving the cast of *Doctor Faustus* a last-minute pep talk.'

'Is she prepared for curtain up?' said Mr Campion as he joined them.

'She's dreading it,' Rupert answered, 'but has to keep upbeat for the sake of the boys as all the parents will be there for the first show and then there's another performance tonight for the locals, but Perdita thinks if they come at all they'll come for the brass band music, not the play.'

'Has Roderick Braithwaite reported for duty?' asked Campion.

'Is he your apprentice detective?' said Amanda.

'Sort of. He's a fine lad – brave one too. He's playing Faustus.'

'Perdita's confident he'll be fine,' said Rupert, 'and he was certainly full of beans this morning. Last night, Arthur Exley called round for his tea at Mrs Braithwaite's as per usual, but instead of going into the house, he opened the door and threw his cap in.'

'And Ada Braithwaite didn't throw it back out.'

'She did not. It seems she's agreed to a new husband and a dad for Roderick.'

'I am so glad,' said Campion, 'and we will be devastated if we're not invited to the wedding.'

'We will?' murmured Amanda.

'Oh, yes; in fact, I fully expect to be asked to be Best Man.'

'You have been busy making friends and influencing people, haven't you?'

'You know I always try to sprinkle a little fairy dust in my wake. Now it's your turn to charm and inspire Denby Ash, darling, which you will do brilliantly. Go give them a Speech Day they'll never forget!'

It did indeed prove a memorable Speech Day. The correct prizes were given to the correct recipients, the applause was heartfelt and polite when it was called for and the cheering (for any mention of a winning school team) was controlled and not at all unruly. The school song was sung with gusto, the Rev. Stanley Huxtable lead the assembly in a prayer suitable for all denominations, the staff looked suitably learned in their university caps and gowns, speeches were listened to in respectful silence and the last oration – Lady Amanda's stirring call to arms to 'Reach for the Stars through Education' – received a standing ovation from every woman, and a fair proportion of the men, in the school hall.

Tea and cake were served in the enforced intermission while the hall was rearranged to accommodate the staging for *Doctor Faustus* and the arrival of Arthur Exley and selected members of the Denby Ash Brass Band.

When preparations were complete and the audience had resumed their seats, the three Campions allowed a prime position on the front row, Brigham Armitage mounted the stage and begged boys and parents for their attention as he had an important announcement to make.

'I have to inform you of a slight change to the cast of our production,' began the headmaster once he held the silence of the packed hall. 'Owing to unforeseen circumstances, the role of Helen of Troy will not be played by Miss Hilda Browne but by Miss Perdita Browning.'

There was a hum of expectation among the boys and of mild curiosity among the parents. The headmaster indicated that Arthur Exley and his musicians, resplendent in their red and black with gold piping bandsmen's uniforms, arranged in a semicircle in front of the stage, could now commence their overture.

As the first notes began to swell, Rupert leaned in to his parents. 'Perdita says to thank you, Pop, and that she's promised to give you a big kiss if she gets through this. How did you manage to get the mad Hilda to step down?'

'I paid her a social call,' said Mr Campion under the music, 'and pointed out that as her late brother was now the subject of a murder enquiry, it might be wiser not give the impression that she was more interested in theatricals than in justice for Bertie. I may also have mentioned that she would surely be expected to appear in court as a star witness in the near future and of course the press would be present there.'

'And she fell for that?' Rupert whispered.

'You know what actors are, my boy. The chance of a bigger role and a mention in the newspapers is usually enough to turn their heads.'

'But what about poor Perdita?' Amanda intervened. 'Haven't you landed her in it at very short notice?'

'She's rather looking forward to it,' said Rupert smugly. 'She doesn't have any lines and she says thanks to you and Marion and Sally, she's sure she'll make a dramatic entrance.'

Mr Campion was watching Arthur Exley conducting his bandsmen with slowing sweeps of his baton and suspected the overture was almost over and the real action about to begin.

'Who are Marion and Sally?' he asked as the lights in the hall began to dim.

'Marion Foale and Sally Tuffin,' said Amanda quickly. 'They designed the outfit I bought Perdita as an early Christmas present in London. Now be quiet, you two, and watch the show.'

When her cue came, Helen of Troy walked regally across the stage and back again. When her second cue came she repeated her statuesque promenade, a beautiful and confident model – as surely Helen was – making the stage her personal catwalk.

The effect on parents, teachers, bandsmen and the boys – especially the boys – was electric.

A few of the women present may have recognized the black-and-white optical check suit and very short skirt she wore from a magazine feature and acknowledged that the long high-heeled white leather zip-up boots and black tights patterned with white diamond shapes added to the Carnaby Street authenticity, but all in the audience agreed afterwards that they had never seen anything so fashionable in Denby Ash before.

The second performance of *Doctor Faustus* took place some three hours after the first. It was more than enough time for the village drums to beat effectively and the hall was packed to the rafters, so much so that Rufus Harrop volunteered to work front of house without any thought of an overtime payment, for the sheer pleasure of turning people away.

That night, Brigham Armitage would say later, was a bad night for television in Denby Ash. Then, remembering his Yorkshire heritage, he would add: 'If only we'd sold tickets . . .'